WAR OF THE HARBINGERS: DEATHWIND

WAR OF THE HARBINGERS: DEATHWIND

✶

BRAD PAWLOWSKI

sunquakebooks.com

Copyright © 2022 by Brad Pawlowski.

This is a work of fiction. Names, characters, places and incidents either are products of the author's imagination or are used fictitiously. Any resemblance to actual events or locales or persons, living or dead, is entirely coincidental.

All rights reserved. This book or parts thereof may not be reproduced in any form, stored in any retrieval system, or transmitted in any form by any means—electronic, mechanical, photocopy, recording, or otherwise—without prior written permission of the publisher, except as provided by United States of America copyright law.

ISBN-13: 979-8-9871552-0-2 (*paperback*)
ISBN-13: 979-8-9871552-2-6 (*hardcover*)
ISBN-13: 979-8-9871552-1-9 (*ebook*)

Cover design and illustration by Jeff Brown Graphics

www.bradpaw.com

PROLOGUE

MASSIVE, WATER-SOAKED CLOUDS gathered above the world of Aureon. As they swirled in a clockwise formation, the glow of a swollen blue star cast a cobalt shine across the storm. With each passing moment, relentless winds fueled the growing hurricane, pushing it inland.

A single raindrop began its descent, joining countless more on their way to the ground. It plummeted through the darkened sky, where it mingled with the others on its chaotic journey. Finally reaching its destination, it sailed into a forest clearing and splashed onto the shoulder of a colossal man.

Shrouded in gray and silver body armor, he was difficult to see in the storm—a helmeted shadow with glowing blue eye slits. Spikes ran down his right arm, from shoulder to hand, which firmly gripped a broken spear. Draped across his back, strips of leather dangled, ready to whirl about with every move. He was the premier commando of the Meraki Dominya, Valor Krell Duma—a nightmare in human form.

Lightning flashed, cracking a whip in the distance and illuminating the clearing. An exhausted man stabbed at Duma with a spear of his own. But honed reflexes kicked in and the commando parried the attack.

Duma countered, slashing through the name "Vander Conak" on the man's military uniform. The spearhead tore through the fabric, ripping flesh and sending blood pulsing down Vander's stomach.

Not willing to yield, Vander spun and bashed Duma's knee with the handle of his weapon.

Ignoring the heated pain, as he'd been trained to do so

many years ago, Duma pushed forward. He whirled the spear in his right hand, distracting his opponent, and connected with a swift head kick. His shin crashed into Vander's skull with a satisfying crunch.

Vander crumpled to the wet ground, mud skipping across his face. His weapon thumped down in the muck behind him. Duma paused, taking a moment to survey his fallen opponent. He paced back and forth, appraising Vander, while giving the man time to recover.

"The Furies welcome you, Consular," Duma said, his voice projected through a speaker in his helmet.

Metal flashed as Vander dove forward with a knife from his boot. He stabbed at Duma with desperate energy, but the move was anticipated. After catching Vander's hand, Duma snapped his wrist backward and drove the knife into his ribs. Even as hardened as he was, Vander shuddered in pain and fell.

Sheets of rain hammered them with machine-gun intensity, drowning out any last words. Vander struggled to his knees and stared up at Duma, eyes full of rage but ultimately helpless.

Duma raised the spear into the sky over the crippled man. Facing his death head-on, with blood running down his sky-blue skin, Vander unleashed a deafening roar that pierced the storm. It was an impressive display of bravery and honor, Duma conceded. A second later, he plunged the spear into the man's chest, piercing his heart and cutting the roar short.

Around Duma's boots, the mud turned crimson as blood rushed out of the wound. He leaned forward and removed a picture from Vander's pocket. Then, with a sharp jerk, he withdrew the spear from the body and raised the tip to the glowing blue eyes of his helmet for inspection.

Lightning flickered, strobing the area as Duma sauntered away, followed by a growl of thunder.

CHAPTER 1

Nathan Stryder struggled frantically for awareness, even though he knew the creatures would be waiting for him on the other side. The moment he reached it, his senses sparked to life with agony. Every muscle in his body seized up, each clawing at him with desperate urgency.

He fought to move, but could only open his eyes. They flashed wildly, searching the darkness in a frenzied panic, still unable to focus. He was standing—no, dangling from the ceiling. Everything was blurring in and out.

A figure approached, at first still a haze, but too tall to be human. It was twisted, distorted. The figure's long, dark arms stretched for him, clamping to his shoulder with a cold, metallic grip. Despite the pain, his attention was fixated on the ominous presence.

Above him, a glowing instrument lowered, closing in on his chest. Strange clicking and hisses echoed around him. Fear, something Nathan had typically controlled, now shot through his body unchecked, turning the world black-and-white. Dizzying bursts of light spotted his vision as the instrument lanced through his skin. A flash of nausea flared in his gut.

He retreated from the pain into his sub-conscious. There, he spun in a world of strange images and bizarre feelings. People, voices, and faces all clouded his head. His mind worked to recognize them.

The images rippled as if he were looking up through a pool of liquid. Blue light flashed, eradicating the faces, replaced by a swinging pendulum from a giant clock. He heard his voice, but it was distant, as if echoing down a hospital hallway.

"Where is she? Is she okay?"

The dark arms returned, spiraling toward him. Forcing himself to focus, he fought his mind for control and awareness of what was real and what was not.

Nathan awoke, gasping for air. A slick, transparent membrane covered his body, smothering him. He lashed out, kicking and clawing desperately to break free. Choking for oxygen, his body convulsed. He was dizzy, but still writhing to get away.

Then, abruptly, he could breathe. For the moment, he was content and his muscles relaxed. As he panted uncontrollably, the sweet sense of oxygen gave way to something else. With each breath, a sour blend of chemicals crammed into his nose, burning a path into his lungs.

The room bucked, knocking Nathan to the floor. Tendrils slithered around him, trapping his arm beneath him and causing the bones in his shoulder to scrape against each other. A groan escaped his lips as the tendrils tightened. He was sure his arm was broken.

Movement to the left grabbed his attention—another creature. More strange clicks. It approached, looming over him like the corn stalks from... however long ago that had been. He had no sense of time. Every ounce of energy left went to twisting or kicking.

He had to get out—he had to find Susan.

The dark figure became motionless, its numerous alien eyes dissecting him. Grinding his teeth, Nathan strained against whatever was holding him down. But it was futile. His energy was fading. Exhaustion ran through his body, settling in. Eventually, he had nothing left.

More tired than he could ever remember being, Nathan drifted into unconsciousness.

No longer plagued by twisted nightmares or painful

visions, his mind desperately grasped for the clearest reality he could recall. The memory was still fresh and alive with vivid detail.

It was the second of April when Nathan had returned alone to his hometown for his parents' funeral, a day he would always remember. That morning, he'd visited Susan, who was recovering in the hospital and still in a coma. Since the accident, everything had looked different. He imagined that everyone he saw had a virtual ticking clock hanging over them, counting down to oblivion. There seemed no point to anything.

The car dipped as he pulled it into the driveway. He parked, stepped out, and took in the yard. It felt empty without his dad out mowing, pulling weeds, or whatever else was on his to-do list.

Nathan climbed the porch steps with heavy feet. The front door stuck momentarily to the frame, then popped open. After a deep breath, he stepped into the house. For a moment, he waited to hear his mother call his name, but there was only silence. The people who'd taught him to tie his shoes and to cook an omelet were gone, and a hollow rift opened within him. So much was missing now.

In his father's office, Nathan watched the grandfather clock as it ticked. He tapped the pendulum. Was that how life worked, constantly swinging back and forth from good to bad? No. He hadn't been to the positive extreme in a while, and now he was swinging quickly back, drawn by misery's irresistible pull. His eyes followed the arc of the pendulum. Would it be so bad to live life in the middle, never to experience the extremes, never to be happy or sad, just empty?

Everything at the house reminded him of them. From the way the place smelled as if his mother's margarita candles were still burning somewhere, to the floor's lonely groans, which would warn him of their approach when he'd stayed up too late.

He stepped into his old room and crawled into his bed, embraced by its familiarity. He was a kid again. Above him was the small, wooden wagon-wheel chandelier that hung slightly to the left. A dreamcatcher he'd made himself still dangled from it, misshapen and missing a feather.

It had been a long day, and he wanted nothing else but to get a merciful night's sleep. His mind raced, as it had always done in the past when he lay in bed, waiting for sleep to overcome him. But soon it did.

It was then that the dream usually came. And it was always the same.

He was on a battlefield, running, attacking. Strange, armored beings lay dead on the ground. Charging at him was a mountainous shadow with four arms. In each was a unique weapon—a pistol, a sword, a flaming ball and chain, and a spear.

Energy grew in his hands, and they began to glow. The dark creature raised its rifle and fired, unleashing a streak of purple. Nathan flung his arm up to block the blast as a translucent shield materialized on his forearm.

The monster roared, and Nathan woke up in a sweat.

The same dream had plagued him since childhood. Lying in bed, he stared up at the dreamcatcher again, trying to decipher it. It always filled him with a strange restless energy, but he'd never been sure what to make of it.

He crawled out of bed, knowing he wouldn't be able to get back to sleep. This was the part of the night where his feelings of being trapped were the strongest. His mind searched for a way out of the puzzle that was his life, but ultimately, he found none.

Unsticking the front door as quickly as he could, he slipped outside. The cool breeze cleared his head, sweeping his cluttered thoughts into the night. With his gaze turned skyward, he contemplated the stars that lit the clear sky. The view made his problems seem so small, so meaningless. Surely there was something more.

He'd raised his arms to the cosmos and released all the anger and sorrow from his parents' deaths—combined with sudden feelings of insignificance, helplessness, and fear, all in one primal scream.

It had roared from the darkest corners of his soul and into the night, echoing across the sky in a slowly fading beacon of angst. Had he reached the extreme of the pendulum yet? Or was there more to come?

It took a concentrated effort for Nathan to fight his way back from the memories. When he reached consciousness again, it only lasted a few cloudy moments.

There was a sense of weightlessness as the creatures lowered him into a cylinder full of gel-like fluid. His body became immobile, and a tacky liquid quickly rose around him. It clung to his skin and poured down his throat, coating his lungs.

Panicked, he gasped for air, quickly drowning. Once he was fully submerged, an intense light blinded him, and the gel instantly hardened, leaving his body frozen. His mind, however, was not.

Rifling through the catalogue of his memories, he hunted for the most recent one, for something that could help him, something that could tell him how he had gotten here. And hopefully how he could escape and help Susan.

Then, he found it.

CHAPTER 2

Earth: Twelve Hours Earlier

Muscles rippled as a karate student's leg flew forward with wild intensity. It collided with a hunk of wood and splintered it into several pieces.

"Stryder!" a gruff voice called from nowhere.

Adrift in his thoughts, Nathan turned from the martial arts class he was watching through a window stenciled with Japanese lettering. As he did, he saw the familiar stretch of small-town America he grew up with. His eyes fixed on the freckled face of Ryan Monshor exiting the bakery next door. It was a breezy afternoon, well past the morning donut rush.

"Have you been out here staring off into space this whole time?" Ryan raised his arms with the question.

"I wasn't staring into space." Nathan motioned to the karate dojo with his head. "I was watching the class." He glanced down at his phone, pretending to check for texts so he could avoid eye contact. Its screen was cracked from falling out of his pocket earlier that morning.

Before he knew it, Ryan flicked his ear, like they'd done to each other since junior high. It stung, but it was a pleasant change from his numbness.

Nathan's hand snapped up to guard from further attacks. "You're still doing that?"

"Sorry, old habit." Ryan smirked. "You still need a ride?"

"Yeah. I thought you were just running in?"

Ryan put his arm around Nathan, leading him to his car.

"Stryder, there comes a time in a young man's life when you meet a girl and lose all sense of time."

"I think you've just lost all sense."

"That's possible!" Ryan said with a skip. "Chelsea wanted me to try her new cupcake creation." A thought stopped him in his tracks. "You should come in and meet her! She's outstanding."

Nathan stuck his hands in his pockets. "Nah, man. Can we just go?"

"You got plans or something? A date? Are you finally out of your funk?"

Nathan shrugged off Ryan's arm, moving away.

Ryan sighed in defeat. "Guess not."

Slumping into the passenger seat of the yellow convertible Mustang, Nathan waited for it to start. It revved like a mountain lion, which was inevitably followed by the whine of the top coming down.

"Do we *need* to put the top down?" Nathan grumbled.

"It's a convertible! Of course, we have to! It's in the owner's manual. And just because your car is broken doesn't mean you can't enjoy this one."

Memories of Nathan's childhood passed in a blur as they drove through town. Blocking them out was easy, just like with everything now. The simplest way to do that was with YouTube videos or scrolling through memes and feeds. It was better than facing his problems. The next time he looked up from his phone, they had just left town.

"Lighten up, will you? Why don't you come out with us? I'll buy the first round." Ryan paused for an answer. When he got nothing back, he pushed. "Mandy will be there. It's her last day before she goes back to MSU."

"I can't. I have some things," Nathan said, almost to himself. He'd hoped that was enough for Ryan to leave him be, but Ryan liked to push.

"'Things!' More 'things!' What are these things?" Ryan slugged him in the shoulder.

Nathan was growing irritated. "Just things!"

"Okay, jackass. Whatever. Can we have the old Nathan back? Remember? The one that didn't take shit from nobody. The one that fought Billy Johnson."

"That wasn't a fight. I hit him one time."

Ryan shifted gears. "Because you broke his jaw! I mean, the kid deserved it, but that was exceptional. Now, we just have zombie Nathan."

They sat in silence as cornfields gave way to trees. There was tension between them as tangible as the wind blowing on his face.

"I'm happy for you," Nathan said, the words leaving his throat roughly.

Ryan's eyes flicked from the road to Nathan.

"Thanks, man! That's good enough, I guess. I know you're dealing with a lot. I'll stop picking on you, for today. But it's gonna start all over again tomorrow! Until I break you." He switched into a bad Russian accent. "I must break you."

Nathan allowed a grin to develop. He remembered why they'd always had so much fun and wished he could break out of his funk. But it wasn't that easy. It was more than that. His therapist liked to throw around words, but all he knew was that he felt like the person he'd been was buried under a snowdrift and couldn't get out.

"Have you ever felt like you knew how your life would play out?" Nathan said, feeling an urge to connect.

"Hell, no! I'm going into the Navy at the end of the month. They could send me anywhere." Ryan waved his arms. "Hawaii, Japan, Virginia! God, I hope it's not Virginia. Anyway, you can't think like that, man. At least not until you're forty!"

He chuckled, then slowed the car to a stop at the place where he always dropped Nathan off.

His face turned serious. "Ten bucks!"

Nathan sighed. He'd known this was coming. "Really? You haven't won this bet in five years."

"I feel lucky," Ryan said with a smirk

Nathan glanced over to the timeworn split-rail fence to his right. At one time it had a purpose, but now it looked like the broken skeleton of a monstrous snake. He recalled the deal they'd made ages ago. It was simple enough—the challenged party must make it from one end of the rickety fence to the other without falling—but he was not in the mood this time.

"Fine. I owe you ten bucks."

"Um, no. No, no, no. You know the rules! You can't back out once you've been challenged. We made a pact. If there's one thing I know about you, it's that you are a man of your word."

Nathan took a deep breath and climbed out of the car. Ryan knew just where to hit him.

He slammed the door. "You said you'd stop picking on me."

"Oh, come on," Ryan said, watching from the driver's seat. "I'll give you two-to-one odds, since you're an old man now. At twenty!" He shook his head. "It's a damn shame."

Nathan hiked to the end of the fence and climbed up. He tried to recall the treacherous spots, but who could know how it had weathered in the two years since the last time he'd done this?

As he stepped forward, a gnarled section of the fence creased his shoe. The wood creaked angrily as he advanced, navigating the first two sections. He hopped the initial gap effortlessly. A sense of pride crept up on him like an unexpected friend as he landed.

The next gap was wider. He'd need to generate momentum to clear it, followed by another gap right after. Leaning forward, he pushed off with two quick steps. He skipped the gap, landed on one foot, and jumped across the second. So far, so good.

"Impressive, Padawan!" Ryan called from the car, followed by some scrambling.

During the next jump, Nathan spotted an object coming in fast. In a flash, his reflexes kicked in. His upper body twisted sideways as he caught an apple in midair, landing on one foot.

The fence wobbled fiercely under his weight, and for a moment he was sure it would break. His arms and leg sprang out like a gyroscope, offsetting his center of gravity. Equilibrium spread quickly like a wave through his body, and he regained his balance.

Nathan smiled. "There you go! Twenty bucks. You want your apple back?"

"Shit! You're like a damn cat! I'll pay you tomorrow. Lucky bastard."

The Mustang's wheels spun. Dirt and rocks launched ten feet behind it. A cloud of dust hung in the air as the car zoomed away.

Brimming with confidence and full of adrenaline, Nathan jumped off the fence and headed home.

The euphoric rush quickly diminished, bringing his mood back down. He'd loved this walk before the universe turned against him. Now, it was a reminder of how things had changed. He wandered down the dirt road with feet that got heavier with each step. A breeze ruffled through the cornfields that stretched out on either side. He closed his eyes, trying to coax the positive feelings back.

Soon, he was in his driveway. He looked up at the house before him. A modest ranch with a varied complement of trees, flowers, and shrubs. It had been home since he could remember. He grabbed a daisy on the way up.

After unlocking the door, he lowered his shoulder and gave it a good shove. It popped open with a tacky sound, like when he pried his teeth apart after mashing down on a candy cane.

It always did that in the summer when the humidity got too high.

Nathan stepped inside and made his way to the first bedroom. "Sue?"

As he entered, a bank of various medical devices and medicines greeted him. An IV stand dangled pouches and hoses down to his older sister. Her black hair hid some of the tracheostomy scars that painted her neck in soft pink lines.

"Sue, did you take your medicine?"

She rolled her eyes and leaned back. "Yes, Nathan. And stop calling me that. It sounds like you're calling a pig!" She wrinkled her nose.

"You prefer big sis?"

"No, I do not." She tilted her head affably. "One: don't call a woman 'big' anything. Two... okay, just one. But it's an important one to remember." She pushed herself up into a sitting position.

Nathan dropped the flower into a glass of water with no fanfare.

"Aww. Widdle brother brought me a flower."

Nathan ignored the comment and got down to business. He switched the IV bag, loaded up a syringe, and injected it into the solution with a practiced hand.

"We need to get more of this."

Susan waved the air in front of her. "I don't need it. It's just for pain. The insurance won't cover it anyway."

"Don't worry. I'll get more." Nathan tossed the syringe into a hazardous waste box.

Then her face brightened. "You remember what tonight is?"

More weight fell on Nathan's shoulders. He'd been looking forward to being alone tonight. But he had promised.

"Yeah. I remember." He tried to sound excited as he opened Susan's wheelchair. It jangled with a distinctly familiar noise that reminded him of all her trauma. After sliding his arms under her, he picked her up and placed her in the chair.

"I'll get some snacks," she said, and rolled away.

It took Nathan longer than he remembered to set up the battle worn telescope on the deck. Twisting the fragile knob ever so slightly, his fingers dialed in the focus. The knob had threatened for years to snap off, and of course, today it did. Nathan sighed, wanting to smash the whole damn thing on the ground. Couldn't just one thing go his way?

By the time he fixed it, night had settled in. Not only was there a lunar eclipse tonight, but there was a meteor shower as well. Susan had been looking forward to this since she'd read about it last month.

Nathan left the telescope to go inside and returned with Susan in the wheelchair, wrapped in a blanket. He maneuvered her chair down the steps one bump at a time.

"I remember when Dad got you your first telescope. You thought you'd see aliens." She leaned back and looked at him with a big smile.

"What do you expect? I was like seven." He allowed himself a small grin before squinting into the telescope. "Check it out."

She pushed herself up and glanced into the lens. "Oh, wow. Wait, what happened?" She took her eye off and looked up.

Nathan rested against the house, crossing his arms, and glanced skyward. Black clouds had drifted over the moon, with more behind them, as far as he could see.

"Figures," he mumbled as he rubbed tension from his face. A headache was slowly surfacing.

"The clouds will pass, Nathan."

He shook his head. "You want to wait out here all night?"

She motioned to her wheelchair. "I'm not going anywhere."

The words struck a nerve. Nothing had gone right since the accident, and she was cracking jokes about it.

"I'm going inside," he said, pushing off the wall.

"Nathan, wait." Susan looked him over. "Are you okay?"

The question agitated him. People had been asking him that for the last four months. He was sure she was sick of the question too, which was why it irritated him even more.

"Am I okay?" It came out like a bursting dam. "Our lives are messed up, Susan! Mom and Dad are dead! You're in a wheelchair. And I—"

He stopped, his arms waving helplessly. "You're joking about it!"

"And?" she said. "And you, what?"

"Just forget it."

"No, I won't forget it. Say it, Nathan." She stared at him. "You what?"

"Why can't we just have a normal life, like everyone else? All my friends are living their lives."

"Are you talking about Angela's Instagram? I saw it. Just because she posted that picture doesn't mean she doesn't have problems. I can post a picture of me dancing and everyone will think my life is wonderful and I dance the days away in some glamorous way. But it doesn't make it true. That's not real life. This is real life." She gestured between them. "Me and you talking. Right now."

Nathan picked idly at splinters from the wall next to him. "It's not just her. Ryan too."

"Everyone has to live their own lives, Nathan. Ryan has always had it easy. But fixating on his life, or anyone else's, isn't helping you live yours. It's making you miserable. Besides, Chelsea is dumping him. His life isn't perfect, but it doesn't have to be, and neither does yours."

"It's not just that." He took a deep breath. "I can't afford to take care of you." His shoulders sank with a heaviness he'd never felt before. "There's just this crushing mountain of debt.

It's not going away—it's just going up! How am I supposed to take care of you? There, I said it. Now you can be pissed at me."

Susan nodded, as if she already knew. "You need to go back to college. That's where you belong. Not here with me."

"Do we have to go over this again?" Exhaling, he spelled it out as clearly as he could. "We. Can't. Afford. It."

Susan cocked her head to the side, giving him a twisted frown. "You have a soccer scholarship!"

"To some school five hours away! We'd have to hire a nurse. No. Just drop it." He turned to go inside.

"I won't be responsible for you giving up your future, Nathan!" She nearly rose out of her chair. "Yes, there was a car accident—yes, Mom and Dad died, and I'm stuck in this wheelchair. But you aren't, and that's not your fault. You don't have to be stuck here taking care of me. I'll be fine. I'm not your responsibility!"

"How? Where are you going to get money? You're not a dancer anymore!" He took a deep breath, attempting to calm down. "You took dance lessons since you were seven. That was your entire life!" Sorrow flared in him, causing his eyes to sting with tears. Clenching his jaw, he blinked the sensation away.

"And this is my life now. I've accepted it. I'm not dead, Nathan! And neither are you! Move on. Move on from this. Go to college, fall in love, make a difference. I don't need you to watch over me."

Unable to think of anything else to say, he snatched up the telescope and went inside, then paused and put it down. Nathan wanted this interaction to be over, but he realized Susan would need help getting back up the steps. He returned and maneuvered her and the wheelchair inside without a word.

A soft smile formed on her lips, and she patted his hand.

The clouds moved on, and the meteor shower ended, but

three hours later, Susan's words still tumbled through Nathan's mind as he lay in bed. Looking up at the dreamcatcher he'd made as a child, he traced the strings with his eyes and tried to find the path out of its maze.

He sat up and rested his chin on his knees. Options, or lack thereof, ran through his mind. Nothing was clear anymore—it was hopeless.

In the darkness, he got up and made his way to the front door. Susan's monitors beeped as he passed her room, alternating with her peaceful breaths. Quietly, he slipped on his boots.

Outside, a gentle breeze blew by, bringing the smell of a lonely summer night and cooling his warm skin. Clearing his head beneath the wide-open night sky was the best part about living in the country, but his worries had followed him.

The field across the road was alive with eternally moving corn stalks. A giant tree sat in the middle of the field a good thirty yards out, looming over it all. As a child, he'd always thought it was out of place. No matter how high the corn was, he could always see the tree over everything else, like a lighthouse in the middle of a green sea. But in the darkness, it was more ominous. There was no beacon of light to guide his path, just the silhouette of a Godzilla-sized monster swaying in the wind.

He closed his eyes and lifted his head to the sky, letting the night seep into his soul. The rustling leaves formed a static of sorts, drowning out all his painful thoughts. For a moment, he enjoyed the symphony—the leaves, the crickets, the calming purr of it all.

A minute or two later, though, he realized that there was something else there, an unusual element hiding within the natural matrix of nature. Encrypted among the wind and the leaves was a soft whirr.

Nathan opened his eyes and scanned the immediate area. It wasn't like anything he'd heard before. It didn't belong here.

He turned left, then right, attempting to triangulate the noise. Soon, he was certain it came from in front of him. Not wanting to lose the sound, he took small, cautious steps. Before he knew it, he'd crossed the ditch, and gravel was crunching under his feet from the road. Fearful he would lose the mysterious noise, he paused to listen.

It was gone.

After slinking to the other side of the road, he waited for it to come back. The swaying corn was loud, but he zeroed it out. Then the hum returned.

Following it, he crept into the field. His view was now blocked by the corn, most of which towered over him. Step after step, the long leaves scratched and pulled at him as he tracked the sound. Visibility was about one foot in any direction, but he could sense where he was going.

His heart was thumping now as his mind buzzed with potential explanations. It came up with none that made sense. This was unlike anything he'd heard before.

Nathan pushed through the endless corn, its sharp stalks scratching against his clothes. The wind triggered a whisper of darkened cornstalks rustling from all around, their leafy fingers grasping at him. He was closing in. The whirr was louder now, easier to detect.

When the rows of corn finally broke, it revealed the clearing around the giant tree. He looked up at it. It seemed alive in the wind. Then it flickered like an old TV, as if two competing channels were fighting for dominance. One was the tree. The other was...

Impossible.

Nathan stared up at the wavering image of a strange craft hovering before him. It de-cloaked from the darkness as if the night sky were a curtain being pulled back from it. He was alone in a darkened field with god knew what, yet it wasn't fear that struck him, but wonder.

The mysterious ship defied physics. In his world, it could

not exist, but here it was. Gripped in a place of amazement and possibility, he was unable to break free.

Everything else was void as he watched purple-white lights dance over the ship's smooth black surface as if they were shooting stars captured in a bottle. Their movement was like the sparkling glitter that swirled in the water globe his parents had given him years ago.

From the ship came the gentle hum he'd followed, which now penetrated his body and pulsated over his stress-filled shoulders.

Nathan's eyes flowed over the craft's surface, drawn to it like a child to the wonders of fire. Moonlight glimmered off the ship's eerie silhouette, giving him a hint of its shape. Three wings swept out from the body of the craft, resembling an inverted 'Y.' Its top rose sharply from the nose, then curved downward midway back. The bottom did the same except for two sloped wings underneath the nose. The wings and body merged perfectly with each other in waved fins.

The craft floated above the corn like a giant, creepy angelfish.

The humming changed to a tone much deeper than before. The swirling lights vanished, and a soft blue glow appeared from the center of the craft. The whirr rose in pitch as the blue became more intense, bathing the clearing in an eerie cosmic illumination. Nathan could even see the cornstalks around him now.

A scream sailed through the night, piercing Nathan's trance. Panic shocked his body taut. He knew immediately who it was.

Susan.

Then, he was ten feet into the field, mowing over cornstalks as he raced back to the house. His legs pumped like a jackhammer at full tilt, bulldozing his own path. Slashes to his hands and face from the sharp corn tassels barely registered in his consciousness as his focus narrowed.

After emerging from the field in a reckless sprint, he stumbled up the ditch, slowing slightly to maintain his balance. Tendons crackled as his left ankle rolled. Pain flashed up his leg, but he refused to acknowledge it as he regained his equilibrium and crossed the lawn in a haze. A few more seconds and he'd be there for her. Lowering his shoulder, he crashed through the front door.

Inside, he paused for a beat to gather his senses. It was quiet and dark, except for the moonlight that streamed through the bay windows in a checkered pattern on the carpet. His heart thundered against his ribcage. An unfamiliar clicking noise drew his attention to the hallway. It sounded like—

Susan's scream tore through the darkness from the backyard.

Nathan charged through the house, his body reacting with soccer-field instincts, twisting and sidestepping the furniture. He was ten feet from the back door.

Then, something new, something out of place, was blocking his way.

A dark shape rose from a hunched position to loom over Nathan, dwarfing him. Fear spread through him like water on a dry beach, seeping into his core. For a moment, his mind grappled with what he saw.

It was not human.

From the shadows, he could see the eyes clearly. There were twelve of them, six on each side of its horrific head, and they glowed from within. Their eerie luminescence speckling the room with a supernatural glow. Spikes seemed to drip from its head, like untamed icicles.

It looked at him calmly, like a gorilla might just before it ripped you in half.

There was a clattering behind it. Nathan knew the sound—the jangle of Susan's wheelchair crashing to the ground. Energy surged inside him.

He darted for the door, but the creature seized him with an icy, powerful grip. Then, something was in Nathan's hand, and he swung it at the creature like a baseball bat. The telescope shattered against its head, the fiberglass shaft snapping in two. The errant half cartwheeled through the air and smashed through the window, causing a whipping wind to surge in from outside.

Nathan tried to move, but the creature's grip constricted. He lashed out and stabbed the now-serrated telescope into the arm that held him. The creature hissed as white gas rushed from the wound, clouding the air. Its hold on him slackened, and he twisted free.

Hurtling past the creature and through the broken window, he landed on the deck in the backyard. Broken glass crunched under his boots, and pain flared from his twisted ankle.

Nathan scanned the area for Susan—she was nowhere.

Another black angelfish craft hovered ten feet off the ground. From it, blinding spotlights lit up wildly billowing trees and an empty deck. A round doorway to the ship spiraled closed.

"Let her go!" he shouted into the night air.

A deafening horn sounded from the ship, and a bright blue glow lit up underneath it.

"Let her go!"

The horn faded as the craft started to rise. Running out of time, Nathan leaped onto the porch railing and raced toward the craft. His body was numb and operating on pure adrenaline. At the railings' end, he launched himself at the craft, reaching for something, anything, to grab on to.

Clasping a ridge of the hull with one hand, he ascended with the ship. He lashed out, desperately seeking another handhold, but found nothing else to grasp. The house was below him now. His muscles burned with the weight of his body. It was too much. His fingers went dead, and he tumbled from the ship, his vision spinning. He closed his eyes and tucked his head, ready for the pain of impact.

And then, unexpectedly, he had stopped. Stopped spinning. Stopped falling.

He'd lifted his head and saw one of the bizarre creatures had projected a pulsating ring of lights at him. Then everything had gone dark.

Nathan's mind churned through the haze and carried him back to his current reality. He was coughing up a slushy gel, and his ears and throat were burning. A sharp pain pinched his leg. Had the creatures come to torture him again?

The scene was coming into focus. It was just out of reach. His consciousness was a misty cloud of senses. There was movement around him. Two—no, three beings. They were smaller, human-like, and spoke in distorted, whispered sentences. Nathan strained to listen. It wasn't the clicks anymore.

They were speaking English!

Before he could piece it all together, darkness encircled him once more.

CHAPTER 3

Meraki Dreadnaught Kai'den: The Present

Nathan floated back to full consciousness and reclaimed control of his eyelids. As he opened them, pain shot through his pupils as if he'd been in the dark for days. A pulsing orange light glowed through a waxy structure that encased him like a cocoon. His ears were filled with a rumbling bass that reverberated all around him as if someone were playing drums in the next room.

As he shifted, the cocoon broke apart and crumbled with a crunch. Nathan climbed from a concave depression within the floor through the fragments of his enclosure. His muscles were rigid and complained about every command, but besides the stiffness, he had no pain or injuries. He stretched and flexed his joints to a point where he was comfortable moving them. His feet were bare, but a soft gray material covered the rest of his body.

Now that he was free, he wasn't about to let the creatures take him again. He had to get out of here and find his sister.

With each pulse of the orange light, Nathan tried to piece together the room. It was small and mostly empty. There were other impressions in the floor for more cocoons, but they were not in use. This seemed like some sort of recovery room.

The thumping bass grew louder as Nathan took a step toward the door. His attention lingered there, his mind slow to realize that the door had no handle. Then, as the light returned, he located a circle etched into the wall and pressed it.

A sudden weightlessness washed over him as his body lurched forward. His hands instinctively latched onto the doorframe, quickly slipping off the smooth metal as an invisible current dragged him forward. His body was being sucked out of the room, along with the shattered pieces of his wax cocoon and anything else not bolted down.

Covering his head in anticipation of impact, he tumbled down a hall, thumping against the walls, first his shoulder, then his hip and arm. Spinning with each impact, he bounced a dozen more times before coming to a painful stop. It was moments before his mind caught up to his body and stopped tumbling. Once the dizziness retreated, his body relaxed, and he lifted his head.

He was in a vast room that was sparsely decorated, with two open levels, the main one he was on and a mezzanine above. It seemed to be an observatory or high-tech solarium. One whole side of the room and half the ceiling was made of glass. On the other side of the glass…

A nebula, floating in deep space. Vivid colors that did not exist on Earth painted a swirling mosaic before him. Thunderstruck, Nathan climbed to his feet and approached the window in a dreamlike awe. Where the hell was he?

His body jolted in surprise as a long, sleek craft roared by and then exploded. Another craft followed. And another. They twisted and spun in a frantic dogfight. Multicolored lasers crisscrossed as the crafts looped and dodged.

The longer he looked, the more he saw. There were other dogfighting crafts in the distance, and a large silver ship with an aura of debris drifting around it.

That was when he realized that the bass he was hearing wasn't music down the hall, but explosions and gunfire. And it was getting closer.

He crept back from the window to the hallway. Glancing out from the cover it gave him, he saw a firefight a few hundred feet away. Lasers of different shapes and noises flashed around the corridor, and the smell of ozone filled his nose.

What the fuck was going on?

Before he had time to consider an answer, his arm twisted painfully. He spun to see a human soldier in red armor about to snap something around his wrist. On pure impulse, Nathan threw a leg out and kicked the soldier's knee with shocking force, knocking him off balance.

Grabbing the back of the soldier's head, he smashed his knee into the man's face. The soldier stumbled backward and dropped his pistol. Nathan scooped up the gun and pointed it at him.

The soldier charged, drawing a knife from his hip. Nathan's finger twitched against the trigger, yet nothing happened.

His attacker thrust the blade at him. Scorching pain sliced through Nathan's skin and spread into his stomach. Warm blood spilled down his side, but somehow, he swung the pistol down and smashed the soldier in the face.

But the soldier wasn't done. He head-butted Nathan to the floor and followed that up with a sharp kick to the ribs. Nathan felt a crack, and his entire abdomen erupted in agony. His vision blurred.

As his assailant drew back for another kick, he convulsed and fell to the floor.

An older man in silver armor appeared, holding a pistol over the dead soldier. Looking like a seasoned veteran in his forties, he pointed a finger at Nathan.

"*Dina feydoor!*" he said.

With a red-hot pain in his stomach and his own blood everywhere, Nathan did not feel safe. He reached desperately for the knife, which had fallen a few feet from him.

The veteran shouted again and kicked the weapon away.

Nathan, untrained in combat, was surprised as his body instinctively spun around, his foot sweeping the veteran's legs out from under him. The man's body hung in midair briefly before crashing to the ground. Nathan lurched forward and elbowed him in the face.

However, sooner than expected, the veteran recovered, rolled forward, and smashed his fist into the side of Nathan's jaw.

✳ ✳

Nathan awoke upright with a headache and no idea how much time had passed. Hanging spread-eagle and feeling like a human X, he took inventory of the situation. His body was suspended from glowing purple energy bands that restrained his wrists and ankles. Somehow, his stab wound was gone.

Expecting to be dead or abducted by those strange dark creatures, it surprised him to see two humans standing before him. Both were male and dressed in light gray military uniforms. Behind them, a woman with teal skin watched, wearing a long white tunic.

Nathan closed his eyes, waited a moment, and opened them again.

"*Kinto idar shok vur?*" the younger officer said with a certain smugness.

Nathan looked up at the man, searching for answers. The second officer was the veteran he'd elbowed. Behind him was another window into space. The nebula was still there, but this time, six ships were traveling alongside them, accompanied by a handful of smaller fighters. The battle appeared to be over.

"*Cumo,*" the veteran said.

Nathan blinked repeatedly. His eyes were still sensitive to the glare of the room. "I don't understand you. What do you want?"

The veteran glared at the woman behind them. She stepped forward. Nathan could now see her sharp eyes and odd ears. Moving between the officers, she grabbed Nathan's head. He struggled, but couldn't stop her from tapping behind his ear.

"Let's start over," the woman said.

The young officer spoke again. "So, he's ready then?"

"The translator is on. Whether he's ready to hear what you are about to tell him is unknown." The woman turned to Nathan. "You've been unconscious nearly three hours."

Questions raced through Nathan's head. "Who the hell are you?"

"I am Master Chief Drelmar Vinn," the veteran said, butting in, then motioned to the others. "This is Chief Ajax Sculic and Doctor Wendalin Rami."

"What did you do?" Nathan asked the doctor.

"Relax," she said. "It's only an implant. Your brain will access it when you hear or see a language that's coded on it. There's another in your throat that will translate your words to the last language you heard."

Nathan caught a second wind. "You can't just cut me open and implant shit in me!"

Ajax tilted his head impatiently. "You were taken by the Vox. You'd rather we left you frozen?"

Drelmar shot an annoyed glare at Ajax. "We found you in a cryo-cell at a checkpoint aboard a High Command ship. From the records, we found your name is Stryder, and they took you from a class-B planet. Is that true?"

Still vulnerable, Nathan hunted for a way out. His mind played out scenarios of escape.

"You are safe now," Drelmar said in a calming voice.

"Safe?" Renewed defiance rippled through him, and he wrenched at his restraints.

"I'm sorry we had to restrain you," Dr. Rami chimed in. "But you've proven to be," —she searched for a word— "aggressive."

Ajax stepped forward. "You're not a prisoner. Just tell us

what you know about the High Command's invasion strategy."

"Then let me go!"

"We just need a few answers first," Ajax said, dismissing Nathan's demand with his hand.

"No! I need answers. Where am I?"

Drelmar waved for Ajax to back off. "You are aboard the *Kai'den*, dreadnaught flagship of the Meraki Dominya, a light-year from where we found you."

Nathan wasn't sure how much of this he was willing to believe. He was in a state of shock. He'd seen a lot—alien creatures, wax cocoons, a starfighter dogfight—and apparently, he was in space.

Drelmar must have been able to read his face.

"We are human like you, with some minor differences. We appear to be prolific in the galaxy." He waved his arms outward in an all-encompassing gesture. "Perhaps a common ancestor, convenient genetics… there are many theories."

He stepped forward and turned off the restraints. Nathan's legs buckled, slumping to his knees without the bands of energy holding him up.

"I don't believe it," he whispered, trying to convince himself none of this was happening.

Ajax leaned close and observed him. "Interesting. Is your world flat, too? Because you just sailed off the edge. I understand you're struggling with this—apparently, your world hasn't contacted other civilizations—but this is real."

Drelmar interrupted. "Behind your ear. Turn off the translator." He motioned to Nathan's ear. "Tap twice."

"Or step out an airlock," Ajax added. "We don't—"

Nathan reached behind his ear and felt a tiny elevated triangle about the same size as the eye of a needle. Tapping it twice instantly turned Ajax's words into an alien language.

After a few moments of this, he tapped it again, and the

words turned back to English. It was as if toggling the audio settings on a foreign movie.

"—convince you," Ajax finished.

As Nathan's mind struggled to comprehend what was happening, words fell out of his mouth. "How? Why?"

The officers made their way to the door, motioning for Nathan to follow.

Leaving the doctor behind, they traveled down a long hall, passing several doors, and entered an elevator. Drelmar placed his hand over a metal plate on the wall. A light washed across his palm, and the elevator began to move. As near as Nathan could tell, they were going up. The doors opened, and another hallway stretched out in front of them.

A few strides later, they stood before a pair of double doors, which slid away, revealing a room that was strangely normal. There was furniture, but alien in design and structure. On the far wall was a couch made from dark, twisted wood. Above it hung a worn map of a planet Nathan didn't recognize. It showed no oceans, just vast channels of water splitting up the land.

"There was one more thing," Ajax started. "The manifest listed another 'Stryder.'"

The words hit Nathan like a sledgehammer. His chest constricted as a surge of panic crashed over him. With everything that had happened, he'd forgotten about Susan.

"Where is she? The 'other Stryder?'" he blurted.

"You know who it is?"

"Of course I do!" Nathan snapped. "Where is she?"

Ajax turned to Drelmar.

Drelmar cleared his throat. "We don't know. You were the only one we found."

A vise closed on Nathan's heart. "What do you mean? What did they do with her? She needs her medicine!"

"Please, have a seat," Drelmar said. "I'll find out what I can. But for now, we're headed for—"

"We're headed for a rendezvous with the rest of our fleet at Sienna," a deep voice rumbled behind him.

Reflexively, Nathan's muscles grew taut as he turned toward the startling voice. A man strode confidently into the room with measured steps. His uniform was more impressive than the others. Black with gold cuffs and collar, it was decorated with medals and insignias. The man's ebony skin blended well with the uniform, as if he were just another part of it.

Behind him was a woman of the same caliber, intelligent-looking and sure of herself. Her uniform was a shade lighter, and her long, white hair twisted into braids that hugged her head.

"Thank you. Wait outside," the man said.

Drelmar and Ajax complied, leaving Nathan.

"I am Lord Admiral Arid Lasal." He paused dramatically. "And this is Captain HaReeka," he continued, gesturing to the woman. "And you are?"

Lord Admiral? Nathan had never heard of such a title. But that sounded about right at this point. He had heard none of this before.

"Nathan Stryder," he said.

"Well, Master Stryder, I like to do as much as I can for refugees like yourself, but we are heading for a critical engagement."

"What about the other Stryder?" Nathan demanded.

Lasal regarded him for a beat. "We don't know. People are often displaced in the war and despite our best attempts to prevent it, it ravages the galaxy. It seems you and this 'other Stryder' were, for whatever reason, caught in the middle and taken without consent. I'm sorry."

Nathan was at a loss for words as his mind wrestled with what he'd just heard. As he tried to make sense of it, his eyes wandered to a sparkling object overhead. A transparent bowl hung from the ceiling, filled with thousands of crystals floating in a thick liquid. The crystals gave off a spellbinding light as they drifted in an almost organized pattern.

"Relaxing, isn't it? They're Gaderian Crystals," Lasal said. "They generate power by floating around and absorbing kinetic energy, which in turn produces the light." He made his way to the couch across from Nathan.

"Who are the Vox?" Nathan said. "They're the ones that took us?"

Lasal appeared to be caught off guard. "The Vox? Where did you hear that name?"

"That's what they said. She was on the Vox manifest."

HaReeka chuckled. "The Vox? They were making fun of you. That's a fable."

Lasal regarded HaReeka briefly. "As far as we can tell, you were abducted from your planet by slavers and sold to the High Command. They would be the ones who have her now."

Nathan's eyes stung. A simmering heat rose within him. "Who is the High Command?"

"The Baraska High Command," HaReeka interjected. "A collective of aggressive expansionists maneuvering to control this wing of the galaxy. We've been at war with them for decades. We encountered this group by accident, and you're lucky we did, or else they would have continued their experiments. It would have been nothing you would want to remember."

Experiments? The word triggered a rise of fluid in Nathan's mouth. He quickly swallowed as dread twisted his stomach. It was as if he were back on the table. The rank smell returned, as did the numerous eyes, and the pain.

He attempted to focus on his senses, on what he felt and saw and heard right now. It was a calming habit, helping him to be present. He focused on the texture of the couch fabric and the floating crystals above him.

"What do you mean 'experiments?' What experiments?"

Lasal sat calmly. "We have no way of knowing for sure.

Regretfully, though, you cannot return anytime soon. At least, not in the near future. We were far from your planet when we rescued you, and we are even farther now. But we will do our best."

He nodded with a reassuring smile, then stood up and looked Nathan over.

"For now, you are aboard the *Kai'den*, flagship of the Meraki Navy," he said, puffing out his chest. "You may stay onboard as a guest. I'm afraid you are stuck with us for a while. We are currently locked into a hyperspace jump that won't be completed for some time. I truly am sorry, but I have millions of people depending on us. Without this fleet, they could all perish."

Nathan nodded, feeling a bit out of his depth. "How do you mean?"

Lasal gave a slight smile, as if he had been waiting for the question. "Well, we are outflanking the High Command. They have seized and enslaved the planet of one of our most primitive allies. The world is useless. It has no strategic value. Perhaps—"

"I don't care about any of that. I only care about finding Susan."

Lasal paused, glaring at the audacity of the interruption.

"You should care, because unfortunately, war spreads, and the High Command are pushing this way. For your planet, and the others in the sector, war is coming. And when that happens, many—including your sister—will suffer."

CHAPTER 4

Arista Conak stepped cautiously into the Crucible, processing what she saw. What challenge awaited her today? In many ways, this room was familiar to her. She had been here many times before, but every time it was somewhere different. Using Altered Reality technology, the room could be anywhere or anything.

On this day, it was a hot, arid desert plain with no end in sight, reminding her of the brief time she'd spent on Naam. The gritty winds tousled her hair and slipped over her red jumpsuit. She gripped a two-meter wooden staff in her left hand, grinding it into the dirt unconsciously as she mentally prepared for whatever was to come.

She kicked the bottom end of the staff and let it swing up over her head. Twisting her wrist, she continued the momentum, whirling it around her. She took notice of its balance, appreciating the smooth grain on her palm at the same time.

For years, they'd intensely trained her as a soldier, developing keen skills in over one hundred forms of armed and unarmed combat. By all means, she was a force to be reckoned with. Her studies had also included various strategies and tactics needed for the art of warfare.

It had been a while since she'd faced anyone who could challenge her on the battlefield. But she was still a student to the man now approaching her, the mighty Krell Duma.

His presence was enormous. Outfitted in coal-gray armor, he stood well over two meters tall and weighed, she guessed, 120 kilograms. With his features concealed in a helmet, she had no clue to his thoughts. Over the years, he had often switched between helmets. This one had an open face when the blast shield wasn't activated, but it nearly always was. His skill for combat was rare and perfected, volcano-like in its explosiveness and violence. Just seeing him as an adversary spread chills across her body.

A leathery sound whispered in the wind as he moved. He gripped the same type of weapon she held. He dwarfed the staff, just as he dwarfed her.

Arista saluted him. She positioned her right arm straight across her chest, hand in a fist over her heart, her left arm tucked behind her at the base of her spine. Duma returned the salute.

Pushing aside the deep current of intimidation that threatened to wash her away, she focused. She'd need every bit of knowledge, technique, ability, and luck she had to come out of this fight without another week in the med bay. This was her fifth actual fight with Duma himself. After the last fight, she'd spent months earning the right to stand against him again—weeks of two new martial arts styles, body conditioning, acrobatics, weapons training, and innumerable full-contact fights. She was not about to let this chance go to waste.

To Krell Duma, she imagined it was another chance to see how well he'd taught her, his only student. When she first met him, she'd been living on a quiet planet a distance from the main star lanes. Trained from a young age by a war matriarch, her grandmother, she'd already had her first taste of battle. After her father died, Duma had taken her under his shield, and taught her not to commit to any one style of combat, but to use them all, making her a more efficient fighter. A fight to the death differed greatly from a sparring match. The more styles one learned, the better the chance of emerging from combat alive.

Duma stabbed his staff into the sand hard enough for it to stand on its own. Then he unclasped his helmet and threw it behind him. In silence, he grabbed the staff again and stepped forward.

The pair locked eyes and silently entered into fighting stances.

Without a blink, Duma slid in, extended his weapon, and struck Arista in the solar plexus. The blow forcefully expelled the breath from her lungs.

"Pay attention!" Duma commanded.

Arista cursed herself. After all these years, she still underestimated his speed. Now she was at a disadvantage, and would be on the defensive until she could catch her breath.

With lethal swiftness, he came down on her, striking twice with the staff and then sending a kick at her ribs. Arista blocked the two powerful blows and quickly covered up her ribs. But the force of the attack sent her sprawling back, and she barely held onto the staff with one hand. He'd beaten her already.

No. She wouldn't accept it. She wouldn't disappoint him.

Arista pushed off her left leg and launched into a textbook back-flip. The world spun quickly around her, then settled back into place as she hit the ground. It was a solid landing, and she quickly regained her bearings.

Duma shifted toward her as she feigned an attack to his right. Falling for the ruse, he thrust his weapon to intercept. But she wasn't there. She released one hand from her staff and spun with her elbow out. It smashed into his head and sent it rocking back.

She couldn't believe it—she'd hit him.

But to do it, she'd overextended and was out of position. Arista rolled forward to get some distance, dragging the staff behind her.

Duma came at her like a locomotive, stomping a heel down on her staff and pinning it to the sand. As she sprang back up into a fighting stance, the staff jerked away from her. He'd disarmed her. Just like that, he had all the advantages.

Not waiting for him to pick her apart with his weapon, she charged ahead. Swiftly ducking and weaving her upper body to avoid his attacks, she closed the gap. Sliding feet-first at him, she tried to surprise him with a heel lock. Duma snatched his foot up a blink ahead of her, denying her the prize.

Wasting no energy, she scrambled to a knee and rammed her shoulder into his thigh. Wrapping up his leg with her arms, she converted her momentum into a single-leg takedown attempt.

Duma released his weapon, grabbed her under the arms, and tossed her into the air. He charged forward and kneed her in the side before she even hit the ground.

※ ※

The sheets were feathery soft and covered her like a blanket of invulnerability. Even given all her knowledge of armor and experience with it, Arista still felt the safest under a warm, plush, fuzzy blanket. Sometimes, she expected to emerge from them as her six-year-old self, safe on Aureon in her grandmother's bed.

But today, she was far from that. Her grandmother was dead, and she lived in space. She wasn't even bundled in sheets or blankets. Instead, she was encased in a waxy shell called a ZIPR coating.

Her fight with Duma had ended quickly after she'd landed her first blow. His controlled frenzy of attacks had been more than she could handle. He moved like someone half his size.

She was grateful for the wonders of Meraki medical technology. On Aureon, it would have taken phases to recover from the wounds she'd just suffered from her mentor.

In her mind, Arista relived the exchange, remembering her mistakes and the damage inflicted on her body: left shoulder, stomach, left thigh, right ankle, and head. They were all perfectly fine now, but a few hours ago, they were screaming for attention.

Knowing her duties and agenda, there was really no time to lie around. The med bay was a surprisingly comfortable place, but she had to return to work. With a quick stretch, she prepared to leave her artificial sanctuary. Breaking out of the shell took little effort and was weirdly satisfying. The material cracked and shattered as she stood up.

"Godspeed, Arista. Don't come back until you break something." Dr. Rami's voice came from an office to the right.

"Is that how you see me?" she asked flatly. "You're hurting my feelings, doc. Do you think you could work on your personality?"

Rami stepped out of her office. "Once again, I cannot," she snapped jokingly. They'd always had a good relationship. She was like an older sibling—one who cared, but liked to pretend she didn't.

Arista allowed herself a moment of pride for her performance against Duma before exiting the room and heading back to her quarters. Today's battle had proven that her skill was increasing, for it was the first time she had struck Duma.

Still, she knew she would be back in the med bay after the next fight. It wasn't negative thinking. It was a grim reality. That reality drove her each day, made her strive to become better and someday match her mentor. She wanted nothing more than to fight for the ideals that her grandmother had taught her, those that the High Command dishonored, and perfecting her deadly art was the only way she knew how.

Returning to her quarters, she discovered several messages left on the haloid. A quick skim revealed the usual: her training schedule, a mission proposal for her to look over and for Duma to approve, and an updated report of the High Command's movements. It was rarely anything new.

Then, the monotony of her daily routine broke as she

watched the little holographic figure of Lord Admiral Lasal appear. He stood straight, shoulders arched in a perfect military stance, as if his back were against an invisible wall. She rarely saw him, let alone received a vid from him. All her orders came from Duma.

Instinctively, she snapped to attention.

"Lieutenant Commander Arista Conak, I am addressing you as well as Valor Krell Duma about this matter. The time is now 0622."

Arista flicked a glance at her clock. It was currently 15:06. The messages had been recorded just after she left for her training session.

"Approximately three hours ago, we secured an individual who we feel has raw talent comparable to yours—Nathan Stryder. Your orders are to train him under the command of Master Chief Drelmar Vinn.

"I expect you to hone his abilities to the peak of their potential, as I have confidence that someday this individual would rival yours and Valor Duma's value to the service. We have great hopes for him and think he can aid us immensely in our campaigns, as you have in the past and continue to do. As you were." The image faded.

Rival Valor Duma? That was unimaginable. The Lord Admiral most likely threw that in to get under Duma's nails. But those thoughts faded quickly as a sense of eagerness washed over her—someone new to train with! It had been such a long time since she'd met anyone new. Outside of Duma and Dr. Rami, she'd seen a rare few people in person since her military career started—except for those she'd killed.

CHAPTER 5

Nathan returned to what he called the solarium. It literally was a room made for looking at the stars. Most of it was made up of windows that stretched from the floor all the way up and even curved to form part of the ceiling. There were two levels that were open to the center of the room, where a projector protruded from the floor. Each level was decorated similarly, with a few simple benches and floor pillows to sit on and large, decorated vases filled with colorful flowers. He estimated that a couple hundred people could fit in here comfortably, but currently, he was the only one.

He'd been told to wait for more details, and this was the room he felt most connected to, so here he waited. His mind zipped back and forth between thoughts, trying to reconcile everything he'd just experienced with everything he had known before. This, it seemed, whether he liked it or not, was his new reality.

Nathan gazed out at all that was before him. The nebula was no longer there, replaced by a weird distortion, a tunnel of swirling green and copper clouds segmented in regular intervals by rings of light. Lasal had said they were in a hyperspace jump. That must be what he was seeing now. Susan was out there somewhere. His heart sank into his stomach, weighted down by hopelessness. How would he ever find her?

Behind him, the whisking noise of the metal door sliding open drew his attention. He turned to see Drelmar, the soldier who had told him about his sister, approaching in a practiced military walk.

"Stryder. I have your resource assignment." Drelmar held out a silver card.

Nathan grasped the card between his fingers and looked it over. It was smooth like plastic and blank on both sides.

"Thanks," he said. More anger clung to his words than he'd expected. A layer of animosity tainted his emotions—he wanted to punish someone for taking him and Susan.

Drelmar read the angst in Nathan, and his tone relaxed. "Things will be difficult for you, I'm sure. But if I may offer some advice?"

Nathan was cynical. What kind of advice could this man possibly have for him? He'd been abducted and tortured. His sister was still missing. But at the same time, he was utterly lost, and didn't know where to turn.

"Sure, why not?"

Drelmar strode past Nathan to the window. "People of all races like to strive for happiness. Sometimes they have this idea of happiness that they will never reach. Like a nebula, even if they reach it, happiness is not a destination that lasts. It's fleeting."

He turned to face Nathan, and their eyes locked. "Instead, focus on resilience. On overcoming or adapting to anything the universe puts in your path. If you are resilient, you will reach your goals much more often. And happiness comes with that. But to be resilient, you must keep moving forward. No matter what. Understand?"

Nathan nodded. He had been expecting something more specific, but it made sense, especially now. Drelmar wasn't just a hard-nosed soldier brushing him aside. He seemed to care, to an extent. But could Nathan trust him with what he felt?

He took a chance. "You said you only found me."

"Yes. You were the only cargo they had. It's possible they transferred the other Stryder to another ship."

The words stung. "Stop calling her 'the other Stryder!' Her name is Susan. I still don't understand. Why us? Why her?"

"I wish I had a better answer." Drelmar paused. "But we don't know why."

Frustration strengthened Nathan's voice. "I have to find her."

Drelmar shifted his stance, stepping near Nathan, his tone graver. "The High Command is a nasty enemy to declare war on."

"Do you think I care?" Nathan retorted.

Drelmar kept his calm. "Let me ask you. Do you know where you are? Or how to pilot a Lima 3 shuttle? Do you even have any combat experience?"

Nathan was reluctant to admit it, but the Master Chief was right. He'd been plucked from a mud puddle and thrown into the ocean.

"It doesn't matter. I'll find a way!"

Drelmar looked him over, as if assessing him for a job. "I have a way."

Pausing for a beat, he studied Nathan's reaction. "We can help you find her. We can teach you what you need to know to survive, and to locate her. I could convince the Lord Admiral to let you enlist. You'd learn the skills you need, and would have access to our resources. You'd be under our command and protection."

The last words came softly. "As would Susan."

Silence separated them as Nathan ran through the options in his head. He visualized rescuing Susan. That was the goal. If only—

"You couldn't even fire that blaster," Drelmar reminded him. "How can you help her if you can't help yourself? It won't be quick. From what we can tell, you've been in a cryo-cell for months—that's a gigantic head start. You'll need patience, but it's your best chance. It's *her* best chance."

Nathan had nothing. Drelmar was right. He was worthless to Susan at this point. As if everything that had happened before wasn't enough, here was more to beat him down. Where would it end?

"If you want to keep moving forward, report to Section 9 at 0600 in two days. There's a reminder on the card." Drelmar nodded.

With the card directing him, Nathan found his quarters fairly easily after that. He slipped it into a terminal and stripes on the floor lit up for him to follow.

Like the other door, there was a small circle next to the one for his quarters. Touching the circle did nothing. He slid the card in and out several times, not even triggering a sound. On closer inspection, he could see a grid of lasers. He leaned closer, and the circle scanned his eye.

There was a beep, and the door opened.

Having been accustomed to one-room efficiency apartments in college, his quarters seemed immense. It included a main living/dining area, a bedroom, and a bathroom.

On a console in the bedroom was a monitor and keypad for him to use. It looked simple enough. Curious about the new technology and devices, Nathan was eager to explore them, but the last two days had caught up to him and were forcing him toward sleep. It would all still be there tomorrow. He collapsed onto the bed, barely able to pull the covers over him before sleep struck its final blow.

The next morning, a menu screen appeared on the panel next to the dining table. With little thought, he scanned the list of items and found something that looked like eggs. The digital image lit up with the touch of his finger, followed by a click. The panel then became translucent and Nathan watched as his meal was 3D printed before his eyes.

Once it was complete, the panel opened, and Nathan tentatively removed his breakfast. It resembled some type of egg casserole. He poked it with utensils that had been printed alongside his meal. After tasting a small forkful, he inhaled the rest. It was good—really good. He couldn't remember the last thing he'd eaten. He ordered another.

After his second breakfast had settled, a soft tone rang from his door. When he opened it, the officer he'd met with Drelmar stood before him. Nathan couldn't quite recall his name.

"Hail," the officer said formally. "I thought you could use some help understanding our daily technology with your primitive mind."

"Jack, right?" Nathan asked, a bit of animosity tainting his words.

He shook his head. "No. *Ajax*. Sculic. Security Chief."

"That's right. Thanks, but I was able to feed myself," Nathan said sarcastically. He turned away, but Ajax followed him inside. Nathan questioned the intrusion with a glare.

Ignoring him, Ajax proceeded. "Very good. There are a few other things I was instructed to go over with you." He pointed to the keypad and monitor. "A haloid: voice-activated knowledge base and holovid comm." He turned to the food printer. "You figured out the food. The water too?"

"It's pretty straightforward."

"Good. Good." Ajax stepped over to a small circular device that reminded Nathan of a Bluetooth speaker. "This is a vidcomm. With it, you can send video messages through the haloid. It is also voice-activated."

His instruction continued for another few minutes, though it was bland and pointless. Everything seemed to be pretty user friendly. Nathan just wanted him gone.

"I think I can figure out the rest," he said, stepping toward the door.

"Very well. One more thing." A bit awkwardly, Ajax pulled a small candle from his pocket and handed it to Nathan.

"Where I grew up, we light a candle for those who are... not with us."

"She's not dead," Nathan said. "But thanks."

"Call me if you need anything else," Ajax nodded on his way out.

Maybe he wasn't such a dick after all.

Later, Nathan fiddled with the haloid, but his mind was preoccupied with memories of Susan, the abduction, Drelmar's offer, and everything else. He lit the candle Ajax had given him and contemplated it all.

The day was gone in a haze, and so was Nathan's appetite. He lay on his bed, staring up at a crudely made dreamcatcher he'd assembled with pieces of a plate that had printed out with his dinner. At least he could look at something that reminded him of home.

He switched off the lights and tried to sleep.

In the darkness, he could hear the clicking noises as the creatures scurried around him. He knew they were there, in the shadows. He could see six rectangle eyes moving together in the gloom. Pain pinched his leg as one of the glowing instruments grazed him.

Nathan jolted awake, slamming his foot into the wall. Above him, the dreamcatcher twisted slowly. He sat up, taking a moment to remember where he was.

He was aboard the *Kai'den*, flagship of the Meraki Dominya, and they were in some sort of hyperspace jump. He'd hoped all of this was just a dream, but it was a blunt reality.

After sliding off the bed, he sat by the window and lifted the shade to see the weird clouds of hyperspace and its flowing rings of light. He wasn't sure what the rings were. Maybe stars streaking by? Whatever they were, they were soothing—their patterns and glow. They didn't waver in their path. Nothing stopped them, nothing affected them.

A soft *ding* echoed from the other room. Nathan released the shade and located the source: the metal card Drelmar had given him. It was pulsing red and chiming. A reminder displayed on the card: "Section 9. 06:00. Keep Moving Forward."

He still had an hour, but could not get back to sleep in that time. He lay in the bed, not wanting to move. The feeling wasn't new. It was his beast. Since his parents had died, and maybe even before that, Nathan struggled with it. There seemed to be no point to anything. He was such a small, meaningless part in all this. It was overwhelming, hopeless. He would never find Susan. He couldn't even fire that gun, and he had no idea what a Lima shuttle was.

A heaviness was on his chest, and he was slowly sinking into despair. But he had to do something. She was counting on him.

Nathan forced himself to move. By focusing on one task at a time, he got up, got dressed, and grabbed the card, which was again flashing with the reminder.

As he opened his door, anxiety sucker punched him. His stomach plummeted, and what felt like a python wrapped around him. Breathing became difficult. All he could manage were short, panicked gasps. Spots started forming in his vision, and ringing filled his ears as vertigo took over. What was he doing? He was in over his head.

Not wanting to pass out in the hall, he retreated inside. He leaned against the wall, trying to remember how the therapist taught him to deal with this. He sucked in a breath and held it for seven seconds, then pushed it out deliberately for eight more. After repeating this process four more times, the vise loosened, and his breathing returned to normal.

Willing his legs to move again, Nathan climbed to his feet and stepped out into the hall. At first, each stride was a chore, but after rallying his courage, he forged it into mental armor and pushed through the intangible wall of resistance before him.

Following the directions on the card that Drelmar Vinn had given him, Nathan made his way to Section 9. It was an enormous ship, and he wasn't sure he could find his way back to his room. But he'd deal with that later.

Before long, he approached large double doors with "Section 9" stenciled above them. Beyond the threshold was his future—and a way to find Susan. Nathan took a breath and strode through. The ash-gray doors slid apart as he did.

On the other side was a bustling interchange of people. Some had noticeable tints to their skin that he detected quickly—he saw red, blue, and green, along with the more familiar skin tones of Earth. They were not all deep shades but were enough to catch his eye. It was a jarring reminder that even though some of them looked like it, these people weren't from Earth. Other differences also stood out when he took the time to look more closely—subtle variations in the shapes and size of their features. The location of their ears, for instance. Some didn't even appear to have them.

The room reminded him of a smaller hi-tech version of Union Station, which he'd seen once on a vacation. There were benches and tables with people lounging and terminals along the wall where others were punching up data and watching holograms. Several lines queued up in front of a dozen streamlined booths.

Before Nathan had time to discover what it was all about, he sensed a strong pooling of energy inside him. It wasn't anxiety, though, he knew that feeling. Adrenaline? It was similar, but not exactly the same. The intensity grew swiftly and with ferocity, rushing through his body like his blood was on fire.

A body jolted into him from behind, drawing his attention. He turned and time slowed. His perception narrowed. Everything around him appeared to blur, except for—her.

Alluring, exquisite, striking—he couldn't find the word to

describe her, yet all those seemed to fit. There was an edge to her, a jaguar of a woman covered in a crimson jumpsuit. A storm of silvery-white, razor-cut hair perfectly complemented her powder-blue skin, its ends teasing her shoulder blades. Immediately, her eyes locked with his. They were a soft rose hue, like a sunset over the ocean. She flowed by him, holding the moment with a smile. Not a full smile, though—one that hinted at a secret.

She cocked her head, signaling for him to follow, then sauntered away.

As he collected himself, Nathan felt something was different now. Call it intuition, or kismet, or something else—whatever it was, a crosswind had hit his sails.

The woman crossed the room without looking back and continued down a hall. Nathan was halfway there before he knew he was following her. The pull toward her was magnetic.

In the hallway, he glimpsed her foot as she turned a corner. He pursued. His heart was racing and his mind had discarded the reason he was even in Section 9 to begin with.

A door slid shut around the corner—it had to be her. Nathan closed in. Something in his brain tried to reason with him. What was he doing? He wasn't supposed to be here and had no idea where he was. But the consideration was brief. He stepped through the door and found a small room.

Inside, a menacing black door stood notably before him, and it had just closed. Hanging on the wall were a variety of pictures of planets, weapons, ships, and the pressure points on several alien bodies. He had so much to understand.

Approaching the black door caused it to open, but inside he saw simply darkness. Regardless, he stepped through.

Only the glow from the open door behind him lit the room, and that disappeared quickly when the door closed. Nathan stood in the blackness, searching for something to focus on.

Before he could ponder what the hell he was doing, the

light began to rise. Slowly, the room was bathed in brilliance, but not from lighting overhead or on the walls or anywhere conventional. An immense, radiant sun ascended in the distance.

As it rose, he saw a jungle spreading out all around him. Lush, vibrant foliage with mostly purple and green hues limited his sight.

Nathan turned to where he'd entered but saw only a giant tree now. With few options, he stepped forward to discover a shallow watering hole, various colors of the jungle mirroring across its surface. Unseen birds cackled in the distance.

He grappled with what he was seeing. Was he not on a ship in deep space?

Then there was a crisp snap behind him. The birds went silent. He spun, but saw nothing. Squinting in the light of the rising sun, a sweep of vegetation caught the corner of his eye, spreading a sudden fear through him. He missed whatever had moved, only catching a wave of teetering grass in its wake, and realized he wasn't alone.

Nathan stepped backward, watching the growth for further movement as the swaying vegetation slowly came to a stop. Pulling his eyes away, he turned to find a safer position.

There it was again—the energy, the fire in his veins. His focus jumped abruptly to a figure standing before him.

Shocked by her sudden presence, adrenaline prickled to every corner of his body. It was the same woman he'd seen moments before, but now she had the wild look of a predator.

Her foot struck him hard in the chest, stripping his breath away. The force sent him stumbling backward, and he fell into the pool of water behind him.

Gasping for air, he scrambled to his feet. She was already moving toward him. His arm instinctively lifted to protect his face, blocking an incoming attack. The other swung down to stop a kick to his ribs.

Then the world spun, triggered by a sharp pain in his ankle

and a sudden weightlessness that overcame him. Once again, he fell hard into the water as she spun and swept his legs out from under him, sending a spray of droplets through the air.

Pouncing on him, she kept her body tight against him, hooking her legs around his, barring him from getting leverage. Nathan lifted his head from the shallow water, searching for a target to strike. However, her head was tucked against his, thwarting his attempts to land a blow.

She grabbed his trachea and squeezed, forcing his head back down. The crushing pressure prevented a full breath. Nathan thrashed for air, striking her in the ribs again and again in a desperate attempt to survive, but it didn't seem to do any good.

The lack of air made his temples pound, and a rush of pain to his head made it hard to think. It was as if his brain were too large for his skull, shoving and pushing for a way out. His punches grew weaker with every second. Slowly, his vision blotted and turned to black.

※ ※

In the Crucible's simulated jungle, Arista remained on top of Stryder's unconscious body for a heartbeat. She could imagine the chaos he felt as he was slipping under, the fear that had raced through his mind. He probably didn't know what to make of all this. She didn't envy him, and she wasn't thrilled with taking him down. It wasn't her call, though. The order came from Valor Duma.

She hopped up and dragged Nathan's limp body from the water. As she wiped a trickle of liquid from her face, she regarded him while the jungle dissolved into pixels. Soon, they found themselves in an empty room with solid black walls. A stretcher floated up and slid itself under Nathan's body. Arista followed it to the med bay.

There, she applied a G-boost patch that would accelerate

her natural healing. She left Stryder in the care of Dr. Rami and headed back to review the vid of the ambush. She knew Duma would be eager to view it as well.

CHAPTER 6

His hands were silent and quick on the terminal, careful not to trigger any fail-safes. With the passcodes etched into his mind, he focused on the information he needed to retrieve. The computer responded like an extension of himself, erasing the memory and deleting all traces of the dangerous information it held. In its place, he set up a blockhead program that would imitate the files, so it would seem as if they were still there.

Without pause, he removed the datagem from the console with his left hand and dropped it into his pocket while continuing to code in the commands with his right. The information downloaded to the gem was vitally important to his cause.

A beep from the terminal split the precious silence he had been careful to create, signaling the completion of his program. Besides the dummy files, the drive had been wiped clean. He ran a search on it again to be sure. There was no room for a mistake.

A bead of sweat made its presence known as it ran down his left temple. Ignoring it, he continued his delicate task.

As rock-steady hands removed a tiny plasma bomb from its case, the click of a boot from the outside corridor shattered his focus, sounding like a thunderclap in his ears. Snapping his head quickly to the left, he paused. If anyone discovered him, it would be a sure execution. He took three slow, deep breaths and waited for the boots to leave.

Then, gently placing the charge on the underside of the terminal, he inserted the capsule that activated it. Feelings of tension slowly dissipated as he stood and hurried back to his quarters.

Two minutes later, an explosion ripped through the prime weapons development lab. A grin forced its way to his face, breaking the emotionless rock of concentration it had been. The design of the horrid weapon had been destroyed.

The weapon itself remained to be dealt with.

CHAPTER 7

Lord Admiral Lasal had just entered the expansive bridge of his flagship when the explosion occurred. There was a slight tremble, even thirty decks up, from where he stood. Perplexed, he couldn't fathom what the ship had hit. They were in a hyperspace tunnel, which would be theoretically empty. Quickly, he regained his composure.

"Status report!" he said, searching the panorama of outer space projected before him. The center of the room was occupied by a three-dimensional display of the ship and its position.

"Level 13, sir," an ensign said. "The weapons development lab just exploded! I'm sending a security team there now."

"And we've dropped out of hyperspace," another voice added.

Lasal straightened his uniform and left the bridge, heading for level 13. Dread twisted sharply in his gut. This was no accident.

Nothing remained of the lab when he reached the hollowed-out section. With barely anything to stand on, Lasal could observe the repair crews on the levels below and above through the enormous holes in both the floor and ceiling. It was a miracle they hadn't all been sucked out into space. Not truly a miracle, however, as the emergency energy field hummed and crackled, its ethereal glow casting an eerie light around them. It was the only thing standing between them from the bone-chilling void of space. A somber reminder of nature's indifference.

He stepped up to the energy barrier and gazed out, scowling at the jagged maw that had once been his advanced weapons lab. After giving orders to his repair crews, he left distraught.

From his office, he summoned the most capable person he knew. Now, sitting at his desk, he took a moment to calculate his thoughts.

"Send him in," Lasal ordered.

His assistant turned sharply toward the double doors, causing them to slide open.

Valor Krell Duma entered, not waiting for the assistant's invitation, halting to stand at attention. Behind Duma, Captain HaReeka entered and saluted as well.

Lasal let the salute linger before whispering, "At ease."

The pair lowered their arms, but remained stiff. Lasal looked them over critically.

"Our saboteur is back," he started. "He destroyed the weapons lab for Project Deathwind."

"What of the prototype?" Duma asked with the cool demeanor of a professional.

Lasal nodded. "It's secure, but I suspect he will go after that next."

Captain HaReeka stepped forward. "I'll have security increased."

Lasal nodded to her, then turned to Duma. "I want Valor Duma to oversee everything. You have proven your capability and value in the past in the most extreme ways. So, I am convinced you—"

"He won't go after the Deathwind right away, sir," Duma interrupted. "He'll wait for us to relax our grip first."

Were it anyone else, the interruption would have been grounds for punishment. Now, however, Lasal let it slide. Duma was technically a lower rank, but Lasal respected him, along with his skills. He knew Duma was aware of the importance of Project Deathwind and would guard it with his life.

"I'll send you the information on our safeguards, then," Lasal said.

Duma nodded, then switched gears. "And Stryder, sir? We—"

"We can't put him back now, can we?"

"Sir, we don't need him. It's a distraction," Captain HaReeka added.

Lasal waved her away. "Stop being dramatic. I will decide what is a distraction, *Captain*." The last word was emphasized to warn her she was close to crossing a line. He knew her intentions were not pure. HaReeka was always looking for a way to challenge him.

"I'd like my objection noted," HaReeka said.

Duma stepped forward. "Then at least put me in charge of him."

Lasal pondered the suggestion while straightening a few objects on his desk.

"Very well. But if he is not trained to his potential, you will be trimming Death Blossom trees on Devonshire." Lasal leaned forward onto his desk. "There's one more thing. Since you've been under my command, I've had no reason to question your loyalty, commitment, or service. But my file on you doesn't go into much detail about Carcosa."

"I was loyal to them until they tried to eliminate me and my team, sir. Carcosa is better without them in charge. By the time the Meraki fleet had arrived, anyone I knew or had loyalty to was dead."

Captain HaReeka endorsed Duma's explanation with a slight nod.

Duma saluted and spun on his heel toward the door. He passed Lasal's assistant, who stood smugly with a vid-board.

"Classic detached morality," the assistant's soft voice piped up.

Duma halted. He turned to the thin man, brandishing a deadly glare.

"Detached morality," the assistant repeated. "It's a clinical condition. As long as you don't know them, you don't care. You can condemn, betray, or eve—"

Duma exploded on the word "betray." He grabbed the assistant by his throat and slammed him into the wall. The vid-board skittered across the floor.

He leaned in close. "*They* betrayed *me*."

Captain HaReeka watched, fascinated with the display.

Lasal, however, had lost interest. "Valor Duma, don't break my assistant."

Duma released him. The assistant quickly scurried away, scrambling for his vid-board.

As the doors closed behind Duma, Lasal looked his assistant over, then turned to Captain HaReeka. "Course correction report?"

She nodded to his assistant. "Your aide has it, sir."

The assistant, still rattled, shuffled by Captain HaReeka to Lasal's desk and fumbled as he passed the vid-board over. Lasal took it, amused.

"Tinook, Primar, Kavka, and then to Sienna," HaReeka stated. "Looks pretty smooth, but Kavka still has a few trouble spots. As you can see, Kavka is still in active revolt. Led by—"

Lasal raised his hand to silence her. He preferred to analyze the report himself. Pausing on the page showing the Kavkin rebel leader, he touched the digital image and flicked it to his desk, which projected it as a hologram they could all see.

"Prymack Vaiirun," Captain HaReeka said, in defiance of being silenced.

"They have horns?" Lasal's assistant blurted out. "Are they beasts?"

Lasal knew the race, but not the man. Kavkins were humanoid. They had skin tones of various shades and patterns of orange and distinct predator eyes. The males grew protective exoskeletal headpieces—not horns, per se, but more akin to crowns of bone that ran from their temples and wrapped around the top of their skulls. He assumed they were from some evolutionary warfare gene leftover by their primal ancestors. Females lacked the bone headdress, but were usually more lightly colored with larger eyes.

Lasal studied the image, admiring the man and his valor. However, once they reached Kavka, he had a plan to put an end to him and his uprising.

CHAPTER 8

Nathan awoke, startled and dazed. He was still in fight mode. The last thing he could remember was slowly dying from suffocation. Sweat dripped down his back as he tried to recall exactly what had happened. Who had choked him?

The memory struck him like a brick—*she* had tried to kill him. But why? Someone must have stopped her after he went unconscious.

It was slowly coming back. Through the thin, latex-like jumpsuit she wore, he'd felt her warm, tense body lying on him, then a crushing pain at his neck. Her lingering scent, which was a surprising mix of mango and vanilla, was still on his shirt.

"Well, hello. I bet you're surprised to see me again. Welcome to Medical Bay 1."

Nathan glanced up and, for the first time, noticed that a woman was at the foot of the bed. It was the doctor he'd seen before, when he'd first awoken on this ship, the one who must have implanted the translators.

Nathan moaned, "Doctor?" His throat was burning.

"Correct," she said with a casual smile. "Doctor Rami."

Pushing a few controls on the end of the bed, she glanced up at him. "How are you feeling?"

Clearing his throat, Nathan forced out the words, "What happened?"

"Well, all I know is from the chronicle when you came in. You had several contusions, specifically on the throat, and a few more here and there. Nothing serious—not enough for the shells anyway. Your unconsciousness was caused by a momentary lack of oxygen to your brain. Not a habit I would recommend."

"How'd I get here?" For the first time, Nathan took in the room. He knew nothing about the machines scattered throughout, but the smooth and minimal engineering made them look like serious medical equipment. There was room for six beds and two depressions in the floor, which seemed to be for those wax cocoons, or shells, as Rami had called them. A separate office with immense windows allowed anyone inside to observe this room.

"Arista. She is training you, I assume."

"She tried to kill me!"

Dr. Rami laughed. "From what I know of Arista, if she wanted you dead, I would be starting a whole other procedure on you—it's called an autopsy. She's always been nice to me. I can't see why she would want you dead."

"Arista?" Nathan rolled the name over in his mind. Feminine, yet strong, it somehow fit her perfectly. He fingered his neck, still able to feel her hand.

Doctor Rami nodded. "Well, you're free to go. I'll see you again soon," she said with a grin.

"Sure." Nathan slipped off the table, looking for direction.

"Just follow the hallway until it ends," Rami said, pointing out the doorway.

Nathan nodded, stood up, and tried to find his way back to where he'd been strangled. He was specifically looking for this "Arista." Despite what he'd thought of her at first, he wasn't about to let her off the hook. Yeah, she was striking, but she'd tried to kill him, unprovoked.

He found Section 9 and traced his steps back to where she'd attacked him. At the end of the hallway, he entered the antechamber with pictures of weaponry.

Quickly, Nathan made his way past the pictures and toward the next room—where she'd ambushed him.

Taking a deep breath, he entered. But there was no jungle, no rising sun—only a thousand-foot square black room. It was dark, but not completely like before. There was light coming from somewhere that made it glow. Other than him, the room was empty.

His fingers glided over the wall. It was cold and like glass.

A spotlight beamed down from above, focusing on him, followed by a woman's voice echoing through the room.

"There you are. I was just on my way down to check on you. How do you feel?" It was Arista, yet her voice had no hint of malice. In fact, it was soothing.

"I feel abused. How do I get up there?" He peered through the bright spotlight, searching for a glimpse of her. Maybe she hadn't tried to strangle him. No, he wasn't about to let her off the hook. But why had she attacked him?

A light clicked on about fifty feet up the side wall, revealing a control room. Arista stood there in her red jumpsuit with a sizable figure next to her.

"I'll come down," she said.

A minute or two later, she was standing in front of him. The woman was built like a kickboxer. Her muscles were not overly developed, but they were defined with an equal thought to speed and strength. Nathan had dreaded her scent minutes ago, but now that seemed foolish. Her aura and smile were disarming.

"We just finished reviewing the vid of our fight," she said casually. "You show a lot of potential."

"Potential?" Nathan blurted. "You nearly killed me!" It couldn't get much more embarrassing for him.

She grinned as if he'd made a joke. "The good news is, your instincts are phenomenal. We just need to teach you how to use them. I am Lieutenant Commander Arista Conak."

"I'm Nathan."

"Stryder. I know. You are here to train, and I am here to

train you. I am your superior officer. You will address me, and all your superiors, as 'sir.' Understood?"

"Yes, ma'am," Nathan responded flippantly.

Arista stepped close to him. "Sir!"

"Yes, sir!" He tried not to flinch at her proximity. Her aroma was even stronger now.

"I was instructed to show you how brutal the training can be and not to go easy on you."

Nathan raised an eyebrow. "By who?"

She flashed him a harsh look.

"By who, sir?" he said, correcting himself.

The door behind Arista slid open, and she fell silent as a colossal man strode in. The room seemed to grow smaller as he entered, and Nathan felt a touch of claustrophobia, forcing him to take a step back.

He wondered if he was among a race of giants. Were the others just an exception? No, he realized, this man before him was the exception. Even aside from his size, the man's cropped hair, broad shoulders, and stern face told him this was not someone to mess with.

Arista pivoted to face the man and saluted. He returned the salute as he stepped toward them. So, he was the one Arista had meant. Nathan had expected Drelmar. After all, he was the one who'd talked him into this.

"I am in charge of your training," the man said in a forceful tone.

"Where's Master Chief Vinn?"

The man's face didn't change. "I am in charge of your training. Is that understood?" he said louder, ignoring Nathan's question.

Arista flashed Nathan an urgent glance. She mouthed the words, *Yes, sir*.

"Yes, sir!" Nathan said.

"Do not test me." The giant took a heavy step closer. "You

are no longer a civilian. Your job is to follow orders perfectly and without hesitation, no matter what they are."

"Yes, sir." To say Nathan was intimidated would have been a vast understatement. He could not imagine who wouldn't be.

The man leaned down into Nathan's face, looking dead in his eyes.

"Down!"

Nathan heard the words, but they weren't processing. He looked down.

"Don't think, soldier! Get down!" the man bellowed.

Then, in a flash, a fist drilled Nathan in the gut. A fiery ball of pain erupted on impact, and he went down.

"I want him ready for combat by the time we reach Tinook. Do not forget to continue your training as well," the man ordered as he marched past them.

"Yes, sir," Arista said.

Nathan struggled for breath. Arista rolled him over onto his back.

"Stay calm and focus on breathing," she instructed. "It's important that you learn to recover quickly from being hit."

A minute passed before Nathan could breathe fully again. He climbed to his knees.

"Who the fuck was that?"

Arista gave him a hand up. "Valor Krell Duma. He's our C.O."

Over the next thirty minutes, she gave him basic instructions on protocol. She explained how to act, talk, and stand in the presence of someone of a higher rank. She included how to salute—right hand in a fist over his heart, arm parallel to the floor—and who to salute, which was pretty much everyone except the doctors. He also learned the chain of command, of which he was at the very bottom.

"If you follow me, I'll show you around." Arista gave him a calm, reassuring look.

Then, without a second's delay, she sprang at him, blocking out the world around him. Nathan marveled at her quickness in the same way an antelope would a tiger's. And like the antelope, he could do nothing to avoid her. She flipped him over her hips and slammed him down, causing a momentary touch of nausea as he fell to the floor and his breath lurched out of him again.

"Rule one, always stay alert. You never know who your friends or enemies are." She rolled off him and stood up. "Understood?"

Nathan remained on his back momentarily, inventorying the pain that had emerged when he landed and forced breathless words out of his lungs. "Yes, sir."

Arista led him on a tour of the interconnected rooms of the training facility. In each, they went through the equipment and devices he'd seen earlier. There were five rooms, the Pit, which was basically the gym, the Crucible, which was the black obsidian room that had changed into a jungle, the Briefing Room, the Control Room, and a small locker room.

From one of four lockers, she removed a neatly folded blue jumpsuit made of a gel-like material and handed it to him.

"Put this on and meet me in the Pit before 0900. And *do not* be late."

Once alone, Nathan stripped down and stepped into the jumpsuit. It was how he imagined sliding into Jell-O would feel like. He tugged it up over his legs and hips. Then it abruptly tightened, coiling itself around him as if it were alive, spreading down his arms and legs. He stumbled backward in surprise, clawing at it, trying to pull it off.

"Holy—" he blurted with no following thoughts as he wrestled with the gel that was covering his body. Then, it stopped moving and took on the properties of a jumpsuit again. With no ill effects, he tried moving around in it. It felt weird, but it was surprisingly comfortable. When he moved, the material moved with him, like a second skin. It was so natural that he had to remind himself he wasn't naked.

Nathan found the Pit easily enough, as he'd just visited it on the tour. Arista wore the same red jumpsuit she'd had on before. Now, of course, he realized what it was. Sort of.

"What the hell is this thing?"

Arista gave him a stern glare.

"I mean—what the hell is this thing, sir?"

"You are wearing a sentient symbiotic organism called a Tanzi warsuit. In time, you'll be able to control its color, shape, and density, by thought. The more you become familiar with it, the more control you will have and the more it will protect you."

She demonstrated by changing the color of her jumpsuit, making it move up and down her arm, and even extending it from her hand into a claw-like tool. "It's insulated and fireproof. It can be used as a re-breather, allowing you to breathe underwater, and even in space." The suit formed a face mask covering her mouth and nose, then totally encased her head, and finally returned to normal.

Then she held out a small, diamond-shaped device. "This is an enhancer. Put this on your temple before you sleep. It works with the Tanzi to train your muscle memory as you rest."

He took the device, which was the size of an almond. The flat side stuck to his skin like Velcro. He peeled it off and placed it in a pocket.

The door whisked behind him, and boots clunked on the floor until Duma strode past him. He was simply an enormous man, something Nathan still had not gotten used to. Duma stopped next to Arista, who saluted him. Then he turned to Nathan. Subtly, Arista motioned for Nathan to salute. He brought his heels together and did.

Duma wore high-tech, body armor. Under his left arm he

held a flat-faced, featureless helmet. The only signature characteristic on it was one long, horizontal visor for his eyes.

"As I am sure you realize, you are no longer a civilian." Duma's voice left no room for questions. "You are a soldier of the Meraki Navy. You will fight with fury and loyalty in the war against the High Command. Lord Admiral Lasal has informed you of the stakes in this war, and surely you understand that soldiers kill and they get killed."

He paused briefly. "There is a significant possibility that you may die. You will accept these risks."

"Yes," Nathan said. "I know."

Arista flashed him another hurried look.

"—sir!" Nathan quickly added. Damn, how was he going to remember all this?

Before yesterday, no one had told him what to do, except his parents. He had never thought of killing anyone. None of it felt real. It was like living someone else's life.

"There are four levels of Meraki soldiers: vanguard, enforcer, stalker, and us," Duma said. "Right now, you are less than any of those. Luckily for you, to do your job, to defend yourself and this nation, you will learn the most lethal and effective forms of combat. Above everything else, you are expected to follow orders flawlessly, no matter what."

Nathan understood the chain of command, but he was resistant to becoming a mindless soldier. He recalled the horror stories he had heard from past wars, about soldiers who were ordered to slaughter innocent people.

"Kick me!" Duma ordered, abruptly interrupting Nathan's musing.

Confused, Nathan hesitated. Why hadn't he been paying attention?

"Don't think, soldier. Kick!" Duma shouted.

Nathan threw out his leg. Duma deftly caught it and flung him into the wall.

"Your training begins now."

Immediately afterward, Duma left, and Arista started the training.

Five hours in, Nathan regretted everything. She'd already driven him through two separate sets of calisthenics, alternating them with an hour of basic martial arts techniques. Wiping the stinging sweat from his eyes with his already soaked shirt, he staggered to the finish of a thousand-meter run, then trotted up to Arista and stood at attention. Five minutes—a good time, considering everything he'd been through earlier.

Shaking her head, she looked at a stopwatch. "Slow. Give me forty push-ups, then hit the drum."

Nathan glanced over to the side wall, where a holographic dummy projected from the floor. They called it a contact drum, but it served the same purpose a heavy bag did on Earth.

He dropped to the floor and began his push-ups. After twelve, a biting pain ravaged his arms, making it hard to focus. Halfway through the next push-up, his muscles cramped, and he dropped to the floor with a *thump*.

Arista took a knee next to him. "I know this is your first day, but Stryder, I want you to realize something. You are not in the gray anymore. You shouldn't be here for anyone but yourself. Once you are in combat, you can't afford to give up, you can't afford to fail. If you lack endurance or skill, then you will die."

It wasn't exactly what he had expected her to say, but it gave him a new perspective on the position he was in. It also gave some insight into her. He saw fierceness, determination, and, for the briefest of moments, something else.

"Now, get up!" she ordered. "Let's get that body into shape."

✷ ✷

Ajax and Drelmar had clear orders—to oversee each of the

rooms that could hold Project Deathwind. One room was a decoy, and the other held the device, but neither knew which was which. Valor Duma had made it so.

Now, they shared a war room where they would scrutinize and select the people who would assist them. Carefully, they went through each candidate. The last thing they wanted was to recruit the saboteur to guard the damn thing.

"No, not her," Ajax said, objecting to the latest candidate. "She's been shipside for a year. That's around the time of the first attack."

Drelmar pushed a new virtual file across the digital face of the table. "So, we select those that came aboard after the first attack. They wouldn't have been part of it."

"It makes sense as far as who we can trust, but they're still green. We are facing a threat—"

The lock on the door disarmed with a beep, and Valor Duma marched through in full stride, his face creased with anger. He rounded on Drelmar, coming within a breath of him.

"You should have left him frozen!"

"Who?" Drelmar said as their eyes met.

"If you're talking about the refugee, sir, the Lord Admiral ordered it," Ajax said.

"He wasn't a prisoner, sir," Drelmar followed up. "We couldn't leave him iced for eternity. It's a living death. And like Chief Sculic stated, it was an order."

"You two might be Lasal's pets, but you are under my command! Protecting the project is your *only* concern." Duma glared at them both.

"Yes, sir," they replied in unison.

CHAPTER 9

It had been three weeks since Nathan started his training. He worked every day on strength and endurance, but that was all he did. So far, there was no combat training. It was exhausting, and he was growing impatient.

Asleep in his bed, he was not at peace. The dream had come again. His body tossed, coinciding with what he saw.

He was outside, on the edge of a burning battlefield. Before him were the bodies of fallen soldiers. He rushed ahead in alien battle armor that somehow felt familiar. Charging at him was the creature that had abducted him as a mosaic of lasers flashed around them. Nathan's hands begin to build energy and glow blue. Instinctively, he raised his arm to block a bolt of purple energy. From his forearm, a translucent shield formed and absorbed the shot.

Suddenly awake and upright in his bed, Nathan scanned the darkness. His chest was tight and his body filled with dread. Susan was still missing, and he had heard nothing about her. With practiced ease, he started his breathing technique.

He wasn't sure what these dreams meant. Probably something about his fear of the unknown. He just wished they would stop.

Having gotten no sleep after the dream, Nathan was drained and annoyed later in the training room. He completed the last pull-up in his callisthenic circuit.

"Good. Now, back to push-ups," Arista said, as she worked on her own sets.

Nathan dropped to the floor and started another set of push-ups.

"On your knuckles."

He sighed, clenched his hands into fists, and started over. Pushing through the pain in his knuckles and arms, he'd completed six when frustration set in and he stopped.

Arista glanced at him. "You still have fourteen more."

"This is all we've been doing for weeks, sir."

"We train hard, so the battle is easy," she said. "You're a soldier now. Everything should be framed around defeating your enemy."

"We're wasting time. I won't defeat anyone by doing calisthenics and stances."

Duma's voice bellowed from behind him. "You want to move on? Let's move on."

Nathan's stomach dropped. He'd thought they were alone. How long had Duma been standing there?

"Yes, sir!" he replied immediately.

"Lieutenant Commander, schedule calisthenics and body conditioning in the morning, and two full combat fights a day, with five classes in between."

Thirty minutes later, Nathan stood in the black-walled room of the Crucible. The walls were unnerving. Absent of light, they pulsated with energy, waiting to transmute into something else. He wouldn't have been surprised to find out that they were also alive, like his suit.

Duma stood across from Nathan as the walls changed in a wave around them, forming a primitive wooden dojo carved into the side of a mountain. They now stood on a large outdoor platform with a dark hardwood floor that alternated with lighter colors in a checkerboard pattern. Tree-sized beams rose from the corners and connected in an open pergola structure above them. Red banners and paper lanterns with strange alien symbols dangled from the beams. It wasn't much more than a fighting platform, but he imagined that was all Duma wanted.

Nathan swiveled his head and watched as the room changed. It really was astonishing. The sky above him was blue and cloudless, a gentle breeze blew across his face.

As he turned back to Duma, a hard orb the size of a softball slammed into Nathan's face. White lights filled his vision, and his face felt painfully flat. He twisted away from the impact, his blood splattering on the ground next to him.

Duma was speaking, but it was muffled. "First, you will condition your body to take damage. *Then* you will learn to cause damage."

Two more orbs joined the first and flew in orbits around Nathan, taking turns swooping in to attack him. He swatted at the first one that dive bombed him, but it slammed into his chest. Stepping back and bending his body, he barely dodged the second. The third kamikazed into his spine.

The pain overload caused his body to go rigid. He was sure something was broken. With a tingling numbness spreading down his legs, he staggered forward.

The first orb completed its revolution and came back to knock him flat.

After an hour, his face was swollen and his body was bruised, but he could parry or dodge the spheres about half of the time. Duma stood in silence, studying him.

Later in the Pit, Arista taught him basic kicks, punches, and blocks. He felt like he was picking it up quickly—at least quicker than he thought he might. The movements seemed strangely natural to him. Maybe this was his calling.

✷ ✷

Four more weeks slipped by, and Nathan was improving rapidly. The locations and situations changed every week thanks to the Crucible, ranging from the alien dojo to a snow-covered forest to a rainstorm in the jungle and everything in between.

Arista was the only constant. Every day they were together. The pain and soreness of training was more than equally balanced by the feeling he got from being with her. Most of his time was spent learning basic maneuvers of unarmed combat until each technique was etched into his mind. Without Instagram, Imgur, or Snapchat, he realized he had a lot of spare time, and he used it to learn about the culture and technology he now lived with.

He learned that his jumpsuit, or Tanzi, was bred and developed to protect its user. Now, it felt so natural to wear. He could change the color and shape of it with a thought, making it cover his entire body or just a specific vital spot. The more he condensed it, the thicker it became, and vice versa when he spread it out. It provided some protection from physical attacks, whether blunt or edged. With a certain level of concentration, he could camouflage it into different colors and arrangements. The more he became familiar with it, the more he could do.

Every now and again, Valor Duma would stop to instruct them both, displaying an exceptional amount of knowledge. He was a grimoire of warfare, both ancient and modern. Duma explained that honing their bodies into weapons was the first step, because actual weapons were unreliable and could be taken away.

It was wholly comforting when Arista trained alongside him, under Duma's instruction. He drew on her strength, strengthening himself in the process. It gave him the feeling that he wasn't in this alone, however absurd that might be. Her presence pushed him to become better, inspiring him to move past the pain of his parents' deaths and to deal with the present.

But Susan was different. She wasn't dead. Every push-up

he did, every wound he received, it was all to rescue her. She was at the forefront of his mind. Always.

Over the next week, Arista fused his training with weapons. In addition to a simple tactical knife, she focused on teaching him something he'd dreamed of since he was five—a laser gun.

Not exactly a laser gun. Specifically, it was the Augur 7A, an advanced pulse energy rifle. Unlike the thin lasers he'd seen in movies, this weapon fired four-inch-wide pulses that could stream, burst, or single fire, depending on how you pulled the trigger. Aside from the primary pulse, it also had a secondary attack that could charge up to explode on impact.

The sound it made was like nothing he'd heard before. It wasn't deafening, like guns he'd fired on Earth, but it had a distinct, satisfying *zing*. The Augur wasn't the only firearm she taught him, some used lasers and others plasma, but it was his favorite.

They switched from rifles, to pistols, to knives—the celestial trinity of weapons, as Arista called it. Over and over, they trained movement, targeting, reloading, and care of the weapons. The trickiest part for him was maneuvering with them. It wasn't a natural skill to carry a deadly arsenal around.

Today, however, they were back to unarmed combat, but he wasn't learning a new combat style or practicing ones he already knew. Today was a test.

The empty, nervous sensation he used to have going into every midterm or final in the past was trying to get him to run. But it had been eight weeks of training, and now he was about to fight Arista again. The intense training and advanced technology had allowed him to learn skills more quickly than he could ever have imagined. Compared to his first embarrassing fight, he felt a hundred times more capable. Yet he knew it would be nearly impossible to overcome her years of experience.

His Tanzi warsuit stretched to cover all but his head and hands. Standing before the sliding door that led into the Crucible, he visualized some of his techniques. What would it be this time? Another jungle? He pushed the thought from his head and focused on the fight before him. This was an unarmed fight, but it was full contact, so he had to be ready for anything.

His heart was pounding aggressively. Determined to keep moving forward, he took a deep breath, then stepped through the doors.

The room was dark but filled with sparkling stars and two moons that dimly lit the rooftop he now stood on. Arista appeared on the opposite side of the roof—she seemed laser focused. Nathan glanced behind him as the door closed and saw what looked like a hundred floor drop-off.

They stepped to the center. Nathan sensed a smile approach his lips, but forced it away. He knew it was untimely and would betray his focus. Besides, Valor Duma was surely watching from the hidden control room.

Nathan bent his knees and raised his hands into a fighting stance. Arista followed. Slowly they circled, locking eyes, trying to read the other's thoughts, to anticipate their strike.

Arista moved first, gliding forward with a front kick to his gut. Nathan swung his arm down. *Blocked!*

Recoiling, she snapped a round kick with the same leg. Her foot slammed into the side of Nathan's head. The impact echoed in his skull, fracturing his vision and triggering the wet, metallic taste of blood on his tongue.

When his slanted view of the world righted itself, he was stumbling backward. The gravel on the rooftop rolled under his feet, making a continuous crunching sound as he regained his balance.

Still on the offensive, Arista accelerated her knuckles at his face. Nathan dodged, sliding off her line of attack, then counter-punched her ribs. Her abdomen was incredibly solid. He felt her ribs compress on impact, but she didn't react. Not even a flinch.

Arista spun to sweep his leg, like she had in the first fight. As Nathan darted in, they collided. Momentum sent them both whirling to the ground.

He rolled away quickly before she could catch him. They both knew he was toast if it came to grappling. He could still almost feel the strangulation from the first time.

Arista landed on her back but instantly coiled her legs and sprang forward, whipping herself to her feet again. Nathan scrambled to his feet with a constant eye on her. She was amazing.

She pursed her lips in determination, probably not even trying to distract him, yet she achieved it with flawless ease. Nathan shook his head clear.

Again, they closed into striking distance. Arista stuttered her step to change up her rhythm, throwing him off. As he faltered, she extended her right leg toward the left side of his face and hooked it back. Her heel found his chin, hard.

Without lowering her leg, she kicked again. It happened so fast, it only registered as one strike to his brain, yet pain flashed on both sides of his head.

She kept the pressure on with a fist to his ribs, followed by a left cross. A stream of blood poured out of his nose.

Then, she kneed him in the liver.

At first it seemed like a normal blow, but two seconds later it was as if someone had injected acid into his stomach. Pointed daggers stabbed his abdomen from the inside, shocking his system and sapping his strength.

"That's a liver shot, Stryder. All the toxins it's collected are rushing into your body."

His legs buckled, and he fell to one knee.

"Stay up," she said. "Fight through it. You're at a disadvantage now."

Nathan scrambled backward, fighting the urge to curl up and die.

"Create space. Buy yourself time to recover. If you can't get away, wrap me up."

Realizing he was on the ground, he staggered to his feet, but Arista was already on him, causing severe damage to his ribs. The pain brought him back to his knees, defenseless.

Buried energy surged up through Nathan. He bowled into her base leg as she brought her heel down. Hooking her knee, he twisted his core and threw her to the ground. He raised his forearm, ready to smash her knee, but paused.

Crack-boom-crack. Three rapid kicks from Arista's opposite leg relieved him of further decisions for the rest of the day.

※ ※

Arista untangled herself from the body of Nathan Stryder and stood up. The rooftop and the surrounding night faded to reveal the walls of the Crucible. She ran a hand over the soreness on her head where his knee had struck her in their initial collision.

"Better." Valor Duma's voice echoed throughout the room. "Take him to med bay."

This will strengthen him, she told herself. *He must learn not to hesitate while fighting.* She'd seen the reluctance in his eyes and knew it would get him killed one day. It was touching that he'd refrained from doing any significant damage to her. Yet, it was a weakness. In the end, it had only hindered him. But it was something she would remember.

An automated stretcher maneuvered under Stryder's body and rose from the ground with a hum. Arista followed it.

Arriving at the medical bay, the stretcher slid Stryder onto the table. Arista stepped up to him and brushed the messy hair off his forehead. Glancing around the immediate area, she found a tissue and wiped the blood from his face.

She didn't envy him. She knew what it was like to be where he was, alone and away from everything he once knew.

"I can do that, Arista," a voice said from behind her. Adrenaline shot through her body before she turned and realized it was Dr. Rami. She had never surprised her before.

"Oh, I know. I just feel bad." Arista glanced back at Stryder. If she only knew how much of an understatement that was.

Dr. Rami walked around the bed, now coming into view of Stryder. She whistled. "Well, I see you took it easy on him, at least."

"Ha ha, Doc." She was hardly amused. "That's my job, I just—" She looked down at her hands. Rami wouldn't understand how much she empathized with him.

"I know. You don't have to explain it to me. You people play by different rules than us doctors." Rami waved a scanner over Stryder's wounds, then switched on the bed, which would chronicle his overall condition.

Why couldn't people see her as more than a trained weapon?

CHAPTER 10

Drelmar Vinn ran his finger over the bumpy material on the table before him as he stared Ajax down, wondering what he would do.

They had served on the *Kai'den* together for two years. They knew each other well, acting and reacting in deadly unison. Collectively, they were the chief security officers to Lord Admiral Lasal, though he was never worried about his safety on the *Kai'den*, which essentially had made them his personal assistants. On board, they carried out his operations, most of which were highly classified. Only when he left the ship did they become his specialized guard.

When Ajax first arrived, he'd been young and straight out of Ragnakor. Despite graduating from the intelligence academy, he'd been green, and Drelmar had done his best to initiate him in the realities of their job, including how to unwind.

Now they were adversaries, sitting across from one another at a Gira table. Three other off-duty officers joined them in pushing their luck. They reserved the last night of every week for this game.

The room was dim, and a hazy nebula of smoke lingered overhead. A single light source was directed at the table from above, making it the only thing fully illuminated in the room.

"So, we found this guy face-down at one of those pleasure houses on Hale," Hamil, the officer to Ajax's right, continued. "Well, after poking him a few times, he finally looked up. He had like six eyes, all on his forehead."

Hamil poked his forehead to indicate where.

"I turned to Scori, the guy that was with me. You know Scori?" He looked to Ajax for recognition.

Ajax shook his head. "Nope."

"Anyways, I turned to Scori and said, 'You don't see that every day.' And this guy, with six eyes, looks at me and says, 'See what?'"

Hamil started to chuckle, but soon it spread across the table like fire, and they were all laughing.

Ajax dealt the next round, having just won the last. "Who's in?" he asked before dealing the next card.

"I am," Hamil spoke up.

"Me too," said Gunder, to Hamil's right.

Drelmar nodded as the deal came to him. A familiar twinge ran the length of his leg, causing him to shift his weight to relieve the pain.

Ever perceptive, Ajax seemed to notice. "Drelmar's getting antsy."

"Old man pains," Hamil added.

Drelmar smirked, weary of the same old jokes, then graced him with a side-eye. "War wounds, child."

The offer came to the last man at the table, who at the moment was still as stone, staring into a mental void somewhere beyond them.

"Xoni?" Ajax urged. "You in?"

Xoni's eyes shifted casually to Ajax. "Yeah."

Drelmar picked up his cards and threw out a distraction before viewing them. "How'd that banderball game turn out, Gunder?" he said.

"Oh, we lost. But it wasn't a total ruin. Hamil got smacked in the roundies!" He grinned. "It was worth it to see him rolling around on the court in agony."

Everyone except Hamil snickered.

Now that the rest were engaged, Drelmar glanced down at his hand. His face was trained not to react, so he didn't need to redirect their attention, but micro expressions were sometimes difficult to control. And as a Tiberian gambler had once told him, "*It's difficult to detect your own tells, so it's a good idea sometimes to throw a monkey onto the table and let it dance.*"

"I guess that put a damper on your plans with what's-her-name?" Xoni inquired, while lifting his cards from the table.

"Funny," Hamil said. "No, as a matter of fact, she brought her friend over—"

Gunder pitched his worthless hand at Hamil along with a few choice words.

"What?" Hamil flashed a grin.

"Ajax, to you," Xoni reminded him.

Drelmar studied Ajax's eyes as he pondered quietly, then placed a card in the middle of three squares on the table.

Gunder moaned. "Damn, I could have beat that!"

Ajax threw two green chips into the pot.

"'And they say her eyes were the green of the brightest emeralds.'" Xoni quoted an old Madison play referencing the bet.

Ajax nodded in recognition of the passage.

All eyes shifted to Drelmar. In his mind, a calm breeze was flowing over a young wheat field, as he focused on keeping his cool. Emotionless, he gently laid down two cards. It was a move that made him more vulnerable but could also win him the game. Of course, everyone knew this, and everyone cursed him—everyone except for Gunder, who had nothing to lose given he had already folded.

"'Yet we came to discover they were twins.'" Drelmar mocked the Madison quote, making up his own line. Flicking his hand out, he released four green chips into the pot, doubling the bet.

"I love this game!" Gunder said. "It doesn't matter who you are, or where you're from, it's your guts that win it." He patted Drelmar on the back. "Even someone twice our age can come out on top!"

He surveyed the other players, stopping on Hamil's disgruntled grimace. Gunder looked satisfied.

Drelmar smirked at him. "Fifteen years, no more, no less."

"Sure, Master Chief, whatever you say." Ajax smiled, joining in on the running joke. "Why is it again that we're the same rank?"

"We are *not* the same rank yet, *Chief*."

"Essentially. HaReeka already started the process."

Drelmar ignored Ajax's ego. "It's a long story, and by the time I finished it, you would be my age." He let the comments roll by. His focus was the game. "Now, let's get on with it. Hamil, it's your call."

"Fold," Hamil mumbled.

Gunder laughed with wholehearted enjoyment.

"Honestly? You didn't win either," Hamil said as he swigged from his mug.

"Yeah," Xoni said reluctantly, tossing his cards. "I'm out too."

Drelmar took control of the deck. He had long ago purged his mind of most indulgences because they interfered with his job. The small feeling of pride he felt at winning this game was his only sin left.

With years of muscle memory, his fingers dealt the last card of the hand, flipping it out toward Ajax onto the red felt of the table. Around them, the others watched. The rounds were usually not this quick, but Drelmar had made a risky move. Now, it was between these two, each pitting their wit and luck against the other.

"Your move," Drelmar declared, watching Ajax's thoughtful eyes.

CHAPTER 11

THE NEXT MORNING, Nathan was back at the alien dojo construct in the Crucible. His arm was currently locked up and being controlled by Arista after he'd tried to shoot in on her for a takedown. They were on their feet, but any slight shift Nathan made sent a jolt up his arm as she threatened to hyper-extend his elbow. She had shown him an escape earlier today, but right now he was having trouble recalling it.

"Do you remember?" she prodded. "Think, Stryder."

He twisted and tugged, but her grip was solid. Wind whisked across them, blowing her hair into his face.

"I'll break it in three seconds. You better get out."

Everything he'd learned today was flooding his brain, but the pain made it hard to focus. One wrong move and his elbow would snap. Flipping through the moves in his mind like the pages of his own combat grimoire, he found it.

Leaning forward, he bent his elbow and jerked it out. He did it! His arm was free.

But Arista just clung to him like ivy, pulling him tighter. Wrapping her arm under his opposite shoulder, she thrust out her hips.

Nathan twisted to face her, but it was too late. She had the leverage.

His feet left the floor, and the room spun as a sick feeling of weightlessness spread through his body.

He knew now what he'd done wrong. He was only thinking about getting out of the armlock, and not what came after. Arista had been two moves ahead, waiting for him to twist, putting her in a better position to flip him.

Nathan hit the ground on his back, shocking his body. She landed on top of him, which was itself another blow. While he reassembled his senses, she grabbed his arm, and pulled it between her legs, then leaned back into an armlock.

Once again, his elbow was hyper-extended, sending lightning up his arm. Nathan rolled, relieving some of the pressure, but Arista rolled with him. During the scramble, he wedged one of his legs between hers and pried them apart, yanking his arm from the vise it was in. He was now on top.

It couldn't last, though. He was too exhausted at this point to think. His energy was fleeting. His limbs wouldn't respond. While he savored his moment of victory, Arista shoved his hips away with her feet.

Before he knew it, she was on him again, putting all her weight on his chest and locking up his arms. They were nose to nose, and he could do nothing.

Arista watched his eyes, waiting for his next move. Nathan stared back, his fuel reserves depleted. Then something entered his mind, something he'd thought about often.

With the last of his strength, he lifted his head and kissed her.

The warmth of her lips filled his body with exhilaration. The feeling rushed through him, like a first breath after being underwater for too long.

Arista froze. The combat ready look in her eyes morphed into bewilderment. She was speechless, motionless, like a startled doe.

Panic gripped Nathan. What had he done? Heat spread across his face as humiliation sparked within him.

"I'm sorry. I thought—" he faltered.

Arista rolled off him and sprang to her feet. She opened her mouth to speak, but didn't. Behind her, the door whisked open, breaking the illusion of the mountainside dojo as Valor Duma entered.

Scrambling to his feet, Nathan joined Arista at attention.

"At ease," Duma ordered. "Lieutenant Commander, with me."

Arista followed Duma out of the room, leaving Nathan alone. His mind whirled. Had Duma seen the kiss? Was she being reprimanded?

A grip tightened on his chest. His stomach was turning. A deep breath in, a long breath out. It wasn't working. He waited for answers, but Arista and Duma didn't return.

It was difficult not to think about the unknown consequences of his action, but right now, it was out of his control. The best way to focus on the moment was to feel, listen, and smell, so he returned to training for the last hour of his day. He pushed himself hard, concentrating on the motion of his body, trying to burn away the nervous energy that overwhelmed him.

He drilled combat techniques until his body failed and he collapsed on the floor. The feeling was still there, like a snake in the shadows waiting to constrict him, but for now it had diminished.

Back in his quarters, he sat at the window as the hyperspace rings streaked by. Watching the rings continue moving on their path, oblivious to his insignificant problems, was comforting, and reframed his perspective.

Frustrated that he hadn't had time to talk to Arista after the kiss, he mindlessly tore up the printed plate that came with his dinner. The food, however, he didn't eat. Why had he kissed her? Had he just ruined things? She'd given him no reaction. And Duma really couldn't have come in at a worse time.

Every thought of her elicited the recognizable coil around his chest. He'd read it wrong, that he knew. But how would he face her? Maybe it was better if he didn't. Maybe he could just avoid all the drama and embarrassment.

No—it was done, he concluded. He couldn't go back and

change it. Nathan forced his mind on the present. He had to keep moving forward.

The next morning, neither Arista nor Duma met him in the Pit. With no instructors, he followed his daily routines and the directions Arista had started him with before, improvising as best he could. Again and again, he practiced the same four techniques until he could perform them perfectly ten times in a row. Each, when performed correctly, could incapacitate or kill an opponent. Two hours later, he accomplished this goal and switched to other moves.

His skills were rapidly improving. The fundamentals of personal combat had found a place in him and were growing exponentially. With the holographic training aids he'd discovered, he'd pushed his limits with learning advanced techniques and new strategies. In just a few months, he had learned more than he'd ever thought possible.

Nathan used the solitude to drive his training. He refocused on Susan. No one had given him any information on her yet, but he had to be ready when they did.

✷ ✷

Ajax Sculic wondered how someone who finished at the top of his class at Ragnakor could end up as essentially an errand boy. *An errand boy for a lord admiral*, he reminded himself. He was on his way up the ranks, but he had thought it would be through battle, not being a nursemaid.

However, at least in his position, he was aware of many things and always had his eye out for an opportunity to advance. And recently, as parts of the ship had started blowing up, he hoped Lasal would take security a little more seriously.

Lasal had sent him with the results of Stryder's training assessment to find Valor Duma. Looking them over on his way, Ajax had to admit the results were impressive. Very impressive. With these results, he presumed Lasal was hoping to prove that the decision to defrost the refugee had not been in vain.

As he entered the war room set up for Project Deathwind, he prepared himself for the reaction. Duma stood at the table, reviewing the security detail Ajax had drawn up earlier. He had been waiting for Duma's approval of the plans.

Duma glanced up, irritated.

"Lord Admiral Lasal wanted you to look this over. It's Nathan Stryder's training assessment."

Duma snatched the datagem from his hand and threw it on the table. The surface lit up with graphs and numbers, comparing Nathan's stats to the historical data of everyone who had been assessed before. Reflex speed, endurance, strength, and power were a few of the statistics measured. These were cross-referenced with time on one chart that Lasal had made the focal point of the assessment.

The visual representation of the stats showed Stryder's progress being at least four times quicker than any others on the chart, except one that was blanked out.

"Lord Admiral Lasal wanted to make note of the fact that his progression is exponentially faster than all but Lieutenant Commander Conak," Ajax said.

The scowl he received was what he'd expected, but he had his orders. Duma was a large, intimidating man, but his stats were not part of the historical data, since he had never been a greenleaf. He had come from a world at war with itself, which the Meraki had been asked to pacify. Even without the stats, Ajax knew the stories, which made him want to test his own talents against Duma.

"He is even surpassing her in some areas for this time scale." Lasal had specifically instructed him to say that part. "He believes Stryder is ready to be activated."

Duma batted the datagem off the table. "Dismissed," he growled.

CHAPTER 12

The light on Nathan's keycard was flashing when he awoke, summoning him to the Briefing Room in full battle gear. He wasn't sure what type of training was next, but it was a welcome change to his routine, which had grown tiresome and lonely.

He wore his living jumpsuit, which he'd named Alfred in the past week, so he had someone to talk to. Alfred couldn't exactly talk back. It was more like feelings, but it was comforting to know there was another living being with him.

On top of Alfred, he wore traditional armor. His boots were made from flexible, light, but amazingly strong material that Arista had called Trinex, with their treads, heels, and toes enhanced with metal. He also wore the same material as leg guards, with hardened areas over his shins and knees. His upper body was protected similarly and covered with a reinforced shell on the chest, back, shoulders, elbows, and forearms.

Around his neck was an inch-wide collar. Unlike Duma, Nathan had no helmet, but in his collar was a device to scramble almost any type of recording device, securing his identity. He reached down and snapped his left leg guard into place. The rest of his armor already conformed comfortably to his body.

When he arrived, Valor Duma was waiting. Nathan immediately drew to attention. Moments later, Arista filled in line to his left.

Though looking straight ahead, Nathan could sense her next to him. A warmth hummed through his body, but at the same time, a viper of apprehension coiled in his stomach. It had been a week of emotional distress and uncertainty since he'd kissed her.

For what seemed like several minutes, Duma made his way around them, as if sizing them up. In the silence, Nathan was bursting with questions for them both, but he held his tongue for now.

Duma's voice growled to life as he stopped in front of Nathan.

"This is not a training mission. You will be entering an active combat zone. Rely on your training. It will keep you alive. Survive this mission, and I will promote you to lieutenant, and your training will advance."

So many things were churning in Nathan's skull. Survive? He was risking his life for the pledge of information on his sister, yet he had gotten none.

"Sir. I was promised updates about Susan Stryder. Is there any—"

"Halt!" Duma commanded. "I do not know what kind of deal you made with the Lord Admiral, but you are a soldier now. My soldier! Deal with *your* problems on *your* time. Focus on coming home alive. Understood?"

Nathan risked a glance at Duma's eyes, which he instantly regretted. An intense and intimidating force stared back at him, filling him with raw fear.

"Yes, sir!" he replied on reflex. The frustration billowing within him was ready to surge out, but this was not the time. If Duma was serious, he would need to concentrate on whatever this mission was.

He would seek out Drelmar, Ajax, or Lasal for answers when he returned.

"With me," Duma said.

He led them down the hallway and through an entrance labeled "Docking Bay 23."

The door slid open, leading them into a dim hangar. As Nathan stepped through the doorway, he was struck with a scent of burning carbon that stung his nose and eyes. He blinked away the sensation.

The hangar was large enough for a dozen house-sized ships, but it was nearly empty, save for one. It wasn't a warship, as there were no visible weapons. It was more of a dropship. Shaped like a bullet, it seemed it was built for speed.

At the base of the ship was the pilot, though his outfit made him look more like a motorcycle racer. Gray leather pants with a yellow and gray jacket covered his slim, teal-skinned body. Patterns on the clothing glowed like they were under a black light.

Duma signaled the pilot and waved Nathan inside the ship. Gusts of hot wind rushed by them, tangling Arista's hair as the whine of the engines ramped up. Nathan ducked inside the aft door and took a seat.

The interior had been stripped down to the essentials—six metal passenger seats with enough room for equipment, along with two pilot seats.

Arista followed him and sat on the opposite side. The engines were too loud to hear each other, even a few feet away. She winked at him and strapped on a headset. Nathan grabbed the headset on his seat and did the same.

"I'm glad to see you are surviving the training," her voice sang through the speakers. "You nervous?"

"Maybe, a little," he lied. His stomach was full of rattlesnakes, and his mouth was dry—he was far from comfortable. But he did his best to appear so.

"You'll be fine. I have faith in you." She smiled.

A pair of Warden sniper rifles broke their gaze as Duma shoved one into each of their hands.

"We've been given a recon mission. You two will take up position at a construction site east of the target and cover me from range. Find your nest and stay put. Don't go anywhere, just cover me. I've sent the mission details, including the extraction point, to your HUD displays."

Those were the information heads-up displays that projected into their eyes. Nathan had been told everything they did, but right now all he could remember was that it told him where to go and what not to shoot at.

The pilot in the glowing jacket strapped in next to a co-pilot Nathan couldn't make out in the dim quarters. He leaned his head back toward them and spoke into the headset.

"Watch your head. Watch your feet. You are now aboard the Roman Drake hyper express!"

"These don't look like our pilots, sir," Arista said.

"No. They're mercenaries," Duma responded. "So keep quiet."

The engines roared louder.

"We prefer the term 'rogues,'" Roman said, giving them a mock salute.

Annoyance flashed on Duma's face as his point was made. "Keep this channel clear."

Several minutes of silence later, the dropship entered the atmosphere of Tinook. Once they cleared the stratosphere, the ship's side doors opened automatically, creating a wind tunnel. The initial shock caught Nathan off guard, but after a moment, the pressure evened out.

It was dusk on this side of the planet, and they were coming in over an ocean.

Endless dark water stretched out as far as Nathan could see. His HUD raised the light level in his eyes to compensate for the setting sun. It showed that they were eight kilometers out from their drop point, which seemed to be a large ocean platform the size of a football stadium.

As they approached, more details filled in—a trio of seven-story buildings with rounded architecture, plus one more under construction. Several smaller structures covered the surface of the platform.

The ship dropped sharply and continued the trip just meters above the water, cutting through the mist created by the rough sea. It was a sickening feeling, like the first hill of a roller coaster, except there were no tracks.

"Electronic jammers activated," Roman called into his headset.

Just before the platform, the ship rose abruptly and hovered over the half-constructed building. Arista slipped from her harness and slung the rifle over her shoulder. Seeing this, Nathan popped the release on his own harness and stood up next to her.

She stepped out of the ship, dropping effortlessly to the building and rolling into cover.

Nathan inhaled deeply, taking in the salty air, hoping to suffocate the dread in his stomach. With one foot forward, he reached the door and froze.

Until now, he hadn't realized how strong his anxiety was. He surveyed the partially constructed building below him. So many things could happen down there, the main ones being he could die or embarrass himself. His legs didn't seem to want to move. He imagined them moving, but they remained still.

Keep moving forward, he encouraged himself.

Once he got going, he could focus on the present. That usually helped. The trick was to start moving. So he did the only thing his body would let him do and leaned forward. Gravity did the rest, pulling him out of the ship and out of the relatively safe world of combat simulations.

Adrenaline rushed through him as he fell, overriding everything else and supercharging his body like nitrous oxide in a race car. As he hit the ground with bent knees, he leaned to his right, letting the momentum carry him into a roll. The metallic floor let out a pinging vibration when he hit.

Arista had already set up position at a window and was

scanning the area for possible contact. Nathan shifted to the next window, flipped down the bi-pod stand to stabilize his rifle, and settled in.

"Just watch. Hold your fire—unless I give the order," Arista whispered in the dusk.

Nathan could see a blue outline of Duma at all times through his HUD, even when he was not in line of sight. Right now, the man was still in the dropship as it glided to a high-rise.

Through the scope, Nathan watched the ship create a dust storm on the roof before Duma jumped out. Then his blue silhouette disappeared. Nathan blinked a few times, hoping to clear up any interference. It didn't work.

"I lost him."

Arista lifted a finger to her lips to quiet him.

Looking through the scope once again, there was no sign of Valor Duma.

Then, the top floor windows blew out in a storm of glass, the shards jingling against everything on the way down like a chorus of sleigh bells. Lasers flashed in the smoke. A moment later, Duma appeared in the window, tearing through four massive, heavily armored guards, each at least a foot taller than him. He threw the last one straight out the shattered window. It was incredible. The clang the gray-skinned body made when it landed on a patio several floors below made Nathan wince.

Krell Duma glided to the next room. Two more guards were waiting for him, but that made little difference. In crisp, measured movements, he took them down so fast Nathan's mind couldn't even process what happened. It was like watching Batman, except he was killing everyone. The last remaining person was a black-scaled alien. It was dark, but Nathan could make out some type of tentacles or antennae on its head.

Duma threw him into the wall and exchanged a few words.

The alien was already shaken and hurt even before Duma slammed a knife into its shoulder. It howled, waving its head around in pain, and its mouth moved rapidly. Once the alien stopped talking, Duma shot it in the eye.

Nathan drew his head back from the scope and glanced at Arista.

"What the hell? Who was—"

A shadow slid in on her. "Behind you!"

A scaly figure plunged a knife at her back. Arista spun just in time, her body twisting deftly, as if she'd predicted the strike. A flash of metal from her hand disappeared into the attacker's chest. There was a small grunt as the lizard-esque creature fell to the floor.

A stream of lasers flashed from the darkness, crashing into the structure around them.

"Head for the exit!" she said, darting out of position for cover.

Nathan was two steps behind her. *Damn, she was fast*, he thought as lasers whizzed by them. Ahead, a small counter blocked their path. He prepared to slide over it, but as Arista approached—she unexpectedly drew her pistol and vaulted it in a one-handed flip. Upside down and in midair, she sent a stream of fire at their pursuers, killing one. She landed midstride and kept going.

It was surreal. Nathan had only seen something like that from an Olympic gymnast or in a movie. Behind him, the guns fell silent for a beat as he slid across the counter.

Three steps later, Arista and Nathan crashed through the door on the far end. Immediately, the only thing Nathan saw was water. The rest of the building was unfinished, leaving a four-story drop to the waves below. The pair screeched to a halt. Alfred, Nathan's sentient jumpsuit, stretched out to wrap itself around the metal framing to help.

"Shit." Nathan looked back at the door. There was no lock.

Without words, the duo took up positions on either side of the door just as two reptilian humanoids charged through. The first one could not stop in time and stumbled over the edge.

Nathan pounced on the second with a hammer fist across his head, followed by a knee to the ribs as Arista's fist found a third guard's throat. From behind, Nathan heard what sounded like an uncoiling spring. As he spun, a net flew by his face.

It hit Arista, wrapping itself around her, the momentum carrying her backward off the platform. Nathan's arm shot out, but it was too late.

Without thinking, he dove off the edge after her.

Entangled in the net, Arista plummeted four stories. Her body twisted until her feet were under her just as she splashed into the rough water below and disappeared.

Nathan plunged into the icy depths only seconds later. For a beat, he was blinded in shock by the bitter temperature, but once his eyes adjusted, he glimpsed Arista struggling with the net. She was trapped and sinking fast.

He swam for her, his arms churning violently, pulling his body downward through the water. When he finally caught up to her, he saw her jumpsuit had encased her head.

He copied that tactic, mentally instructing Alfred to do the same. It was a weird sensation, feeling the Tanzi slip over his face. But breathing underwater wasn't a natural instinct, and he instead attempted to hold his breath for as long as he could.

Sliding his fingers into the net, he slogged up toward the surface. It was much slower, and he was nearly out of oxygen. Black spots spread over his vision with each kick, and his brain functions slowed. Finally, unable to take it anymore, he exhaled. Figuring he'd suffocate when he took his next breath, he was ecstatic to feel more oxygen in his lungs.

It took him a moment to get used to breathing this way,

as it was strange, and the oxygen was still not all his body needed, like breathing through a wool hat. He paddled his feet again and slowly dragged Arista to the surface.

Hauling her to a ladder, he drew his knife and cut her loose. The jumpsuit retracted from her head, and she gasped for fresh air. Alfred slid back as well.

"Are you okay?" he said, panting. He searched her face, finding her eyes wild with fear. For the moment, she seemed uncharacteristically shaken.

"I couldn't move. I didn't think you'd—" Arista paused and wiped a hand over her face.

"It's okay," Nathan said, trying to reassure her. "You're okay now."

Two deep breaths later, she collected herself again. "We have to make it to the backup extraction point."

The ladder led to the mesh floor of the ocean platform. As they reached the top, black domed buildings surrounded them like high-tech igloos. Waves crashed over the structures and drained harmlessly through the flooring.

"I signaled the ship," Arista said. "Do you still have your sidearm?"

Nathan reached down for it but found an empty holster. "No. I lost it in the water." He handed her the knife. "Still have this."

"Looks like we do this the rough way."

Clinging to the buildings for cover, they prowled across the platform until they came to a group of six more of the mermen. Nathan didn't know what else to call them. Aquamen? They were humanoid but had scales with various color patterns instead of skin. Their heads were more squid like—angular, with short tentacles on top and two green eyes with U-shaped pupils. He couldn't tell if they even had a gender, and if so, what it was.

Arista signaled for Nathan to start from the left. He nodded sharply and stalked closer. She did the same on the right, casually flipping the knife blade down and plunging it into the first one's neck before it could react. However, its flailing tentacles alerted the rest.

Taking the cue, Nathan hit the nearest guard with a strike to its throat. The skin was tougher than he expected, but the merperson staggered backward, its tentacles wrapping around the wound.

Arista slid close to the next guard and twisted the rifle from its hand, using the butt to break its knee. She fired once, burning a hole in its chest. The others were on her now, grabbing her arms. Arista turned, clutched their limbs, and redirected their momentum, cranking their joints until she found an opening.

With lightning speed and finesse, she waded through their attacks, blocking, dodging, and counter punching her attackers. As she saw an opening, she struck one in the jaw, taking it down. A second opening. *Crack*. She snapped another's neck.

Nathan circled to the left of his opponent's attack and countered with a strike to its torso. A high-pitched screech escaped its throat. He pressed forward with a leg kick and parried its wild swing. Bobbing the next attack, he connected with an uppercut and transitioned into a spinning kick, knocking the creature back.

A razor-sharp fin sprang from its forearm, catching Nathan off guard. It sliced through his skin, sending a flare of pain across his arm. It lashed out again, swinging the fan-like blade in a giant arc, ripping through the armor and into Nathan's stomach.

Blood washed down his abdomen. The exposed wounds were quickly covered by Alfred. The merperson pressed forward, its scaly forearm crashing against Nathan's face, inflicting further damage. A groggy fog overcame him from the sudden blood loss. *This isn't training*, he reminded himself. If he lost here, he could die.

Fighting the blazing pain in his gut, Nathan spun around, catching his opponent in the head with his heel. He pressed in and wrapped his arms around its legs, tackling it to the ground. Warm blood continued to stream from his wound, even after Alfred's attempt to stop it. The world around him was getting darker and more muddled. He knew he didn't have long before he passed out.

Scrambling on top of the creature, Nathan unleashed a flurry of blows to its smooth head. He rained down elbows for as long as he could, each one growing weaker until he collapsed from blood loss. He wasn't aware of much else, but he hoped he'd at least knocked the merman out, for Arista's sake.

Everything was blurry now, but there was a sudden reddish-orange glow around him. Energized balls of light were waving about. Trying to focus, Nathan saw Arista still fighting. The glow moved in sync with her. For a fleeting moment, he reached a flash of clarity. It was coming from her hands.

A sharp *clack* of energy followed every impact she made, one after another after another after another. Until it was quiet.

Then she lifted him to his feet.

"Come on, Nathan. Hold on," she said.

It was a grueling journey to the rendezvous point. Every step seemed to tear the wound even more. Nathan's vision faded in and out. He'd never felt a cut that deep before. He was dying. Not realizing he had passed out, he awoke face down on the mesh. Arista pulled him to his feet again and dragged him forward.

The shuttle doors flew open with a heavy clunk. Arista hauled him inside and strapped him into a seat. His eyelids flickered, and his gaze caught her worried eyes. She leaned in, her voice filled with determination, ordering him to stay awake. Despite his pain, he mustered a weak smile, grateful for her care.

"Did we win?" Roman said, before leaning back in the pilot's chair to see the pair covered in blood. "Shit! Guess not."

Valor Duma stepped in and slammed the door shut.

"Go!" he commanded.

CHAPTER 13

ARISTA OBSERVED AS Dr. Rami chronicled Stryder's condition. She had seen him unconscious before—usually when she'd made him that way—but this was different. His bloody body was splayed out on the table, and she was constantly watching to make sure he didn't stop breathing.

"He'll be okay," Rami said. "We'll get him in a ZIPR shell as soon as I'm done." A laser extended from Rami's wand to Stryder's heart. "Yep, his heart's still there." She grinned.

"He saved my life. He had no hesitation."

"Saved your life? That's a new one. Concern, too? Another first."

Arista shrugged. "I have a heart too, you know."

Rami tapped a button, and the table lowered into the hollowed-out impression in the floor. An imprinter lowered from the ceiling and began constructing the ZIPR shell coating, starting at his feet.

"I need your opinion," Arista exhaled.

"Sure, go ahead."

"I think I'm growing fond of him." She winced, wishing she could take it back. The words sounded ridiculous even as they left her mouth. She stood up straighter and recomposed herself in an attempt to look more professional.

"Fond of whom?" Rami asked distractedly, looking over the chronicle report.

Arista bowed her head toward Stryder.

Rami glanced up in surprise. "Oh!"

"It's just—I really haven't met too many people since I started training," she said, feeling a need to justify herself. "I don't know if I truly like him or I'm just grateful to have some company." She was trying not to undermine any authority or respect by opening up like this, but Rami was the only one she could talk to who wasn't part of her chain of command.

"Well, you know, the Tithe of Valera is a few weeks away. Maybe you should take him to the party and get to know him outside of bruising his face."

Arista's head tilted sharply, accompanied by a half-hearted glare. "Don't you remember the last time I went to a party? I ended up here."

"Right. I'm sorry. But, seriously, do you see him outside of your training? He might be a totally different person. Then you can make your judgment."

Silently, Arista shook her head. "I haven't been to the Tithe of Valera since I was home, before I started my service here."

"It's much different here on the ship. It's simply spectacular. I went last year with my spouse. We had an amazing time. Everyone's out of uniform and in a relaxed environment. I think you and Nathan would have a wonderful time. You'll know if you like him then."

"Maybe." It made sense, but Arista was skeptical. Plus, Dr. Rami always had something up her sleeve. What was it this time?

After Rami left, Arista took a wet towel and kneeled next to Stryder, who was now up to his chest in the shell coating. As the machine continued to cocoon him, she gently cleaned the grime from his face, tracing his cheek with her fingers. Leaning in, she stole a moment to linger by his lips, contemplating the kiss they'd shared a few days ago.

It was her first kiss, and although it had surprised her and wasn't how she'd imagined it, she felt close to Stryder—intimate and vulnerable, like she never had in the past.

✷ ✷

Nathan woke up inside a shell again, surprised to be in one piece. He ran his hands over the gashes on his stomach and face, relieved to detect no lasting damage or even pain. It took him a moment to put it together—Arista had saved him and dragged him to the ship. There was something else, though, something that slowly floated to the front of his mind. Lights dancing around her. He struggled to remember, but it was a blur.

Regardless of how he'd survived, he'd nearly died on that planet, and he didn't know why. The only reason he'd agreed to do this was so he could find his sister—there was no other loyalty than that. Drelmar had given him nothing yet, and as he'd learned, Valor Duma couldn't care less. They were taking advantage of him, and it pissed him off.

He left the med bay with anger in his veins and marched into the solarium, which was ironically where Drelmar had convinced him to join the Meraki military. The target of his hostility was sitting on the floor in a lotus position, wearing a gray tunic and facing the massive window to space. His manner was unexpectedly serene. Which only pissed Nathan off more.

He marched up to Drelmar. "You said you'd help me find her! I'm done being a toy soldier." He stepped closer. "I've played your game, and I almost died! I can't save her if I'm dead."

Drelmar opened his eyes and lifted his head to Nathan. "Sit, Stryder," he said in a calm voice. "That's an order."

"No. I told you—I'm done with all this!"

"These things take time, Nathan."

"I don't have time. *She* doesn't have time!"

"I understand how you feel. But I told you it would take time. You are not the first person to lose someone. My kin were slaughtered in their beds."

Nathan choked on his next words. If there was a way to screech to a stop emotionally, he'd just experienced it.

Drelmar locked eyes with him. "Now, sit. Please."

Nathan reluctantly took a seat on the floor. "I'm sorry."

"First, empty your mind." Drelmar closed his eyes again.

Nathan complied, letting out a breath he hadn't realized he was holding. Some of the tension flowed out with the air. And after a few breaths, he felt better.

"What are you doing?"

"Breathing," Drelmar responded.

"Yeah, I saw that much."

"Close your eyes, Stryder."

Again, Nathan grudgingly complied.

"I've been following a few vapor trails so far. Nothing solid yet," Drelmar said, in answer to the lingering question. "Breathe in," he continued, "and imagine that each breath is a level of a waterfall that starts in your mind, falls to your chest, and pools in your stomach. You are breathing in the universe. Let it flow through your body and breathe out your suffering."

It was a fresh perspective on the breathing techniques Nathan had practiced to control his anxiety. The breath rushed into his lungs and washed up over his mind, then cascaded down to his chest and filled his stomach.

"You need to learn to tap into your inner strength. Breathe deeply. Feel for it."

A few breaths later, Nathan could feel it. Either he had a great imagination, or it was working. He let the universe saturate his soul like a waterfall.

"You can make a difference in this war," Drelmar said.

The waterfall fluttered. "I just want to find Susan and go home."

"You can't go home, Nathan. Even if you find her, this is the world you live in now. You can't ignore that."

Nathan had known that in his bones, though he didn't want to admit it. It took a little focus, but the waterfall settled again. "I suppose you're going to tell me to stop thinking of myself and fight for the greater good?"

"No." Drelmar spoke calmly, his words no longer disturbing the waterfall Nathan imagined. "We all have to write our own stories."

"And what piece would I play?" The words came out before Nathan could review them, but he was genuinely curious where he fit in. He felt so out of place here.

"That remains to be seen." Drelmar's words lingered. "There was an empire—an old empire, that is long extinct now—called the Coda."

The word hit Nathan like a train. A brilliant flash blinded his mind's eye, and his body shuddered. The waterfall was gone. He was on the deck of a space station, covered in bizarre, translucent armor. Before him was a creature with several arms and a dozen eyes. It was covered in spikes. Somehow, all of this was familiar. He slammed his forearms together, reached back with both arms, and then threw them forward. Crackling energy streamed at the creature.

"They genetically bred their warriors," Drelmar said, continuing the story, "to have amazing skills. Each one could wreak terrible, massive havoc on their enemies. They called them Asante."

Again, Nathan's mind quaked. The space station fell away, and he was now standing on a walkway above a cavernous room filled with enormous, high-tech reactors that were harnessing miniature stars. He leaped from the walkway and spun like a gyroscope toward the ground, in the way an Olympic diver might. As he whirled, he could feel a buildup of energy. He hit the ground in the middle of a dozen soldiers and sent a shockwave out in every direction. The flooring buckled and cracked like ripples in a pond, throwing the soldiers backward as if they were rag dolls.

Nathan's eyes snapped open to the present. Drelmar sat

across from him with his eyes closed, still talking as if nothing had happened.

"Asante means, 'The resolve of one can eclipse a legion.'" He paused. His eyes opened and examined Nathan's face. "You alright?"

Nathan nodded, not knowing what to say. "Yeah."

Drelmar locked eyes with him. "A war isn't won by an army, but by the blood and sacrifice of individuals."

He stood and made for the door, stopping briefly to look back at Nathan. "Be patient. The time will come."

* *

Ajax put his feet up and watched from a vidscreen in his office as Drelmar and Stryder talked in the solarium. That was a benefit of being the chief of security, being able to watch everyone and studying their motives.

Five cycles ago, when he was deployed to the *Kai'den*, Drelmar had taken to him and groomed him for this position. The Master Chief was the first person Ajax felt he could trust to have his best interest at heart. Together, they ran the security detail for Lord Admiral Lasal. It seemed silly to use "mentor" to describe Drelmar, but he couldn't come up with a better term.

They'd installed all these Overseer recorders themselves. The *Kai'den* had security vids all over, but the Overseers, Drelmar explained, were the next step of security. They monitored a person's heat, eye movement, heartbeat, and breathing, as well as what they were actually doing. It was the best way to get inside someone's head without a brain implant.

Of course, as much as Drelmar was his mentor, he didn't know about the extra Overseers that Ajax had installed. Chief of security was a pleasant job, but Ajax had bigger ideas about his future, and knowing more than everyone else was the best way to outwit his adversaries.

Drelmar was notorious for having one of the best Gira faces around, a virtual plate of granite that told them nothing. But as great as Drelmar was at that, everyone knew it, and so they knew what to expect. What was harder to read was the person who loses a bit, has apparent tells, and might not take the game seriously. This was the person who had other motives. The one who might lose the game, but walk away with everyone's money, nonetheless.

And now, as he watched the vid of Drelmar and Stryder, it was time to interpret their motives. Stryder's was easy. The man wanted to find his kin, but he didn't know who to trust. He seemed to trust authority—Lord Admiral Lasal and Drelmar. Drelmar had been kind to him and had a gentle, but tough, personality.

The trick Ajax saw was reading Drelmar. His behavior tracked. The way he treated Stryder was the same way he'd treated him. It sparked a bit of jealousy; he had to admit, but not more than he could suppress. Did Drelmar have other motives, though? That was the question.

His stomach felt uneasy when he thought about the future. How everything he had become comfortable with here would come to an end. How everything would play out. What it would be like to handle everything alone, without a mentor.

As he contemplated the future, the Overseer feed abruptly washed out, and instead of Drelmar, Stryder, and the Solarium, it was a white void.

Ajax's feet dropped to the floor. "What in the devil?"

He leaned forward and cycled the feed back to when it had cut out. Drelmar was telling a boring story about the Coda, one Ajax had heard several times from him—a fairytale Drelmar had probably been told on his backwater planet as a kid. Then, whoosh. The feed was gone. No, not gone. Ajax tweaked the levels of contrast. It was still there, recording. It was just overloaded.

Then it came back. Drelmar stood up and told Stryder to

be patient. Stryder sat by himself for ten more minutes until a group of people came in and he left.

Ajax had never seen an Overseer act like that before. Could it have been a glitch or power surge? Whatever happened to it, at least he didn't have to hear that stupid story again.

Sliding over to the haloid, he called up Captain HaReeka. A hologram of her appeared. He'd always been fond of working with her. Perhaps it was her confidence or their shared ambition.

"Captain. I have more for you."

"Send it," she ordered. "Anything on Lasal?"

"No, nothing yet, Captain."

CHAPTER 14

Nathan had often used the haloid in his room to learn about his new life, researching planets, weapons, and common laws. He'd discovered that the Meraki Dominya comprised nineteen systems, but there wasn't much on the High Command, and nothing on the Vox. Now, though, he looked up something different—a holiday called the Tithe of Valera. Dr. Rami had suggested it to him. It was coming up, she'd said, and Nathan should at least know what it was.

He asked the device, and instantly, there was a response. Valera had been the astronomer who discovered the constellations on the planet Nava. They were thought to be entities that watched over each person for the gods. Each "Watcher," as they were called, had a group of people to watch, categorized by their date of birth. There were twelve major constellations, and they divided the year into twelve parts.

Each year, on the same day they were discovered, the people would offer their Watcher a tithe, or gift. This would encourage the Watchers to tell the gods good things about them, so the gods would bless the individuals with an auspicious year. Over the years, it had turned more commercial as people gave gifts to their loved ones.

The gifts were traditional, and each had a different meaning. They included different varieties of flowers, wine, jewelry, art, and food. The haloid went on to mention the constellations, or Watchers, some of which contained the same stars as the Zodiac constellations of Earth.

Learning astronomy had never gotten Nathan much back home, but now it seemed to pay off. It was fascinating to him to compare the things he'd learned in college to the facts he saw before him. Some of the star systems thought to be uninhabitable as seen from Earth proved to be the home of prospering civilizations. Whether they were altered naturally or by technological advances, they differed vastly from how they appeared from Earth.

He glanced at the clock on his monitor. It was already 21:00. With his eyes heavy and his body lobbying for sleep, he flicked off the haloid and slid into bed. Nathan dozed off and ushered in another night of restless sleep.

The next morning, he followed his daily schedule. Routinely, before he entered the Crucible, he would pause, wondering what he might walk into. In the same way, every time he entered the Pit, he would recall the first time he entered and saw Arista. After that first day, she'd nearly always been there, waiting to start his training.

Today was different, though. She wasn't here. Instead, a massive form stood solidly in his way. There was no avoiding the figure of Krell Duma—with his eyes projecting an icy stare into the depths of Nathan's soul. It would have been enough to send rational people fleeing in terror. It seemed the fun part of his training was over.

Nathan hurried a salute.

As if on cue, apprehension attacked him, clawing at him from the inside. Swallowing the feeling as best he could, he raised his chin as Duma's voice commanded his attention.

"I have set up a training program for you. Until now, your training has been soft and basic. For the past several weeks, you've learned the fundamentals of almost every form of unarmed combat, but your performance on Tinook was pathetic. It was the same underlying theme as your fight with the Lieutenant Commander—you hesitated, you were always on the defensive, and you failed to commit your power."

Nathan swallowed his embarrassment. The "fun part" *was* over.

"We have taught you knowledge and skill," Duma said. "But those are worthless if you don't have the conviction or fortitude necessary to use them. Without those, you will never master the art of warfare. You will never be a competent warrior. I suggest you find them, or else in a universe of war, you will become a statistic."

With a *clink*, something sprang from Duma's forearm, which was now aimed at Nathan. A fibrous web struck him with tremendous force and propelled him backward into the Crucible. His body was racked with a hammering pain as he slammed into a wall.

Now thirty feet away from where he'd stood just seconds before, the webbing pinned him securely to it. As the pain subsided, he assessed his predicament. Struggling to pull his left arm from the web, thin lines of blood formed where the tension of the wire sliced into his skin.

He molded Alfred to thicken the parts of his body touching the wires. With increased protection from the armor, he struggled again to break loose, determined to free himself before Duma could get to him. A burning ran up his arm as his muscles reached their limit. He thought they might tear out of his skin, but one strand finally snapped, then another. With enough broken, he untangled himself and dropped to the dusty ground.

Glancing up, Nathan expected to meet a dark helmet and glowing blue eyes, but instead, he saw a wall built from what looked like hardened sand. Remembering what room he'd just flown into, he wasn't at all surprised.

Crouching, he made his way to the edge of the wall and peered around it. What he saw was an endless desert surrounding the village he was in, which included a dozen houses and small buildings.

Nathan cautiously made his way around the corner, looking for his armor-clad opponent. Instead, he saw six guards in tan body armor patrolling the area.

Duma's voice boomed through the room, yet the soldiers seemed oblivious to it.

"There is a building on the far side of the village that is the operations hub for this outpost. Your job is to take out the sensors. Everything you need is in the village. This is a High Command asset, so use lethal force at all times. Innovation is your greatest ally."

Nathan observed the soldiers. *Lethal force?* He was determined to show Duma how much he had learned, even if it was only against holograms.

Nathan's warsuit changed shades to match the sunbaked mud used for the buildings. He willed Alfred to cover his hands, then shaped it into small claws. The front and bottom of his feet took the same form. They were the best he had at this point, since he hadn't completely mastered control of the Tanzi yet.

Spiking his claws into the wall, he slowly climbed. Pieces of the structure crumbled and rained down under him. He struggled to clear the last ten feet and crawled over the top, landing on a brittle roof. Visible waves of concentrated heat rose from the shadowless surface.

The next rooftop was a good jump away. From here, he could see there were nine structures. Right now, his primary concern was to find the armory, if there was one, and collect some explosives. If he could do that without drawing anyone's attention, this might be easier than he'd thought.

The desert wind blew across his face, stirring up a twister of sand from the rooftop. In a crouch, he cleared a pathway on the roof, removing rocks and debris.

Starting at the end of the runway, he braced his feet against the edge of the roof. Then he pushed off and bolted ahead.

Within a few strides, he was at a sprint. Now oblivious to everything else, his vision narrowed as he timed his steps to fall at the edge of the roof. When the drop approached, it looked ten times farther than before.

His leg muscles compressed as he hit the edge of the roof, uncoiling a second later to launch him into the air. The jump was executed perfectly. It was flawless. The landing would have been perfect too, if a bird hadn't been hidden by the edge of the roof.

As he hit the surface, the frightened bird squawked out in terror, drawing a guard's attention.

He flung himself flat against the roof, hoping no one saw him from the adjacent buildings, but laser fire began crisscrossing the area around him. A shot grazed his left arm, slicing through Alfred and lancing into his flesh. He had to move.

Jumping up, Nathan sprinted across the surface. With no time to stop or gauge his next jump, he couldn't be certain how far the gap to the next building was.

At the edge of the roof, he threw himself forward into the desert air. In mid-flight, he was glad to see the gap was shorter than his previous jump, but so was the building. He cleared the distance between the buildings and prepared for the inevitable impact.

His body came together in a punishing crunch as he hit the surface and rolled into a hard slide. The momentum propelled him uncontrollably across the top of the building on his stomach. Loose gravel grated into his abdomen and arms with little remorse as it ground under him. He clutched and grabbed at what he could, trying to stop his momentum.

With space rapidly running out, his last chance before going over the edge was the claws he'd made earlier. They tore into the hardened mud, spitting out fragments in all directions, as it slowed him to a stop.

Wasting no time, he found an opening in the roof and

peeked inside. Seeing no one, he jumped down into the building.

Once inside, he took inventory and realized his luck had changed. Around him was the largest collection of guns, ammunition, and explosives he had ever seen. The walls were loaded with racks of energy rifles and pistols. Grenades filled three rows; clips and ammunitions filled another two. At the opposite end of the ammunition, he recognized two powerful detonating charges.

Thirty seconds later, the timer on the first charge was set, his fingers stringing together the correct sequence to activate the bomb with trained precision.

A guard entered the door behind him just as he finished. "Halt!"

Nathan darted for a wooden crate before the order was even completed. The guard sprayed the area with laser fire, missing everything but the wall. This was an awful place for a shoot-out. Any stray shot could send the whole place up in a fireball.

There weren't many places to take cover in here, but Nathan crawled toward the rear doorway until he came to a rack of grenades, slowly lifting one from its slot. Activating it, he tossed it behind him and sprinted outside, securing the extra detonator under his arm.

Just as he made it clear of the building, the armory exploded in a spectacular wall of fire. Accompanied by a heat wave, the force of the blast flattened him to the ground. Nathan covered his head and tried to protect the detonator from the shrapnel with his body.

After a moment, he peeked up and located the operations center a block away. It was the only building loaded with sensors on the roof.

He changed Alfred's colors to match the guard's uniforms, which would hopefully give him a bit of a disguise. He did his best to look the part, pretending to search for the intruder.

Maneuvering through the buildings toward the sensor outpost, he lost sight of the guards.

Clear of prying eyes, he set the timer on the detonator. Once he activated it, he'd have a minute to reach the minimum safe distance.

Slipping inside the doorway, he saw four guards and a handful of computer operators. None of which fell for his weak disguise. Before they raised their weapons, Nathan fired, dropping the nearest one. As the remaining guards returned fire, he dove behind a terminal, releasing three wild shots as he did.

Then, before they could organize, he leaped back over the terminal and shot the nearest guard twice in the chest. Now, within striking distance, he swept away the rifle of the next guard and kicked him hard in the stomach. A spinning elbow dropped the last one. Thankfully, the rest had fled out the back.

With the room clear of enemies, Nathan gently laid the bomb on the terminal and activated the detonator, leaving the building at a sprint.

Outside, there was no one in sight. The village looked deserted except for a red light in the distant sky. His arm still throbbed where a laser had struck him, but other than that, he was doing great.

He made his way toward the designated end point, when a storm of lasers unexpectedly rained down on him. A blast struck his left shoulder, and another seared his cheek. A scorching pain caused splotches in his vision, but he dodged to his left and raced for cover.

The red glow descended in a roar of fire, landing with a heavy *clunk* in front of him. A hulking robot, bristling with rockets and a Gatling gun for an arm, now stood in his way.

Nathan dropped to his knee and fired a burst of shots. The barrage deflected off its armor with little effect. The robot responded promptly by backhanding Nathan in the ribs. He was thrown backward by the blow and sent spinning to the ground. His knee twisted violently.

Knowing there wasn't much time left on the bomb, Nathan struggled to his feet and staggered for safety. His hand dropped to the ground to stabilize him as he wobbled forward. Dragging his leg, he pushed on. Safety from the explosion was only thirty feet away.

Behind him, he heard a whirl as the arm cannon on the robot began to spin up. It would fire any second. Why hadn't the detonator blown yet?

With only his right arm and left leg functioning, he hobbled the rest of the way. Inch by grueling inch, he grew closer to the finish. Nathan's eyes watered as he tried to hold back the pain just a little longer. He grasped the edge of the safe zone just as the operations center gushed upward in a geyser of fire and flame.

"Halt program." Duma's voice invaded the room.

The image dimmed, but Nathan didn't notice. He lay sprawled on the ground, his wounds throbbing, his throat burning, disappointment filling his gut.

"Congratulations, you accomplished your mission. However, you are dead." Krell Duma motioned at the robot, which was frozen in midfire, like someone had hit pause on a TV.

In fact, the entire scene was paused. A motionless explosion engulfed the robot, but a dozen laser pulses from its gun streaked toward Nathan.

"Perhaps I didn't make it clear. You can die in here. Permanently. Now, get up! And report to the Pit."

Nathan struggled to make it across the surface of the Crucible. He turned the idea over in his mind—had this been real, he would be dead. There was a finality about it that had never occurred to him before.

He stumbled into the Pit, hoping desperately to find Arista, the same woman who'd nearly killed him twice before, waiting to catch him if he collapsed. With that thought, he realized just how desperate he really was.

Her being there was a fantasy, however. Instead, he hobbled in to see Lord Admiral Lasal. Nathan fought through the aching in his body and attempted a salute, but his legs operated like Slinkies, and he came up way short of adequate.

Lasal spoke softly. "It's all right. I will excuse the salute today. I have been watching your training session this morning, and I am impressed. A short time ago, you didn't even believe that other intelligent beings existed. Now, you fight alongside us. And from what I have seen, you display much talent in doing so. I am pleased with your progress. It has been rapid, and so will your advancement be if you continue your path."

Nathan stood motionless except for his eyes, which followed Lasal.

"I believe you have an important future as a member of the Meraki Navy. As of now, I am activating you. You will still train as normal, but you will also be assigned missions and gain experience in the field. By recommendation of Lieutenant Commander Arista Conak and Valor Krell Duma, I am promoting you directly to lieutenant." He placed a hand on Nathan's shoulder. "Don't let me down."

Nathan was utterly stunned, and at the same time proud. For a moment, he was outside himself, away from the pain and exhaustion.

"Additionally, I've been informed you seek an update on the status of your kin. I have a lead, and I have sent our best stalkers to follow up. I should have more information in a week."

The pain faded from Nathan's body as his thoughts turned to Susan.

"Thank you, sir. What is the lead?"

"We tracked a signature from one of their engines. With

luck, your sister will train beside you." He smiled. "But like I said before, there is a chance we might be too late."

"We won't be too late, sir. I'll go with them."

Lasal shook his head. "No, no—they have already left. Lieutenant Stryder, as you were," he said, then strode away.

Moments later, Nathan heard the door slide open and looked up to see the large black boots of the only person he did not want to see. He winced as all his pain seemed to rush back.

"Attention, soldier!" Duma ordered. "Your training is not over."

In misery, Nathan brought both feet together and balanced his weight evenly.

"You must learn to control your pain. It hampers your performance. Now, concentrate. Block it out. Stand at attention. Don't let the pain dictate your movements.

"Feel your nerve endings—imagine a dial and turn them off. Regulate the pain. Don't let it control you. Feel it gradually fade until you feel nothing. A good soldier feels nothing: no pain, no grief, no pity, no sorrow. No remorse. Those are the things that make you hesitate. Those are the things that get soldiers killed. We don't have time to feel, to judge if someone is worthy of living. We are not the judges—we are the executioners."

Nathan studied Duma. "Arista isn't my enemy, sir."

"When you fight her in the Crucible, she is! Do you see Arista hesitating? That is why she's still alive after years of war. She doesn't have any problem with killing! She doesn't feel pity, and she doesn't hesitate!" There was a slight pause as Duma allowed that to sink in before continuing. "The enemy has your family. The enemy deserves everything they get. And never forget it."

Duma took a step back. "Now, kick me."

Nathan winced at the thought, remembering the last time

he'd tried. He must be in hell, and Duma the devil incarnate. Where was Arista?

He hurled his injured leg at Duma's head. It was brushed aside, and what felt like a hammer slammed into Nathan's ribs. A whimper escaped his lips as he collapsed to the floor. He was sure Duma had broken something—multiple things.

"Don't leave your ribs open when you kick. Some bastard might do *that* to you."

Nathan remained on the floor. He hardly noticed Duma had stuck a G-booster on him until it took effect. It caused his wounds to tingle with heat and goosebumps to slither over his body as it healed him.

Duma loomed over him.

"You are too reckless, and at other times, you hesitate when you shouldn't. Your technique needs work as well. Let's start with the basics. Show me the first three forms you learned."

Nathan made it through two of the memorized string of techniques Arista had taught him before he made a mistake, flailing a weak reverse punch.

Duma spoke deliberately, his words a warning.

"Do not do that again." He lifted a wooden staff from the wall display. "Snap the punch!"

Nathan resumed, but he hurried another crude reverse punch. The exhaustion was affecting him. His muscles weren't responding properly.

The staff swung down with a whistle and struck Nathan on the wrist, making a sickening snap. Staggering pain crashed up his arm and shocked the breath out of him.

"I said, don't do that again," Duma repeated, twirling the staff to a default position at his side.

With tired eyes, Nathan continued the routine more slowly, with precise intent. Duma scrutinized the movements, giving no emotion.

Behind them, the door opened, and Ajax leaned in. "Valor. Lord Admiral Lasal wants a word."

Duma nodded and turned to Nathan. "Hopefully, we won't have to repeat this lesson. Wait here, there's one more test," he said, then left him with his thoughts.

Nathan closed his eyes. This was too much. How was he supposed to learn when all Duma did was torture him? But he knew if he wanted help finding Susan, he needed this training. Now that there was a lead, there was a distant light in the tunnel. Using those thoughts, he recommitted himself to doing whatever he needed to save his sister.

Opening his eyes again at the sound of the door, he was ready for whatever this madman wanted of him.

"Try to sense my attacks," Duma said.

Without a twitch of an eye, he slammed his glove into Nathan's face, cutting his cheek. "Not just my eyes, my body positioning. Sense my movement."

As they circled, Duma struck with a lightning kick to Nathan's groin. Thankfully, that was a place he'd reinforced with the Tanzi. Even so, a deep ache radiated from the impact.

"Do better," Duma said.

Eventually, Nathan came to a point where he could anticipate some attacks. In an actual fight, it would be impossibly more difficult, but each step brought him closer to being prepared to rescue Susan.

"Good. Now let's fight. You go full power, full speed."

Duma slapped his helmet on, and instantly Nathan could no longer read his eyes.

If he couldn't defend, he decided he would attack. With his nose bleeding, his rib cracked, his wrist fractured, and numerous other swellings, not to mention the wounds he'd suffered earlier from the laser fire, Nathan charged in on his enormous opponent, and remembered nothing else.

CHAPTER 15

A WAXY SUBSTANCE surrounded Nathan, blocking his vision. He lay there at one with the ZIPR shell, melting in its comforting fortification. Inside, he felt protected from the world.

He missed Susan. With the possibility of new information, he was thinking more about her. She was older, but he'd always felt he had to protect her. He'd failed. As a child, his parents had dragged him to her dance recitals. Now, he would have given anything to rewind the years and see that again. A twister started in his gut, sucking his hope into it. He strained to push it aside. Dwelling on the past would accomplish nothing. It was out of his control for the moment.

But Susan didn't have that luxury. He had to keep moving forward, for her if nothing else. With one last breath of serenity, he poked his fingers through the material and watched it crumble. As he climbed out of the shell, he saw the smiling face of Dr. Rami approaching him. He wasn't sure how long he had been in the shell, but his pain was gone, though a bit of grogginess remained.

"So, we meet again," Dr. Rami said.

"It's destiny," Nathan croaked.

"It's funny, the mention of destiny… I happen to know a certain someone who is going to ask you to the Tithe of Valera celebration."

"Who?" he said, trying to clear his mind.

"Oh, come now, Nathan Stryder. How many people do you know on this ship? And of that many, how many are…" She outlined the curves of a female figure with her hands and waited for a response.

His thoughts were still murky, and he was slow in putting together what Dr. Rami had said.

"Arista! Arista, you fool!"

"Really?" His mood brightened.

"Of course. Why else would I say it?"

Finally, the pendulum was swinging back in his favor.

"Did you read the history of the Valera celebration?" she asked. "That you have to give an offering to your watcher and your companion?"

Nathan pulled himself away from pleasant thoughts of Arista. Susan was still missing.

"I really don't feel like a party," he said.

"It might feel safer to stay in your quarters, but you never know what could happen. Going to the Tithe could change your life. It might not, but nothing is going to change just sitting in your room. And, as for the gifts, don't worry about that."

Dr. Rami's eyes searched for her next words, and she grinned wickedly. "What is important is that I know Arista's favorite flower."

"Hold up. How do you know that? And why?"

Dr. Rami waved her hand to dismiss the questions. "Oh, I'm devious. No one told you?" She laughed.

"What is it?"

"A red-and-white philtre aphrose," she said, as if it were a profound secret that would change his life.

"A what?"

"Oh, just go to Level 16, Section 44, and tell them Wendalin sent you. Hurry, though, you only have a week!"

✸ ✸

Valor Krell Duma was not pleased with his current assignment. Splitting his time between watching over a neophyte who should have still been in cold storage and guarding a top-secret prototype seemed like the two most divergent tasks imaginable. Now, he was being summoned to Captain HaReeka's office.

They'd had a fairly pleasant relationship over the twenty cycles Duma had served the Meraki, and sometimes it went even farther than that. Her intelligence and confidence had drawn him in more than once. She had always shown him due respect, unlike some of his superiors in the past. However, she was also always working the system, which annoyed him greatly. Others who played those games had burned him, and he was not about to let it happen ever again. These days, he kept his guard up around her.

Stepping into her office, he saw a clear vine of smoke climbing to the ceiling from a wooden incense burner on the windowsill behind her. A strong aroma of gala fruit, a scent that brought up memories of his assignment in Sontarey, filled his nose. He'd been charged with protecting her from a zealous local faction she was trying to quell. It had been a time in which they'd inevitably grown close. A time when he called her by her first name, Venea.

Duma's boots thumped together as he stopped before her, drew to attention, and saluted.

"Sir!" he said, declaring his presence.

Cool, sterling irises glanced up and took him in. "Valor." She returned to her work, leaving him to remain at attention.

Eventually, she rose from her chair and sauntered over to him. HaReeka's harsh, yet tantalizing eyes surveyed him with each step she took, as if she were preparing for a meal.

"You are quite a paragon, aren't you?" she said as she continued a tour around him. "I remember that solid frame, those powerful arms. I wouldn't be here if not for them."

She traced her fingers down the side of his head and neck.

"I know what's under that armor, my scarred, tattooed beast," she whispered in his ear, sending prickles through his body.

The woman knew how to draw his heat, but this wasn't the time. He was in control.

"At ease, Valor Duma."

He slid into the position innately.

"I have information that I find disturbing, and that I need your assistance on," she said, leaning on her desk.

"Of course, sir."

"I've uncovered facts I need someone to verify. It concerns the sabotage of the ship."

He did not want to get drawn into whatever she was planning. "We have security teams for that."

"And what a wonderful job they've done so far." She cocked her head in an exaggerated motion. "And what if they're in on it? I need you to investigate the Lord Admiral. I believe he is working with the saboteur."

This didn't surprise Duma. He just never expected her to bring him in. She had ambition and drive. It was attractive, but those were also traits of the people who'd turned on him in the past. For some, it made them incredible leaders. For others, it made them backstabbing snakes.

"Spy on a commanding officer?" he said. "Some would call that treason."

"It's just you and me here, Krell. You trust him? He is Andromin. Andromere, Petra, Jin. You can't trust anyone from the Cadre."

"The Cadre? That was over thirty cycles ago. They are all one with the Dominya now. Lasal grew up in the Meraki Navy. Why would he suddenly turn on all that?"

"He's a loose cannon." She pushed off her desk and approached him again. "We both know that."

Duma ignored her statement. "I was still on Carcosa."

"What do you mean?"

"Thirty cycles ago—I was still on Carcosa. I hadn't joined the Meraki yet. Am I on your list as well?"

"Krell," she said in a wounded tone.

The sound of her tailored uniform gliding against her thighs filled his ears as she stepped closer. He resisted the memory it produced, instead focusing on her micro expressions. Then, the warmth of her fingers rested on his hand, again bringing up their shared time together. "You did what you had to do. You had no choice."

Duma let her touch linger before moving his hand away. "Regardless, I have other duties that cannot be ignored. I do not have the time, nor the subtlety."

"Just keep an open ear. And let me know if something is amiss." She turned from him and strolled back to her desk. "Dismissed."

Before Duma could reach the door, her voice rose again wistfully. "Krell, do you ever think about what we had in Sontarey? We're stationed together again. We could pick up where we left off. Don't you want to see if that flame still burns?"

Duma paused and reflected momentarily. "That was a second life, Captain."

※ ※

Nathan went back and forth on the idea of attending the Tithe a thousand times as he sat in his room watching the stars, going over all the awkwardness of not knowing anything about the customs or what to do. Would his lack of knowledge fool anyone? He might stand out like a weed in a flowerbed. And what if Rami was wrong? Could he even trust her?

Mentally fighting away the questions was pointless. They continued to crash back like waves. Eventually, he took Drelmar's advice again and kept moving forward. Fixing his mind into the front wedge of a train, he pushed the questions aside as they came. He didn't need to be in control of everything. He didn't need to have all the answers beforehand. It was scary to take a dive into the unknown, but he kept reminding himself that once he was in the water, it was usually not as bad as he expected it to be.

Nathan lay down in his bed, put on the enhancer, and closed his eyes, focusing solely on the blackness he saw. A few months ago, he'd had trouble falling asleep, but now, with the physical exhaustion of training all day, he only needed a few moments.

The next morning, his mind was ready, and he headed to the Pit early, planning to arrive first. However, Arista was already there practicing a precise routine of martial arts, sharp yet fluid, tailored to cause damage. It was not a kata that he had learned yet, but she had it mastered.

"Are you ready to spar?" she said without breaking her concentration.

The words didn't register as he watched her athletic form work through the sequence. The curves of her body shifted and contorted as if they were built for it.

Arista paused mid-technique and eyed him.

"What exactly are you looking at?"

Nathan snapped back from his thoughts. He slid his leg through a stretching belt about waist high and leaned in.

"Just stretching the glutes." It was a weak attempt, but it was all he could think of. He hadn't really meant to stare. He was simply dazzled by her movement.

"Oh," Arista said, clearly unconvinced. Transitioning away from her kata, she whipped her foot at his head.

He stepped back, barely avoiding the kick as a blast of wind rushed by. His hips spun in a fluid motion as he threw a kick back at her, which she skillfully blocked before assuming a fighting stance.

"Oh, we're doing this?" Nathan taunted as he found his own stance.

Arista tracked back and forth around him. "We sure are."

Nathan feigned a takedown, causing her to step off the line of attack and drop her hands.

"You're learning." She smiled, then slid at him, throwing a kick and two punches. Nathan's arm instinctively blocked the kick, and he bobbed around the rest.

"What are you doing later?" Nathan changed directions, moving to her left.

"What do you mean?" she asked as she faked an attack.

Nathan retreated. "Later. Like after training. I thought we could do something."

She connected with a combo. *Ba-bam.*

Nathan stumbled but quickly recovered. He darted in, grabbed her core, and tied her up in a clinch. Arista dropped her center to defend, which put them close.

"I don't understand." Her breath was on his neck.

"You know. You. Me. A bar. A drink?"

They struggled against each other's position. In her effort for control, she attempted to drive her hands under his arms for leverage, but Nathan held tight, pressing his head firmly against hers. *Where your head goes, you go,* she had once instructed him.

Arista pushed back. "I'm not thirsty."

She kneed him in the stomach. Too late to block it, he prepared for the impact, tightening his core. It hurt, but he still had his breath. More importantly, his grip was still intact.

"No," he said between breaths. "I mean, just hang out."

"Hang what out?"

"No. I mean, talk." This was not going well.

She ground the top of her head into his chin. "Do you need help with your training?"

Was she serious or just playing with him? She had to know what he was asking. Either way, he played along.

"Yeah. I could use some help with..." He struggled to divide his attention between talking and their grappling battle. "...uh, battlefield tactics."

Arista took a moment. Maybe she was having the same trouble. "Perhaps. If you can get me to the ground."

Nathan expected it wouldn't be easy asking her out, but hadn't thought it would be this difficult. He wasn't about to give up, though. He dropped to grab her leg, but she kneed him in the head.

Sneaking his leg behind hers, he pushed backward, but she quickly stepped out over his foot and circled away. They slid along the wall, trying to gain position.

The door to the Crucible opened as they inched closer. Nathan pushed her toward the entrance, hoping she didn't see it.

Arista was much stronger than she looked, but eventually, he maneuvered them in front of the open doorway. Pumping his legs faster, he drove her backward into the Crucible. Without the wall behind her, she stumbled, falling to one knee, which was enough to stabilize her as she bounced back to her feet.

"Clever," she said, regaining her balance.

The Crucible already had a program running, which Nathan assumed was from a previous session. They were now in a grassy hilltop grove of what looked like apple blossom trees, except the tiny flowering petals were orange. A constant breeze sent random petals adrift in a parade to the ground around them.

Posting her heel behind his, Arista shoved, trying the same trip he had earlier. Nathan recognized it in time and stepped over it.

If he couldn't out-position her, he'd use his strength as an advantage and Hulk out on her. He had other options, like wearing her down with knees to her thighs or body shots, but he was trying to ask her out, and he didn't think that would help.

Nathan squeezed her close, connected his hands behind her, and twisted his upper body. He could feel her lift into the air. He had her!

Then, he sensed her feet entwine around his leg and hook together, anchoring her to him. It was just enough to stunt his upward momentum, causing him to lose balance.

He unclasped his hands and dropped one to the ground to stabilize himself. Arista took the opportunity to climb onto his back and wrap her legs around his throat. Now top-heavy and unable to breathe, Nathan found it even harder to right the ship.

Arista threw her upper body back in an arch, and they spun into the grass, sending fallen apple blossom petals wisping into the air. She released him and stood up.

Nathan's head was pulsing, and he was sucking in as much air as he could now. His body felt like jelly. Despite that, he stood up and charged her again. He wasn't about to give up.

They continued for the next five minutes. She'd thrown him down or wrestled him off her a dozen times, it seemed, but she was slowing down now too.

"You want to discuss tactics more than anyone I've ever met," she said in deep breaths.

Nathan was too tired to respond. He was focused on breathing and taking her down.

"If you give up now, we can talk about tactics at the Tithe," she said.

"That party?" He sounded like a caveman as he eliminated unnecessary words to save oxygen. "No. Don't like"—he took a deep breath—"parties. Too…many people."

Nathan shot in again for her legs, but his body lagged behind the intent like drying concrete. His unresponsive fingers slipped off her thighs and clutched a knee. Arista pushed down on his head and spun out of his grasp.

Nathan remained face down in the grass, gasping. His body was numb. Slowly, he rolled over to face the sky.

Arista sat next to him.

"Your technique and reflexes are much better." She took a deep breath before continuing. "But you still need to work on conservation of movement."

His head turned subtly to her, his eyes focusing on her mouth as he considered her words. He was hardly worthy of a compliment. He had failed.

She lay beside him and looked up at the sky.

"Well, I'm on the ground. Still feel like that drink?" She smiled.

Nathan tried to laugh, but it turned into a winded cough.

"You got it."

CHAPTER 16

Underneath the transparent floor of the Stardrift Oasis Lounge, glowfish gently drifted down the river. Each one was illuminated from within via a multitude of alternating colored lights. The one Arista watched swam under her table and turned from turquoise to magenta to emerald and back again. None of them were real, but it was easy to forget, just as it was with the fireflies that floated around the room, blinking in pre-determined patterns. The nighttime oceanfront background displayed on the walls was also fake, but not to the extent of the Crucible's reality. Only the nearby trees and plants were real, and that was enough for the facade to work.

Places like this were necessary for most people stationed indefinitely on spacefaring ships. They allowed you to reconnect with nature, to the point you could with a simulation.

Sitting at one of a dozen tables, Arista wondered how her plan would have turned out this morning had Stryder not upended it all.

She'd arrived at the Crucible early to prepare a simulation she'd reconstructed from a childhood memory on Aureon. On that breezy spring day, she'd sat in the passion triloba orchard and looked at the clouds. The complete scene was supposed to be a tranquil, scenic setting in which she could invite him to the Tithe of Valera.

She wasn't upset at what had happened instead. In her profession, things rarely went to plan. In fact, she was delighted that he'd taken the initiative and asked for a drink, but a morsel of disappointment sat in her belly as she wouldn't get to go to the Tithe with him.

A warm prickling started at her tailbone, rose up her spine, and quickly filled her with exhilaration. He was here. She felt it every time he was close. And sure enough…

"Good evening, milady." Stryder's voice broke into her thoughts, and a flash of excitement sparked to life in her stomach.

A curious smile brushed across her face. She rotated in her chair to greet him.

"'Milady'? What does that mean?"

He greeted her with a smile that put her at ease. "It was a name for a woman during the Middle Ages on Earth, a title. Like Ma'am or Sir. Reserved for the wealthy and respected."

She beamed. "And you find me wealthy?"

"Um. Well, no. I meant it more for respect."

Arista didn't know how to reply. Respect was something she hadn't expected. She had always respected Lord Admiral Lasal and Valor Duma, but being respected was new to her. It was warming.

He sat across from her. His head tilted as his eyes took in the ambiance of the room.

Arista spun the menu display around on the table to face Stryder. "What will you have?"

He regarded the menu. His face contorted, befuddled, and his eyes went back to her.

"I have no idea." He chuckled. "Like always, I'm at your mercy."

She ordered two Purple Phase combinations. "Hush. You've only been here a few phases. You're still learning."

"Just to clarify, phases are months, right? Around thirty days?"

"Yes. The translator isn't perfect, but it should pick that up now." She nodded as the barista brought them their drinks.

Stryder's right eye twitched the moment he took a sip.

"Yeow, that's tart," he coughed out. His hand jerked up to hide the spasm.

A smirk grew on her lips. It was a wonderful reaction. She found herself studying him.

"Careful, Stryder. It's got some smite. Medic!" she called out.

His eyes lit up as he laughed. "What's this called?"

"A Purple Phase. You like it?" She took a drink.

"If it doesn't kill me."

"Good. It's from Aureon. It's named after our star."

"A purple star?"

"Well, it phases between blue and purple about every thirty days." She spun her glass in her hands, watching him put it all together.

Stryder gestured in understanding. "Which is why you say phases instead of months. That circled back around fast. Wait, is that why your eyes are rose-colored? Because of the color of the sun?"

"I suppose. What color is your star?"

"Yellow."

"I read somewhere that we evolved to see colors differently because of the influence of the color of our star. My eyes filter blue light differently, for instance. So, we might look at the same thing, but I'd see a different color. And the translator takes that into account when it interprets our words for colors. Some races can see wider spectra, others only black and white."

Stryder's eyes narrowed as he pondered the idea.

"Damn. I never thought of that." He lifted his glass and took another sip, looking prepared for the bitterness this time. "Don't you miss your home?"

"At times. But I've been here six years. The longing fades. I bet you miss yours."

"Yeah. I tried to find it on the maps in the solarium, but it's just a dot. It helps a little."

"When I find myself missing those things, I like to look to the future, not the past."

"Wise advice," he said, raising his glass in the air. "To the future, then."

She looked at the glass, then back to him for an answer. Was there something in it? What was she missing?

His smoky brown eyes regarded her with amusement. "A toast. Lift your glass." He raised his a little higher.

Awkwardness and confusion tangled inside her as she lifted it to the same height. Stryder clanged the glasses together, forming an unexpectedly pleasant chime.

"To the future," he said, smiling. "You say it now."

"To the future," she said with a laugh. "Now what?"

"Now we drink."

A sip of the Purple Phase washed over her tongue. The sweet sting reminded her of Aureon, bringing a smile to her face. It had been a long time since she'd felt normal, not like a soldier, or a lieutenant commander, just herself.

"So, what are your people called? Aureonan? Aureonese?"

She nearly choked on her drink, barely holding it in with a gurgling snicker. She forced herself to swallow.

"What are we called? What a strange thing to ask."

"I mean, you know. Your race."

"My 'race?'" The last word came out sharper than she'd intended. She tried to hold it back, but the laughter rose from her gut and burst through her pressed lips. Once she started, it was hard to control.

The question had an endearing purity—ignorance, but purity. She peered over her drink at him, but that only made it worse. The laughter resurfaced.

"What?" Stryder's expression was an invaluable mixture of bewilderment and awkwardness, all tinted a blushing red. "I don't know. Are we even the same species?"

The muscles in her stomach cramped from the sudden exertion. She couldn't stop laughing. She had to, but she couldn't. Everything he said was making it worse. Gradually, she regained control and her stomach relaxed. She hadn't laughed like that in forever.

"You know, I never know what is going to come out of your mouth," she finally said, suppressing a giggle and watching Stryder squirm. "Aurein. The people from Aureon are called Aurein." She shook her head, amused at the conversation.

"And, yes, we are the same species. Anyone who can mate and produce offspring are the same species." Her words came to a halt after realizing what she'd said.

Stryder raised an eyebrow.

The subject had already been clarified with Dr. Rami, but she wasn't about to tell him that and didn't wish to give it away with further discussion.

"What about you? What are your people called?"

"We are called…" He paused, frowning. "Earthlings? No. I never thought about it. Earthies? Earthers! No." He threw his hands up in defeat. "No idea." His eyes lit up with a chuckle.

"And what is Earth like?"

"It's amazing. Really. That's probably what everyone says about their home, but it's true—blue skies, cornfields. At least where I live." He paused. "Well, lived. There are also oceans and mountains and deserts and cities! And jungles and snow. Man, I wish I could see it again."

His excited rambling was endearing, warming her from the inside.

"What is the story behind that? I heard you were a refugee. Is that true?" She tried to be delicate with the question, but she wanted to understand him more.

He took a heavy breath. "My sister, Susan, and I were taken. I was rescued… she wasn't."

"I'm so sorry. I didn't hear that part of it."

"Have you heard of the Vox?"

Arista searched her mind for the word. "No. I've never heard of them."

A hush settled between them. Arista sipped from her drink to rationalize it. Stryder, it seemed, was doing the same. The silence lingered as she took in the artificial décor of the room. Each tree had a thin, decorative rope clipped around it to alert anyone before bumping into it.

Somewhere in the back of her mind, she recalled his invitation.

"You know, Stryder, you haven't said one word about battlefield tactics."

An exaggerated wave of surprise passed over his face. "No? Are you sure?"

He glanced at the empty floor to their right and gestured to it. Arista wasn't sure what he was doing, but she followed him as he stood up and led her to an open spot.

"Now, say this is the battlefield. And you are my objective."

She laughed.

"Shh. This is serious," he joked. "What would be the best way to approach you?"

The unorthodox tactic intrigued her. He was a puzzle box of curiosity. "Well, if you're looking to overwhelm me, just a straightforward approach."

Stryder took a step closer. "Like this?"

She cocked her head but didn't step away. She liked the feeling of his closeness. Gazing into his eyes, the fingers on her right hand explored silently until they found what they were looking for.

"You can call me Nathan, by the way."

She smiled. "Nathan? There's no going back. You're sure?"

A faint *click* behind her made her cringe inside, but she resisted the urge to show it. The palm of her left hand found his chest as she slowly circled him. Her fingertips danced across his sternum and taut shoulder, then over his muscular back until she was back to where she'd started.

"And then I might try a pincer move?" Nathan said as he

placed his hands on her hips. He looked as lost in her eyes as she was in his.

"That is a solid maneuver. But, *Nathan*," she said, emphasizing his first name, "do not underestimate lures and misdirection."

She turned on her heel and walked toward the door. A scuffle behind her told her that he'd tried to follow. Arista glanced over her shoulder to watch him stumble as he realized she had bound him with the decorative rope clipped to the tree.

"I'll see you at 0800." She winked.

CHAPTER 17

Since his promotion, Nathan's training had picked up in intensity, but now that he knew Arista was interested in him, everything seemed different. He looked forward to training now, despite the punishment and pain he often felt from it, knowing he would see her.

Occasionally, a thought passed through his head about why he trained as an isolated soldier and not in a large group with other cadets. They couldn't train all their soldiers one-on-one like this. However, they were on a warship and not at an academy, after all, so he gave less thought to such ideas as the weeks passed.

They continued training his physical skills, while also adding more specialized ones, like demolition and infiltration. Arista had taught him to bypass and defeat a range of security systems with fingertip prowess. Right now, he was learning about small, but focused, explosive charges in the Pit.

On the table was a horseshoe-shaped device. Arista had gone into the technical name for it, but Nathan remembered it by its common name—a plasma bomb. She showed him how to arm it and went over its uses. There were settings that could control the direction and radius of the blast. Then she switched to several other types of explosives.

"Lieutenant, accompany me to the next room."

Nathan followed her into the Crucible, which was now an open wheat field at sundown.

In the sky, a recognizable red glow descended on them. It

was the colossal robot that had "killed" him in Duma's training program. His heart skipped as he searched for a weapon.

"At ease," Arista said, as the robot landed with a *clunk*. "Today's lesson is weakness. You have weaknesses, Stryder. As do I. As does everything. This is called a Cyber. It's an armored drone. It's outfitted with an arsenal of rockets and a rotating pulse cannon. And even this monstrosity has weaknesses. The back armor is weaker, and its joints are vulnerable to precision attacks. You won't be able to overpower most enemies. You must learn to exploit and attack them where they are weak. You must learn to fight smarter."

"Yes, sir."

Back in the Pit, she ran him through a series of calisthenics that ended with push-ups.

"What will you do?" Arista said, standing over him.

"Attack their weakness!"

"Pick it up, Lieutenant, you're only on fifty. You still have twenty more."

Nathan pushed against the floor again, slowly raising his body. Once his arms had straightened, he counted it out loud. "Fifty-one!"

"Do I sense a challenge in your tone?"

Stepping around to the front of his prone body, she lowered herself into a push-up position. "Well, how about this—I'll race you to seventy, and whoever wins gets to pick the next stage of today's training? Deal?"

Nathan grunted from the strain of his next upward push.

"Good." She smiled. "I'm glad you agree."

"Fifty-two," he announced once he'd completed the push-up.

As he lifted himself the next time, he was only vaguely aware of her voice counting, and of her body rising and falling in front of him. The numbers rose rapidly, but the blood was already rushing to Nathan's head, making it hard to keep track of her total—or even his.

A grueling minute later, it was over, and Arista had narrowly won. Nathan lay on the floor in the midst of a gasping fit. His arms were jelly, a familiar feeling he was not a fan of, and his lungs burned. Arista was talking, but he could hardly hear what she was saying, catching only the end. She was panting hard too, speaking between extensive breaths.

"Which means I get…" She inhaled deeply. "…to choose…" Another pause for air sent her chest heaving outward. "…what you do next." After a few more breaths, she finished her thought. "Now, Lieutenant, give me fifty more. And no slacking this time."

Nathan knew what she was doing. By being harder on him, she was making sure the lines of their personal and professional lives didn't blur. What he didn't know was whether she was doing it for his benefit or hers.

A random thought popped to the forefront of his mind as he lay panting on the floor.

"Wait! So that means I'm an Earthin?"

Still gasping for air, Arista chuckled, which caused Nathan to as well, and the effect snowballed into more laughing. But the laughs quickly turned into coughs as neither had fully caught their breath.

"Yes!" she yelped between coughs. "You're Earthin."

Floundering on the floor a few feet from each other, Arista was still giggling when Nathan grabbed her ankle and tugged. A grunt escaped his throat as she slid across the smooth surface and ended up next to him.

She smiled at him with the last vestige of her laugh. "Hey!"

"Would you go to the Tithe with me?" Nathan asked plainly.

There. He said it. It was done. The thought of a party caused him all sorts of ill feelings, but she wouldn't have asked him before if she didn't want to go. Plus, it was another reason to see her again outside of training.

Looking dazed, Arista eyeballed him. "Wh—You can't just ask like that," she sputtered. "We're still training."

Nathan rephrased the question. "Would you go to the Tithe with me, sir?"

✳ ✴

The door to Lord Admiral Lasal's office slid open.

Stepping through the doorway, Duma saw he had interrupted Lasal's thoughts. He loved to catch him off-guard. It served to remind the man of his skills.

"Sir, you requested me?"

Lasal turned away from a white marble sculpture—which looked to Duma like a glob of panphin dung—and returned the salute without getting up from his chair.

"Yes. Have a seat." He motioned to a chair. "It has been months since our saboteur struck last. As you predicted, he seems to be waiting for us to relax our grip."

Duma remained standing.

"What I want to know, Valor, is whether you're any closer to finding out who it is." He stared Duma dead in the eye.

Without a hint of submission, Duma returned the gaze.

"No, sir. Nothing definite. They are sophisticated and highly trained. I have Master Chief Vinn and—"

"I don't care how well they're trained!" His voice raised a notch. "I want them stopped."

Duma had never seen him lose his temper. Self-control was something he knew Lasal took pride in, but right now the man looked to be on the brink of losing it.

"Sir, I requested your classified personnel files last week. Without your access code, I cannot open them. Clues to the saboteurs could be sealed in them. I need to see them, sir." He should have already had the information he needed.

Lasal fingered a smooth rock on his desk. "I will grant you access to them tomorrow."

"I would appreciate them as soon as possible, sir," Duma insisted.

"That is as soon as possible, Valor!" Lasal sounded insulted. "Do you think I want these saboteurs running around blowing things up?" He shot out of his chair. "Making a mockery of my ship?"

"No, sir. I simply wish to have everything I need to do my job."

"So do I, but there are certain channels to go through. I don't like it any more than you. There's simply no way around it."

Bureaucracy was a facet that sent Duma into the red zone, and with the saboteur running around, it seemed to be getting worse. He didn't like people standing in the way of his job, especially when he could take other routes. None of them, however, would be acceptable when dealing with his superior. He found it so much easier to deal with the enemy when he could use his deadly skills without restriction. It seemed he would have to wait. As much as he hated it.

"Sir, I think we should bring Captain HaReeka in on this. She is highly quali—"

"Bring her in on what?"

"Deathwind, the prophecies—everything, sir. She needs to know to do her job."

Lasal sat down again and looked over his desk. "No. We can't. The circle starts and ends with us. It's out of my hands. But there is one more thing we need to discuss."

Duma remained still. The words indicated it was something he would not like.

"As you know, your training of Lieutenant Stryder is highly classified."

Duma nodded, waiting for the sledgehammer to drop.

"At 1747 today, Lieutenant Stryder purchased a red and white philtre aphrose from outside his restricted perimeter."

Duma kept an outward calm, even though he felt heat in his veins. There was nothing worse than a soldier disobeying an order, especially a soldier under his command.

Lasal continued, "Last week, Lieutenant Commander Conak submitted a request to attend the Tithe of Valera. She has been restricted from attending for the past six years. In light of these two events, and much to your disapproval, I'm sure, I have granted her permission to attend with Lieutenant Stryder. If all—"

"You granted them permission to go to a party?" Duma interrupted through clenched teeth, attempting to push down the rising magma inside him. "*Before* you granted me access to your files? Have you confused your priorities?"

"Don't question my priorities, Valor!" Lasal raised his voice again. "Have you confused your rank?"

Their eyes locked into the bloodless battle that had started the moment they met. Duma knew his place, but Lasal was tying his hands and risking his mission over this absurdity.

A slight pause, a shallow exhale, and Lasal was ready to continue where he had left off before the interruption.

"As I was saying, allowing them to go will not only make Lieutenant Stryder more comfortable in his situation, but it will also strengthen his conviction to stay in our service. And if they were to fall in love... then he would definitely be under our control."

Duma stepped closer. "Love?" Pressurized, seething anger coursed through his body. His eyes hardened and his vision narrowed. He smashed a fist into the desk, scoring the wood. "I speak of stopping a saboteur, and you speak of love!"

Lasal rose from his desk to meet Duma's challenge. "You know the importance of Nathan Stryder. He could be the final piece in a very big, complex puzzle." His voice was on the verge of shouting. "He has the potential to be our best! Even better than you."

"Don't threaten me with his potential. I'm not afraid of how good he could be," Duma thundered. "And what would happen to your scheme if they both ended up in med bay for the next week?"

"Valor Duma," Lasal said calmly, "I refuse to fall for your attempts to annoy me. But, in any case, if they aren't in shape to attend the celebration, I will have you arrested and thrown in the brig."

Fury filled Duma's eyes. "You just try it." This was his first assignment with Lasal, and it would be his last.

"Relax, Valor. We are both on the same side. I was simply pointing out what would happen if you interfered with the interests of the Maelidor and continue to question my authority. We've been warned that the Harbingers' dawning is at hand. They must be securely under our control."

"I am just as concerned with the interests of the Maelidor. It's you I don't agree with, and your decisions. The prophecies can't be used to find the saboteur. And neither can *love*." Duma spat the word.

Lasal straightened his jacket. "Your disapproval is noted, Valor, but I felt I should inform you they are my plans, whether or not you like it."

"If that is all. I will await the access to your files. Sir."

Duma lifted his hand from Lasal's desk. *Intolerable, incompetent fool!* He would have the boy under control, in his own way, without Lasal's ridiculous plans.

"That is all, Valor."

Duma turned and exited through the double doors like lightning through a tree.

The next morning, Valor Duma stood in front of Lt. Commander Conak and Lt. Stryder.

"Neither of you are aware of this, but there is a saboteur

or multiple saboteurs on this ship. They have destroyed some important information and given away our position periodically in the past. They must be stopped. I have some leads, which you two will help me follow up on in the next week." He paused.

"But for now, as you both are attending the foolish celebration—and I am aware of what you have planned…" He looked directly at Stryder. "You will watch everyone. You will suspect everyone. If you see anything, report to me immediately. They will try something soon."

"Yes, sir!" they said in unison.

The day went fast, even as the pair annoyed him. He could see the excited looks they gave each other. Years of training to suppress Arista's emotions were failing. As his frustration kicked in, he ordered them to train separately, discouraging their distracting relationship as much as he could.

Aggravated, yet focused, Duma spent the rest of the day at the computer console, continuing his attempt to hack into Lord Admiral Lasal's personnel files.

CHAPTER 18

At Nathan's request, Doctor Rami gave him instructions on what to do and how to dress for the celebration. He tried on the clothing he had to wear while Rami explained the order of events.

The room would have holographic images of the constellations floating overhead toward the ceiling. At the appropriate time of 21:00, he would need to stand under his Watcher's constellation and throw his offering into the air. He and Arista would exchange the gifts for each other an hour after that.

"Though, one suggestion I will make," Rami said, "is that I've always thought that exchanging gifts with your companion at the party was impersonal and—well, to be honest, tacky. I like to get away from all those people, just one-on-one someplace private. You have to romance it."

Nathan nodded. "Got it, but that might be easier said than done."

"The trick is to surprise her."

"I'll think about it." He smiled and fastened the wrap-over flap that reached across his chest like an old-fashioned pilot's jacket. It had been uneven three times before.

She patted the jacket flat. "Exactly. Now, can you remember all that? I don't have time to come and dress you before the party."

The next day, Nathan was in the Pit, already halfway through his daily schedule. Arista paced around him, providing instructions on various escape tactics. He was standing at ease, absorbing to every word she said. A few feet away, Duma worked diligently at the computer, maintaining a quiet focus.

"Let's take your escape route from last week as an example," Arista said. "Having set the bomb, you charged out of the building and ran straight through the middle of the village. Your route offered no cover and was perfect for an ambush, which, in this scenario, turned out to be the case. Now, considering what happened, would you say this was a good escape route?"

"No, sir."

She was close enough that her aroma was distracting. In addition, the closer she got, the more sensitive he became. It was a certain excitement that flowed through him, like adrenaline. He experienced it every time he was near her. It seemed almost insubordinate, even illicit, to feel that way with Duma still present, which made it altogether more thrilling.

She corrected his escape route and ran it through a computer, showing him the best path in his situation. "All factors must be considered when you plan an escape. After all, your life depends on it."

They switched to sparring with the wooden staffs that Duma had used to beat him with a few weeks before. Although Nathan was becoming more skilled, it was not enough—Arista gracefully thrashed him in every way possible—though he managed the day without ending up in the Medical Bay. A few bruises and a slight limp were tolerable. When training was over, they made plans to meet later in the solarium.

Once in his room, he removed his clothes and stepped into the shower. Duma had always instructed him to wear the Tanzi warsuit for two reasons: first, so he would become more familiar with it, and second, because *"you must always be prepared for war."* Duma was either paranoid or just a fantastic boy scout.

Nathan decided Alfred wasn't needed in the time it would take him to shower. The heat of the water was soothing on his wounds. He imagined it widening his veins and letting his blood flow to heal the injuries. Once out of the shower, he ran the towel over his body and slid back into the Tanzi.

That was when he noticed a light flashing on his haloid. He tapped the light, expecting more orders from Duma, but hoping for a message from Arista. What happened was far from either of those.

It was not a figure, but a single sentence in gold letters glimmering like stars, floating before him and illuminating his room in an eerie twinkle.

"Their lies lead to the truth. Seek the Vox."

The last words hit him like a brick. Nathan studied the letters as they hovered in the air. "Seek the Vox?" Were they real? Had they abducted him?

Then he noticed the message's point of origin. It was right here, in his own room.

His reflexes took over and he quickly spun around, anticipating someone behind him.

Nothing.

Nathan scanned the room, looking for anything out of place. Who could have written the message, and how did they get into his room? He checked the door for signs of a breach but found none.

Possibilities crisscrossed through his head, trampling each other. Then they stopped and pointed to the only logical explanation: the saboteurs. He leaned forward, running a hand down his face. But why would they contact him? After all, he was insignificant. He held no power, no influence. He wasn't even fully trained.

A blaring buzz from the door shattered the silence, making Nathan's heart skip and turned his whole body cold. Frantically, he switched the message off.

It didn't matter who was at the door. The message could

easily get him charged with treason. He took a few deep breaths to calm himself as he stepped toward the doorway.

He activated the door, which promptly slid to the side. In front of him stood—Valor Duma.

Instantly, Nathan saluted as his superior stepped into the room.

"As you were, Lieutenant."

Nathan attempted to put up a calm facade, dashing a hand through his hair, but he couldn't relax. A message from the saboteur, addressed to him, was just a few feet from them. He foolishly glanced at the haloid, mentally cursing himself the moment he did.

Duma motioned to Nathan's apparel, and he realized Alfred was still molded into boxer briefs. With a thought, Alfred expanded to cover Nathan's body, forming a jumpsuit.

This was bizarre, Duma coming to visit him like this. Did he know about his relationship with Arista? Was it about the saboteur? Did he know about the message? Nathan's mind cluttered with incriminating thoughts.

Duma quickly interrupted them. "Lieutenant, you've had extensive simulated experience, but little genuine experience. The time has come to change that. In seventy-two hours, you will take the next step in your transformation into a soldier."

CHAPTER 19

Gripping the barrel of the rifle he held to his shoulder, Nathan slowly entered the four-story complex. Once in, he found cover and swept the area with his eyes as the HUD adjusted the light intensity. It was too dark for minor enhancements, so the device switched to a night-vision setting. His finger twitched impatiently on the side of the rifle as he waited for the signal.

With three days still to go before the actual mission, Valor Duma had sent him here, to the Crucible, to run yet another training program as preparation. Duma would lead the mission, with Arista assisting him. Apparently, Nathan was just being brought along for experience and would have a limited chance for action. His stomach growled, reminding him he'd had to skip breakfast because of the briefing for this exercise.

The signal came as a soft buzz in his right ear. In a crouched position, Nathan cautiously inched toward the metal stairwell, carefully covering all directions. When the first dark stair clanked against his metal-lined boots, his breathing stopped, and he froze in place.

As the echo subsided, he swept the surrounding area. That was a mistake that could have cost him his life. Nathan remained still until he was satisfied no one heard it. Step by step, he continued to climb the staircase. The beam from his rifle's laser sight danced across the wall and over a row of shadowed crates.

As he crept into the room, he used the crates as cover, crouching behind them. Then one of them creaked. He stopped and amped up the light in his HUD. From the crates came soft, shallow breathing.

With a measured hand, he dragged off a tarp off the nearest crate, exposing the metal bars of a cage. Inside, a young girl scurried away into the opposite corner.

It was Susan.

The realization struck like lightning. Nathan grabbed the cage and searched for a way to open it. Then he noticed she was younger and had no scars—it wasn't her. The woman, with a face steeped in terror, stared at him. The other cages started weeping for help.

Then he remembered—he was still in the Crucible. This was all fake. Rage filled his veins, and he stepped back. Valor Duma had put this girl here on purpose, to see what he would do. If that was what Duma wanted, then he would show him what he could do.

He covered his trail in silence, making sure no one was behind him, and secured the first floor. Tapping the sensor on his wrist with two quick raps, he signaled this to Duma.

A shadow stirred to Nathan's left. He gently lowered the rifle and drew his knife. Stalking the shadow in silence, he approached. He was a predator now—an assassin. Coming up from behind, he slid the knife through the shadow's throat.

Helping the man to his final resting spot on the floor, Nathan inadvertently looked into his eyes. Guilt made him pause, before he reminded himself it was a hologram, an illusion created by the Crucible. When it came to the real thing, he wasn't sure if he hoped he could kill to protect his life or that he couldn't to save his humanity.

The second floor was now secure. Again, he reported his progress to Duma, then ascended the next staircase. One careful step at a time, he advanced up the stairs, trying to anticipate the next encounter. At the top, he saw another room littered with large metal crates. He cleared the sweat from his forehead. This was a perfect place for an ambush.

The soldier leaped from behind two of the crates, striking out with his left hand. Nathan spotted the shine of a blade before sweeping the rifle across his body in defense. Forcing the knife to the side, he swung the butt of his weapon up, hitting his assailant in the temple.

Following up with a jab to the soldier's throat, Nathan caused him to falter backward. Relentlessly, he continued the attack, moving in with strikes to a knee, a kidney, and finally the man's throat as he fell, lifeless, to the ground.

Nathan reclaimed his rifle. Third floor secured.

The rest of the way up the building was less violent. The top level had emergency lights on that bathed it in a red glow. His HUD switched off the night vision.

From across the room, he saw Arista. She motioned an "all clear" sign, waving him over.

"We have executed the primary directive," she said, almost immediately. "Valor Duma is on the roof, waiting. We have two minutes to reach him and evac."

Something didn't feel right about her—something was different. A rushed feeling of exhilaration always accompanied her presence, but not now. Perhaps his mind was exaggerating, romanticizing the memories of how he felt around her.

She had already secured the upper floors, so their journey to the roof was swift. Once they arrived, their evac ship waited. It was a vehicle Nathan had learned to recognize as an ACSE. Small, fast, and lightly armored, the ship was designed for a quick departure from hostile territory.

Nathan trotted toward the ship's hatch, its ramp already extended.

Halfway there, an explosion blindsided him and sent him flying backward. Fire and light sprang from everywhere as figures emerged from all around them. The simple extraction had turned into havoc.

Nathan pivoted to confront his closest enemies. His rifle jumped as he fired off two short bursts, clearing away a pair of the attackers. A high-pitched whine rose from his weapon, and it stopped firing. Options flashed through his mind.

He had little choice but to rush the rest, letting his trained instincts take over. The quick-twitch muscles of his legs responded instantly to his command, driving each step like a jackhammer against the roof.

He glimpsed more figures rising out of the smoke, and with a few strides, he closed the gap between his assailants, but not before one had sent a volley of plasma his way. A shot ripped through his ear, igniting it in pain and sending a sizzling vibration down his spine. Ignoring the wound, he did the best he could to remain focused.

Once in range, he quickly drew the knife from his forearm sheath and twirled it into a stabbing position. With deadly precision, he drove it deep into the closest guard's chest. The blade slid easily through his ribs and lung before puncturing his heart.

Locking in on his next target, Nathan spun to his left. With the force of his momentum, he drove the heel of his boot against the second man's temple, dropping him instantly.

Regaining his balance, Nathan pulled the knife from the first man's body and flung it at an oncoming attacker. The handle slid gently out of his hand, filling him with the confidence of a perfect release.

The small knife spun end over end at its target, quickly lost to Nathan in the lingering smoke. His body reacted almost instinctively, attacking and blocking in the haze of figures and chaos. One after another, he dropped the oncoming soldiers until…

"Freeze program!" Duma's voice boomed out.

The battle, the lasers, Duma, Arista, and seemingly time itself froze.

"Very good." Duma said, but not from the frozen figure of him.

Nathan scanned the motionless battle.

Hidden speakers came to life with Duma's voice again. "Do you feel that? The heat, the exhilaration?"

The images of the battle faded as the Crucible reverted to its original black. But this time was different. The lasers faded, the fire faded, the rooftop faded, and even the images of Duma and Arista faded. Everything faded except for the four lifeless bodies that surrounded him. Four dead soldiers remained.

Nathan turned to ice as shock, confusion, and realization all hit him within seconds.

"Congratulations, you have killed the first of our enemy, the High Command. Your first kill is the hardest. But you're past that stage, Lieutenant Stryder. You've killed your first four, and now there is no longer a reason to hesitate."

Duma's voice trailed off in Nathan's head. Gradually, his hands turned to fists as a horrifying chill spread through him. *These are real people? WERE real people?* What had he done? The lifeless expression of the soldier's eyes was all he could think of. He was speechless, oblivious to everything now. The world was just a muddled fog.

A vague presence approached him, then a hand landed on his shoulder. A firm pat on the back was enough to knock the pendulum back toward the ill-favored extreme.

Nathan turned to glare at Duma, hardly surprised to find his face cold and expressionless, except now with a slight grimace of contentment.

"You may think you have the luxury not to kill, not to get bloody, but you do not. You are not fighting for you. You are fighting for everything you care about. If you die, then your family dies, and anyone you've ever known dies. Do you want your family back?"

"Yes, sir," Nathan answered through a clenched jaw.

Duma leaned toward him and shouted. "Do you want your family back?"

"Yes, sir!"

Duma nodded with satisfaction. "You have power. Those with power must use it to create the world they want."

He turned and strode away, leaving Nathan stunned and alone with the guilt of stealing four men's futures. He hadn't meant to. It was all a simulation.

But that changed nothing. They were dead, and he was responsible.

CHAPTER 20

It was an exhilarating feeling to swipe the perfect brush stroke—a feeling of being in tune, at one, with your painting. At least, that was how Arista defined it. It felt as if what she'd imagined was manifesting itself right before her eyes, through her arm.

She dabbed her bristles into the brushberry blue paint on her pallet and attempted to repeat the feeling. It was the final stroke in the vast ocean of a planet she had never seen. The only thing she knew about it was what Nathan had relayed to her in his excited description at dinner. Without a detailed account, she'd started with a blue planet of water. Where she would go from there, she wasn't sure.

An alarm bleeped softly to her right, reminding her to meet Nathan. She paused to admire her work, then cleaned out her brushes and headed to the solarium.

It was nearly empty, as usual. People got sick of looking out into space when they spent months at a time lingering in it. Her eyes took in the room and locked onto a figure on a viewing bench. It was Nathan.

When she saw him, the anticipation and nervousness in her chest quickly hardened into a rock that dropped to the pit of her stomach. He looked as if his mind were in another star system. His face was tired, and his eyes were dark.

"Nathan?"

He glanced up and smiled somberly. "Hey."

"Nathan, what's wrong?"

He shook his head in silence, then stared back at space.

"You're rattled. What is it?" She spoke as softly as she could, hoping to comfort him.

He rubbed a hand across his face and took a slow, deep breath. "I killed four people today." His eyes lifted to hers, pleading for help.

She had known this day would come—the day Stryder stepped out of the gray and joined the fight. She also knew the swirl of shock and revulsion he was currently experiencing.

The feelings were familiar to her. Though, in her case, she had confronted them long before Duma had ever entered her life.

✳ ✳

Duma reviewed the battle, watching the efficiency in his student's movements, intuition, and reaction time. The novice from Earth was coming along nicely. Stryder had the raw potential and reflexes to outmatch even Arista someday.

Yet, that day was still in the distant future. Duma had trained her intensely for years, pushing her beyond what she perceived as her limits. He'd taken much pride in training her. She was his first student since the others had died, but much more skilled than anyone he'd ever taught. She rarely disappointed him.

Finishing the review, he decided to check in on her. He'd been monitoring her progress by computer and assumed the latest codebreaker program might be completed by now. As he walked in to see the empty computer terminal, he noted it was only in battle in which she rarely disappointed him. Since her introduction to Stryder, she had become distracted. Duma realized he would have to put an end to that as soon as Lasal would let him.

There was little doubt where she was now. He sighed and shook his head, tapping a code into the Overseer console. An idle haloid flicked on, and the image of Nathan and Arista filled the screen. They were on the observation deck, completely unaware of the intrusion.

Arista spoke softly. "I was where you are once. I know how this feels. But you need to realize this is our job. We are trained to kill."

She paused, took a breath, and started over. "When we are sent out into the field, that is what we do. We aren't the judges—we are the executioners. It's for the right cause, Nathan. We fight to preserve the lives and rights of others. No one wants to kill, but there are seriously dangerous forces out there that will impose their will if someone doesn't stand up to them. And they don't always listen to words."

Duma enjoyed a moment of satisfaction at hearing her speak of her duty. Years of molding her body had brought her to physical perfection, and her skills were rising to a masterfully polished peak. In that time, her body was not the only thing he had molded. Her mind was strong, stable, quick—and his. Nothing could change that.

He finished watching his students' interaction with interest. Arista had done her best to convince Stryder that what they did was right, that it was necessary for them to preserve freedom and defend the defenseless. It was a romantic sentiment, even if it didn't reflect the grim reality of how things were.

✶ ✶

Nathan's bed shook lightly, signaling the unwelcome start of his day. He removed the training device from his temple, got dressed, and made his way to the Pit for his morning briefing.

Arriving there, he discovered only Valor Duma, and begrudgingly saluted. He was still pissed at the man, but Arista's words had made sense—they were at war. Someone had taken his sister, and he needed to do anything necessary to get her back. But the way Duma had tricked him still didn't sit well.

"Report to Bay 75 by 0615 in full battle gear. I will brief you en route." Duma turned on his heel and left the room.

Nathan hurried off to get equipped. His heartbeat quickened as he slid his boot knife into place. This was the mission he had killed four people training for.

At Bay 75, he realized he didn't have the code to get in. Alfred retracted from his wrist so he could see the clock on his commlink.

A moment later, a shadow shot past him and stabbed in the code. Adrenaline jumped through Nathan's body as Duma strode past him into the bay, silent as ever. Briefly, he considered running up and stabbing Duma in the back for making him kill the soldiers, but he dismissed the thought.

When he entered the docking bay, he noticed it fit just one ship, which immediately came into view. Its black surface shone in the light, at the same time clinging to the shadows. The hull seemed in constant motion, or at least never in focus.

From the angle Nathan approached, it appeared sleek, devoid of hard angles, only curves. It reminded him of a devil ray, with wide, flat wings that sloped down and then narrowed into a long tail. It was larger than the fighter jets he knew from Earth, probably to accommodate for a moderate amount of equipment and a few passengers.

By the time the pair reached the ship, the strange distortion deactivated. A narrow opening appeared on the side of the vessel, revealing a red glow from within.

Once onboard, Duma stomped to the front of the ship and into the cockpit like a mythical dragon returning to his lair. The interior of the ship had an elaborate arsenal of weapons stowed meticulously around the hold. There were also four tightly cramped seats with restraints that pulled down overhead, like rollercoasters Nathan had been on. They looked rather primitive compared to some other things he'd been introduced to recently.

Nathan took the seat closest to the cockpit, noticing that there were no windows, nor any other way to view the outside world. He secured his gear and pulled down the harness, then massaged his temples, trying to coax the headache he felt coming on into retreat. With a deep breath, he blew out the anxiety churning within him, but it gave only temporary relief. Despite his efforts, he couldn't prevent the metal heel of his boot from rapping nervously against the floor.

He swirled in a pool of confusion, struggling with the memory of killing those men in training, of Duma's ruthlessness, and of possibly killing again during this mission. Arista had said it was necessary to preserve freedom, to protect billions of people who wouldn't ever know. It was a sobering fact of war—to kill.

The ship's hull rumbled as the engines came to life, and it lifted off, exiting the bay. Within minutes, Nathan could feel the ship beginning its descent into the atmosphere.

From the training, he remembered they would enter on the dark side of the planet. After stabilizing from entry through the atmosphere, the cloaking device would engage, and from ground level, the ship would look like a small meteor.

A short, rough ride later, the ship landed. Coming forth from the cockpit, helmet secured in place, the dragon approached.

"You know what to do," Duma said.

The interior lights flicked off, and the outer door slid open. Nathan rushed out, dropping two feet to the ground with the wind whipping around him. The sky was overcast. He felt a slight sprinkle of rain as he took cover to the right of the ship. As it was still cloaked, he couldn't see it, but he knew it was there.

There was a mile jog before he reached the target building.

He initiated the countdown on his watch, signaled Duma, and started the trek. It took him just over ten minutes, with his HUD magnifying the light enough for him not to trip over anything.

The bushes crackled in the wind, providing him suitable cover for the sound of his footsteps. He settled behind a grouping of thick vegetation as thunder growled in the distance. A slight squeeze to the communicator on his wrist signaled Duma.

A signal came back, and Nathan prowled up to the main entrance. The security seemed lax. The door locks looked Earth-like. He removed a small device from his pocket. With hours and hours of practice, he'd learned to use this simple, yet highly powerful, explosive with precision and speed. Focusing it on the weak points of the door made it most effective.

After finishing, he retreated cautiously and waited for Duma. As Nathan looked up into the rain, he saw lights dotting the eighteen floors. He took a deep breath, held it for a five count, and exhaled.

Several floors up, the windows abruptly blew outward from a fireless blast. The shallow pop of the explosion echoed in his ears. Soon, the debris from the windows would fall around him, but he was prepared for it. He protected his head and neck, patiently waiting while the glass and fragments bounced off his armor.

He was to give Duma a few seconds before blowing the main door. When his count reached ten, he detonated his charge, blowing the door off its rails. In a crouch, he cautiously entered the complex.

Concealed in the darkness, with his rifle held snug to his chest, he waited inside.

The signal came from Duma. Nathan took a deep breath and sprang into action, sweeping through the floor. He found nothing—no guards, no cages. At the top of the stairway, he signaled to Duma that the floor was clear.

The next level up was when he'd met his first enemy in the training session—the one whose throat he'd cut. Here, Nathan spotted a gray-skinned humanoid crouching beneath the steel staircase, unaware of his presence. He scanned the area, but since Duma had blown the generator, the room was pitch-black.

Like a tiger, he stalked to within arm's reach of his prey when the guard turned directly at him. Nathan froze, blending into the darkness, as Duma had shown him.

As Nathan hid in silence, his confused and racing mind was haunted by a vision of the man he'd stabbed in training. A faint buzz stung his ear when Duma's signal came in. His stomach clenched up, freezing him in place. Hopefully, the guard hadn't heard it.

Time seemed to stand still as the guard turned, checking for enemies in the opposite direction. There was a perfect time for a commando to strike, and it was now.

With a powerful blow, Nathan brought his rifle butt down on the soldier's head, causing him to slump to the floor. He kneeled to check his adversary's pulse. Relief settled over him. He had avoided a kill.

The second floor was secure.

Each step seemed to echo so much louder now than in the training session, and the scratching of two days of facial scruff against his collar sounded like deafening radio static.

Sweeping the third floor, Nathan discovered another guard in a similar spot. This time, the guard was waiting, and quickly fired off two shots. The first hit Nathan in the leg. He clenched his jaw and fired back. The target dropped to the floor with a *thud*.

The Trinex armor had done its job, preventing any significant damage to his thigh.

In a crouch, he inched his way to the downed guard. His shots hit him twice, in the throat and chest—the man was dying. The sight of the man's dead eyes made him sick. Holding back a wave of nausea, he took a deep breath. It wasn't a simulation anymore.

Nathan secured the third floor.

Duma signaled again, this time to meet on the roof.

✷ ✷

Duma's part in this mission wasn't easy, but it was nothing he couldn't handle. After blowing out the windows in the explosion, he'd swung down into the twelfth floor unchallenged. Having killed most of the people on this floor in the blast, he wasn't worried about resistance.

The visor on his helmet illuminated, tinting everything he saw in a blue glow as his spectral vision clicked on. It was a fusion of various imaging technologies that granted an authentic perception of his surroundings.

As he stepped over a distorted and mangled body sprawled on the floor, he turned down a short corridor. At the end of the hall, a metal staircase descended to the level below.

His first objective was on the eleventh floor. It was paramount for this mission and the only thing on his mind. Project Deathwind had been left in a vault on the ship. Though normally, Lt. Commander Conak would have been stationed to guard it. In the past, she could have been trusted, but now, he'd noticed a difference in her, and he wasn't taking any chances.

Edging closer, Duma glanced down the staircase. He tracked three guards on the landing to the eleventh floor. Two of them crouched low to the left, and a third on the right. The staircase blocked any clear shot at the pair on the left, but the third was out in the open.

Duma took him out with a single, silenced projectile

round, the third setting on his rifle. He switched back to the second setting—rapid fire—before the guard had slumped to the floor. The remaining two guards swiveled toward the crash of their falling partner, which gave him just enough time to navigate the stairway.

From behind, Duma's knife slid easily between the first guard's ribs and through his heart. He closed a hand over the victim's mouth to make sure no sound escaped as he lowered him to the floor.

One step back, and the shadows wrapped themselves around Duma like a mother protecting its child. The remaining guard searched in the blackness, now unable to find either of his comrades. He found only one thing in the dark, and it appeared in front of him.

Duma struck before the guard even had time to gasp in recognition of his end. These men probably didn't even know what they guarded, or who was after it. They were cannon fodder in a war for the stars.

Moving on, he found the room he was searching for. The door responded to nothing now that he'd blown the power, but he had a way in. He checked all exits and sealed the floor before he began.

✶ ✶

Nathan deactivated the seal on the tenth-floor stairwell, still checking behind him for opposition. He wasn't sure what the seal was made from, but it clung to the doorway, and the small strip of metal he held deactivated it. Almost nothing could get through it, or so he'd been told. Yet, when deactivated, it shrank back into its case and fit easily in his pocket.

With the HUD, Nathan could see a collection of bodies on the floor. Glass popped under his feet with every step as he maneuvered around them.

So far, he'd run into only two guards, but on this floor

alone, six lay dead. A quick flash of the ones he'd killed in training sprang into his head. Shaking his mind free of the memory, he forced himself to stay focused.

None of it really seemed clear anymore. He'd cursed Duma for making him kill those men. Now he was helping him sweep this building, and for a reason he didn't even know. Yet he felt safe knowing that Duma was here and on his side.

Reaching the eleventh floor, he deactivated the seal and found three more corpses littering the floor. Another buzz from Duma told him to make it to the roof as soon as possible.

As he emerged from the stairwell and stepped onto the roof, his lenses switched to a brighter setting. The clouds were dark, but it was lighter here than inside. Two pale moons hung low in the sky, giving the rooftop a soft glow.

Duma's devil ray ship decloaked, shedding the night sky from its body and hovered before him. In the session, this was where all hell had broken loose. Keeping the memory of that disaster at the surface of his thoughts, Nathan approached the ship.

Two steps from the ship, he realized he could do nothing to open the hatch. Crouching under it for cover, he signaled Duma.

A rapid clanging rose from the stairs that he'd just exited. His stomach whirled—he had forgotten to seal the door. Anxiously, he watched as the clanging grew louder. Nathan leveled his rifle at the stairway and waited.

A red-faced guard crashed through the door and charged onto the roof. Once he spotted the devil ray, he opened fire on it. Nathan's reaction was only to watch, as the shots weren't hitting anywhere near him. The guard angrily fired nonstop, with no effect. The lasers were just reflecting off the hull.

Then, from behind the furious guard, a blue-eyed demon arose from the shadows. Gliding across the roof, it enveloped the guard in its darkness. Two more shots escaped, and then all was silent.

It turned to Nathan, its blazing blue eye-slit coldly searching his soul. The beast approached, almost in slow motion, its long casual strides silent against the roof. It seemed to take forever for it to step from the shadows.

The hatch on the devil ray sprang open.

"Get in," the low growl of Valor Krell Duma commanded.

The voice startled Nathan out of his brief delusion. Hearing the order, he promptly climbed aboard the ship and strapped himself in. After lifting off the roof, they cloaked again, hovering a short distance away. In that moment, Nathan took a deep breath, releasing the tension and doom that had taken up residence in his body.

A blast shield on the wall opened, and for the first time, Nathan could look out. A thick woodland surrounded the building they had just left.

He felt nothing when the missile dropped from underneath his feet, but after it cleared the bottom of the ship, it was all he could see.

The warhead entered through the tenth-floor wall before it exploded. Hellfire erupted from the building. The blast cascaded through each floor, shooting its fury from every window as it extended its reach over the structure. The eruption shattered the foundation, forcing the building to fall in on itself in a fiery display. Trees surrounding it burst into flames like flash paper, blazing in the night.

Nathan's mouth slipped open at the scene. Awe filled his body.

"My god," he said, as the blast shield slid back into place and the ship left in the wake of obliteration.

Duma's and Arista's words echoed in his head—they were the executioners.

CHAPTER 21

Nathan struggled through the next four days, fighting to keep his mind off the destruction they'd caused. The waterfall breathing technique helped as he strained to focus on the present.

Currently, his attention was on the flower he held in his hand. It was still in a tight bud. It had the appearance of a rose, with ten pedals that alternated between red and white. The stem, on the other hand, had an intricate design of intertwining red and white trails, giving it an artistic, hand painted look. Nathan ran his fingers over the colors to make sure they weren't actually paint.

The clothes he wore were part tuxedo, part WWI pilot's jacket, with variations including a short collar, decorative shoulder armor, and a wrap-over chest flap. And like a tuxedo, it was uncomfortable. Stretching the sleeves and flexing about didn't seem to change that.

The door buzzed, forcing his stomach into a cartwheel. A whirling stream of apprehension flowed through his body and emptied into his gut. In an attempt to cool himself down, he tugged on his collar, feeling the sweat on his neck. He made for the vent in his room and messed with the panel until it blew out cool air. Then he took several deep breaths.

The door buzzed again. Still feeling unsure and nauseous, he took one final deep breath, straightened his coat, and touched the sensor to open the door.

As it slid open, he saw Arista, and all his trepidation disappeared. A wave of pure exhilaration crashed over him. She was simply magnificent.

Her legs were strong—he'd known that, but he'd never really noticed how long they were until now. A billowy dress partially covered them, reaching down to her ankles, but with slits on both sides that revealed glimpses of their length. Her dress was lavender and shimmering with sparkles. It fit neatly over her smooth hips and sculpted curves, accented by her hair, which whirled down her shoulders like mercury. Entwined in her hair was a scarf that matched her eyes. Then, under each eye, were three evenly spaced gemstones.

Eventually, his eyes met hers. "You look absolutely enchanting."

Her face lit up. "Your Darcian looks amaze me as well." With that, she placed a finger on Nathan's cheek and let it slide down his face as she sauntered by him into the room.

Darcian looks? That explanation could wait until dinner. He made note of it to discuss later, when he ran out of things to say. He had no desire for any uncomfortable silence between them later.

"Shouldn't we be going?" he said.

"In a moment. I want to make sure we're clear." She paused. "Tonight will be a little complicated. We are still on duty and have orders to investigate anything out of the ordinary, so keep that in mind, but things will be different. I want this to be like a normal engagement, not one between two people who claw at each other every day. Afterward, when we go back to training, it goes back to the way it was. Understood?"

"No need to even say it," he said nonchalantly, as if he already knew. She was his superior, and if that was how it had to be, he was fine with it.

They smiled uneasily at one another as silence settled in.

He held out his arm for her. "Shall we?"

She smiled and took his arm.

The pair entered a grand hall where the Tithe celebration

was being held. The ceiling was dark, and images of the constellations floated around in a dazzling spectacle. Nathan's chest swelled as he glanced over at Arista again and savored the moment. There were already about two hundred people in the room, but no one was close to the level of radiance that stood next to him.

✻ ✻

Two guards lay dead by the access hatch to an out-of-the-way laboratory. Two more lay dead on the inside.

He disarmed the auxiliary security system for the hatch and pried it open. Already, he had re-routed the power for this section of the ship, plunging it into darkness. The cameras, the sensors, and all mechanical devices powered down. After clicking on his flashlight, he swept it through the room until he saw it—Project Deathwind, a weapon that could shift the tide of war.

Its core was housed in the steel container before him. Cutting through it took time, even with a highly concentrated plasma torch. As practiced, he cut a hole about eight centimeters wide through the side of the container.

With that completed, he retrieved a hand-crafted explosive charge from the backpack. It slid through the hole perfectly. The last step was activating the device using three razor-thin discs.

He checked his watch. There was now just enough time to shower and shave.

After all, there was a party to attend.

✻ ✻

Arista found a host who escorted them to their seats. First, there would be dinner, then the celebration would begin. Anticipation tingled through her veins. It was hard to believe this was happening. Every day for the past six years had been nearly the same for her, apart from occasional missions.

Tonight, the walls shimmered like water. Holographic stars and crafted decorations floated overhead in an antigravity field, and there was a buzz of exhilaration from the guests. The lighting, the fashion, the ambience, it all gave the whole thing a dreamlike rareness. It was a challenge to avoid all that and focus on her orders.

"Okay," she said. "What is your assessment of the room?"

Nathan glanced around. "A crowd with access to any number of sharp objects. Four main entryways, and a ventilation system. We can't cover all this."

"We are only to watch this exit." She gestured to the closest exit with her head. "That is why we are sitting here."

"Ah." Nathan pulled out a chair and offered it to her.

"Do you have anything like this on Earth?" she asked as she sat down. It was first on her list of questions. The silence that had spread between them in his quarters was something she didn't want to repeat.

He took the seat across from her. "Not really. New Year's would be the closest, I guess. It's celebrated at the beginning of every year, but we don't offer gifts. That's like Christmas."

"Christmas?" She leaned forward. "What's that like?"

"Well, it started as a celebration of the birth of the son of a god, but kind of turned commercial with people giving each other presents. That's one religion, anyway. On Earth, there are many religious beliefs. There's a lot more to it, but you'd have to see it in order to understand."

She nodded. "There are quite a few religions on my planet, too. It was first set up as a free colony thousands of years ago, but we lost contact, and then started developing on our own. I didn't know about the Tithe of Valera until I was here. It wasn't something we celebrated."

"We? Your family?"

She squeezed his hand. "Let's talk about something else."

The conversation paused awkwardly. Scat. She didn't mean to end it, she just wanted to stay away from depressing topics. Duma was really the only person who knew about them.

Nathan took the time to look at the menu. Lines formed on his brow, and his head tilted slightly. Looking as if he were trying to solve a crypto box, he glanced from the menu to her.

"I think I'll let you order again."

Arista winked. "I'll get you something weird."

"Two tentacles or less, please." He smirked.

Unable to keep the regret from her mind, she stepped out from behind the walls she'd built up for so many years and took a chance.

"Can we go back? About ten seconds, when you asked about my family? It's just that no one has ever asked about them, and I'm not used to opening up."

Nathan nodded with a smile. "Sure."

"My mother died when I was born, so I was raised by my grandmother."

"That must have been rough. I'm sorry."

"No. It's okay. I didn't even know her." There was still sadness there, but she continued. "My grandmother trained me to become a war maiden until I was twelve, when she died. My father was in the military, and since there were no other women in my family, he raised me for two years, until he was killed in battle. Then, Duma took me in. And now, I'm here."

It felt good to talk about, to let someone know where she came from.

"Thank you," Nathan said. "For sharing that with me."

"Enough of that. Now you get three tentacles!"

He laughed. "Fair enough."

"Do you know anyone here?" she said, watching the people coming in.

Nathan nodded at Chief Sculic, who nodded back, before turning to a woman at his side.

"There's one. Ajax. Do you know him?"

"I met him once. About a year ago at a party for Captain HaReeka. He told me some old story about the Codi."

"Was it the Coda?"

She tapped a finger on her glass, trying to recall the story. "Could be. It's a haze."

Nathan chuckled. "I heard that one too. And the Vox."

"Is that why you asked me about the Vox before?"

"Yeah, basically. Captain HaReeka said they were fables."

Arista glanced to make sure no one was in earshot. "I'm not supposed to tell anyone, but she told me once that she and Valor Duma were together. Back when he was assigned to protect her. He's never mentioned it, though."

"Duma? Large, menacing, pain distributing Duma? What happened?"

"I don't know." She shrugged. "He got transferred. She got promoted. Life, I guess."

"Well, you think you know someone."

Arista ordered two plates of smoked Sitka Harpon Cazo, a delicately seasoned fish she'd had only once before. They talked more over dinner, mostly learning more details about each other rather than about their training or people they knew.

After dinner, Lord Admiral Lasal made a speech acknowledging the tradition of the celebration and its history. A deep bass and rhythmic chords began playing when he was finished, and nervous energy rose in Arista's chest.

This was the moment she'd been anticipating since Nathan asked her to the Tithe. Though she'd never been to the celebration, Dr. Rami had painted the picture for her, complete with music and dancing. She wanted an excuse to be closer to him, and dancing was a perfect justification.

Someone tapped on her shoulder. Everything in her stomach flipped when she turned and saw who it was.

Prinji. The woman wore the same fake smile as the last

time Arista had seen her, when Prinji spent the night insulting her.

"Arista! It's been an eon. Isn't this just breathtaking?" Prinji said as her eyes drifted to Nathan. "How has your night been going?"

"Brilliantly." Arista stood up and slid her hand into Nathan's. "Would you care to dance?" she said, already pulling him away.

"Well, I—" Nathan gave up trying to talk when she didn't wait for his answer. She pulled him to the dance floor and wrapped her arms around him.

"What was that all about?"

"Nothing." Her voice took on a hurt tone she couldn't control, which embarrassed her further. Then it spilled out. "Last year she accused me of being 'mank and plain.'"

"Her?" His head dipped in Prinji's direction.

Arista nodded.

"Mank?"

Arista glanced at Prinji over Nathan's shoulder. "She said it in a roomful of people. She just wanted to embarrass me or impress her friends. I could have killed them all right there!"

Nathan chuckled.

Taken back by his reaction, she eyeballed him. "Why are you laughing?"

"I'm sorry. I'm not laughing at you." He looked up into her eyes. "I'm laughing at her. I don't know what 'mank' means, but plain? Arista, you are the baddest ass here!"

Shocked, Arista stopped dancing and stepped back. *Why would he say that?* she thought. *Her ass, was bad?*

"What do you mean? I don't understand."

"I mean, over the last few months, I've seen a lot of craziness—aliens, spaceships, insane technology… I mean, just wild things I've never seen before. But out of all those things, you are the most extraordinary. There's nothing plain about you. Not only can you do things I've only seen in movies, but you're strong, beautiful, intelligent, and someone who I look forward to seeing every day. That's the exact opposite of 'mank' to me."

"'Baddest ass' is the opposite of mank?" She laughed. "What a weird thing to say."

"I'm sorry. That's Earthin talk." He smirked.

Arista consciously attempted to relax her fingers from the tight fists they were in. His words were pleasant, and they felt good, but were they genuine? She searched his face for deceit and found none.

Swaying with the music, she lingered in his words like a warm bath. It was strange for her to feel this way after years of strict military protocols and training—years of not expressing this part of herself. The song ended as she contemplated the contrast between the two parts of who she was.

Nathan dipped his head to catch her gaze. "You still with me?"

"Yeah, I'm fine. Thank you." She wasn't about to let anything ruin this night, especially Prinji's hurtful glare.

The band started another song.

"Another dance?" she said.

"Love to." His breath washed over her neck, sending a shiver through her body.

Her job was to survey the area for any irregular activities, and she found that dancing was a good way to scan the room behind Nathan for anything suspicious. At least, that was what she convinced herself.

✶ ✶

Krell Duma sat at the idle computer console, waiting for his access into Lasal's files. He had been waiting all day, and his patience was thin. All his attempts to break-in had been unsuccessful. The files contained personnel items not listed in the ship's records, and he was sure clues to the saboteur were among them. But apparently, Lasal did not feel the same way.

Duma ran his fingers over the stubble on his cheek. The man was probably lollygagging around at that stupid party. Duma had no patience for incompetence. Lasal had maddened him yesterday, and this waiting was not making him any friendlier.

The saboteur would strike tonight. Duma was certain of it. At the moment, he felt a little like both predator and prey. He had to catch the saboteur, and at the same time protect Project Deathwind.

He tapped the screen under his fingertips as he once again checked the security systems set up around vital areas of the ship, combing for any loopholes he might have overlooked. He inspected everything—the energy flow throughout the ship, the haloid circuits, and all his security staff's commlinks. All was in working order.

Then his stomach clenched, and his breathing paused. There was a jam in the haloid sub-server. With a few strokes of his fingers, he traced the problem and pinpointed its location. The control center for calls to grid seventy-one. The same grid that supplied power to the section of the ship where the Deathwind was secured. However, the power was on. The instantly recognizable taste of bile came to his lips. Something was massively wrong.

Duma snatched his helmet and hurried to the control center. When he arrived, he strode to within centimeters of the door before coming to a halt. It didn't open. He stabbed in the passcode to activate the door, but nothing happened.

"Damn!"

He grabbed the emergency handle and jerked it to the side. The door remained in place. Again, he tried to wrench it open, this time setting his foot against a system jack next to the door. His body stiffened into a rigid force, his muscles constricted, and his breathing stopped as he pried the handle.

The system jack snapped from the wall and tumbled down the corridor.

Duma exploded in anger and frustration. It was the final crack in the dam. First Lasal had butted in with his training of Stryder and Conak, then he'd threatened to throw him in the brig and delayed his access to the files. And now this. He knew it was the work of the saboteur. One of his men had let him slip by.

A wild rage flashed through him. Now, things would be done his way.

Placing a small, focused charge on the locked door, he slapped on his helmet but didn't bother taking cover. The door disintegrated in a fiery blast, shooting debris everywhere. Chunks of it ricocheted off his helmet and armor.

Marching through the smoke, Duma entered the control center.

Filtered by the tint of thermal vision, he saw his two guards and four technicians dead. With a simple glance, he could tell that they had died at the hands of the saboteur, not the explosion. Their color in his thermal sensor told him they were at least an hour cold.

Tiny lights flashed everywhere on the console, indicating unanswered calls on the haloid. Duma jabbed at one. A face promptly appeared, complaining of power loss in level five. How could that be? He had just checked the power flow himself.

His fist reactively crashed down on the haloid casing, destroying the image.

Scanning the room, he noticed the handiwork of a true expert as he unraveled the chaos. The saboteur had rigged a connection to the overall power flow, bypassing the downed section, which made it appear to have power from any console but here, where he'd locked the door.

Duma charged out of the room and sent a message to the

guard station. He knew he was now racing against the clock. His prey already had an hour's head start.

Rushing through the ship, now with four guards in tow, Duma made it to Project Deathwind in five minutes flat. Two men lay dead at its entrance.

He entered quickly and bolted straight for the weapon. The four guards followed him in. A bomb rested inside the protective container, as he'd suspected. He knew there was a timer inside that was silently counting down, but unfortunately, he couldn't see it and had no clue how long was left before it blew.

Carefully, he reached in the hole that had been hollowed out for the bomb. The tips of his fingers stopped just short of the detonator. The bulk of his armor prevented his hand from going any farther.

Someone had put a lot of thought into this operation.

Duma flung off his gauntlet and tried again, but the bomb was still out of reach, and there wasn't enough time to disassemble the casing. Leaving his arm as far in as it would fit, he concentrated on his devoted servant. A black snake-like extension emerged from under his sleeve as his Tanzi slid forward and coiled around the bomb. It constricted and hardened, preparing to lift it. Then it halted.

Working through the placement of the device in his mind, Duma realized there would undoubtedly be a tripwire. Slowly, he ordered the organism to release the device and slither toward the three discs. One would cut the power and deactivate the bomb, but the others would detonate it instantly.

He knew which disc to pull on a standard device, but so did the saboteur. If the saboteur had constructed it personally, he could have switched it.

A drip of sweat tingled against his scalp. He had been chasing the saboteur for almost a year in a game of deception, skill, and a bit of luck. Which disc had the saboteur switched?

Duma's decision would either end his life and those of the soldiers around him, or deactivate the bomb and continue the game.

The Tanzi hung patiently over the three discs. Then Duma knew what to do. Gently, the Tanzi lowered and glided the middle disc out of position.

※ ※

It was 19:50 now, and Arista and Nathan were still dancing. In the time they spent together tonight, his touch had become familiar to her.

"Do you know what Watcher you were born under?" she said into his ear over the music.

"Well, no. Not really. The stars are all different here. Can I just pick one?"

"I guess, but that ruins all the fun. Not that anyone believed in this stuff anymore."

"Which star are you from?"

She pointed to Fumera, the blue star at the center of her solar system.

He glanced back at her. The holographic constellations glittered in his eyes, and suddenly, she was lost in the moment. Even just a few weeks ago, she never could have imagined this. She felt so alive.

With Nathan at her side, she'd almost completely forgot about Prinji. Their hands were tangled together loosely, yet it warmed her entire body. She hadn't felt this close to anyone in a long time, if ever. Tomorrow was going to come too soon—she'd have to stretch out the night.

Strangely enough, they ran into some specialists that Duma had allowed her to train with from time to time, all of whom she quickly re-examined as possible saboteurs.

The first they ran into was her only genuine friend, Mirra Cardin, who had taken Arista on a survival expedition to the planet of Kantar. Mirra's expression when she'd returned to camp covered in soot from an unexpected ash eruption was seared into her mind and always there when she needed a laugh. Arista stored it with her most cherished memories. They got along great, but as a survival guide, Mirra traveled frequently.

Then there was Cornileus Grift, an expert in demolitions. There were no fond memories of him, just boring lectures on explosive ordnances.

As the night progressed, dancing with Nathan was Arista's favorite part. She loved to feel his arm around her, holding her tight like a warm blanket. Barring the run-in with Prinji, the night had been perfect so far.

Through the years she had trained with Duma, she'd forgotten anything outside of fighting or killing. Tonight, Nathan opened her eyes again, and it was wonderful.

At 20:58, it was almost time for the offerings to begin. Tradition dictated they were to stand beneath the sign of the Watcher they were each born under. Most of the people had already moved under their signs. Couples would traditionally start with the Watcher of the oldest person, and while Arista wasn't sure how old Nathan was in Meraki standard time, this was his first time, so she wanted to start with him.

Realizing they were the only ones still dancing, she panicked. "Hurry, get the offering to your Watcher!"

Hustling off the dance floor, they jogged over to their table, where Nathan had put the gift, a bottle of Alevian wine representing a worthy quest.

"What's your sign?" she said, tugging on his arm in a hurry.

The enormous clock on the wall had begun the countdown at thirty seconds.

"Lyman," Nathan said. "At least, that's my best guess."

She tugged harder as she maneuvered between the other guests. "Hurry." She pointed. "Over there."

They made it under the Lyman constellation with ten seconds to spare, just as the crowd joined in the countdown.

"Five!"

"Four!"

"Three!" She smiled at him.

At two, he slid his arms around her again and leaned in close, centimeters from her lips.

"One!"

With a tile of his head, Nathan kissed her. A warm flash of connection rushed from their lips to her chest and then to every point of her body. Her senses crackled with bliss.

Miniature fireworks exploded in the room, and the crowd cheered, but Arista was oblivious to it all as her heartbeat doubled and euphoria washed over her. All she could hear was the symmetry of their hearts. She felt weightless. For a beat, she wondered if they had somehow gotten tangled in the anti-gravity field above them.

When it ended, they lingered near each other. His smell was sweet, like sunberry cookies.

Then someone bumped into Nathan, making them stumble. Energy shot through her veins, and instinct took over. She rushed into action. One hand grabbed the man's arm, twisting it backward, and the other was ready to strike.

"Whoa. Hey!" he called out, stumbling.

Her mind instantly analyzed several distinct aspects before determining he was harmless: soft hands, no weapons, out of shape, alcoholic breath, and a wobbly equilibrium.

The unsteady man glanced at Arista's hand as she released him. Then, as if nothing had happened, he motioned to the wine Nathan carried.

"Yer saving dat for next year, or what?" he said, sending a powerful stench of alcohol in their direction.

Nathan chuckled, then tossed the wine up toward his Watcher. The bottle spun cap-over-bottom until it reached the constellation, then froze in midair, where an anti-gravitational field held it in place.

Hundreds of other offerings also floated overhead: bottles of wine, gold statues, fruits, and flowers.

"I have to go do mine now!" she said, finding it difficult to control her excitement.

Nathan smiled at her. "You got it."

They strolled with Nathan's arm on her back to the Watcher sign of Omni. To her Watcher, she threw a single bow. It was white and had many loops, each with its own separate string of material.

"What does the bow mean?"

"It has two meanings." She paused, forcing Nathan to wait.

He tilted his head toward her curiously.

"Do you want to know?"

"Yes, of course!" He laughed, making his eyes crease in the corners.

"First, it means that, like the bow with all the interconnecting loops and bonds, my relationship with someone will grow stronger. The second meaning is a secret."

"A secret, huh?" His hands found her shoulders and squared her to him.

She nodded, then hummed an affirmative.

"Really?" He leaned in, putting his arms around her.

"Really. But don't worry—we get to exchange gifts now!"

"I'll have to go get mine," Nathan said.

She eyed him suspiciously. "Why didn't you bring it with you?"

He laughed. "Do you want to come with me?"

"Yes, I do!" Arista grabbed his hand and started for the exit.

Nathan resisted at first, pulling her back.

Stepping close to him, she put on a stern face, trying to resist a smile. They were merely centimeters apart.

"We can walk there nicely, or I could knock you out and drag you."

He laughed again, then took her hand and weaved through the noisy crowd toward his quarters. Arista's heart sung with anticipation. He was hitting all the right notes.

✶ ✶

Krell Duma returned to his training facilities with the Deathwind weapon in tow. He stationed four guards in every room and programmed the Crucible for zero-g and a complete vacuum. With the Deathwind safe in the Pit, he sat down at the computer console and again tried to hack into Lasal's files.

At 21:13, he still didn't have the access codes. He jabbed a finger at a guard.

"Go find our glorious Lord Admiral," he said, full of contempt, "and tell him I need those access codes now!"

✶ ✶

Nathan confined Arista to his couch as he went into the bedroom to get her gift. She had her present to him tucked safely in her purse. Humming a favorite song from home, she waited.

"You sure are taking your time in there," she called to him after a while. Gently biting her bottom lip, she leaned out, trying to get a glimpse of what he was doing.

Nathan emerged from the bedroom just as she stood up to go after him. A box wrapped in white paper appeared from behind his back.

"Well, here it is. But you can't open it for another half hour, according to your traditions."

"Ah, yes, tradition," she sighed.

Nathan waved the box in front of her. "While we're waiting, can you show me your quarters?"

"Why?" Arista rested her hands on her hips. Her quarters were off limits for Nathan. It seemed a pointless formality, though. What trouble could possibly come of it?

"I haven't seen them yet, and they've got to be livelier than this place." He gestured to his half-empty room.

"Hmm… We can. On one condition."

"That being?"

"That being…" She paused and eyed his impatient expression. "That you never forget me, or tonight."

Nathan stepped forward, taking her hand gently in his. "I think I can handle that."

He leaned in to kiss her. She tried to resist, but she couldn't wait to feel the rush again. It was a shorter kiss than before, but just as rousing.

She pulled Nathan toward the door, which opened at her approach, then glanced out into the hallway. Duma never had to know.

They arrived at her quarters a short time later. Before entering, Arista let her security system identify her. The door slid open to reveal the refreshing colors and sprightly mood of her living room. It was a haven for her, an escape from the drab blues and grays that were regurgitated uniformly throughout the rest of the ship. She was proud of it and enjoyed every feature of Nathan's face as he discovered it.

He eyed a painting on the nearest wall as she activated the rest of the lights. It was her second-favorite. It captured a wide shoreline stretching along a far-off ocean, a sun and two moons hanging on its horizon as a flock of birds flew by. It wasn't any place she had been—it was something that had come to her in a dream.

Nathan took a step closer, viewing it with interest.

"You like it?" she asked hopefully.

"Yeah—it's so detailed. It looks familiar. Where'd you get it?"

"Thanks! I painted it." The night was getting better by the moment. He liked her paintings!

"Amazing. Do your talents ever stop?"

Arista walked into the kitchen. "I sing horribly, if that helps," she said before returning with two glasses of sparkling wine.

"What's this?"

"It's called Quadesa Le Ro'n."

Nathan drank from the glass. "Mmmm." He raised an eyebrow. "Did you make this too?"

"No. I've been saving it for a special occasion." *And this is it,* she thought, as she lifted the glass to her lips and sipped. The wine was something her grandmother used to drink. Another lifetime ago. It was the only thing she'd brought from home to her new life among the stars.

"How long do we have now?" Nathan said as he took another drink.

Arista glanced at her wall clock. "Seventeen minutes by that clock."

"You wanna open it now?" Nathan said as he sat on her overstuffed couch.

"No, no." She waved the thought away, sitting down next to him. "So far, we've done everything according to tradition. Let's keep it that way."

Nathan shrugged. "If that's how you want to play it."

They spent the next fifteen minutes talking about her paintings. It was the first time she'd had a chance to speak about her passions in what seemed like forever. She recalled for him her first "floor painting," as her grandmother had called it, when she had dipped her feet in paint and pranced around the house to record new dance steps on the floor.

At the beginning of the night, a lull in conversation would have terrified her, making her think something was wrong or their chemistry was off, but now, after the last few hours, she was comfortable with Nathan. She slid her hand into his and waited for the last minute to tick by.

"Okay, what'd you get me?" she asked the instant time was up. "Oh, wait. No, you go first!" She removed the small box from her pocket and handed it to him.

Leaning forward, Nathan kissed her on the cheek as he took the gift.

"Thank you," he said, sitting back to unwrap it.

An uncontrollable smile extended across her face as she watched. She had two presents ready to give him, depending on how the night went—one relatively common and meaningless, in case the night went flat, and this one.

He opened the box with care and withdrew the small device, a long ribbon connected to a tiny igniter. It unraveled smoothly. Nathan's face was full of wonder as he tried to deduce what it was. His curious eyes flicked up to meet hers.

"What is it?"

Holding out her hand, she asked, "Do you trust me?"

"Of course."

As she pressed the igniter between her fingers, it clicked and lit the ribbon, which started burning slowly. The igniter dropped off and the smoldering ribbon gently floated between them. It was smokeless and burned away completely until it reached the end. Then, a single spark emerged and hovered between them. It was a plasma spark, and she'd been lucky to find it deep in the bowels of the market section on the ship.

Arista held her right hand out to one side of the spark. She nodded at him and waited for him to do the same.

"This is going to burn, but we have to hold it for ten seconds. Trust me and hang on."

Gently, they clasped hands around the spark as if they were arm wrestling in midair. A tingle came immediately, then burning.

"Ten. Nine. Eight," she counted down.

His eyes watered as the sting intensified. Her body was reacting the same.

"You sure know how to entertain," he said through clenched teeth.

Their eyes were locked, and their grip grew tighter with the pain, but their resolve remained. Arista did what she'd been trained to do with pain: imagine a dial and turn it off.

"Five. Four."

As she reached three, she leaned in and kissed him sweetly, returning the kiss from the Tithe countdown. Their hands released, and Arista pulled him toward her. A tear that had been caught in her eye from the painful ritual ran down her cheek and onto his.

Her lips slid from his mouth as she lifted her hand to compare it to his. The spark was now seared into their palms in the shape of a starburst.

Nathan ran a light finger over the burn. "I truly don't know what to say. You're one of a kind." He smiled. "I don't think I can top that, but hopefully, it won't hurt as much."

He chuckled, and it was a wonderful sound.

"Nathan, I'm sure I'll love it."

He handed the white box to her.

She snatched it playfully, laughing and more excited than she had been since she was a little girl. Unwrapping the white paper wildly, she pulled out the red-and-white flower. Her eyes widened, an awkward heat rose in her body. She blinked. An aphrose? Warm blood flooded her cheeks.

"Nathan, I… Do you know what this is?"

"Sure, it's a red and white philtre aphrose," he proclaimed proudly.

"I mean, do you know what this means?" she said, surprised she could get the words out.

"Dr. Rami said—"

"Dr. Rami?" Arista interrupted. "I should have known."

Nathan looked baffled. "She said it was your favorite flower."

Sighing, she made a mental note about the esteemed doctor. "Well, it seems that Dr. Rami has played a trick on us."

"Why? What do you mean?"

"A red-and-white philtre aphrose is called 'the Love Blossom.'" She studied the flower, dazzled by its beauty.

"Seriously? Wait. You mean…" His voice trailed off.

Arista nodded. She'd never been this close to anyone before, but the more she contemplated it, the more comfortable she became with the idea. It had been a night of happiness, one she would never forget. The corners of her mouth turned up, followed by a tickle on her spine.

"Maybe." The flower twirled between her fingers.

"It's not—I mean…" Nathan paused.

"Are you trying to get out of your obligation?" she said suggestively. A newly gained confidence rang through her voice. "You're the one who gave me the flower."

"No, I—"

Gently, she put her hand on his. "Are you afraid of me?" It was her turn to play.

"Of course not, it's j—" His expression made her laugh.

She placed a finger to his lips. "Nathan, it's okay. I'm just toying with you. It means we have to kiss." A kiss wasn't the real meaning, but she didn't want to embarrass him any further.

"Oh." He smiled, then leaned in.

His lips pressed against hers in the softest kiss she'd ever known. The tingle resurfaced all over her skin.

"You know what I would like to do, though?" She grinned. "I want to hear you."

"Hear me? What do you mean?" He chuckled. "You can't hear me?"

"We've never heard each other's true voices—only what

the translator interprets as our voices. I want to hear *your* voice."

His head tilted as he pondered it. "You're right. I never thought about that. How do we do that?"

"Easy." Arista slid her finger behind his left ear and tapped twice, then guided his hand to hers and allowed him to do the same.

They spent the rest of the night in their naked voices and native tongues, laughing, drinking, smiling, and doing their best to understand each other. They even created a few new words by mispronouncing and mangling languages together, like "sny'quon," "ronya," and "ensolo."

Arista had never felt this close to anyone before. It was intoxicating. Staying awake with him was the only way she had to savor it.

* *

The party had died down after 02:00, but there were still many people around exchanging gifts. Confetti and balloons shaped like stars and hearts were still falling. The music played on, and lasers, reduced to a harmless intensity, made for a wondrous display. The colored beams shot all around, entertaining the guests as the crowd drank and caroused into the night.

Lord Admiral Lasal had just exchanged gifts with his spouse, Thesa, who stood next to him. Now, he was conversing with two of his friends and a visiting ambassador from the Caspian Cree.

The Caspian Cree were the oldest known race in the galaxy. Evolving millennia ago, they had mostly reptilian qualities with natural scales, large triangular heads, and wide mouths. An alliance with them would provide a wealth of information, including answering some long unknowns about the prophecies. This one didn't look like it was enjoying the holiday.

Then, two of the decorative lasers hit the wall next to Lasal, leaving a burned crater in the metal. A jolt of panic sent Lasal diving to the floor, followed by the Caspian Cree ambassador. Thesa lay lifeless next to them. The rest of the crowd remained ignorant to what had happened as the party lasers continued to flash.

Lasal was cursing the saboteur when an explosion ripped through him and everyone else within a three-meter radius. The music halted, but the lasers and confetti continued.

People scattered in every direction, not knowing where the blast had originated or what would follow. Medics rushed to their aid, yet none of them could change what had happened.

Lord Admiral Lasal was dead.

CHAPTER 22

THE RIFLE BROKE down into six parts and packed perfectly into its case. With practiced speed, he climbed across the flipside of the party hall's ceiling, careful not to make a sound. He had hoped to take out Lasal without a big incident, which would have made his escape much easier. Unfortunately, he'd missed the shot, which had triggered the bomb, but he was confident the blast had finished the job. It had taken some expertise to rig the explosion to go off only if he missed the shots, but it worked and that's all that mattered.

He knew much about Lasal, and in a way respected him, but his usefulness had ended, and now, his death was worth more than his life. It made for many more options in the chaos that would follow. He'd been an obstacle, and with him out of the way, the plan could move forward. It wouldn't take long for someone to break the passcodes that were now locked in the dead Lord Admiral's mind. Then they could open the personnel files.

Time was precious now. He had to play his hand carefully.

✳ ✳

As the blast ripped through the hall, Dr. Wendalin Rami didn't hear or feel the explosion. She was enjoying a peaceful word puzzle back in the Medical Bay. The emergency klaxon, however, sparked her into action. The sound reminded her of air-raid sirens she had heard as a girl during the raid of New Waygo.

She knew there would most likely be casualties. Her job

now was to minimize them. After tapping the emergency button on the console to summon the personnel under her command, she grabbed a medical bag. She prayed most of them would be sober enough to help. Shamus, her primary apprentice, had requested the evening off, but he was in for a harsh recall.

Once at the scene, Wendalin acted on pure instinct. Choking smoke and deafening noise faded out as she homed in on the injured. Time and patients blurred by her.

She delegated what she could to her staff and had them triage the victims. They would organize the ones who could not be helped, those who needed ZIPR coatings, and the ones whom a simple G-boost could heal, and then she would move down the line to stabilize them in the order they had designated. The task would have been easier with Shamus, but he was noticeably absent.

A shock hit her when she realized he might be one of the victims. Her pulse quickened as she searched the wounded faces. She didn't see him, but it was hard to tell with blood and debris distorting their features. Body after body, she checked and rechecked.

"Are there any more dead?" she asked, frantic now.

Then she saw him as he rounded the corner, out of breath and ready to help.

"Shamus! Thank the lords!"

He dropped to one knee. "Where can I help?"

✳ ✳

Drelmar Vinn hurried to the war room that Duma had set up to safeguard the Deathwind, summoned by an urgent message. The time was 02:16—just fifteen minutes after the explosion. The death of Lord Admiral Lasal had triggered several events, and this was not something he needed right now. He'd been in the middle of locking down the scene, but Duma seemed more concerned about the Deathwind than about Lasal's murder.

As the door slid open, he immediately picked up Ajax's voice.

"This is not the priority right now! We need to find the assassin!"

Stepping into the room, Drelmar realized he had walked into a standoff.

"Continuity of command is the top priority," Duma declared.

Ajax's face was flushed. "Captain HaReeka is the next in line! It's mutiny!"

Piecing together the dialogue, Drelmar had an inkling about what was happening, but wanted clarification.

"What in the bloody death is going on?"

Valor Duma turned to him. "Master Chief, give me the Lord Admiral's security permissions to everything. I'm taking over command of the ship."

"It's mutiny," Ajax repeated.

The law was clear, and they all knew it. Captain HaReeka was next in the chain of command. There was obviously more to this. The muscles in Duma's face twitched with intensity as he waited for an answer.

"Valor, we can't do that," Drelmar said. "Military law states—"

"Security of the ship supersedes law!" Duma interrupted. "There are saboteurs—assassins—on this ship! We must take measures that the current chain of command is not capable or willing to make."

Behind Drelmar, the doors opened, and Captain HaReeka entered with six guards. Immediately, all the attention shifted to her. She was flanked by three guards on each side, their weapons drawn and directed at Valor Duma.

A groan quietly rose in Drelmar's throat. Six guards were not enough. He'd heard stories and seen reports of Duma handling twice that many. Sure, they were probably exaggerations, but nevertheless, six were not enough.

What felt like a ball of molten iron dropped into his stomach when he recognized a face among the guards from their weekly Gira night. It was Hamil.

Even if Drelmar and Ajax fought alongside the guards, it would not go well. It was still a toss-up. Why hadn't she brought more?

Duma shot a poisonous glare at Ajax.

"I was following protocol, sir," Ajax said. "She had to be notified."

Duma addressed HaReeka. "By authority given to the rank of valor, I have taken command of this ship."

A valor was technically equivalent to captain, but existed outside the chain of command. Drelmar only knew of one time a valor had taken command of a ship, and that was after the captain had died in battle. It was a gray area, he'd admit, but right now they were in hyperspace and had no way to contact anyone to clarify it.

HaReeka took a step forward. "Valor Duma, you do not want to do this."

"Captain, there is more going on here than you know!" Duma said sternly. "There are more important things at stake."

Just outside the doorway, more guards arrived, to Drelmar's relief. However, the knot in his stomach twisted tighter as they included more faces he knew. Xoni and Gundar.

Acknowledging the additional guards, HaReeka's voice grew in confidence. "You have one chance to avoid the consequences."

Drelmar's mind was whirling with outcomes. He couldn't see either HaReeka or Duma backing down. The guards outside gave HaReeka more of a chance, but many could die, including his friends. His eyes flicked over to Ajax, who was clearly doing the same shrewd calculations. Right now, the odds were close to even, but what worried Drelmar was the unknown relationship Ajax had with HaReeka, and that he'd always spoken about going head-to-head with Duma. If that was his wish, then this was his chance.

Drelmar's attention shifted from Ajax to Hamil, who showed great courage given the position he was in. However, Drelmar knew he was terrified. Reading his face every week had made it easy for him to see that Hamil knew his odds were iffy.

The silvery eyes of Captain HaReeka were locked on Duma, but they seemed to be searching for something within. A flinch of resolve? An unsure emotion? A reluctant loyalty to her authority?

Then, in a blur, all bets were off.

Duma's arm flashed forward, propelling a black streak into the door panel, triggering the blast door. It crashed down with a *thud*, cutting off the guards outside and creating a fulcrum shift in the showdown.

From there, the room erupted into chaos. With a quickdraw, Valor Duma produced a pistol and eliminated the two farthest guards with a pair of precise shots.

It escalated swiftly after that, as the remaining guards opened fire and Drelmar's choice was made. He drew both his sidearms and started firing.

Thankful that his apprentice had come to the same decision, Drelmar acted in harmony with Ajax, as they always had. The rest was a haze of laser fire and blood. Duma was hit several times, but it didn't seem to slow him down. He attacked with uncommon speed and accuracy, dropping guard after guard.

It was over in a handful of seconds, but the din of battle remained in Drelmar's ears, the adrenaline rush still warm in his veins. Bodies lay twisted and lifeless on the floor, making the room seem significantly more confining.

With little fanfare, Duma stepped over to HaReeka's limp body and carefully removed his dagger from her chest. Her breaths were shallow and labored.

"Now," she murmured, her eyes locked on Duma. "We'll never know…" Her voice trailed off as life drained from her face.

Duma stood up and turned away.

Finding Hamil's body, Drelmar silently wished him Godspeed in whatever afterlife he believed in.

Then Hamil gurgled, and his eyes flickered. He was still fighting to live.

CHAPTER 23

O6:00 CAME QUICKLY and without remorse. Arista's head was pounding from the wine and lack of sleep, and her body felt like lead. The ding of her alarm sounded more like a shrill, echoing yip.

She woke up to see that Nathan was spooning her on the couch, and it was all replaced with a warm tranquility. Their Tanzis were all that separated them. It was as if she was in Ryliea, as if everything in the universe was right, and she—was complete. The heat and warmth generated from their bodies was a luxury she didn't want to give up, but she knew it had to end.

She wiggled her shoulders to wake him up. "Nathan Stryder," she whispered.

A smile crossed his face, then his eyes opened.

"You were faking?" she said with a laugh.

He shrugged and pushed himself up with his arms. As he did, their Tanzis peeled apart from one another like sticky leather on a summer day.

"I didn't want to wake you. You seemed at peace."

Arista grabbed her boots. "We should get going."

A half hour later, they stood in the briefing room, waiting for Duma and the day's briefing. Something was wrong. Duma was never late.

Moving to the Pit, she opened a channel to him. He could always be reached. He'd made sure of it. A vid-link had been installed in his helmet for just that purpose. Nathan followed her into the room as the link connected.

There was no picture, but Duma's cold, dry voice was unmistakable. Arista came quickly to the point.

"Valor, Lieutenant Stryder, and I were uninformed of a change in our briefing schedule. We wish for—"

Duma cut her off. "There has been another act of sabotage. The Lord Admiral is dead. Continue with your training. You will be briefed on the haloid."

A brief pain surfaced in her chest, but then it was gone. She'd felt a special bond with Lasal. She wasn't sure why. He just had a calming influence. But she was accustomed to death—Duma had made sure of that. It was something that happened to everyone, and in war, it was all to be expected and accepted. She felt nothing for Lasal now. He simply no longer existed.

Nathan's hand slipped onto her shoulder. "Are you alright?"

"Yes, Lieutenant," she said, bitingly. "It's war. People die."

It came out more brutal than she had wished, but the news of Lasal's death frightened her. After everything that had happened last night, what would it feel like to lose Nathan? Would she feel anything? Was she conditioned so thoroughly that she would shut it out? She was too ashamed to think about the answer.

"Well, let's get started," she said, masking her thoughts.

She began their training, hoping it would divert her attention from any further soul-searching. Despite everything that had happened the night before, a sense of doom seemed to overshadow it. It was amazing how quickly things could turn around. Last night, she'd felt good about herself, normal, but now Lasal's death reminded her who she was, and the cold emptiness within reminded her what she was trained to be.

They practiced in silence. Arista prayed the person she had been last night was the real her.

✴ ✴

The silence was eerie. Nathan sensed he should say something, do something, but just what it should be escaped him. Arista's mention of war had hit him harder than it ever had before. Sometimes his life here felt like a dream, or a movie he was acting in. Besides the two missions he'd gone on, it was mostly training. He was insulated from the reality of it.

As he watched her eyes, his mind wandered to how many people she might have killed. How it had affected her. She looked so different now than she had last night. A hard shell seemed to spring up and encase her, swallowing the light that he'd seen within her the night before, and completely blocking him out. Of course, he knew Lasal's death must have devastated her. He could understand that, but there seemed to be something more.

At 14:00, Arista dismissed him early and disappeared before he could say a word. Nathan's feelings yesterday had been so clear and simple. He'd been eager to see Arista and attend the Tithe. Now he felt alone, unsure, and confused. Everything seemed a blur. Arista knew the importance of Lasal's death more than Nathan, but he felt that something else was terribly wrong.

Back in his quarters, a message awaited him on the haloid. Valor Duma's form materialized and explained the situation—how Lasal had been killed, and how his death would affect their duties. Duma was now in charge of the ship. Arista had been reassigned, and Nathan was confined to his room for unexplained "security reasons." The message ended, and the figure of Duma dissolved.

Nathan was pissed. Security reasons? What did that mean? He'd spent all this time training so he could find Susan, and now he couldn't leave his quarters?

He wandered around the small room for most of the day, driving himself crazy with questions. With each that popped up, he would lose focus on the previous one. He had to reheat his lunch three times because he kept forgetting he'd made it.

Nathan was starting to realize his role in all this. There had never really seemed to be a war, and he had never really seemed to be a soldier. With Arista around, it hadn't sunk in. But now, with the Lord Admiral's death and plenty of time to think, he realized, maybe a little too late, just what he'd gotten himself into.

He was being trained to kill, to extinguish life. *The enemy deserves everything they get*, Duma had often reminded him. If the High Command was enslaving entire worlds, abducting people, then maybe he was right.

The mysterious message was still his secret. The words rolled over and over in his head, echoing through his daily routines. *Their lies lead to the truth. Seek the Vox.* What did it mean? The second part seemed to suggest that the Vox *had* taken him and Susan from Earth.

He had to concentrate, to find his center. There was so much going on, and he couldn't process any of it—Susan, Arista, Duma, saboteurs, his new orders.

Closing his eyes, Nathan felt the imaginary waterfall form inside him, starting in his mind. As he drew a breath in, the universe filled the top level, then flowed down into his chest, finally pooling in his stomach. Exhaling, he expelled the troubled feelings and chaos. He did this over and over, only allowing himself to think about the waterfall, and with every breath, his mind became clearer.

When his eyes opened, he was at peace with his situation and had a new clarity. He accepted his reality. The changes that swirled around him were happening, and most of it he could not control. Lord Admiral Lasal was dead. Nathan was restricted to his quarters, and he would not be training with Arista.

Along with that, there was one more important decision.

There were dark forces out there that had taken his sister. He would confront them. He would kill them.

He would destroy them.

CHAPTER 24

Wendalin Rami meticulously watched Hamil's condition, checking in on him every fifteen minutes. With the Tithe explosion fresh in her memory, it took a conscious effort to wipe the vision of Lord Admiral Lasal's corpse from her mind. There was no sign of that kind of damage here—no shrapnel or burns. Nothing but precise wounds to the windpipe and left knee, and internal bleeding in the liver. She took extreme care in examining the wounds. His condition was critical.

She'd given him a dose of G-T624, commonly called G-booster, which would accelerate his natural recovery rate. One dose was enough for a healthy individual to heal a broken bone within a day. She'd waited until now, hoping that his liver would recover, but it looked worse. The damage was irreversible, even with modern technology. It seemed as if, somehow, something had simply crushed it. He had an incredible bruise on his back in that location, but the damage to the liver was like nothing she had ever seen. Even a new liver wouldn't respond to the damaged nerves.

Now, there was no choice. She would have to remove the entire section and replace it. It wasn't that she worried about him surviving, but that she could do nothing to save his liver. She was helpless, defeated.

Behind her, the door slid open, and the booted footsteps of Master Chief Vinn approached. She turned to face him.

"He's okay, I trust?" he said, his voice emotionless.

"Well, actually, it was very touch and go in the beginning.

His vital signs were faint. I was extremely worried about him pulling through at all."

Drelmar gave her a small smile. "I know he's in excellent hands."

"From there, he has improved. Now, his liver—"

"Doctor, that's not why I came."

Wendalin stuttered to a stop. "I—ah…What?"

"Where were you after 2100 hours during the Tithe of Valera?"

She pulled off her gloves. "You mean when Lord Admiral Lasal was killed?"

Now she understood. He hadn't come to check up on Hamil. He was here for an interrogation, and she was in no mood for it.

Drelmar nodded. "Yes."

"Well, I was cramped in the air vents, crawling around for the way out. They are much more confusing than they appear to be." Sarcasm laced through her response.

Drelmar studied her with piercing eyes.

"I am a doctor. And unlike an assassin, I heal people, not kill them. Now, if you will excuse me, so I can heal this one." She turned back to the unconscious patient on her table.

"No, doctor," Drelmar said, "I will not excuse you. This is not a game. Lord Admiral Lasal is dead. Now, tell me your location at the time."

Wendalin turned slightly, resenting his tone. "I was in my bed and sleeping by that time," she said with an edge to her voice.

"And your companion? Can they support your alibi?"

She turned back to face him. "She and the others were out in the living room, drinking and talking. Having drank too much, I was feeling ill, so I went to bed."

"All this medicine, doctor, and you had nothing for your ailment?" Drelmar motioned around the room.

"I didn't feel like walking down here."

He considered this. "Is there an air vent in your room?"

"Yes, of course there is." She paused. "Are you—"

"Thank you, doctor. Now, you are excused." Drelmar turned away from the conversation and exited the room.

Moments passed before her irritation subsided. A figure slowly emerged from the operating room wearing a surgeon's jacket. Wendalin glanced up.

"Shamus!" She brought a hand to her heart in surprise. "I forgot you were here. Did you prep the room for the operation?"

"Yes. We can move him in now."

"Good. Help me with the door." She glided Hamil's table into the operating room. "This whole thing has my nerves rattled."

Shamus glanced at the door that the Master Chief had exited.

"You too, I see." She winked. "We'll get through it."

✸ ✸

Though confined to his room, Nathan wouldn't let others decide what he did or when he did it. The best way to do that was to learn how to travel and navigate space. He alternated his time between studying the fundamentals of astronavigation and piloting, doing grueling calisthenics, and hacking the lock on his door. Duma had locked it, but he saw that as a way to learn a new skill.

Two days had passed since everything changed, and solitary confinement was wearing on him. On top of all this, the dream was coming more frequently. It was the only one he could ever remember having—the battlefield, charging into combat, fighting, destroying.

Then the beep of the haloid woke him.

Floating to consciousness, he opened his eyes. He searched the corners of his mind and pieced the dream together. There seemed to be additional parts now that he couldn't fit into place.

A sensation he hadn't felt in a while crawled across his soul. Loneliness and futility threatened to smother him, but using the breathing, meditation, and mindfulness techniques, he was able to move past it. He was getting a better handle on things. Forcing himself to his feet, he dialed into the present, ignoring the past and future.

When he finished the last of his reading, Nathan looked to the four questions on his monitor. After keying in the answers, he stood up and stretched. There had been no mention of punishment for disobeying Duma's orders, and he'd had enough of his room, so he decided he would risk it. He needed a change of scenery, and space, even hyperspace rings, calmed him.

Hacking the door turned out to be easier than he thought. Still, it had taken him eight hours. But now that he could open it, he launched himself toward the solarium.

The path was mostly clear. Those he passed, he didn't know, but each was given a walking salute accordingly. Concern for getting caught was overpowered by an eagerness to escape his isolation. Even just the stroll was refreshing.

As the door to the solarium slid open, he halted. He'd already had a heightened sense of risk that elevated his heartbeat and adrenaline levels, but it all doubled when he saw Arista. Her back was to him as she looked out into space, but he was sure it was her. Her distinct stance, sky-blue skin, and silvery hair.

She was alone.

He quickly ducked behind the corner where the room controls were, and tapped in the sequence to put the room into projection mode. The lights dimmed, and metal shutters closed over the windows.

Arista spun immediately toward the control switch, dropping to a combat stance to assess her situation. Peeking out,

Nathan watched her reaction with the help of his HUD augmentation. Hers was no doubt activated as well.

"Stryder?"

Biting his lip to suppress any sounds of amusement, Nathan tapped in another command.

Without a response to her question, Arista rolled to her right and drew a knife, now in full battle mode.

In a blink, the room burst with the twilight of holographic stars. Their light sparkling in her eyes.

Taking a brave step out from the corner, Nathan strutted toward her with a smile he just couldn't help. Arista visibly relaxed upon seeing him.

"Well, you almost got yourself killed."

"Don't underestimate lures and misdirection," he said proudly.

Flipping her knife around, she stowed it back in the leg sheath and smiled.

"You *do* listen."

A few steps more, and her aroma filled him with comfort, washing away his stress.

"I didn't know you came here," he said suspiciously.

"I don't. Usually. You mentioned it, so I thought I'd try it again."

Not ready to let her off the hook, he made a show out of weighing her answer.

She chuckled nervously. "What?"

"Nothing." He grinned, bolstered by the idea that she'd come here for a chance to see him. "Which one of these is your star?"

Pulling her eyes from him, she took her time and surveyed the constellations.

Nathan stepped behind her, closing one eye, trying to see what she saw. Arista questioned him his proximity with a glance, then slid over to a large star and tapped it. The star turned blue with her touch.

"This one. Fumera—it's a giant blue. Which one is yours?"

Nathan marched over to a smaller star and dinged it yellow. "Right here. That's home. We just call it...the Sun. Super creative, I know. Around it is Earth. Terra firma."

"I have something for you," she said, holding up a tiny crystal.

A little too eagerly, he reached for it. "What is it?"

Arista snapped her hand back. "I'm not sure I should give it to you, after your prank."

"I said I was sorry." He smiled innocently, reaching for it again.

She knocked his hand aside. "No, you didn't."

"Okay—I'm sorry." Now more eager, he used the other hand, hoping to surprise her.

It didn't work. This time, she countered with her free hand, which Nathan instinctively blocked, more determined to take the crystal now than ever. The whole thing quickly escalated into a game of close-range hand techniques. They danced around each other, evading and deflecting.

"Someone's been practicing," she said mockingly.

Raising the stakes again, Nathan quickly stepped in and ignored the crystal, grabbing her body. With a twist of his torso, he hip-tossed them both to the floor. Arista's foot swung around as she flipped over his body, crashing into a flowering plant in the chaos.

Nathan pinned her. Leaning in from on top, lips just inches apart, he asked again. "What's on the crystal?"

"You think you can break me?" Arista grinned, playing along.

His eyes caught sight of a broken flower on the floor, prompting him to lean over and grab it. With careful intent, he drew the petals down her cheek and over her lips, then caressed her neck. She watched him, patiently. When he was done, she tenderly slid her hand to his throat.

"Not so fast, hotshot." She tightened her grip on his trachea. "I could take you out with a flick of my wrist."

The words hung in the air, empty, as Nathan gently leaned closer, daring her to do so, but she put up no resistance. Her warm hand slid to the back of his neck, and she pulled him in the rest of the way, kissing him. It was a tender kiss that lasted but a few moments, yet it filled him with electricity.

Arista took a deep breath through her nose, then bucked hard against Nathan's hips and locked his elbow. Before he realized it, he was upside down and crashing to the floor behind her.

She quickly rolled on top of him, smiling down as she studied his face.

"That was an interesting reaction," he huffed.

She placed the crystal on his chest in humble victory. "This should make you feel better."

Climbing off, she pulled him up. He nodded in respect of her skills, then stepped over to the projector. The crystal slid in and clicked into place.

The stars around them were replaced with a large hologram of Earth.

Nathan was thunderstruck. He wasn't sure what he'd been expecting, but it wasn't this. Mesmerized by the sight, reality vanished as feelings of home welled up inside him. It had been so long since he saw it. The well-known shapes were all long lost friends—the familiar continents, the blue oceans, the boot of Italy, the mitten of Michigan.

He was able to pull himself away from it long enough to look at Arista, who was glowing with happiness as she watched his every expression.

"I never thought I'd see it again."

"Now you can see it whenever you want."

Warmth rose in his body, and he drew her close. He kissed

her more intensely than before, their arms wrapping around each other. An irresistible passion intensified between them as Nathan pulled back and Arista persisted. She eased him gently backward into the hologram until his legs met a viewing bench, and they kissed as Earth rotated around them.

Arista pushed him down onto the bench and straddled him, keeping her lips on his. Nathan was filled with an awareness, a growing desire that had built to this moment—a desire to be close, intimate, and part of her world.

The holographic stars twinkled overhead, illuminating quick glimpses of their passion below.

✷ ✷

Valor Krell Duma was priming himself for more pain. Severe pain. Self-inflicted pain, necessary for him to survive. The injuries he'd received in the battle with HaReeka were serious. He'd been shot several times and had only kept his poise because of the Tanzi warsuit, which covered the damage as quickly as it was inflicted.

Isolated from the rest of the ship, his quarters were soundproof and secure. He needed them to be in order for him to implement this process.

Duma sat in a specialized, reinforced chair and pulled on the straps that would hold his legs and torso in place until they were taut.

With stable fingers, he loaded the Q particles into the injector. Once in his blood, the particles would rejuvenate the nanites that were already there, but the injection was not simply to heal his wounds, that was a side effect. The primary reason was to augment his body and control the disease that ravaged it.

Placing a bite guard between his teeth, Duma activated the injector. Particles lurched into his system. A mind-numbing pain coursed through him like a seething firestorm as the nanites were charged. The nanoscopic machines augmented his strength, healing, and reflexes while fighting the ravenous Echo virus that was hell bent on killing him.

As the nanites flared within his body, they illuminated his blood, bones, and muscles in emerald radiance. The glow penetrated his skin and filled the room around him as he bit down on the rubber safeguard.

Once every fourteen days, this process brought him back to the first time he'd experienced it. Lying in the gutter on Carcosa, he'd watched the blood drain out of him from several exit wounds. The crimson stream mixed with the dirty, gray water and greasy oil that leaked from his decimated vehicle.

The initial attack had come from the skybots. Blaze projectiles and cluster bombs had been the first wave, taking out most of his team. Then, the government soldiers had converged. The remnants of his team had destroyed a good chunk of the hit squad, but it was not enough. One by one, they fell, Krell Duma being the last.

Coherent enough to drag himself into the sewer drain before the shooting stopped, he'd rolled onto his back. It was all instinct and pointless in the big picture, as he would be dead from the virus in a few months anyway.

In the murky filth, he'd faded in and out of consciousness, vaguely aware of the government soldiers celebrating their victory and collecting the bodies of his battle mates. Soon, their clatter had morphed into twanging explosions and, eventually, silence.

Duma could not see, only hear, as they dragged him from the gutter.

"We've been watching. We can help," a low, raspy voice told him.

First, they'd injected the nanites, which flooded his veins in a cold rush. Then, the Q particles—a fiery pain like he'd never felt before, invading every nerve in every inch of his body. Bones, tissue, organs, they were all ablaze. Duma roared in agony as it shocked his system.

Now, as he was strapped to the chair in his quarters, he was already dizzy from the wounds, and the pain caused him to lose all sense of reality. Time twisted around him. Past and present merged; his childhood, his military training, killing the ones who betrayed him, handing Carcosa to the Meraki, Arista, Lasal's death, and HaReeka.

His psyche lingered on HaReeka and the time he'd spent protecting her, and embracing her, on Sontarey. It was the most intimate he'd been with anyone in his entire life.

Then, skipping to the moment he'd pulled his bloodstained dagger from her chest, the haze started to dissipate.

Slumped forward in the chair, he stared at the injector, which was now on the floor. His wounds were healing, itching as new cells grew.

HaReeka stuck in his mind like a poisoned thorn. A feeling of emptiness rushed into him, followed by crushing regret. She was dead now, by his hand, and he couldn't take it back.

CHAPTER 25

Returning to his room from the solarium, Nathan felt every cell in his body humming with exhilaration. In the middle of all this fog, this darkness and chaos, Arista was his beacon. She made him feel a part of something when he was so far out of his element.

That elation left his body instantly when he saw the message waiting for him.

A beep on the haloid echoed through his room as he entered. Nathan eyed it cautiously. Ever since the strange recording from the saboteur, he had been anxious about answering his vids.

The vise on his chest was tightening again. Previous unanswered questions ran through his mind—the saboteur's intentions, his motives for contacting Nathan, and his identity.

Nathan forced himself over to the haloid. Sucking in a lung-full of air, he exhaled all the noise that was swallowing him.

When the message came up, a hot coal dropped into his stomach. It was as he feared. His body tensed the moment he saw a dark silhouette, and a heaviness filled his soul. In his mind, he knew it was nothing good. He knew it was the saboteur.

A mechanically distorted voice echoed from the shadowed image.

"Now that Lasal is dead, you can understand. His passcode and other material are on a datagem hidden in the ceiling above your haloid. This will only be good until someone breaks the code. I've also arranged for the security lift to the Level 10 corridor to be unlocked between 2100 and 2200. It's time you knew the truth."

A quick glance at the clock revealed it was 21:25 now. That left him thirty-five minutes.

The door buzzed behind him, flinging Nathan's heart into his throat as adrenaline fired into his veins.

"Close message!" he blurted.

The door slid open as the computer responded, "Closing."

Chief Ajax Sculic stepped into the room, his penetrating eyes giving the area a once over. Nathan had expected to see Duma, but this wasn't much better. Their relationship was antagonistic at best. Even if it weren't, he didn't trust anyone with the message.

Ajax eyed him curiously. It was then that Nathan realized he was out of his chair and in a fighting stance. He relaxed his hands and straightened up, no longer taut and ready to strike out.

"Sorry. A symptom of my training." He forced a friendly grin, knowing that although it wasn't Duma, this was a precarious situation. Ajax's priority was no doubt finding the saboteurs.

"I thought I locked that," Nathan said jokingly.

Assuming Ajax had heard the final computer response, it was more than suspicious when he gave Nathan a slight smile and didn't pursue the matter.

"I'm sorry. I just popped in to see how you were doing. I haven't seen you since the Lord Admiral's demise."

"Yeah, I guess it has been a bit." Nathan tried to use a casual tone.

"So, what is it that the Valor has you doing?"

Nathan shrugged. "Nothing, really. I train most of the day, and then read a few files he assigns for me. Mostly catching me up on everything, like history and technology."

Ajax nodded. Apparently satisfied, he continued to look

around the room, wandering over to the haloid, below where the data crystal was hidden. Nathan did his best not to look up.

Wait—had Ajax just glanced at it?

"Did you enjoy the Tithe?" Ajax said. "I mean, besides the death and destruction. I imagine your planet wouldn't have anything like that."

"Besides the 'death and destruction,' it was magnificent," he said, ignoring the obvious dig at Earth. "I really enjoyed it. Although I wasn't there when the explosion happened."

"Really?" Ajax paused and cocked his head. "Where were you?"

"Oh... well I was... with Lieutenant Commander Conak."

"The Valor's protégé?" Ajax said. "That would make sense. What did he have you doing?"

"We were searching for the saboteurs." It wasn't exactly the truth, but it was close. Those had been their orders anyway.

"But you weren't there during the attack."

"We had to um..." Nathan struggled with how to phrase it.

Curiosity gave way to understanding as a smile crept onto Ajax's face.

"Ahh." He winked. "Have no fear. I'm not here to judge your casual pursuits. I'll leave you with your studies."

On his way to the door, Ajax stopped and turned back to Nathan.

"One more thing. I'd keep that last part from Valor Duma. He doesn't react well to insubordination."

Nathan purposefully locked the door the moment Ajax left. It had been an awkward interaction. However, there was little time to put too much thought into it. His window of opportunity was closing.

Climbing onto his desk, he took apart a ceiling square and reached inside. His fingers flailed around until he found the datagem.

When he placed it on the haloid panel, it lit up and displayed a virtual photograph, one that was all too familiar to him, one that he'd been looking for since his parents died. It was a picture of him clinging to Susan when they were kids at a barbeque with his mom.

Nathan rotated the virtual picture over to see the back. "Nathan – 8 yrs. Susan – 10 yrs." His father's handwriting.

His heart pounded heavily. His vision blurred, forcing him to wipe his eyes clear. He had thought his mind was cluttered and racing before with questions, but now it was simply spinning out of control.

As the shock wore off, he flipped to the next image.

He had to talk to Arista.

CHAPTER 26

After their encounter in the solarium, Arista returned to her post at the quantaframe center, where she tried different codebreaker programs to splice into Lasal's private systems. Duma seemed sure there was information there that could lead to the saboteurs: personnel files, criminal records, and whatever else it held. Focusing on the task was difficult. She tried to block out thoughts of Nathan and how she felt, but she was failing miserably.

Everything had changed for her. There was more to her life than missions and combat now. There was someone whom she cared for, and who cared for her. Her heart was tingling blissfully. There was a sense of being surrounded in a warm bubble.

She worked on the code-breaking program until 21:00, then returned to her quarters for dinner. She would head back to the quantaframe afterward.

As her food was being prepped, she mixed colors on her palette. She had time to work on the boot-shaped peninsula of Nathan's homeworld while she waited. Now that she had the image from the long range scan she'd given him, she could continue it.

She selected the finest brush and painted the land mass three times before she was happy with it. Her mind wandered to what this place looked like for real, and if she would ever see it. The next time she saw Nathan, she would ask him about it. No—she couldn't! Not until the painting was done, or it would ruin her surprise.

The door chime startled her mid-stroke, producing an

unintentional green island in the waters around the boot. Carefully, she set the brush down and answered the door.

There was barely time to smile as Nathan hurried into the room.

"Something's not right," he said frantically.

"Okay. What's wrong?"

He paced to her couch and back. "I don't know. I—Something's not right. With Valor Duma. With what we're told. Something just isn't right. When I first woke up, before I knew anything, Lasal told me they rescued me from the High Command. That they were far from Earth. Too far to go back."

"That's right." Arista grabbed her paint cloth and wiped her hands. "Why?"

"Then how did Lasal get this?" Nathan thrust the datagem at her.

"What is it? Where did you get this?"

"It doesn't matter where I got it. It has a picture of me." He swallowed. "And my family, from a long time ago, on it. Me and Susan, and my mom."

She shook her head. "Wait. Nathan. What? There must be some misunderstanding."

"Misunderstanding?" Nathan said, in an exasperated breath. "No."

Arista was in shock. Just a few moments ago, she had been happily painting. She'd never seen Nathan like this. She tried to understand, but he wasn't making much sense.

Nathan took a breath, but it didn't seem to help. "There's a picture of you on there, too. From a long time ago. We are being lied to. Both of us!"

"Lied to? About what?"

"I don't know—why we're here? The High Command, the Vox?" His voice fluctuated with uncertainty.

"Nathan, you're not making any sense. I've fought the High Command for years. I've seen what they can do. And the

Vox? That's just a story. You need to go to Valor Duma about this. There's probably a simple explanation."

"What? No way! He's probably in on this. He probably has my sister!"

"Nathan, that's ridiculous. Why would he do that? Just take it to him. I'm sure he can explain."

"Why are you defending him?"

"I'm not. I—"

"Arista," he interrupted. "Look at the pictures! I don't have time for this right now."

Speechless and confused, she watched as he charged out. He was obviously unnerved by this, which was understandable, since it had to do with his family. But it was like a puzzle that was missing pieces. Somehow, he believed these pictures meant… what? That Duma had killed his parents?

Placing the datagem on the haloid, Arista did as Nathan asked and examined the pictures. The first was what Nathan had said: a young boy that looked a lot like him, and his family. The second was…

A picture she'd never seen before. Of her—and her father.

CHAPTER 27

NATHAN COULDN'T WAIT around and let whatever was happening to him—or whatever was about to happen—to occur. The conversation with Arista hadn't gone as well as he'd thought it might. Why would she brush it off like that? If he'd had more time, perhaps he could have convinced her, but time was lacking right now. Hopefully, the picture of her would be enough.

Armed with Alfred, a five-inch blade, and a few pieces of equipment he'd taken from the training center, Nathan made his way to the Level 10 corridor.

The halls echoed with his hurried footsteps reverberating off the metal. He picked up his pace when he saw how empty they were. Was everyone else on lockdown too? Was this a trap designed to test his loyalty? Shaking the thoughts away, he trudged on through his fears. *Keep moving forward.*

Reaching the elevator, he selected level 10 and exhaled deeply. As the doors closed, it felt like a point of no return. He was blindly trusting this anonymous person, but he had to know what was going on, and he wasn't getting answers from anyone else.

Focusing on his breathing, Nathan grounded himself in the present. The elevator doors opened, and he stepped into the corridor. In front of him stood sealed blast doors.

As he stepped forward, the doors slid open, revealing what appeared to be an airlock. The space was dim, but illuminated by yellow triangles every five feet along the walls. Ahead on the right was something dark.

Inching closer, Nathan drew his knife.

The HUD amplified the light in his vision until he could see what it was. When he could, he choked on his breath. Crippled by a pure, unfettered wave of fear, he stared at exactly what he was looking for, something that he'd hoped never to see again.

The creature—the Vox—was inches from him, staring back, sending Nathan's heart into overdrive.

Adrenaline spiked, switching his world into black and white.

Recalling the knife in his hand, he lashed with as much force as he could summon. The Vox's skin gave way, the knife ripping through it and slamming into the wall. The impact raised a shrill sound as it scraped on metal. A cold liquid poured out of the cut and over Nathan's arm. He stumbled backward, away from the alien, which released a startled hiss as the knife pulled away.

A foul, white gas sprayed from the wound. The air between them grew heavy with vapor, making it difficult to see. The stench was there, but it was much more subdued than he'd remembered.

Nathan took a step back, his hand running over the icy wall behind him.

Creeping to his left, he attempted to get a better view of the creature's condition through the haze. His stomach had been tight since he entered the hallway, but now it was an unyielding knot. Wide-eyed, he took another step closer, watching the Vox for the slightest move as the hissing slowed to a stop, returning the room to silence. The floor glistened with the watery liquid.

The creature seemed totally inanimate. Hesitantly, Nathan reached out to feel its black, ghostly skin. It was like smooth, hard plastic. But it wasn't the Vox, it was an empty suit.

They'd captured one.

A quick glance ahead revealed another door, leading him

to conclude it was the creature's cell. He placed his ear on the door, listening for activity on the other side.

Then, from his pocket, he pulled an electric jammer, another tool that Arista had taught him to use.

He kneeled at the door and placed the instrument against the lock. After splicing two wires to the device, and he quickly checked the hallway again.

Nervous and impatient, Nathan tapped his foot against the floor as he waited for the lock to open. A light clicked on the device, which signaled the completion of its task.

He stood up, tightened his grip on the knife, and opened the door. A new hallway stretched before him, eerie and narrow. Around a hundred feet to its end. This one was much darker, but just as empty. A thick fog hung in the air, obscuring his vision and making it difficult to breathe. The smell was stronger now.

He prowled slowly through the mist, creeping forward to an intersection. As he approached, he crouched down and carefully scanned the fog in every direction. Satisfied no one was near the junction, he inched by it, stopping once he reached the next.

Then, the wicked stench he remembered all too well overwhelmed him, transporting him back to the Vox ship, where he had been utterly powerless and suspended over the floor. Tubes and wires snaked in and out of his body as one of the Vox jabbed a strange tool into his leg, cutting through his skin. His roars echoed from everywhere.

But that was before. Now, he forced himself to keep moving forward.

Gripping the knife tighter, Nathan knew he was no longer helpless, and all that fear melted into rage. These things had his sister. If the Meraki hadn't found out where they had taken her, he would.

The haze got thicker with every step forward. Past the third crossing, he thought about retreating before he pushed his luck too far, but just as the thought invaded his mind, he spotted something to the right—a glowing line of red lights.

Edging his way there, he came to a row of glass cases. Immediately he noticed the one that read "STRYDER."

A riptide of emotions whipped inside him as he inched closer. His hand reached for the case and smeared fog from it.

It was Susan.

She was wearing the same tunic he'd woken up in, and her skin was terrifyingly pale. Even her neck scars were void of color. Her eyes were closed, and her body lay still. Nathan pushed depressing thoughts from his mind as he searched for a way to assess her condition.

He slid the knife into his boot sheath and tapped a panel. It lit up with cryptic numbers and abbreviations he couldn't understand. Then he saw something he did.

A holographic display blinked to life on the glass. It was an image of Susan from long ago, on Earth. Next to it was a video showing her restrained on a table. Screams of pain lurched from her as a red glow illuminated her body. Then everything went silent, and the video ended. The video was stamped with the words:

> "Asante: Stryder. Cessation of life force during genetic conversion, 15:58. Project Failure."

A chasm of agony ripped open inside him when the panel confirmed his fears. The scene blurred as tears filled his eyes and his throat tightened. His fingers jabbed frantically at the lighted buttons, clawing at the joints in the case in a futile attempt to get her out.

Then, a beep sounded, and the case opened with a hiss. Nathan leaned in and wrapped his arms around his sister. She was cold. Too cold. He listened for her heart, for her breath, for anything. But there was nothing.

Overloaded with pain, tears rolled down his face as he clutched her dead body.

"Susan. No... No!"

Memories of their childhood flooded back—how she cared for him when he was sick. A game of hide and seek. Staying up late together to watch superhero movies.

Whispers rose from the fog, jolting him from his trance. It was a soft voice, too soft to make out.

Nathan gently put Susan down and closed the case. He would come back for her.

Two taps to his left ear, and the translator switched off instantly. A series of clicks whispered through the mist, just like they had during his abduction, destroying any doubt in his mind—it was the unmistakable sounds of the Vox.

Pain turned to anger and anger to rage. His hand clenched the knife in a white knuckled grip as he pushed through the mist, determined to find the source of the haunting voices that had tormented him for far too long.

As if trying to stop him, the mist clung to his face, pulling across it like a spider web. As it passed, it revealed the dark silhouette of the whispering Vox.

Nathan froze. Agonizing memories of his abduction rushed him again, but this time he successfully fought them back as he watched the creature, hoping to understand it better—to find its weaknesses.

Removed from its suit, it looked completely different. It was about five feet tall, black and round, with several webbed tentacles. It was reminiscent of an octopus, but with a thick spine that allowed it to stand erect on four of its tentacles. The head, however, was flat, wide, and ridged, evoking images of a dragon or a samurai demon helmet. Four horns extended backward for at least a foot, covered with spines.

Two diamond shaped displays hovered in the air before it, each showing a different image. It seemed to be communicating with them. The left screen held the image of another Vox that looked more like the one Nathan had encountered on Earth. The right screen showed a humanoid wearing a Meraki military uniform—Valor Krell Duma.

The truth tore through Nathan's world like an unstoppable force of nature. This Vox was not a prisoner—it was working with the Meraki.

With fury surging through his veins, numbing his fear and clouding his rationality, Nathan charged at the creature. Instinct took over as he readied himself for combat.

The Vox spun almost instantly, rising to a towering height. Its leg-like tentacles slammed to the floor with heavy, hoofed feet, and its body morphed from a rounded, fluid form into something more combat ready, covered with spikey protrusions.

A giant maw opened on its head and released a piercing shriek.

Nathan closed on it quickly as two tentacles veered at his head. He ducked and swiftly slashed out with the knife. The blade hit one and sliced easily into its rubbery skin. Liquid poured out of the wound, and the tentacle quickly retracted.

With a thrust of his leg, he launched himself off a metal pod, dodging another whipping limb. He soared into the air in what seemed like slow motion and stabbed at one of its eyes. But before he could make contact, something struck him—hard.

He flew backward into the wall. A concussive ripple ravaged his body, knocking the wind out of him. Not far away, the knife clinked onto the floor.

Sucking in air, Nathan scanned the area for the weapon and climbed to his feet. He was vaguely aware of pain in his back, but his adrenaline had numbed it.

The creature approached him cautiously, clicking furiously and extending its webbed tentacles in a display of dominance. He took note that the tentacles could morph—some were sharp, while others were blunt.

While it was grandstanding, Nathan explored the floor with his feet. The knife couldn't be that far away. The Vox was huge and ominous, but its skin was soft. He would have to use that to his advantage.

Then he spotted the knife, just a few feet away.

Feinting to his right and drawing nearly all the tentacles that way, Nathan dove to the left, grabbed the knife, and rolled in close. Swinging the blade in an uppercut motion, he aimed for the Vox's neck.

A crushing pressure wrapped around his ankle, and all his forward momentum came to a sudden stop. His arm arced upward, but it wasn't enough. The knife stopped just inches from its target. Another tentacle slithered around his knife hand and lifted him off the ground. The grip was like iron.

The creature's giant, sloping head examined him closely, as its other tendrils coiled around him.

Full of pain and rage, Nathan struggled to escape the claustrophobic and crushing embrace just as he had so futilely before, during his abduction. But this time was different. With his every muscle pulling, utilizing all the strength he had, a force—a power—intensified inside him, spreading prickling heat throughout his body.

Every eye the Vox had widened in shock as the energy coalesced and vibrated until it was radiating outside Nathan's body. His hands glowed blue, then his chest. It was building, magnifying, until it exploded in a wave of force and divine brilliance.

Flesh, horns, spikes, tentacles—everything the Vox was made of was obliterated as the blast sent an energy wave through the room, annihilating everything in its wake.

Nathan dropped to the floor, disoriented, the whining explosion still reverberating in his head. He wasn't sure what had happened, or how.

A siren filled his ears.

Stumbling to his feet, he staggered toward the room where

Susan's body was kept. But everything looked different now. The fog was gone, and the hallways were blocked with steel blast doors. There was no way to get to her.

Unsteady, his mind in a haze, he retreated to the airlock. He quickly reached the jammed outer door. Then he was out in the main hall. With a sense of deep dread, Nathan hurried to his room and searched his haloid for the origins of the saboteur's communications. He fired off a message to each, hoping the mystery person would get one in time. It was a risk he had to take now.

Just as he sent the last of the messages, the computer warned, "Door lock override."

Nathan quickly spun and came face to face with Valor Krell Duma.

"Lieutenant Nathan Stryder, you are under arrest for treason," Duma said, without a hint of emotion.

CHAPTER 28

As soon as Arista reviewed the datagem Nathan gave her, she returned to the quantaframe and ran another codebreaking program. It would give her cover in case anyone questioned her next move. After contemplating the consequences, she decided to search the late Lord Admiral's office to disprove Nathan's claims. And more importantly, to give him some peace when she did.

Apart from a few security guards, the corridors were practically empty. As she approached the first guard, she held a breath for five seconds to calm the fluttering in her stomach. What she was about to do would risk her career. Never before had she questioned authority like this. But what if Nathan was right? She trusted Duma with her life every time she went into battle. He'd given her a purpose when her life had been shattered. It didn't add up.

Arista strode by the guard, returning his salute without meeting his gaze. Her footsteps slowed as she neared the restricted area, her mind heavy with doubts. As much as she cared for Nathan, she knew he had to be mistaken. Still, she would do this for him—to clarify the misunderstanding, to help him move on.

When she reached the last turn before Lasal's office, she peered around the corner and spotted two guards blocking her path halfway down the hall.

Slowly, Arista pulled her head back and leaned against the wall. This was the point of no return. She couldn't kill her own guards. That was going too far. She needed a way to distract them.

Footfalls echoed from behind her. She was boxed in. She'd have to try another time. Pushing off the wall, she began walking toward her quarters, away from the restricted area.

Two guards appeared as she rounded the corner. The moment they saw her, they moved to block her path and saluted.

"Lieutenant Commander, Valor Duma has ordered us to return you to the quantaframe and so you could continue with your project."

Arista nodded. "I was already on my way, Lieutenant."

For a moment, she thought they might question her presence in this part of the ship. Even if they had, Nathan's secret was safe behind her lips. She had to give him time and help him realize his mistake.

Hoping Nathan had steadied himself and hadn't gone any farther with his accusations, she headed back to the quantaframe. She vowed to find another way to prove him wrong, but for now, it would have to wait.

Coding was something she enjoyed almost as much as painting. It relaxed her, taking her mind off everything else. Typically, it was something she liked to take her time on, but Duma had been pressing her from the beginning, and now she was on the verge of breaking Lasal's codes. It wouldn't be much longer before she did, and with that completed, Duma could identify the saboteur, and all this would be over. She hoped.

She toiled over the codes for a few hours in silence. The last program narrowed down the millions of possibilities to four different languages and numerical systems. She could now insert the results and it should pinpoint the correct ones, then run through every combination for the twenty-character password and the six-digit encryption.

The weight of Valor Duma's presence was heavy as he entered, settling on her shoulders.

"I have arrested Lieutenant Stryder for treason."

The words hit Arista like an avalanche. Her fingers stopped tapping on the keyboard, and the room became silent. Shock radiated through her body.

"He was communicating with the saboteur and in possession of sensitive material that links him to the assassination of the Lord Admiral. Would you like to go on record with any knowledge of this?"

Arista shook her head, still staring at her monitor. "No, sir."

She didn't dare turn to face him. She knew he would see through her the moment she did. To hide the swell of emotion that threatened to betray her, she began typing again. Then, everything Nathan had said the night before came rushing to the forefront of her mind. His words had been critical, almost incriminating. Could the saboteur have persuaded him to commit treason?

"I'm disappointed in how easily he manipulated you, lieutenant commander," Duma said in a disapproving growl.

※ ※

Every corner of the gray cell looked the same as Nathan paced it over and over. So much was spinning through his head. Susan was dead. The Vox had taken the two of them with the help of Duma and the Meraki. Did Arista know? Had she betrayed him? She'd looked so innocent the night before.

He was trying not to let his mind whirl about, but what else could he do? He figured he'd been here about three hours, but there was no way to be sure.

Despite checking over the room for the tenth time, Nathan still saw no chance of escape. It was simply a ten by ten-foot room with three walls, a floor, a ceiling, and a yellowish force field of some kind blocking the only way in or out. There was no choice but to wait.

The saboteur, ironically enough, was the only chance he had.

Valor Duma entered the detention center flanked by Master Chief Vinn and Chief Sculic.

"I told Lasal it was a mistake to thaw you," he said.

Nathan stepped up to face him. "You didn't have to kill her! Why kill her and not me?"

"That is unimportant now. You have been charged with treason and will be imprisoned until a day of execution."

"Execution? I wasn't—"

"Save it. I've heard everything from Lieutenant Commander Conak that I needed to hear. Her testimony is enough. I'm disappointed in you, Stryder. You had potential."

Nathan could barely control himself. He had little proof, but he knew Duma had something to do with Susan's death. He'd never willingly wished to kill anyone, but now, with every sense of who he was, he wanted to strangle the man before him. The man who'd forced him to kill, deceived him, lied to him, and now confirmed the worst-case scenario—that Arista had turned on him.

"You murdered the only family I had! Who will be executed for that?"

Fueled by pure emotion, he stepped forward, but the barrier sent a jolt through him.

Feeling completely alone, defeated, and exhausted, Nathan glared at Duma, who held his gaze, then turned on his heel and left. Drelmar and Ajax followed a step behind.

The lights in the outer chamber flicked off when the door closed behind them. The only source of light remaining was the yellow barrier that separated him from freedom.

He turned, facing the back of his cell. He was now in a world where everyone was his enemy. Frustrated with his inability to do anything, his mind raged like a violent thunderstorm. This was part of Duma's torture, no doubt.

As Nathan slammed his hand against the wall, he experienced an indescribable and familiar sensation. She was here.

"You? What do you want?" he said.

With no answer, he turned and saw the twinkle of rose-tinted eyes.

Arista looked him over. "I came to see how you were. Duma said that you were helping the saboteurs."

"And you believed him?"

"He showed me a message you sent to them on the haloid. Is that where you got those pictures? You went too far, Nathan. Why? I told you to wait. I was looking into it."

It infuriated him that after all the moments and memories they'd shared, she didn't trust him. And then, like a bursting dam, everything he'd bottled up from his encounter with Duma came out.

"Why? I told you why! They took my sister. Now she's dead! They came in—" He struggled with the words. "They came in and destroyed my life, my family! I've already waited too long."

"I don't know what they were telling you, but you can't trust them. That picture proves nothing. There's—"

"It proves whose side you're on," he said coldly. "You lied to me!"

"I never lied to you! You think a picture and a misunderstanding are going to make me give up everything I believe in? These saboteurs have betrayed everything I stand for. And you're working with them?"

"And what is it you stand for? You're an executioner. You kill who they tell you to kill."

He paused, hoping she could convince him otherwise, but she remained silent.

"Let's get one thing straight," Nathan said. "I'm the one that's been betrayed, lied to, and deceived! My only mistake was trusting you, thinking you cared for me."

Arista's expression turned to bewilderment. "How can you—"

"Duma told me why I'm here. He told me what you did."

"What *I* did? Nathan, I never said anything to him."

"Don't play innocent with me, Arista. It's all a game, anyway, isn't it? I was fooled. Congratulations." Nathan's eyes stung as words leaped from his mouth without warning or thought. "But now I see what you are! You're just a cold-hearted assassin, like Duma."

Arista's eyes glazed over, the light of the force field shimmering in them. She spoke in a whisper, tears welling in her eyes. "I can't believe you just said that."

Without another word, the woman he thought he'd been falling for turned and left.

Boiling with fury and frustration, mixed with feelings of regret, Nathan crushed it all within his fists and leaned against the back wall of his cell. He slapped a tear away from his eye before it could reach his cheek.

✷ ✷

Master Chief Drelmar Vinn rubbed the palm of his right hand as he entered the brig. His tendinitis was flaring again. With long strides, he approached Hamil's cell, and his onetime gambling mate looked up to meet his eyes. He came to a halt two steps from the cell and planted his feet. Crossing his arms, he looked Hamil over.

"You look better than the last time I saw you," he said lightheartedly.

"Just because you're out there and I'm in here doesn't make you right," Hamil said.

"The world isn't always black and white, Hamil. Most critical moments in history happen in the gray."

Hamil rolled his eyes. "Skip the history lesson. Why are you even here? Ajax took my statement."

"Did he now?" Drelmar knew Ajax had been angling for a promotion, but he was overstepping if he'd interrogated Hamil already. Was he running his own investigation? "What did he ask?"

"Aren't you two usually on the same page?" Hamil grinned as if he enjoyed knowing more than him.

"What, did he ask?" Drelmar repeated.

"Probably the same questions you're about to ask. Am I the saboteur? Was HaReeka? Are *you*?"

"Me?"

"Or maybe not. I don't remember. Maybe this is all a big game of Gira. Am I bluffing you? Was he bluffing me?"

"You love games, don't you? This is not a game, Hamil, people are dead! People we both cared about. And if we don't find these insurgents, a lot more could be. Now, if you aren't one of them and want to help people, then let's talk about what happened."

Hamil turned swiftly and took a few paces to his left, measuring his options. He tilted his head with a shrug.

"Very well," Drelmar continued. "Where were you when Lord Admiral Lasal was killed?"

"I was asleep."

"And how did you end up in the confrontation with Captain HaReeka and Valor Duma?"

"I was called to station after the assassination."

"Summoned by?"

"Summoned by my C.O., Commander Partan. He's dead now. I believe you killed him."

Drelmar considered that. "Let's back up. Had Captain HaReeka recruited you to keep tabs on other officers of the ship? Chief Sculic, perhaps?"

"Ajax? No."

"Did she request for you to keep tabs on anyone?"

"No, but if she did, I would have followed her order. She is my superior."

"Was," Drelmar said plainly. "She *was* your superior."

"Wait, do you think she was part of Lasal's assassination?"

He ignored the question. "Dr. Rami—when was your last contact with her? And remember, I can check with the Overseer systems."

Hamil threw up his hands. "I don't know. My yearly physical?"

"Have you been in contact with Lieutenant Commander Arista Conak or Lieutenant Nathan Stryder?"

"I barely know the Lieutenant Commander, and I don't know the other person."

Drelmar lifted his eyebrows and focused on Hamil's pupils. "And Ajax? Before your interaction with him today, when was the last time you contacted him? Either in person or through the haloid."

The pacing stopped, and Hamil faced him. "Why aren't you asking about Valor Duma? Wouldn't it make the most sense for him to kill Lasal? So that he could take over the ship, just like he has?"

"You're avoiding the question," Drelmar pointed out. "I'll do what I can to shield you if he or someone misled you. I know he's crafty."

"No. No one misled me. I didn't do anything! I was just following orders. Commander Partan ordered me to protect the captain. So that's what I did."

"It's unfortunate, if what you say is true. I want to believe you, but there is more to this story, isn't there? What else did Ajax come here to say to you?"

"Why would I trust you anymore than Ajax at this point?" Hamil's eyes flickered angrily. "You're all mutineers. I was following the chain of command. I was loyal! I was doing my duty. Just because you're out there doesn't make you right."

"Yes, I can see how you would think that. But as I said, sometimes things aren't so clear. You know that a valor is technically equivalent to a captain in rank? Traditionally, a captain would take over, but a valor has never asserted authority when a captain was available. So, it's all in how you look at it. But yes, to the layperson who hears about what happened, we would probably be considered mutineers. The question is, are you able to accept the ambiguity here? Are you able to see what we did as clarifying the merit of a valor's authority? And if not, accept the consequences?"

"I'll accept the consequences," Hamil said defiantly.

"That's noble of you." Drelmar looked him over with admiration. "But I'm afraid that doesn't leave you with many options."

※ ※

Ajax and Drelmar were ordered to escort the prisoner planetside. Since Duma wanted the whole thing kept quiet, there was no other choice. The fewer people who knew about Stryder, the better.

The pair marched side by side on their way to the brig. They would take the prisoner to a transport and fly him down to Kavka. The ship also carried fresh supplies and more troops to join the ones already holding the planet. It was a medium transport, by most standards. It could hold up to five hundred soldiers and two thousand kilotons of cargo.

Lights flicked on as the pair entered the outer room of the prisoner's cell. Stryder watched them as they approached.

"It's all lies, isn't it? You knew she was dead. Why string me along?"

"Let's keep this easy and smooth, Lieutenant." Vinn ignored the question and tossed a metal device through the yellow barrier. "Slip your hands in."

Stryder glanced down at the device, then back at them.

Reluctantly, he picked it up and slid his hands in the two holes on one end. The device hissed and clamped around his forearms. Only then did the barrier come down and Ajax move in. Stepping behind the prisoner, he placed a mazer on the back of his neck.

"If you do anything that we don't want you to, this will send a paralyzing bolt of energy through you," Ajax threatened. "Now move."

※ ※

Arista played the scene repeatedly in her head. What the hell just happened? She had just gone down there to check on him, to be there for him. How did it turn into all that?

After the confrontation with Nathan, she'd returned to her quarters and begun the practiced routine of suiting up into her battle gear. The *Kai'den* had dropped out of hyperspace and was entering orbit around the planet Kavka. Her orders were to escort the transport down to the planet, to make sure that the transfer and resupply went as planned.

Kavka was in a violent struggle for control. A minority group had revolted, taking up arms against their government in civil war. The government had called for Meraki support to control the rebels. As with most uprisings, the rebels' use of guerrilla tactics was hard to pin down, so there was no telling what could happen. Whatever happened, though, she would be prepared for it.

Pushing her personal drama aside, she cleared her head and focused on her mission.

※ ※

Valor Duma sat quietly at the desk that had once belonged to the late Lord Admiral, waiting for the codebreaking program to finish. The desk still contained all of Lasal's items, personal and professional. Duma hadn't bothered to clean it out, nor was he planning to. He had little time and trusted no one else with the information it contained.

He had branded former Lieutenant Stryder a traitor. For this, he would be executed, but according to military protocol, he was to be judged first. Right now, Duma had too many other things to worry about. And Stryder was a special case. If anything happened to him, the Vox would need a good justification, and Duma had too much to explain to them already.

The virtual screen he watched displayed a black box centered in the middle around the words "Secured Personnel Files." Arista had informed him to wait until the program finished. Once it did, it would lead him into the files.

Where she was, he didn't need to guess. He would bet his skin she'd gone to visit Stryder. She'd been visibly shocked when he'd informed her of Stryder's involvement with the saboteur, even after Stryder himself had told her he had communicated with them. That was Arista's only weak point—her emotions. Duma had trained her to ignore most of them, especially when she was in combat, but this one was a lot stronger than the rest. He made a mental note of it. He would have to train her to ignore love.

Within the next fifteen minutes, light from the vidscreen bounced off Duma's eyes as the screen jumped past the security access page. It ran through a few others and halted on the secured personnel files. He scanned the files, searching for a clue to the saboteur's identity.

And before long, he found it. As he saw the words on his screen, HaReeka's voice haunted him. *"No one from the Cadre can be trusted."*

CHAPTER 29

Nathan was on the transport now, sitting in his new cell, which looked identical to the last one. His hands remained restrained, and the device was still on his neck. He had no way of knowing, but he guessed this wouldn't be a long trip. As he wet his parched lips, he realized the last time he'd eaten or drunk anything was yesterday morning.

A rumbling vibrated through the hull as the transport took off.

After a few minutes, the door slid open, and the outer light flicked on. It was Drelmar and Ajax again. They marched in, silent and calm, looking Nathan over carefully.

"By the authority of the Meraki Dominya, you are to be executed at the garrison on Kavka." Drelmar said. "Your crime is treason—willfully abetting the saboteur onboard the flagship *Kai'den*. Lieutenant Nathan Stryder, do you understand these charges?"

Nathan peered into Drelmar Vinn's dark eyes and nodded.

"Good." An awkward silence spread through the room before he spoke again. "I've always been impressed with you, Stryder, since the day we met. I won't lie to you. I will be disappointed the day you die. The Meraki will let you admit your crimes before your execution, so that you may be forgiven in the afterlife."

Ajax stepped behind Drelmar and drew the sidearm from his holster.

"Hands where I can see them, Master Chief," he said, moving to a safe distance.

Drelmar glanced behind him in surprise and lifted his hands. "What is this, Ajax?"

Ajax raised the weapon at Drelmar. "You've been recruiting us all to do your work."

Nathan watched in surreal disbelief, struggling to understand the situation.

Drelmar turned slowly to face the weapon. "Ajax, what is going on?"

The pistol moved to Drelmar's head. "It's too late to play dumb. I figured it out. You took me under your wing, but not to help me—to use me. You thought I was some naïve recruit. You thought you were smarter than me. But I've got you."

Behind them, the door slid open, and a guard stepped in.

Ajax glanced back, but quickly returned his focus. "Arrest him for treason and the assassination of Lord Admiral Lasal."

"Sorry, Chief," the guard said, then pulled his weapon and leveled it at Ajax.

Ajax took a second look at the guard, stunned. "Hamil?"

Drelmar seized on the diversion, stepped forward, and cracked Ajax in the head.

※ ※

Duma slammed his fist down onto Lasal's desk, making the objects on it jump.

"Damn it, it's Vinn!" He activated the haloid. "Security! Secure Prisoner Stryder and arrest Master Chief Drelmar Vinn!"

The response came almost immediately. "Vinn escorted the prisoner to the transport, sir."

Heat rose through Duma's body. He waved his hand violently to the right, clearing the haloid, and then brought up the only person capable enough to deal with the situation.

"Conak! Secure the transport and search it for Master Chief Vinn! He'll be with Stryder."

✷ ✷

Drelmar went through the rest of the plan in his head as he removed the restraints and shock device from Stryder before they left the cell. So far, it was going his way. Hamil kept his word, and Ajax didn't pull the trigger when he could have.

"Hold still," he said as he waved the quantum gauge across Stryder's neck. "I'm deactivating the HUD system so they can't track you."

As soon as Stryder was free, he slammed Drelmar against the bulkhead. "You? You lied to me. About my sister! How long has she been dead?"

Drelmar understood the anger and confusion. In another situation, he would have explained it, but not now. Meeting Stryder's gaze, he tried to remain calm despite the urgency of their situation.

"There's no time, Stryder. You have to trust me."

"We've got to go, Master Chief," Hamil said.

Stryder reluctantly nodded, releasing him.

The trio hurried down a slim corridor toward the access entrance by the starboard aft thruster. They were passing the thruster's engine when a siren went off, synchronizing with emergency lights. The corridor was flooded with an eerie, urgent red glow.

"Hurry! We're running out of time!" Drelmar yelled over the siren. He'd had weeks to plan this escape, but this was the first time he'd had to run down this corridor in the dizzying vertigo of emergency lights and sirens.

Drelmar jerked his head to the side, suddenly aware of a low-hanging conduit. This definitely wasn't a place to lose his concentration. He hoped Nathan and Hamil would be nimble enough to keep up with him, having never been down here before. But right now, he didn't have time to turn and check as they rushed to their goal. From behind, he could hear shouts and commotion.

The noose was tightening.

Drelmar slowed to let Stryder and Hamil pass, then arced his rifle behind him, squeezing the trigger. As lasers slammed into the wall in the distance, the glitter of return fire helped him gauge their pursuer's location. So far, they weren't close enough to get an accurate shot.

"They're firing blindly." Drelmar picked up his pace again. "Hurry—straight ahead!"

Stryder took up the lead. The end of the corridor was now in sight. A dim green light marked the access hatch.

Drelmar hopped over a raised vent, closing the final distance. Once he reached the others, he turned around, lifted the rifle to his shoulder again, and took aim at an exhaust pipe back down the passage. The pipe burst with his first shot, spewing a poisonous gray cloud and obstructing the pursuing army that was surely after them.

He handed Hamil his rifle. "Watch the corridor."

Free from the weapon, he reached behind a large metal protrusion from the engine, pulled out a bulky bag, and untied it. From the bag, he retrieved three pentagonal jetpack harnesses and a datagem.

Grabbing Stryder, Drelmar spun him around and strapped a harness to his back. Down the narrow walkway, the hiss from the pipe stopped, and voices could be heard again in the lull of the pulsating siren.

Hamil began firing in measured bursts. "They're closing!"

Drelmar handed Stryder the datagem and activated the harness on his back, quickly stepping away. It lurched open and expanded into a jet powered glider.

"Listen to me, Stryder—everything they told you is reversed. The Meraki Dominya is working with the Vox. They have conquered half the galaxy."

"And killed my sister!"

"I'm sorry. I couldn't help her. I had to get you here."

"But why?" Nathan said, his eyes pleading for answers.

Drelmar glanced back to check on Hamil, who was still firing. Then he looked dead into Stryder's eyes.

"There's a prophecy. The Vox take it for truth. First, they thought it was her, but now they think *you're* the Harbinger. Your abduction was no coincidence. They've been looking for you for a *very* long time."

"What Harbinger?"

"*The* Harbinger. The messenger. The precursor. Some say of change, others of destruction or rebirth. It doesn't matter. They think you're it!"

With that, Drelmar blew a hatch to the exterior of the ship, and a torrent of wind whipped through the opening.

He pointed to the datagem and shouted over the wind. "If you want revenge, if you want to stop them from doing this to others, then here is your chance. That gem has information on Deathwind. Make sure the High Command gets it."

Stryder grabbed the edge of the hatch, fighting the force of the wind that was sucking him out. Laser blasts lit the hallway behind them.

"Go!" Drelmar said. "It's pre-programmed to fly for you." Reaching into his pocket, he pulled out a G-booster and slapped it onto Stryder's wrist.

"What about you?"

"I'm right behind you, soldier! Go! Find Prymack!" He shoved Nathan out of the hatch.

He turned back to Hamil just as two shots hit his friend in the chest, and he slumped to the deck.

"Hamil!" Drelmar shouted, the wind roaring in his ears. "Hamil!"

But there was no movement, and Meraki soldiers overtook his position.

Drelmar dropped to his back, landing on one of the remaining gliders. It activated with the contact, springing into position. With practiced speed, he strapped it around his chest. Locking the last latch into place, he sat up, ready to move to the hatch.

He heard nothing over the wind that whipped by, but looking up, he saw a seething Ajax in front of him, his rifle aimed and ready.

Their eyes locked. Ajax gazed in disbelief.

"It wasn't supposed to end like this," Drelmar said over the howling wind.

"I trusted you!"

"I know." Drelmar's eyes flicked to the hallway, then back to Ajax. More people were coming.

"How could you betray the Dominya like this?"

"I'm sorry, Ajax. I betrayed you. There was no choice. I tried to convince you!"

Ajax brought the rifle tight to his shoulder. "There's nothing you can say now."

"Then once again, my friend, it's your move." Drelmar quieted his mind and searched for a decision in his friend's eyes. He found it.

Rolling to his right, he lurched desperately for the open hatch. As he did, Ajax pulled the trigger.

Moving with Drelmar, the glider revealed a warning on the wall behind it: "Danger: Extremely Explosive." Ajax's eyes grew wide as he spotted it an instant before his plasma pulse pierced it.

A blinding light flashed, and then a terrifying explosion.

※ ※

Arista charged down the main hallway, too far from the traitors' position to get there in time. In her hand she gripped a Warden sniper rifle.

A rumble cascaded around her, vibrating the ship. Sirens and emergency lights came to life, and everything changed. What had once been an organized and calm corridor was now chaotic and full of dread. It felt like her entire world was suddenly upside down.

Crashing through an outer hatch, she climbed down to a catwalk on the outside hull of the transport. There, she quickly set up her rifle and settled into a firing position.

CHAPTER 30

Nathan was approximately one hundred feet from the hatch when the explosion tore through the engine. The hammering blast and accompanying billow of purple-orange flames sent his glider spinning out of control.

Shrapnel struck the jet, causing it to leak fuel, which ignited. Unable to catch the plummeting glider, the flame chased after it, leaving a burning trail in its wake as he tumbled from the sky in a spiral of fire and smoke.

The engine sputtered, slowing his descent, but did nothing to stabilize it. Spinning crazily, Nathan saw this world for the first time in a whirlwind of light. Orange-white-yellow-black, the colors swirled around him in a wild cyclone of distortion.

As he fought to free himself from the harness, the trailing flame was gaining, threatening to ignite the glider. He was trapped in what was now a time bomb.

He managed to release the first latch, only to be thrown off balance as the glider lurched up, spinning him backward. The jolt pinned his finger under the remaining strap, forcing him to unlatch it with one hand. He fumbled with the mechanism, trying again and again but failing to open it, the flame inching closer with each passing moment.

Twenty feet from the planet, the harness released, sending the erratic jetpack shooting off untethered. Nathan smashed into the ground with a bone-crushing thump.

The pain was incredible, coming from everywhere, but he had to keep moving.

Willing himself to stay conscious, he lifted his broken body from the crater he'd made in the dirt. His head was pulsating, and his body ached as he fought to keep it from shutting down.

A bombed-out city surrounded him, giving him plenty of places to hide. Dragging his left leg, he limped toward the cover of the nearest rubble.

✷ ✷

Two perpendicular lines intersecting in the middle of Nathan's back marked the shot's trajectory, tracking him as he ran. The opportunity was perfect, the scope crystal clear—until it blurred.

On the catwalk, Arista pulled the scope from her right eye and smeared away a tear. After everything they'd had together, it came to this.

Pressing her eye back to the scope, she placed her finger on the trigger and watched as Nathan hobbled for cover.

The last intimate moment she'd spent with him and how it felt popped into her head—his touch, his kiss. She blinked away another swell of tears. So much had changed since then. How had it turned into this?

The headset interrupted her musings as it sparked to life.

"Status, Lieutenant Commander," Duma said.

"Explosion in aft engine. Target in my sights."

"Kill him!"

She squeezed the trigger. A streak of blue light sailed from her rifle on the catwalk of the transport and raced to the planet's surface. It struck Nathan in the back, causing him to stumble and collapse in the dirt.

Arista stood up. "Target is—"

A massive explosion rocked the transport, tossing her to the right and sending her cartwheeling over the railing. The blast roared in her ears and vibrated her teeth.

Through instinct alone, she flung her hand out to claw for a lifeline. Her fingertips glanced off the metal catwalk, but there wasn't enough to hold on to. Nanoseconds before she plummeted to her death, the Tanzi shot out from under her armor and attached to the walkway. The momentum swung her underneath, and she crashed into the hull with a shockingly brutal bounce.

CHAPTER 31

Kavka, Brevetta City

An MZ9 guided missile, fired from a portable Spark launcher, slammed into the transport, causing a collapse of the port side engine, severe hull damage, and one devil of a diversion.

Prymack drew his eyes back from the scope, lowering the launcher.

"Phase two, you're on," he spoke into a headset, then to the rest of his team. "Alright, let's see if he's still alive."

Here, on the rooftop of a bombed-out building, were four of his rebellion—Nur, his pledged mate, and three of his best trained soldiers. They wore battle-scarred armor, just as he did. It wasn't pretty, but it did its job.

Silently, they descended from the roof in a rehearsed formation, something Prymack had conditioned into their reflexes. The thunder of another rocket pounding the transport rumbled through the building, shaking loose dust and debris as they exited from the ground floor.

Burning in the night sky, the transport illuminated everything as it arced toward the ground. The Spark launcher was now on Prymack's back, replaced by a rifle in his right hand.

Forty meters from their target, they met opposition. Laser fire danced around them from the left.

Immediately, Prymack dove to a prone position and returned fire. "Cyn, left flank! Pollo, suppressing fire!" he yelled over the roaring concussion of their projectile weapons.

The Meraki's laser weapons were lighter, easier to reload, and quieter, but his team didn't have the resources to maintain them. Gunpowder and bullets could be easily made.

"Their air support will be here soon," Prymack said. "Nur, cover me!"

He rolled to his right and pulled a halo grenade—the last one they'd stolen—from his vest. He snaked through the mud, closing on the Meraki position. After covering half the distance, he lofted the halo in their direction and buried his head.

The spherical device arced through the air and dropped to the ground by the invaders. A pulse of energy released from the bomb in a circular pattern, expanding to eight meters. When it reached the maximum distance, the energy ring exploded, ripping up the ground. Then it shrank two meters and exploded again. The ring continued the deadly intervals, exploding four times, until it collapsed on the central device.

Wet dirt rained down around him until it was over. Prymack peered up and saw nothing but death and muck where the bomb had hit. There was a brief, peaceful silence before the hum of Meraki thrusters filled his ears.

"Let's move. They're on their way."

Prymack leaped up and continued on. The others fell into formation behind him. They raced toward the unconscious body, now thirty meters away. Jet fighters closed rapidly, whirring like a swarm of murderous hornets. Over the headset was a report of the transport retreating.

From the darkness to his right, a familiar but bloodied soldier appeared.

"Diis, where's team two?"

"I'm the only one left."

A Meraki fighter jet streaked overhead, strafing the area and ripping the ground apart.

Two more fighters were closing on them in the distance.

The launcher had only one missile left, which meant their only option was to run, and there was no time to waste.

"Diis, you're with us," Prymack said as he took off toward Stryder's body.

As they closed in on their target, the lead fighter swung around and positioned itself for another pass.

"Stryder!" Prymack called into the darkness.

Cyndron pointed out a dark lump on the ground. "Over there!"

Closing on them, the fighter began to fire. Flickers of lasers streamed toward them, tearing up the ground. Prymack knew it was going to be close.

In a dead sprint, he silently prayed to Kyr that today would not be their day to die.

Then, to his right, Nur abruptly stopped. She turned to face the oncoming jet. Raising her rifle, she unloaded on the fighter with a fierce war cry. The rifle rocked her slight frame. But she held firm, legs apart, with the weapon pressed tight to her shoulder. Her body rumbled as the stream of bullets raced from the barrel.

Prymack turned at the sound of gunfire. A familiar ache of dread filled his chest.

"Nur! No!"

The fighter zoomed forward, seeming to focus on her now. Around her, the ground exploded from the lethal ordnance, making her war cry grow louder. Prymack could only watch the showdown for endless seconds until, finally, the fighter streaked past them.

Nur stood motionless for a beat, took a deep breath, then turned and caught up to the others, dodging his distressed gaze.

He couldn't believe what he'd just witnessed, but he shoved it to the back of his mind as he focused on his objective.

Barely breaking stride, he grabbed an arm of the unconscious body and pulled it along. Niikapollo, the largest member of the team, grabbed the other, helping with the extra weight.

They had been lucky so far, but that ended as Corii, the last member of the team, took a shot to the chest. His scream was drowned out by the continuous fire from the air.

They were still in the open—and vulnerable. What remained of a commercial district lay another hundred meters ahead. They would never make it there before the fighters picked them off. Fortunately, that was not where they were headed.

Prymack heard the whine of the jets pulling around to come at them again as he entered a bombed-out garage. Under the cover of the building, he set Stryder on the broken ground and flipped a drain cover to the side. Pollo crawled in and caught Stryder as Prymack stuffed him down.

"Nur, in!" Prymack reached out to help her.

"Cyn, get in," Nur said, ignoring Prymack's order.

Cyndron didn't argue and climbed down.

Only then did Nur hand Corii's body down, then followed. Prymack was the last to enter the dark tunnels, replacing the cover behind him.

✶ ✶

Back onboard the *Kai'den*, Duma was beyond furious. Arista stood at attention alongside the pilot of the transport, preparing for the verbal reprimand.

"Who gave you authority to retreat?" Duma barked. "We needed the bombers onboard to blow the sewers!"

"I—The transport was heavily damaged, sir," the pilot said.

Duma inhaled sharply, clenched his jaw, and tilted his head. "Heavily damaged? The fighters were already deployed! We have air superiority, in case you forgot! They were all on the run, and you decide to retreat?"

Duma stood looming between the pair. He veered to Arista. "And the prisoners?"

"Nathan was taken by the rebels, sir. And Vinn wasn't seen after the explosion." She paused. "Neither was Chief Sculic. They are both presumed dead."

Behind her, the door slid open.

Duma leaned into her. "'Nathan?' You refer to the traitor by his first name, still? The person you put your trust in? He, who betrayed us? Who used you? He was your ally!"

He paused, knowing that they had been more than that. "But now, he is your enemy, and you will kill him. It's that simple!"

Arista flinched, but held her emotions in check. A badly wounded soldier limped up and filled in the space next to her.

Duma stepped in front of the soldier. "Chief Sculic, who ordered the prisoner to be transferred to Kavka?"

Arista's eyes flicked back to the soldier next to her for a second look. Covered in bandages and burns, he wore a makeshift patch over his left eye. Buried under the trauma, she barely recognized the broken man, but it was him. It was Ajax. She swallowed a gasp.

"You gave the order, sir," Ajax said.

"That wasn't me, you fool—that was Vinn! Stryder was to be brought to Sienna!"

A look of shame crossed Ajax's face before it turned to resolve. "Stryder is still alive, sir."

Duma considered that before turning back to Arista. She had dreaded this. She knew eventually Duma would learn she hadn't killed him.

"You said you had him in your sights. Why isn't he dead?"

"I—" she stumbled. Several responses zigzagged through her head. "He must have had body armor," was the one she hastily chose.

"Tell me you can find him, Sculic," Duma said, his glare still focused on Arista.

"The rebels have retreated underground. The prisoner, Lieutenant Stryder..." Ajax glanced at Arista. "...was taken to a safe house."

"You have the location?"

"Yes, I do, sir."

Duma glanced Ajax over. "Then you are in charge. I will return the *Kai'den* to Sienna. You both will stay on the planet until you find and eliminate Nathan Stryder. When I return, you'd better have his body. He is too dangerous to live."

He then turned back to the pilot. "The supplies will be sent again. And they will get there this time."

Arista knew how long it took to get to Sienna. She calculated the round trip and possible delays. That gave them a few phases to complete their mission. By that time, if all went well, Nathan Stryder would be dead.

※ ※

Nathan woke up in the dark with a splitting headache. He was lying on a cot, a thin blanket covering him. The small amount of light there was, came from a crack under a door to his right. The air was musty, carrying a slight hint of stale smoke.

Stepping down, he could instantly tell he was no longer on the *Kai'den* or the shuttle. The floor gave under his weight and creaked, like his room on Earth used to. He had on only what they had given him to wear in his cell. But this wasn't a cell. He couldn't be awaiting an execution in here. So where was he?

The last thing he remembered was spinning, trying to get the jetpack unstrapped. Recalling the swirling lights made his head hurt even worse. His legs and chest ached too.

Something bulky in his pocket drew his attention. From it, he retrieved the datagem Drelmar had given him. He rolled it between his fingers and returned it to his pocket.

Seemingly from nowhere, raspy whispers filled his ears.

For a moment, he thought they might be ghosts of the men he'd killed, but the murmuring led him to the door. The floor groaned with every step closer, almost as if it were alive and warning someone.

Reaching out into the darkness, his fingers touched the wooden door. With his right hand, Nathan reached up to see if he still had the translator. He did. Straining to hear through the door, he could make out four distinct voices, but nothing of what they said.

A gruff voice startled him from behind. "Hear anything?"

Instinctively, he spun, crouching into a fighting stance, but it was too dark. Someone had the drop on him. If only the HUD hadn't been deactivated, he'd be able to see them.

A lamp snapped on, breaking the veil of darkness, and revealed a being kneeling calmly on the floor. Like everyone Nathan had seen, except the Vox, it was also humanoid. From its appearance, he could tell it was built for survival—muscular and lean, with sharp eyes. Its face was angular and covered with smooth skin, or possibly scales. It seemed to be male.

In the dim light, his skin looked dark orange, accented with a jagged golden pattern. What Nathan had initially thought was some type of helmet he now realized was a bony head wrap that curved and intertwined over the top of his skull.

"So, you're the famed Nathan Stryder. Drelmar spoke much of you."

For the first time, Nathan noticed a shotgun-like weapon on the man's lap.

"We risked our lives to save you. I hope you're worth it."

Rising from the floor, the man reached about Nathan's height. With a practiced flip, the shotgun swung to rest on his shoulder as he tromped past Nathan and opened the door.

In the hallway, silence struck as the five people who must have been making the whispers spotted Nathan. They had similar appearances, each with varied shades and patterns on their skin and bone crowns ranging in thickness and shape. They looked worse for wear, with battered armor, dirty faces, and tired eyes. A few had noticeable scars.

"Cyn, where's Nur?" the man with the shotgun asked.

A wry smile formed on the one called Cyn. "Don't know, boss. Haven't seen her."

Just then, a female of their race appeared in the stairway. Petite, with an inclined nose and thin lips, she reminded Nathan of a girl he'd dated in high school, but aged by time and stress. Her skin was lighter, with no patterns. Instead of a headpiece, she had medium length strawberry blonde hair. At first glance, she seemed harmless, but the anger and purpose she carried with each step forced him to reconsider as she marched into an adjacent room.

"In there, boss," Cyn said with a smirk.

The man with the shotgun followed Nur into the room. Behind them, the door closed.

Cyn stepped over to Nathan and raised a fist to eye level as if he were going to stab him with an invisible knife.

"Stryder, we receive you as a friend in arms. Welcome to clan Yiiga."

With Cyn's fist still raised toward him, Nathan mirrored the gesture. Cyn knocked the bottom of his fist against Nathan's, then pulled it back.

"Name's Cyndron, but call me Cyn." He gestured clockwise around the room. "The big one, that's Niikapollo. We call him Pollo. Masemada—we call him Mase. That's Xantani, we call him Xan. Hopefully, you sense the pattern here."

"And that..." He turned to the fifth man, but he was gone. "Where'd Sundiis go?"

Xantani shrugged.

"Well, that was Sundiis."

"Let me guess. You call him Sun?" Nathan asked preemptively.

"No. Diis." Cyndron chuckled.

The voices behind the door grew louder, eventually leading to barks of anger.

He jerked a finger to the door. "Oh! And that's our valiant leader, Prymack. And his…" He struggled for words. "…soul mate, Nur."

The shouting grew so loud that the closed door seemed pointless.

"They're a bit passionate, if you can't tell." Cyn turned to leave. "Let's let them to plan the next maneuver. I'll show you around."

Before Nathan could take a step, Mase moved in front of him. "Corii was a friend. He died saving you. Why are you so special?"

Cyn laid a hand on his chest. "Mase, it wasn't his fault. And the mission was to stop the transport. Corii died for Kavka."

"I'm sorry," Nathan said. "I didn't—"

"Leave it, Stryder. Let's go." Cyn made his way to the stairs.

As they left, Nathan overheard part of the muffled conversation behind the door.

"Foolish, Nur—just foolish! You couldn't do any damage to that fighter!"

"No, but it gave you time to reach him!"

"Sometimes, I think you disobey my orders just to spite me."

Cyn led Nathan down a flight of crumbling stairs, leaving the argument behind.

"The Meraki invaded five cycles back," he said, flicking his thumb. "Some tried to resist, but after the executions, they forced most of the clans to fall in line. Our clan and a small portion of the others couldn't accept it. We aren't enough to go head-to-head with them, so we use Jiinmaru."

At the bottom of the stairs, they turned a corner into a burned-out room filled with debris and splintered furniture.

"Jiinmaru?" Nathan asked.

Cyn nodded. "The way of one, against many."

An orange light from outside drifted into the room through boarded windows. The rumble of an engine soon followed.

Cyn tugged Nathan to the ground as a heavily armored Meraki tank rolled by. It passed with a slow, methodical intent, stopping briefly to re-scan the area with the spotlight. When the lights receded and the rumble faded, Cyn stood up.

"We survived, somehow, by going underground. This is one of our safehouses. As safe as it can be, I guess. There were rebels all over Kavka once, back in the golden days. That number has dwindled. Prymack pulled together the fractured clans into ours, here in Brevetta, where the Meraki made their capital. Others, not many, are scattered around the planet in pockets.

"The Meraki are brutal when dealing with anyone that opposes them. In the beginning, they executed people by the hundreds, making sure we knew to obey. The technology they wield scares people. It's much more advanced than anything we have, though we get lucky on an occasional raid and snag something really ripper."

Nathan scanned Cyn for the same desperation he was feeling, though it didn't seem to show. What he found was a tranquil quality of someone who seemed able to roll with the punches.

Pulling back a torn rug, Cyn flipped open a trapdoor to expose a hidden ladder. He gestured to Nathan.

Descending the rungs, Nathan discovered a surprisingly large room. Half of it was a makeshift kitchen, while the other half had rickety cots and worn tables. A few Kavkins—he used the naming device Arista had taught him—were eating at one table.

"Let's get something to eat, then I'll show you where you can get some rest."

After an odd meal of something he pretended were noodles and snow pea pods, Cyn showed him a room he could sleep in.

Alone now, in the corner of a small room, Nathan sat on a cot as uncertainty tightened in his chest. He contemplated how different his life was now from a few months ago. Even the idea of aliens was debated on Earth, yet here he was on another world, in the middle of a war. He was so lost.

After months of feeling displaced and lonely, he'd finally created a life with the Meraki. Arista had become a bright spot of that new reality. However, it had all turned out to be a crushing fantasy. Susan was dead. He was a pawn in some scheme he didn't understand, and he had no idea where the woman he'd fallen for was now. Even if he did, she had betrayed him and he couldn't trust her.

Peering through a gap in the boarded-up window, this was the first chance he'd had to see where he'd landed. Two small moons hung on the battle-scarred horizon, dancing on the edge of his view. A third giant moon was high in the sky, casting a pale amber glow on the city.

From what he could tell, it seemed like it had once been vast, but much of it was in ruins now. Five massive skyscrapers, the only structures that remained intact, loomed in the distance. They were all hexagonal at the base but gradually narrowed to a point, like elongated pyramids.

Around the immediate area, no building stood over three stories. There were no clear roads, just piles of rubble and what was left of shattered lives. Any walls that remained were riddled with bullet holes and laser burns.

A bombed-out complex blocked his view to the northeast with hundreds of darkened windows, dead to the world. The weakened foundation had collapsed at both ends, making the building look like a giant frown with most of its teeth missing. From what he'd seen, it seemed a fitting metaphor for the planet. A world knocked on its ass.

This world had been ravaged by the forces to whom he

once belonged. He couldn't help but feel his own guilt. Sick with shame, he wondered if he helped cause this type of destruction on other worlds. Duma had never told him what the missions they went on were about.

Like he had before, it was time to accept what had happened, where he was, and that things would not go back to the way they were. With that, he could find strength and move forward. The Meraki Dominya had taught him well—taught him to kill and to destroy. But now they were his enemy. And so, he concluded, was Arista.

The floor creaked behind him.

"I know it's not fair," Prymack said with pain in his voice, as if reading his mind.

Nathan turned his head from the window. "What do you know about it?"

"I know. Your home. Your sibling. Drelmar told me about it. You're not alone in that pain. Most of us had families before all this. My mate and son were killed during the executions. I couldn't save them. There are millions of stories like that. You need to understand what you're fighting for, and what will happen if we fail. If not for this world, then yours."

He was right. Nathan was falling into the abyss. He had lost a lot, but that was the past, and dwelling on it would not help. However, he could help these people, help them fight the ones who had destroyed his life. At the same time, he might even atone for the things he'd done. He had to keep moving forward.

Reaching into his pocket, he pulled out the datagem that Drelmar had given him.

"Can you read this? I need to get it to the High Command."

Prymack took the gem in his hand and examined it. "This is beyond our tech," he said, narrowing his eyes in thought. "However, we might be able to steal some of theirs. But even if we do, the Meraki have blocked all our outgoing transmissions. We are in this alone."

"That's what I was afraid of."

"What's on it?"

"It has information on it about something called Deathwind."

"And what's that?"

Nathan glanced out the window again to take another look at the devastated city around him. It could have easily been Earth.

"We need to find out."

"I'll do my best," Prymack said, then turned and left.

It took Nathan a long time to fall asleep, but using the waterfall meditation Drelmar had taught him, he finally calmed his mind and pushed out the thoughts of Arista and all the things he couldn't control.

He was abruptly awakened by a firm shake of his shoulder. It was still dark, but he could hear movement and whispers. It took a moment to realize where he was, but it hit him instantly when he saw Cyn kneeling beside him.

"Come on, Stryder," he said.

A large group had gathered in the basement, about fifty people already dressed in armor and brandishing weapons. He and Cyn were among the last to enter, squeezing into the back of the crowded room. Prymack stood at the front, his figure elevated by a step in the floor. Silence spread over the room as he took center stage.

"Last night, we struck a major blow to our oppressors," he began, looking out over the crowd. "We crippled their supply ship, forcing it to retreat. But now, they will try again, and our task will be much more difficult. They will be ready for us.

"Our first and overall aim is to stop the transport. That means destroying it if necessary. But we also need the supplies and technology on that ship. We will take out the engines first and force it to the ground so that we can attempt to capture, salvage, or raid it."

Prymack explained the details of the attack. They planned to strike from four sides. Each team had two of the Spark launchers they had used to hit the transport before.

"If we are all in sync, let's gear up and move." Prymack stepped down into the crowd.

Watching the room, Nathan noted the quiet strength that seemed to emanate from each of them. Their home had been invaded. Everything they had was gone, and everything they hoped for was at stake. To get it back, they had to drive the enemy from their world, and they looked prepared to die for it.

The crowd seemed to function as a single being, each person moving to form their teams, leaving Nathan to wonder about his place here. Slipping through the crowd, he made a line to Prymack. He wouldn't be on the sidelines anymore.

"Why don't I have a team?"

"Stryder, I didn't want to speak for you. Are you ready for this?"

"They killed my sister, lied to me, and tried to use me. You don't have to convince me of anything. I'm all in."

Prymack grinned. "Fantastic. You're with me. Cyn, get him a weapon."

Cyndron returned with an automatic pistol not too different from the kind Nathan knew from Earth, a comm headset, and some worn pieces of armor. The gun differed from what he was used to—the Meraki mostly trained him with energy weapons and other more advanced technology.

"It's all we got," Cyn said.

"It's fine." Nathan pulled the chamber back and tested the weapon. "It'll do the job."

CHAPTER 32

Prymack led his team into position. They coiled through the city, following paths they'd memorized which provided suitable cover from the scouts and satellites that were no doubt searching for them. He'd grown up in Brevetta, but the streets he'd learned as a new fang were no longer the same. Fallen buildings and missile strikes had made the city nearly unrecognizable.

Each of the four teams established positions on rooftops across the city, forming the four points of a diamond pattern around the target area. As soon as the transport hit the center of the kill zone, they would strike.

He'd assigned a handful of team members to stay at ground level as reconnaissance for any land-based counterattacks. The rest were on the roof, some with smaller anti-aircraft missiles for the jet fighters that were sure to come.

Prymack kept Stryder by his side, wary of him getting lost in the maze of the devastated city. He wasn't sure why Drelmar had risked breaking his cover to free the man. Vinn had been a crucial contact, supplying them with useful information for months through one-way transmissions. The only thing he did know about Stryder was that he'd been well-trained, and that was something they needed right now. Their numbers were thinning by the day.

Prymack broke the silence with a whisper. "Have you noticed our greatest disadvantage yet?"

Stryder considered the question. "Technology."

"Yes, and no. We've been able to even the scale by raiding some of their weapon caches. Our biggest handicap is the sky.

Look at it." Prymack lifted his hand to the dim sky, which was clear except for a few clouds and two faint moons. "What do you see?"

"Nothing."

"Exactly. They keep only a minimum number of ships here, but they still maintain control of the skies. We have these Spark missiles, but they have limits."

"How can they do that? With only a few ships?"

Prymack shrugged. "When they arrived, they took out our fighters with ease, which is uncanny, since they had thruster-based engines, which are eons behind our grav engines. We should've been able to fly halos around them. A few of the pilots who survived say that everything just went crazy, their engines went dead. The Meraki captured most of our remaining fighters. Since then, we've found that the Meraki have a device that counters the way antigravity engines work. We've recovered and repaired a few fighters that were downed in the battle, but we can't get any of them to fly."

Cyndron crouched up behind them. "How long do you think we'll have to wait, boss?"

"Not sure, Cyn. Might be awhile. Dig in."

The sun was rising in the east, spreading out over the area, lighting the stage before the show. A warm breeze from the west drifted lightly over the rooftop.

Raising the long-range scope to his eye once more, Prymack scanned the distant horizon. "Or not…"

In the dawn's early light, the transport broke through the clouds. It was still a few kilometers away, but it wasn't hard to see. Seeming to glide toward them, it was following the path he'd predicted.

"Lock and load! Here she comes," Prymack called out.

Lifting the Spark launcher, he set it on his shoulder. The second launcher was at another corner of the roof, easily resting on Pollo's broad frame.

The transport's course would take it directly over his team

on its way to the garrison for unloading. But before it could do that, it would have to make it through the kill zone.

"Ground status?" Prymack said.

Their headsets crackled. "All clear."

"Stay frosty. They're out there."

Lightly closing one eye, Prymack pressed the other to the scope on the launcher, monitoring the oncoming target. The scope kept track of the distance to the ship, counting down meter by meter. If his math was right, he would fire when it reached 3060 meters. They'd have a small window to hit the engines severely enough to down it before it reached them.

He'd taught Stryder to reload the launcher, and even now, he was ready with the next missile. Reloading was a simple procedure, and having Stryder do it freed up another gun he trusted and who knew the area. It also made sure he was close.

Roaring engines reverberated in the air as Prymack spotted the transport approaching. The bow of the ship was harpoon shaped, same as the last one, and it sent clouds swirling as it broke through them. His range finder clocked it at 3100 meters, closing steadily.

"Pollo, on my mark," Prymack said.

"Forty, thirty, twenty." He counted the meters. "Ten. Mark!"

The two missiles fired simultaneously, joining six more smoke trails from the other rooftops. The sight was strangely beautiful. The smoke and light from the missiles seemed to go perfectly with the sunrise as their trails crisscrossed the sky.

Prymack slammed the back end of the launcher down, as did Pollo, resetting the weapons for the next round of missiles. Stryder dropped a new missile in, pulled the arming pin, and took a step back. Prymack retargeted and fired a beat quicker than any of his counterparts. The missile ripped through the air, seeking its fate with the transport.

✳ ✳

Arista had flown ahead of the resupply in a fighter jet. After landing several kilometers away, she took charge of a strike team that had already been stationed in the city. Throughout the morning, they scoured the area for probable strike points. She knew the rebels would challenge the transport, but so far, they'd found nothing.

"3100 meters," the transport pilot called out over her earpiece.

Seconds later, a rooftop two blocks away erupted with loud hisses and flashes of flame.

"The fighters should be in position now," Arista said, as they ran to the rebels' rooftop position. She signaled her team to slow down as they approached the building, but it was too late. They'd been spotted.

The cracking sounds and flashes of projectile rounds exploded out of the shadows. It had been a long time since she'd heard the sounds of those primitive—yet effective—weapons. Two soldiers beside her fell to the ambush.

Her team dropped into prone positions and returned fire as they had been trained to do. She rolled to her right and broke off to flank the enemy.

"Suppressing fire!" she commanded.

Their rifles lit up with a steady onslaught of laser flashes. Once they were set to cover her movement, she retreated to a better position.

Slinging the rifle over her shoulder, she quickly climbed the pitted, collapsed structure to her left for a better view. At that point, it wasn't difficult to verify the rebels' position. They were dug into the bottom floor of what looked like a battered vegetable shop. She immediately spotted signs of antipersonnel mines around the foundation.

Working her way toward the building through a course of unstable and warped support beams, bombed-out windows, and broken ledges, she found herself on the floor above the rebel fox hole. She grabbed loose wiring that dangled throughout the building and fastened it to a beam.

Moments later, Arista hung a few meters above five of the rebel extremists. She slid smoothly down the cabling, not making a sound.

The two below her were back-to-back, behind a wall for cover. At intervals, they peered out and fired on her strike team, ducking back inside after their shots. Carefully, she timed her attack to when there was a break in their shots.

Arista dropped hard onto one of their shoulders in a sitting position. Quickly leaning back, she reached out for the other soldier and found his head. Her thighs closed around the first rebel's neck as she made an elbow lock around the second. They struggled to break her grip, clawing at her legs and hands.

Without giving them time to fight back, she violently twisted her body, snapping both their necks at once. Their bodies went limp and flew over her when she spun onto her side.

As the others turned on her, she swiftly rolled and hurled a knife into the throat of the nearest one. She drew the sidearm from her hip and let loose two shots into the chest of another, then two more into the first as he landed on his back.

Without hesitation, she dove toward the last one as he fired on her. Tucking into a roll, she closed the distance, then burst up and grabbed his weapon.

Caught off guard, the soldier unexpectantly rammed his head forward, colliding with her face just as she squeezed the trigger. The shot went wild, and her vision blinked out.

As it returned, she found that she still had a grip on his weapon, but hers was gone. They struggled for control of the pistol as the spots in her eyesight gradually faded.

Then, with intricate knowledge of the weapon, she ejected the clip and stripped the slide from the gun, making it useless.

With the pistol neutralized, they both dropped it.

Deflecting a flurry of fists, she reflexively struck out with two successive jabs, splitting the soldier's nose open. Crouching low, she brutally extended her fist into his groin, doubling him over, then shot back up to catch him full in the face with an elbow. His head thrashed back from the impact, flinging blood on the ceiling as he fell to the floor.

That was enough to give her team the advantage they needed. They pressed ahead, flooding the first floor on her signal. Two more Meraki soldiers fell as they charged the rebel dogs, but eventually, they secured the site.

* *

"They found us," Nur heard over the headset. "There's about ten now. There might be more moving to flank us."

She turned to Prymack. "I'm going down to help."

About to fire his fifth missile, he paused to make eye contact with her. "Be careful."

She nodded. "Cyn, Mase, Xan. Come with me."

They followed without question. As they navigated the stairs, she tried to focus and push thoughts of Prymack from her head. For the past two hours, he'd only sat a few meters away for that entire time, but they hadn't made up. As much as she hated to be fighting with him, as much as she'd wanted to clear it all up, neither had said a word.

Now, she had to concentrate on the battle that lay at the bottom of the stairs. They would make up later, she convinced herself. They always did.

The sounds of the fire-fight rose from the stairway to meet them.

"Make sure you're in position to fall back up the stairs if needed," Nur said as they descended. "Keep an eye out for the others."

At the bottom, Cyndron darted out to the left, Masemada

and Nur to the right, and Xantani forward, making sure not to clump together.

※ ※

It was the first time Nathan had really viewed the transport from the outside. When he'd boarded, he'd been in restraints and not entirely interested in its appearance. It was larger than he'd expected. He thought they'd run the entire length when they were escaping, but now he could see he was wrong. From this distance, it looked to be about the size of three football fields.

At ground level, he watched helplessly as Meraki jet fighters strafed two rooftops across the way. The missiles there, however, kept firing. The transport was hurting badly, flames and secondary explosions spotted its hull.

It surprised him to see one of Prymack's missiles stray off target. He hadn't missed one yet. As Nathan watched, it intercepted a fighter that had been strafing team two's position. The blast sent the craft spiraling out of control into a building. No doubt already weak from previous bombings, the building collapsed as the fighter crashed into it, sending up a plume of dust and smoke.

Prymack turned his stoic face to Nathan and winked.

Gunfire and shouts from the others came in over his headset. They were falling back up the stairs. Shouldering the launcher, Prymack fired another missile at the slowly moving transport, which was now losing altitude.

"Fallback to the roof and regroup," he said into the headset, then hefted the launcher back onto his shoulder, its weight beginning to show on his face. "Diis!" he yelled as he fired another missile. "The zipline!"

Sundiis, a tall Kavkin with black swirls on his maroon skin, retrieved a strange-looking gun from his pack and made his way across the roof. The gun made a whipping noise when fired, launching a harpoon projectile and a rope line across the street. It attached to the broken remains of a building fifty meters away.

Prymack's launcher slammed against the roof, snapping Nathan back to his duty. He grabbed one of the two remaining missiles and reloaded the launcher.

The transport was uncomfortably close now and in a wild tilt.

The stairway came to life as Nur, Cyn, and the others came charging up.

"They're right behind us!" Mase yelled.

Prymack shouted over the hiss of the next-to-last missile. "Everyone down the zipline!"

Pollo, who'd caught up and passed Prymack's pace, fired his last missile. Then he slung the launcher over his shoulder and jogged with the others to the zipline.

Finally, the debilitated transport thundered to the ground, crashing toward them. The noise was overwhelming, as if an avalanche was roaring down a mountain. He and Prymack stumbled sideways as the building bucked under their feet. Only Nur and Cyn were still there with them. The rest had disappeared down the zipline.

"Hurry! They're coming up the stairs!" Nur said, peering back to Prymack as Cyn rushed her to the zipline. "Prymack! That's it. Let's go!"

Picking the launcher back up and setting it to his shoulder again, Prymack was too busy to notice her concern.

The transport was skidding across the ground now, hurtling toward them in a mound of flames and explosions. Large chunks of earth were thrown upward as the charging freight of twisted metal tore a path through the ruined city.

Prymack, ignoring the oncoming disaster, spun the launcher around and aimed at the stairwell.

"Stand back!"

Nathan dashed to the zipline as Prymack fired the missile

into the stairway. The blast reverberated off the nearby structures, causing a twanging echo, followed by a firestorm of flame and debris that blew back at them from the stairs.

Prymack ducked toward the zipline, oblivious to the flaming debris that had landed on his back. He tossed the Spark launcher to the roof, then hooked his handle to the line and held an arm out.

A moment before grabbing Prymack's forearm, Nathan squashed the flame out with the palm of his hand. Then he was jerked off the roof by the momentum of the steep zipline. He dangled over the ground as they sped down the cable. Hitting the pavement at the end of the line, Nathan rolled with the impact.

Behind them, the burning and wrecked transport ground to a halt, meters from the building. Prymack was on the headset again, already giving orders.

"Scavengers, it's your turn. Be quick before they cut their losses and blow the whole damn thing."

* *

Arista and her unit were charging up the stairway when a missile surprised them all. The blast descended on them, surging its way down the stairs with wild fury. The trooper in front of her burst into flames, howling as he was swallowed by fire.

Her Tanzi instinctively spread to cover her entire body, protecting her from the fire and heat. She was knocked unconscious the moment the blast hit her, throwing her down the stairway and out to the ground floor as the explosion triggered the collapse of everything above.

CHAPTER 33

Erratic, drunken laughter filled Nathan's ears as acoustic music pulsed through the air around him. They were in a safehouse of sorts—a makeshift underground bar, from what he could tell. This was the rendezvous point for after the battle. He sat at a table with Prymack and Nur, watching others play simple drums and stringed instruments.

"The original bar was bombed by the Meraki at the beginning of their occupation," Nur explained, sipping her drink. "We put up this one below it. They don't have a clue."

Three hours had passed since the battle, and it seemed as if everyone who had survived was already here. However, as Nathan glanced around, he saw only about thirty people. And not everyone was celebrating.

Prymack caught Nathan's assessment of the room.

"The rest are confirmed dead," he said somberly, then took a long draw from his glass.

"I know it's hard to deal with, but they died fighting for what they loved, for what they believed in," Nur said in a reassuring tone. "There isn't a better way to go."

She watched Prymack for confirmation, but got only a guilt-stricken glance her way.

Then she turned to Nathan. "I'd guess it wasn't this violent on Earth."

He eyed her curiously, as if she'd discovered a well-kept secret. "How do you know where I'm from?"

"Drelmar contacted us occasionally. He told us about you and planned your escape with us. We were hoping to meet him in person, but something went wrong during the escape. We have heard nothing from him."

Nathan glanced down at the table, uncomfortable with looking Nur in the eyes. "He was still in the engine when it blew."

She nodded. "That's war. I think we need another round." She stood up, putting a hand on Prymack's shoulder, then left slowly for the bar.

That was an opportunity for Cyn to stumble over, stone-drunk.

"Heeeeyy. Stryfer, there you are!" He grabbed his arm. "Come 'ere. These two need to be alone. Besides," he whispered. "There's someone I want you to meet."

In what could have been an attempt to wink, he ended up blinking erratically at Nathan.

"Go on. We'll just depress you further." Prymack grimaced. "Try to have some fun."

Without waiting to hear Nathan's response, Cyn yanked him up, nearly knocking himself over. Nathan had to smile at the man's antics as he followed his swaying guide to a corner where six people lounged.

"Got 'em!" Cyn announced, louder than necessary.

Introducing Nathan took longer than anyone wanted. Cyn was trying to tell the story of when they'd found him, but somehow strayed off the topic and never really finished the introduction before he sat down and drank again.

Four of the people Nathan was somewhat introduced to were men he'd never met before. Niikapollo was the fifth, and the last was the woman sitting on his lap with her arms draped around his neck. Each looked as if they had a system full of alcohol.

Cyn pulled Nathan into the seat next to him. "Have a seat, have a drink." He attempted to slide a glass Nathan's way but gave up after a few inches.

"Now, the reasons I drug ya away from there was her." He motioned to a woman about twenty feet away.

Nathan followed his gesture to the dance floor, where a woman was swaying her body like a vixen in heat. A green mask with gold accents covered her face as she fluttered paper fans around her like butterfly wings. In a blink, she brought the fan up to briefly cover her face, and the mask changed to white with red lips. Then again, the mask switched to a blue face and white eyes behind the fan. In a split second, the masks were gone, exposing her actual face. She glanced at him, this time firing off a smile.

"She's..." Cyn drew out the word. "...been watching you. Her name is Ven. Well, it's Vendala, but Ven. You know. Come on, I'll glive ya an excellent introduction." He paused to consider what he'd just said. "Glive?"

Nathan eyed him. "I bet you will."

"Here, take this." He tapped his finger on Nathan's glass, then tried to stand. "Well? I'm drunk, fool! Help me up!"

✳ ✳

Nur watched the others in the bar as she returned to the table with drinks. This was as hopeful as she'd seen them in a while. A moment worth savoring.

"Cyn grabbed him," Prymack explained when she sat down.

"I know—I saw them from the bar." She pushed a mug to him, studying his somber face.

Prymack nodded quietly. He glanced around the room before touching his drink.

"I know that look," Nur said, sensing his turmoil. "We've been through this before. You've convinced everyone else that death and sacrifice are part of the war. When will you convince yourself?"

Prymack took a healthy drink. "It's different."

"How is it different?" She'd hoped this wasn't going where she thought it would.

"It's different if your friend or the others in your unit die. You followed orders then. You have no decision in that. They just died. The war killed them. There's no blood on your hands. But when you, yourself, give those orders—when you send your friends, your unit, to their deaths—you think you could have planned it better, so more of them would have come back."

She placed her hands on his, feeling his warm skin. "No matter what you think, everyone here volunteered. They all have choices, and they choose to fight. They are free to walk out at any time. Their deaths aren't your decision, but theirs. They chose to follow you. No one else could have planned that attack better. Dread! If anyone else planned it, that thing would have landed on us!" She grinned, attempting to bring some levity to the conversation.

He didn't look amused. "Any one of my decisions that I have confidence in could turn out like Hewl's. He thought what he was doing was right and look what happened."

She knew Prymack well. Never once had she heard him call his father by anything but his first name. Templar of Defense Hewl Vaiirun was the man who'd opened the door for the Meraki to invade. At least, that was how the world saw it. Now, Prymack lived in his shadow, forced to right his wrong—to slam the door on them. Mentioning his father's name always ended the conversation.

They sat in silence, comforting each other with their presence. Prymack finished his drink and started on the one left for Nathan. With a distant look in his eyes, he fixed his gaze on her. She could see the thoughts racing behind them.

She sipped her drink. "What's on your mind?"

He took a few moments before responding, his eyes glazed over. "Eventually, because of me, you'll be dead."

Nur slammed her drink on the table, splashing most of it out of the glass.

"Damn it, Prymack!" She scowled icily at him. "You're impossible! We had a good week. We stopped their resupply. Twice! And we rescued Stryder. 'From our enemy will come our savior,' remember?"

Prymack stared blankly. "I think you're the only one who still believes in that."

"I have to," she said, rising from the table. "It's all I have."

✶ ✶

After Cyn's less than terrific introduction, he laid his head down on the bar as Nathan took a seat next to Vendala.

"How do you do that with your face?" Nathan said.

"It's an ancient art. Passed down from the clan mothers. I don't suppose I should tell its secrets to the first alien who asks, should I?" She grinned.

"Well, it's fascinating. Better keep it a secret, then."

"What about your secrets, Natan Stryder?" Vendala's aqua-green eyes shone in the dim light of the bar. "I've heard a few things about you."

"It's Nathan," he said with amusement. "And what have you heard?"

"You escaped from the Meraki and destroyed a transport in the process."

He raised an eyebrow. "Not—"

"Tally ho!" Pollo shouted over everything.

"Hoo-Hoo-Rah! Hoo-Hoo-Rah!" the rest of the rebels responded, slamming glasses, fists, or feet onto anything that made noise.

Before Nathan could really see what was going on, Vendala placed her hand on his cheek and gently turned his head to face her.

The warm touch reminded him of Arista's the last night

they had been together. Her face jumped to the front of his mind—her soft, curved lips, her deep rose eyes. He tried to ignore it. She had betrayed him. It was over.

When he looked into Vendala's eyes, Nathan didn't see what he had in Arista's the night they were together. He didn't see tenderness, affection, or devotion. He saw only lust.

But he couldn't have seen all that in Arista's eyes. He must have been mistaken. If she'd felt that way, she wouldn't have turned him over to Duma.

Vendala whispered into his ear, her warm breath tingling his skin. "Natan, you look ready to fuse. You want to put that body on me?"

The question took him by surprise, stirring a swell of conflicting emotions in his stomach. She intrigued him, but it was all too sudden. Then he remembered Cyn, who had fallen asleep next to him.

"He'll be fine," Vendala said, reading his face. She stood up, unsteady on her feet. Grabbing his hands, she pulled him after her.

"I don't think we're the same species," Nathan blurted out, in an effort to head off where this was going, cringing at how lame it sounded.

But it only made her chuckle. "Let's have fun finding out."

She guided Nathan to the side door and out into the stairwell. There, she turned around and pressed him against the door with a kiss. An aroma of gunpowder and honey emanated from her skin. He fought back vivid memories of Arista—how she kissed, what she smelled like.

Vendala tugged him toward the stairs.

"I'm sorry," he said, sliding her hand away. "I'm not ready for that."

Her expression shifted from delight to confusion and then to disappointment as she processed his words, nearly making him ill. He winced inwardly, knowing that his words caused it, but also knowing this wasn't what he wanted.

"It's not about you, really," he said, before turning away and ascending the stairs, seeking a place to be alone and sort through his thoughts.

"Damn," he cursed himself. Why couldn't he just find peace? He inhaled deeply through his nose, holding it as long as he could, before exhaling it from his mouth. He tried it again, but it wasn't working.

Overwhelmed, he stopped to lean against the wall, trying to sort things out. Everything he felt about Arista flooded him at once—all the hope, warmth, passion, admiration and...

Glancing down, he realized his fingers had found their way to the starburst scar on his right hand. It had been created on the night of the Tithe during a moment of true intimacy.

Then a rush of treachery, lies, and despair crashed down on him. It didn't matter how he felt about her, because it was over now.

Anxiety, his old enemy, squeezed his chest. His breathing became shallow and laborious, as if everything were suddenly closing in on him all at once.

Pushing off the wall, he hurried down the hall and stopped at the stairs. He had to get out of this place, but he couldn't go down—everyone else was down there. Taking the steps two at a time, he went up, his panic growing. He had to get outside.

At the top of the stairs, he reached a locked door. His breaths came quicker, and shorter, making him dizzy. He needed air.

Stepping back, he stomped his heel into the lock. The force splintered the doorframe, slamming the door outward.

Nathan's momentum carried him out onto the roof, where fresh air rushed into his lungs, filling him with a sense of relief. Above, the sky was overcast, and rain drizzled down on him. His panic was subsiding, but it changed nothing. He was still trapped on this planet, he'd still failed Susan, and his relationship with Arista was still a disaster.

He drifted to the edge of the roof, struggling against the currents of helplessness. His world was out of his control. He rested his hands on the four-foot-high parapet that prevented him from falling off.

Water trickled down his face. Where did it end? He didn't know, and it didn't matter. Nothing mattered.

Trying to control the swirling storm within, Nathan stared into the distance, where a skyscraper was barely visible through the rain. Somehow, he knew she was in there, and even knowing everything they'd had was over, he still longed for it. He was sinking into the crushing depths of despair. Convinced the universe was working against him, his rage surged. Balling his hands, he clenched his jaw in a struggle to endure the pain.

With his white-knuckled fists pressed against his temples, he tried to hold it in. Unable to contain it, he smashed them down onto the parapet, releasing everything he felt. The impact shattered the concrete, sending fragments bursting out in every direction. Nathan staggered backward, shocked.

His hands were humming and churning with radiant blue energy.

※ ※

Her brush gently stroked the sea foam green paint across the canvas. It blended with the cerulean blue water, giving the illusion of algae. Arista stepped back to study it, touching the handle of the brush to her lips in thought. Then she leaned in and touched up the shoreline with a few short dabs.

After the battle, she'd awoken cocooned in the Tanzi warsuit with a broken arm. It had taken two hours for her to dig herself out of the wreckage. Her other injuries included a bruised kidney and some internal bleeding, but now she was fully recovered and painting a quiet pond that her grandmother had taken her to as a child.

Painting had always been an escape that calmed her—it let her imagination and thoughts flow out onto the canvas, distracting her from her problems. Switching to another brush, she dabbed the yellow dash on her palette. A frown passed over her lips when she discovered there wasn't enough left.

Marching to her drawer of painting supplies, Arista withdrew another tube of yellow. Duma had let her bring a few things down to the planet before he'd left. Thankfully, he didn't have restrictions.

As she returned to the canvas, her eyes floated over a painting that sat in the corner. It was one of hers, and one she was proud of, although now she couldn't stand to look at it.

It was a picture of the planet Earth. She'd given it the title "Ronya"—a word invented by Nathan and her the night of the Tithe, when they'd disabled their translators. A combination of the Aurein word for happiness and an Earthin word for excitement it was meant to define what they'd felt that night.

Everything they'd once had together was in that painting, and Nathan had just tossed it aside when he'd elected to do the same to her.

A wave of frustration crashed over her. She'd been cultivated and trained to control her emotions, but it was one she felt often lately. If only he would have just listened to her. Why had he chosen the lies of a saboteur over her?

With her eyes closed and lips pressed together, she focused on controlling her feelings. She was good at it, but this time, she couldn't do it. She grabbed the painting off the floor and pitched it across the room. All she could do was stand there, caught in the crossfire of her own emotions.

"Why would you do that?" she whispered to herself. "I thought you were happy. I thought you loved me."

Letting the tube of yellow slip from her fingers, she curled up on her bed, attempting to fight back her emotions. A single tear rolled slowly down her face as she tried to convince herself that she hadn't fallen in love with Nathan the night of the Tithe.

CHAPTER 34

A WEEK AFTER they took down the transport, there was still no word on the equipment they'd recovered. Nathan had made it a priority to be notified if they retrieved something that could read his datagem.

In the meantime, Prymack kept him by his side, explaining the tactical situation they were in. There wasn't much of an overall strategy other than to hold on, resist, and hope to bleed the Meraki enough that they would give up. With the numbers they had, there was no hope for any type of decisive victory.

He also made sure Nathan was familiar with their weapons, but having been taught by the Meraki, Nathan was already ahead of the game. There were weapons he had never encountered in Duma's training, such as the halo grenade, but those were rare, especially for the resistance.

It was late afternoon, and Nathan was outside under a hastily built shelter designed to hide them from satellites. He was just finishing up a circuit of calisthenics, trying to keep a routine to his days. Things were easier for him with some kind of structure.

Working on a set of push-ups, he spotted Cyn approaching him out of the corner of his eye. Then felt the man's boot on his back.

"Stryder. I'm here for your crash course in Jiinmaru."

Nathan gave him a friendly glare out of the corner of his eye.

Cyn removed his foot. "It takes years to learn, so you might as well start now."

This was good. Nathan had been trying to keep himself busy, so he didn't have to think about Arista or how he felt, and this was something else he could focus on.

"Cool. Let's do it," he said, jumping to his feet.

Cyn clasped his hands together. "The art of Jiinmaru is not only physical but also psychological and spiritual. It is a way to understand yourself by learning your strengths and weaknesses. Through this, you'll learn about you, and find your purpose. If you take it seriously, it will help you to choose and follow the right path."

"That's quite a pitch." Nathan grinned.

"Like I said, if you take it seriously." Cyn paused before continuing. "I won't be teaching you strict technique. We will hone your natural instincts, not force you into forms or moves that feel strange to you. By doing this, it will help you focus and unblock your inner power."

That was a welcome change. Nathan had all the forms and technique he could take. They had been drilled into him and were now simply reflexes.

Looking around, Cyn grabbed a large bag of grain and dragged it into an open area.

"Let's start with something simple so I can demonstrate. Punch this."

Nathan was skeptical. "We're starting with punching?"

"Trust me."

Shaking out his muscles from the workout, Nathan bounced around, then threw a solid punch that dented the grain bag.

"Whoa! Ripper. Real good!" Cyn assessed him. "That had power, but there was still a lot of tension there—rigidness. Right now, your power is constrained, like a kinked hose. Try it again, but more fluid. Focus on the energy you're sending down your arm. Not the punch."

Again, Nathan tried a punch. This time, he thought of the power he'd felt the other night on the roof—the power he'd crushed the wall with. He tried to gather those emotions again as he struck out, but this time his hands didn't glow.

Cyn tilted his head, looking confused. "No, no. What did you do? That was worse!"

"I thought of everything that made me angry."

"Ah. All emotions carry power. But destructive emotions, fear and anger, cause stress, tension. You want to flow." Cyndron made fluid gestures with his arms to emphasize. "Focus on the positive emotions, but remember, do not let them take control of you. Do not make rash decisions because of them, just channel their energy. Are we in sync?"

Nathan nodded, pushing the frustration and anger he'd just called up to the back of his mind. He shifted to positive emotions, focusing on happiness and excitement. *Ronya*—the word popped into his head. A word he and Arista had clumsily created for what they had felt the night of the Tithe.

He focused on ronya.

This time, his fist flared blue as he swung. The grain bag exploded on impact.

Cyn's mouth dropped open. "Wha..." He gestured at scraps of the bag. "Yes! Like that!"

Nathan shook out his fist, but it was more of an unconscious gesture, because it hadn't actually hurt. In fact, his hand was tingly. He wasn't sure where the energy came from, but at least he might be able to control it.

Then, a vague, surreal memory of Arista swinging light around her as he was bleeding out on Tinook drifted to the front of his mind. She said she didn't know when or how it happened, either.

"Stryder." Cyn was still in shock. "How did you do that?"

"I'm not sure."

"Try it again!"

They worked together for most of the day. His movements were getting more fluid, but he could not consistently replicate the power or glow he'd had in that punch. He would have liked to keep going, but Sundiis interrupted them.

"Stryder. The boss wants to see you."

Nathan nodded, then bowed to Cyn. "Until next time."

"Remember, you want to be fluid. Jiinmaru is the art of one against many. You can't get locked into single combat when you're outnumbered. You're constantly moving, neutralizing the nearest threat to you, and then moving on in an ever-widening circle."

Sundiis led Nathan into a cave that the rebels had dug out from the surrounding hills. Prymack was inside, studying a map, when Nathan found him. He turned the moment he heard him approaching.

"Stryder, walk with me."

Nathan took up a pace next to him, unsure where they were going. Prymack led him into one of the three tunnels that branched off in different directions.

"You've proven yourself to be a worthy soldier." He grinned proudly and placed a hand on Nathan's shoulder. "You learned that from them?"

Nathan nodded, but he couldn't decide if he was proud or ashamed of his skills. He decided to redirect the whole conversation.

"I'm still kinda new to these weapons."

"They aren't too much different." Prymack lifted a rifle and looked it over. "I've used the Meraki's energy weapons, and I almost prefer ours. Reloading is a pain, but they just feel more natural."

"They do," Nathan agreed. "They remind me of Earth weapons."

They strolled in silence for a while before Prymack started again.

"I have faith in you, Stryder. Even though you were once a Meraki, you are here with us now."

"I can't change how I got here, but I *am* with you."

Prymack hesitated, as if something else was on his mind. Finally, he spoke.

"Nur and I have a meet tonight. We'd like you to come along. I can't tell you with who, or what for. You'll just have to trust us."

Trust. The word had a whole new sensitivity to it now. The only person who hadn't broken his trust was Drelmar. And Drelmar had sent him here. Nathan had to believe it was for a good reason.

"There's not much I can say then."

"Good."

After sundown, Nathan, Prymack, and Nur exited their camp through underground tunnels and came up a mile out from the safehouse.

Without the HUD system, it took Nathan's eyes about thirty seconds to adjust to the dim moonlight. They ducked through a few empty structures, some of which could hardly be considered buildings anymore, just piles of rubble marking what once was. They were heading away from the center of the city, away from the bright lights of the pyramid skyscrapers.

With a sudden gesture, Prymack signaled them to halt and take cover as two Meraki vanguard soldiers, followed by a heavily armored vehicle, came into view. A figure atop the vehicle carefully directed a searchlight, scanning the area. Next to the light was a hefty gun that swiveled with it.

Slowly, the unit rolled by, patrolling the area and enforcing the sundown curfew. As he kneeled in the shadows, Nathan noticed a dark, bloodlike stain on the street surrounded by shards of glass and bullet casings. Across the street, beyond that, was a tattered wall marred by plasma burns and bullet holes. In the moonlight, he could make out what looked to be graffiti.

Nathan pointed it out to Prymack. "What's that?" he whispered.

"It's an old symbol for freedom," he said somberly.

As the last soldier passed from sight, Prymack signaled again for the all-clear. Nur emerged from the shadows and took a slight detour to the curb across the road. She kneeled and picked up a small object.

"What is it?" Prymack said.

"A toy." Nur held out a stained, ragged doll to show them. For a moment, she inspected it before putting it in her pack.

The trio slipped down an alley and paused at the backside of a rundown, two-story house. Prymack unlocked the back door, and they hurried through it.

Inside, it was just light enough to see a narrow stairway. Each step groaned with age as Prymack climbed them, with Nur close behind. Nathan was last, instinctively stepping on the sides of each step to make less noise, like he'd done sneaking to bed after staying up too late as a kid.

The room at the top was fully lit, throwing light and shadows down the stairs. A man was waiting there. He was Kavkin, though his skin was darker than others Nathan had seen and covered in unique patterns. In each outstretched hand, the man held a glass filled with a green liquid. Apparently, they'd reached their destination.

"I knew you'd come tonight." The man lifted a glass to Prymack.

He accepted the offering. "Of course. What help would you be if you didn't?"

"Stryder, I'd like you to meet Siigur," Nur said, motioning to the man.

Siigur nodded to Nathan in recognition and spoke one word: "Asante."

Everything in Nathan's mind came to a crashing halt. He knew that word. His brain tried to make connections and trace the word through his memories like a zigzagged puzzle. Someone else had said it. But who? Ajax? Drelmar?

Nur and Prymack exchanged bewildered glances.

Siigur shook a fragile finger at Nathan. "I'm sensing an ancient soul. An heirloom of war."

He gave the remaining glass to Nur, then ambled to a large chair.

"What do you mean, 'heirloom of war?'" Nathan said.

Siigur shook his head. "I don't always know what I see. I'm sorry, I don't have more. Please, have a seat."

Nathan glanced at the drinks, wondering why he hadn't been offered one. Then, as he took a seat in a chair to the left of Siigur, he discovered a glass resting on a small table in front of him.

Siigur smiled. "There's your drink, Nathan Stryder."

Nathan looked him over. Something odd was definitely going on here.

Prymack must have sensed the confusion. "He's a mind-walker, Stryder."

Siigur frowned. "You love to ruin my fun, don't you?"

"It's in my contract." Prymack smiled half-heartedly.

Siigur nodded and turned to Nur. "And you, lovely Nur. How have you been?"

"Still here."

Nathan picked up the glass and sipped the green liquid. It was tangy, like the kiwi he used to eat at his grandparents.

"Now, what is the important question that led you all the way out here?" Siigur said.

"Two years ago, we had Deluca infiltrate the Meraki's ranks as a double agent," Prymack began. "We lost contact with him three months ago. All our efforts to find him have failed."

Siigur became still. "And you believe I can."

"It's worth a try. We have no other option. He was our best chance at finding out more about the Meraki, so we could hit something big—something that would have an impact on them."

Siigur nodded. "I'll find him, then. Do you have anything of his?"

Prymack pulled a scrap of paper out of his breast pocket and handed it over. "This was the last thing he sent us."

Siigur gripped the item lightly as he took it from Prymack and closed his eyes. Nathan watched the strange event unfold, sipping his drink throughout.

The mindwalker turned his head back and forth as if trying to see something hidden. He released the paper. It would have been a simple victim of gravity anywhere else, but here, now, it hung in the air, turning slowly. Siigur placed his hands on the armrests of his chair.

Prymack glanced at Nur. He seemed to expect the uncomfortable look she returned to him. Nevertheless, she watched intently. Her glass was already empty on the table.

"I see him. Deluca." Siigur's fingers contracted, clenching the armrest. "His head hangs." The floating paper in front of him stopped spinning.

"Now we look out a window." Siigur's mouth hung open with his last word, straining to see something. "We're saddened, disappointed. Out the window are prisoners, slaves. Their futures are doomed. We know it. They lead four of them to a wall."

Siigur winced, pausing for a moment. "They are struck down. The guards beat them. We watch. We have to—to punish ourselves for not being able to help them.

"A child runs toward them, crying. A sudden fear. We run to the door, out to the prisoners! The child reaches out to one of them, tears streaming. Desperation, our legs are heavy, not moving fast enough—stop the child! The guard raises his club to strike again. No! The child holds his hand up to stop the guard's blow, still crying. No!"

Simultaneously, all the glasses shattered, including the one Nathan was still holding. The paper slowly floated to the floor.

Siigur opened his eyes once more and looked directly into Prymack's. His pupils were now an eerie liquid black.

"Ten kilometers southeast of Fettis. Please don't come again."

"I'm sorry you had to see that, Siigur." Prymack's voice was somber.

"See it? I didn't just see it! I was there, I experienced it. I felt the wind, smelled the blood."

"I know. I know it's difficult, but we need your help. You can't turn your back."

Siigur calmly stepped up to Prymack. "That child was a young male. He had brown eyes, filled with fear and love. He didn't die with the first blow, or the third. He bled to death, next to his dead father. I'll see that, every day, for the rest of my life."

Prymack nodded. "Nur, Stryder. Would you wait downstairs?"

CHAPTER 35

THE NEXT MORNING, Prymack issued orders for everyone to pack up. Traveling posed a challenge, especially with the tight restrictions imposed by the Meraki. Fortunately, they'd managed to restore an underground rail train that had been decommissioned following Kavka's civil war. It was one of the secrets they managed to keep hidden. Now, with most of his team on board, Prymack had a rare moment to delve into his thoughts.

Nur was still upset about using a mindwalker. He knew she didn't trust them, but he did. Siigur, at least. As always, he tried to keep their disagreements low key. It wasn't good for morale when the troops overheard them arguing. But that wasn't easy with her. Once they were alone, he shared with Nur what Siigur had revealed.

"It is only a sense, a feeling. I know nothing more, only that the Meraki are aware of your moves," the man had said.

After that, Prymack had left Siigur to his own internal horrors. Although it was unpleasant to expose Siigur to such things, guilt was a familiar feeling, and this had been necessary.

It didn't make sense. He knew every member of his team and couldn't imagine any of them turning against him. Siigur must have felt something else.

For the time being, Prymack simply watched the people who followed him as they talked and interacted on the ten-hour trip that would take them underground and eventually underwater to an old research station. It always surprised him by what he could learn from just watching people.

Cyndron had come up from the back of the train to sit with Stryder, asking about some details between him and Vendala. Apparently, things hadn't gone well, at least from Cyndron's point of view. Prymack observed Vendala, remembering the day he'd met her, when she was scared, orphaned, and digging through garbage for something to eat. She'd come a long way.

When they arrived at the underwater station, he couldn't help but feel a sense of relief and awe. The massive structure was remarkable. He was impressed to see there were significantly fewer leaks than last time he was here. The station had a reputation for its constant battle against water infiltration.

Riid, the man in charge, greeted them. Prymack had known him well over the years as the leader of a small clan of insurgents in Fettis, and they were more than glad to share resources. The underwater station was their principal base of operations, but they also had control of a cluster of bunkers on the mainland.

After getting everything set up, and in place, Riid led him away from the others. Under a great picturesque window of a coral reef, he rolled out maps of the prison that he had recently acquired, marking points of attack. Prymack didn't have to wait for long before he caught sight of Stryder searching for him.

"Is that the prison?" Stryder said as he approached.

Riid immediately rolled up the maps, eyeballing him.

Prymack motioned to Stryder and led him aside.

"I should be in on the planning," Stryder said.

Riid spoke up, apparently still able to hear them. "I don't trust you, pup."

Prymack understood the hesitation. He trusted Stryder, but then, he also had Drelmar's word to go on. "Look, he doesn't know you or what you lost."

"I know the Meraki better than anyone."

"Do you? You were with them for how long? Less than a year? We've been fighting them for six, very long years."

"I have inside information! I know their training and tactics."

Prymack rested a hand on Stryder's shoulder. "I get it, but we are using his men and his maps. Therefore, it's his call."

"That's bullshit!" Stryder brushed the hand off his shoulder and turned to leave, but Prymack grabbed his wrist.

"I know you want to hurt these people, and we will. But we need his help." He turned to Niikapollo. "Pollo, I want you in on this."

After the exchange, Prymack, Niikapollo, and Riid structured their battle plan for hours, leaving the rest to wait. Prymack knew they didn't mind the delay, for in a few hours he would lead them into battle, and some of them likely wouldn't be returning.

Twelve hours later, as the sun fell and with only Dala, the smallest moon, visible in the night sky, the rebel army was in position outside the prison, their units ready. The structure reminded Prymack of a giant crown. Gun turrets placed along the rim of the circular building each formed a point of the illusion. Their flashing red lights were the jewels. And like those who once wore the crowns of Kavka, a great evil lurked within. The flat, grassy area around the prison made it an intimidating silhouette in the moonlight.

Prymack had hand-picked six of his soldiers to go in first, set charges, and take out the enemy spotters. He'd split the rest into two forces, his with sixty-four soldiers, and the other with seventy-five, led by Riid. As with the transport skirmish, he kept Stryder near him. He was still a new fang. Prymack could see it in his eyes. Plus, he felt he owed it to Drelmar to keep him safe.

With all the pieces in place, Prymack spoke into his headset. "On behalf of the fallen, we are unwavering. We are unbreakable. Blindfold, you're on."

Stryder was next to him at the front of the unit that would hit the compound from the east. Nur was on his left.

Through the headset, team Blindfold's footsteps rasped against the knee-high grass. A strong wind vibrated against their microphones. Then, distinct sounds of silenced weapons.

Six shots and three confirmed kills later, the team called in the first charge.

"Units two and three. Make your way up. Get as close as you can before you blow the door," Prymack said.

"Copy."

He signaled for his team to approach from the east. It was amazing how quiet sixty-four people could be. The only sound he heard was the grass sweeping by their feet as they skulked through the brush, watching for anyone hidden.

He checked on Stryder, who was right on his heels. The new fang's skills were impressive, as well as how easily he picked things up. The Meraki must have taught him quickly. Still, he lacked the eyes of a hardened soldier.

In twenty seconds, they reached the east wall. The cold metal was a relief to Prymack's overheated skin. The single door on this side of the prison was small—it could only fit one at a time. He would make a much grander entrance.

On the north side of the prison, the first team's charge blew with a satisfying concussive blast that lit up the field. Immediately, the prison sirens wailed, their deafening noise shrieking through the darkness. Rapid drumming of machine guns echoed in the distance as the main force attacked from the north.

Starting the countdown on his wristwatch, he glanced back and grinned at Stryder. Catching the wary look in his eyes, he knew the young warrior wasn't accustomed to this yet.

✶ ✶

Commander Ajax Sculic's new cybernetic eyes quickly analyzed the reports that had just come in from Fettis. It took him mere seconds to determine what the rebels were up to. The prison housed some of the Meraki's most valuable assets—captured spies, terrorists, and even a Kavkin general. Freeing them would be a strategic victory and would boost their morale.

Just as he finished the report, the door to the command room opened, and Lieutenant Commander Conak strode quickly by his guards.

"Commander, I need a hundred soldiers to accompany me to Fettis," she demanded.

"One hundred soldiers? Is that it? How about a tank battalion? You realize I have a rebellion to put down?"

"You're aware of my clearance, Commander. Admiral Duma has given my assignment higher priority than oppressing the revolt here."

Ajax could see through her tactic. She used admiral instead of valor for more leverage, even though Duma was not officially an admiral and probably never would be.

"*Valor* Duma," he corrected. "However, our interests align. When you arrive in Fettis, there will be two platoons waiting for you to lead."

"My pleasure, sir," she said, and pivoted on her heel for the door.

※ ※

"Flashfire!" Prymack shouted as he kneeled in the grass outside Fettis prison and clicked the remote detonator.

Nathan heard the call and immediately dropped to a knee, covering his head. The explosion ripped a ten-meter-wide hole in the prison wall, sending pieces of it flying everywhere. Grit from the pulverized concrete peppered him as a concussive blast followed, blowing through his clothes and hair.

The rebels rushed into the smoking hole before Nathan

could even stand. Controlled bursts of gunfire rattled at irregular intervals as he jumped to his feet and followed Prymack and Nur toward the jagged opening. Muzzle flashes lit up the smoldering entrance.

He hurdled the foot-high rubble and made it inside. The air was hot and thick, almost choking. Emergency lights strobed overhead. In his haste, he stumbled over a body on the floor. He didn't have time to identify which side it was from.

"Cyn, take a group and find the prisoners," Nur ordered.

He nodded sharply, then gathered the rebels around him and advanced down the hall.

This was far different from what Nathan was used to, what Duma had taught him. He'd always been on his own in the Crucible. Even on Tinook, there were only a handful of enemies. Now, there were people everywhere. He didn't like it. There was no order. He couldn't possibly take in everything that was going on.

Prymack led Nathan, Nur, and four others up the stairway at the end of the hall. They were the first to reach the second floor and the first to draw the guard's attention.

The scene erupted with a fierce exchange of lasers and bullets, vying for dominance.

Nathan dove to the floor and squeezed his trigger, trying to give cover fire to rebels still in the crossfire. He could see what must have been twenty guards firing back.

"Stryder, get behind cover!" Prymack shouted over the din of battle. He was on the floor too, with Nur and a bloody rebel body. Climbing to one knee, Prymack dragged the body to cover with lasers dancing around him. Only then did he notice that the man was dead.

Nathan rolled to his right, away from the crossfire and into the shelter of an adjacent room.

Nur was still in the hallway, facing death head-on. She lofted a grenade at the Meraki guards as lasers whizzed just over her head, missing by centimeters. Before the first grenade had even gone off, she grabbed a second, tossing it to the other side of the room.

"Pollo!" Prymack said. "Grab her!"

Pollo inched forward, shooting periodically. Nathan leaned out of the doorway and unloaded his clip, giving him cover. Nur returned to firing as the grenades went off.

Flying shrapnel and sparks sprayed the room.

Most of the Meraki took cover from the grenades and the rebels' relentless gunfire. Others lay dead. Amid the confusion, Nathan counted six bodies on the blood-stained floor, but keeping track of anything seemed impossible.

Finally within reach, Pollo grabbed Nur's ankle and hauled her back, pulling her into the room with Nathan. Oblivious to being dragged, she kept firing without pause, her face twisted in a relentless snarl.

Nathan's heart froze as enemy fire blasted the rebel next to him in the face. The smell of burned flesh and blood streamed into his nose.

Prymack and two rebels retreated into the stairwell and now fired alternately, keeping a steady barrage on the Meraki. The ratio was probably close to even now, thanks to Nur's grenades. The battle reached a standoff. Both sides were dug in and unwilling to come out.

Everyone except for Nur.

✶ ✶

Arista was halfway to Fettis, flying at six times the speed of sound, when she heard the call from the prison outside of the city.

She wasn't used to flying in an atmosphere, since most of her training was for space combat. Even the little in-atmosphere training she'd undergone was with anti-grav ships, not ones powered by thrusters. Of course, there was a good reason they couldn't use the anti-grav vehicles. The dampening field was suppressing the Kavkin's air force, which only used antigravity technology.

"We're under heavy fire," an anonymous voice called over her radio. "The rebels have broken through our defenses. We need reinforcements!"

She wouldn't have time to meet up with her new unit at the garrison after all. Cursing, she turned her craft toward the prison and flipped on the afterburners. Within a second, its thrust pressed her against the seat as she accelerated to hypersonic speeds. The fighter generated sonic booms in its wake, disrupting everything she passed over.

Then she contacted the garrison at Fettis. "Send the soldiers waiting for me to the prison." Hopefully, it wasn't too late.

"Understood, Lieutenant Commander. They're on their way."

Coming through the other side of a cloud, she met the teal sky again. She was ten minutes from the prison—but battles could be over in less time, especially hit-and-runs.

Arista flipped off the commlink and stared ahead. If only she could go back and have her last conversation with Nathan again, things might be different. It was a silly thought, and she knew it was pointless to dwell on, but she had a hard time keeping it from her mind.

* *

No sooner had Pollo turned his attention from her, had Nur charged back out into the firefight. She sprayed the prison hallway with wild abandon just as new gunfire came from behind the Meraki's position.

Feeling he needed to back her move or watch her die, Nathan charged forward as well. Prymack and Pollo laid down a suppressing fire to cover him.

Taking a bead on the closest enemy, Nathan squeezed the trigger, rocking the soldier with bullets. Then he dove forward to make himself less of a target, flattening himself on the floor. Targeting another, he fired a three-round burst, hitting him in the chest.

Pollo and Prymack fanned out behind Nur and concentrated fire on three others.

Then, muzzles flashed behind the Meraki forces, rattling the area with bullets. Surprised and overwhelmed from the rear, the guards were trapped, helpless, and easily routed.

As he rushed around the corner with his group, Cyn's voice called out, "Damn, you guys aren't prisoners. Have you seen any?"

"You haven't found them?" Prymack said, lowering his weapon.

Cyn shook his head. "No, sir. We circled around. Nothing."

Prymack clicked on the mic from his headset. "Has anyone found the prisoners?" He paused, listening closely to a reply, then relayed it to the others. "They found a central room barricaded on the first floor."

Cyn started down the stairs.

"Wait!" Prymack examined the interior wall behind them, tapping it in a few spots. "This wall should lead to it."

Pollo handed him a charge.

The others moved behind cover and waited. Through his headset, Nathan listened to the battle taking place on the first floor, though he couldn't discern any voices.

"Joesee, can you get in to lay a charge?"

"Negative. They have it covered."

"Then roll in a grenade!"

An explosion roared into the headset.

"Got it—it's clear. Joesee, set it!"

A few moments of gunfire passed before they heard anyone else.

"It's set. Go, go! Tap it!"

The floor under them trembled, vibrating up Nathan's body.

"Flashfire," Prymack said, and the group crouched. As he hit the detonator, the explosion blew a hole three meters across, sending debris flying.

Nathan sprang up through the breach, opened by the blast. Prymack grabbed his arm and pulled him back.

"Stay behind me," he said, then charged through the smoking gap, followed by Pollo and the rebels from Cyn's group. Nathan trailed behind them, and Nur took up the rear.

The smoke burned his eyes as he passed through. Once clear of the opening, he saw a balcony that formed a complete circle. Its inner wall was made from immense glass windows that overlooked a central room forty feet below.

The place was in complete chaos. There were no boundaries, no clear picture of who was where. It was a dizzying battle of scattered shootouts and hand-to-hand combat.

Prymack and Nur charged to the right. Nathan was about to follow, but his eye passed over Sundiis. A Meraki soldier had him pinned on the floor with his arm back, knife in hand.

Not wanting to risk a shot that might hit Sundiis, Nathan charged over to the struggling pair and punted the Meraki in the ribs. It wasn't anything Duma had taught him, just instinct, from years of soccer. The man's ribs collapsed from the force, knocking him off Sundiis and into a writhing ball.

A laser pulse fired past Nathan's leg, slicing through his pants and searing his thigh. Spinning, he raised his pistol and squeezed off two rounds at the shooter, who dropped dead to the floor.

More prison guards poured down the hall in a stream from the left, charging into the chaos, outnumbering the rebels by what seemed like two to one.

Nathan killed the lead guard with two slugs to the chest. But before he hit the floor, two more rushed in. The next one he crippled with a quick strike to his throat. The third he dropped with a kick to the ribs.

As the situation unfolded, he started getting overwhelmed and what felt like a hammer hit him in the side. With a shoulder driving into his ribs and arms wrapped around him, he was slammed into the glass. Another guard moved in and whipped a baton against his hand. The stinging pain forced him to drop his weapon, which skipped off his leg and fell away.

Nathan brought a free elbow down into the first Meraki's back, causing him to crumble instantly. Then, he stomped the knee of the other, folding it backward.

Swiftly sliding past them, he kept an eye out in case either still had fight in them and noticed that this new wave of guards was armed solely with batons. He also noticed there were no familiar faces in the crowd. Somehow, he'd gotten ahead of everyone else.

Remembering Cyn's words about Jiinmaru, Nathan attacked in a circle, moving outward. As another came at him, he grabbed the guard's wrist and twisted. Feeling the crack of bone, Nathan slid by him, striking out at the next nearest Meraki, trying not to expose his back to any of them. If he didn't keep moving, they would overtake him.

Six Meraki guards now surrounded him.

The first fell when Nathan smashed him with a groin kick. After that, he blitzed through the soldiers in a whirlwind of techniques etched into memory. A kinetic frenzy of elbows, fists, knees, and feet followed. The onslaught was simply a haze in his mind.

Surprised by a blow to his chest, it sent him reeling back toward the window. An additional Meraki crouched low and charged him like a linebacker.

Off balance and distracted by pain, Nathan knew he was going to get hit and hit hard. A second before impact, the guard put his head down, exposing a brief opportunity.

Shifting all his weight to his back leg, Nathan halted his momentum for a split second. Then, like a spring, he popped his knee straight up, catching the guard full in the face. The impact rocked his head and shattered teeth, leaving Nathan more off balance than before as he fell backward.

Grabbing at the dazed guard, Nathan pulled him along. Falling to his back, he pushed his foot against the guard's stomach. The force of his kick and the backward momentum flung the guard over him and into the glass.

The window flexed momentarily before the weight of the soldier's body shattered it. Shards of glass sprayed everywhere. Slivers flung back toward Nathan, slicing into his cheek. The guard fell, surrounded by an aura of jagged glass, crashing into the room below.

Nathan twisted to his feet. The rest of the soldiers lay incapacitated around him. He didn't recall taking them out, but he must have. Everything had happened in a blur, as if his instincts had completely taken over.

Through the broken window, he spotted Prymack and Nur across the gap on the other side of the circling balcony. Heavy fighting had caught up to them as well.

Peering down into the center room, he witnessed a chaotic scene below. As the rebels pushed into the chamber, a mounted laser cannon unleashed its fury on them. The deafening roar of the weapon sent shudders through the air.

His instincts told him to join the fray, but the soldier he'd flipped through the window had attracted some attention. During all the fighting, he'd been oblivious to the elevators that connected the room below, but now they lit up, announcing even more company.

Nathan collected a rifle and two clips as lasers started whipping past him. He estimated five Meraki soldiers coming from each side, pinching in on him.

Springing off his back leg, he darted toward the shattered window, pausing only to fire a zipline. If this didn't work, he would most likely plummet to his death, but right now, it seemed his only choice. The bolt hit the ceiling over the central room, solidly piercing the metal. In his hand, the gun whirled as it reeled in the extra slack, yanking the zipline taut.

Nathan locked the cable as a laser bolt struck him in the thigh, searing his flesh. He clenched his jaw, attempting to control the pain. This already wasn't looking good.

Sucking in the anxiety the situation triggered, he leaped out of the shattered window. The floating emptiness that followed induced a strange air of euphoria. For a moment he was no longer concerned with the deadly lasers that were streaking past him, his focus was fixed to simply hanging on.

With the zipline gun in one hand and a laser rifle in the other, he swung like the pendulum of a giant grandfather clock. His vision blurred from the pain in his leg and the dizzying motion of the swing.

At the bottom of the downward arc, his momentum was at its strongest, and the weight of the gun pinned his finger tight against the trigger, causing it to fire continuously. At that point, he couldn't discern which hand held the zipline and which the rifle. Closing his eyes, he put all his energy into clenching his hands and holding on.

Gradually, the forces pulling him apart relaxed, and he opened his eyes again. Now on an upward swing, he was heading irreversibly into the glass window where Prymack and Nur had been moments before. Seeing this, he tucked his head, gritted his teeth, and waited for impact.

※ ※

Prymack squeezed off two more shots at the Meraki who had just backhanded Nur to the floor. Blood spurted on the glass as he nailed the soldier in the head and chest.

Nur was just getting up when the window behind her exploded into shards. An unidentifiable mass came flying through and slammed into a Meraki guard, crushing him against the wall. Prymack crouched instinctively at the sound, putting up a hand to shield Nur from the shattering glass.

The color of the object matched the blue rebel armor, but what was a rebel doing flying through windows on the fifth floor? Rushing over to the unknown soldier, Prymack immediately identified him as a flash lit the room up from Nur, gunning down an enemy soldier behind him.

"It's Stryder," he said, appraising him. The man was unconscious, but thankfully still alive. Grabbing the nearest rebel, he pulled her down to the floor with him.

"Ven, take him to cover."

Vendala glanced down at Stryder before her eyes quickly returned to Prymack's. "We're already outnumbered in here."

"Get him out of here!" he said as two lasers darkened the wall over his head.

"Heard," she said, slinging her rifle and grabbing his wrists.

"Nur, give her cover!"

Prymack picked up the extra rifle that had flown in with Nathan, gripping it in his off-hand. Using both weapons, he stood up and swept the enemy's position in a merciless barrage of automatic projectile rounds and laser bursts. His intended targets dove quickly for cover. Nur joined in, adding her weapon to his suppressing fire.

Vendala struggled past them and made it safely out with Stryder in tow.

Prymack gathered the remaining rebels from the balcony. He needed to regroup downstairs with the rest of his soldiers. The battle would be won on the first floor. With nine of his soldiers by his side, he did a quick calculation and found roughly sixty were unaccounted for—much more than he'd been prepared to lose.

"Everyone in the lift!" he said, giving them cover fire.

Acting promptly on the command, his soldiers rushed into

the elevator. Then he fell back to join them. It was a tight fit, but they all made it.

"Pollo, I need a ten-second burn!"

Niikapollo activated an incendiary device and tossed it out the door. Then Nur stabbed at the panel, and the elevator quickly closed. The queasiness that always accompanied a quick descent sprang into Prymack's gut.

Above, Niikapollo's fire-bomb detonated, unleashing a towering column of flames in both directions, engulfing the circled balcony. The destructive blaze roared through, devouring everything combustible in its path. Its sudden heat blew out every window on the floor, sending a shower of broken, splintered glass to the raging battle below.

Once at the bottom, the rebels streamed out of the lift in a tactical formation. Prymack glanced up at the balcony, making sure the firebomb did its job. Scanning the room, he quickly took inventory of the situation. With his reinforcements, they took control of the space.

"There's about ten of them left, sir," Joesee said, pointing to a corner. "We have them pinned behind those cells. The locking controls for the rest of the cells are back there too."

Prymack nodded. "Outstanding work."

Then, without warning, the remaining Meraki soldiers threw out their weapons and called out their surrender. They came out, hands raised in an orderly and uncharacteristically docile fashion.

With a circular motion of his hand, Prymack signaled the rebels to gather the remaining soldiers. "Open them up."

A hydraulic whine echoed in the room. As the black cell doors lifted, a yellow fog drifted out of each one.

"Gas!" Prymack called out. "Get back! Find the fans. Get some ventilation in here."

A minute later, a distant whirl began gathering the gas in an upward cyclone. As the cloud lifted, the bodies of the prisoners became clear. Their skin was blistered and, in some places, melted to the bone. Blood ran from their bodies—not from any distinguishable wounds, but from everywhere.

A devastating coldness filled Prymack's stomach, and his mind went numb. He could not fathom the wickedness it had taken to do this. Nur and Cyndron both had to turn away, as did most of the others. Only the hum of the fans kept the room from complete silence.

Nur stepped up to Prymack and placed a hand on his arm. His mind was in a daze and barely registered it. He took a step toward a cell, but she pulled on him to stop.

"Prymack, don't," she pleaded.

He shook her off and continued. Reaching the first body, he kneeled down next to it. The eyes of the corpse were burned and bulged inhumanly out of the skull. It would have been impossible to tell who or what it was if he hadn't already known.

With his mind completely out of focus, Prymack shifted from body to body until he found something he recognized. On one of the corpses, he found—a small emerald with a lightning bolt etched in it. The surface was worn smooth from years of rubbing. He'd given it to Deluca for luck. As he turned it over in his hand, memories of that day filled his mind.

There was a hand on his shoulder—it was Nur again. She led him back out, away from the horrifying scene.

A rebel's voice echoed through the cells. "We have a survivor!"

Within five minutes, three groups reported back to Prymack. They had swept the building, recovering their remaining wounded. Everyone was accounted for.

He gathered the Meraki captives inside a large cell, then returned outside to check on Stryder's status. While still unconscious, he was strapped to a gurney, and seemed stable.

"Cyndron." Prymack's voice took on a dark tone.

"Yes, boss."

Prymack paused, peering into Cyndron's eyes. "Take a group and blow this place. Leave nothing standing."

"What about the prisoners we took?" Cyndron's gaze darted to Nur and back to Prymack.

Prymack turned away. "We don't take prisoners."

"But, we can't—"

"Let them burn." Prymack turned back to Cyndron, a wild fury flaring within him.

Cyndron's eyes shimmered with disbelief. "I can't."

"There are no innocents inside that prison! They invaded our world. They invaded our lives. They killed our loved ones. The same goes for any collaborators that sold us out. They all had a choice to fight this war. We didn't."

He knew Cyndron didn't agree, but Prymack's job was to make sure they would never kill again. Everyone in there was the enemy—the same enemy who was trying to destroy them.

Cyndron remained defiant.

Prymack turned away. "Joesee, blow the prison."

Nur was in agreement, he knew. She had expressed herself many times to him in the past. She hated every last one of the Meraki for destroying her life. They all deserved to die for what they'd done.

With the structure in flames, Prymack ordered the rest to fall back into the forest.

✶ ✶

Arista saw the smoke from ten kilometers away. Drawing back on the throttle, she slowed her velocity as she approached the prison. She could see nothing on the ground from this side of the blaze, but knew it was too late. Her troops would not get here in time.

Zooming into the corridor of smoke rising into the air, she hoped to find a trail to the rebels on the other side. The thick haze curled around her fighter's sleek hull as she passed through the curtain of soot.

Now without obstruction, she found exactly what she wanted: Kavkin rebels. Four lines of the radicals who'd attacked the prison were retreating east toward the cover of the forest. They scuttled like bugs, their lines broken and uneven. *Not a sign of disciplined soldiers*, Duma would say. But uniform lines were the least they had to worry about now.

Seconds after emerging from the smoke, Arista opened fired on the unorganized strings of rebels. They scattered as her blasts tore up chunks of dirt and grass.

A flash to her right grabbed her attention—ground missiles launching! Lights and alarms from the dashboard alerted her to the incoming dangers.

Igniting the maneuvering jets under her right wing, she jerked to the left, easily dodging the first one. Flipping an overhead switch, she activated the countermeasures.

Flares, chaff, and electronic decoys sprayed out in a swirl of colors from the fighter's wings to confuse incoming missiles. Then, diving in lower, she undercut two others while getting a better shot for herself.

Tapping the panel to her right, she switched on the HUD tag assist. Now, the ship's weapons locked onto everything she focused on. One by one, she picked off the missile operators, evading their missiles as she did.

After her first pass, she'd taken out four launchers. Then quickly tried to angle for another run before they reached the trees.

Her body slammed to the right as a missile detonated with one of her countermeasures. The blast rocked her ship. Its response convinced her that at least one engine and possibly a stabilizer had sustained damaged.

Arista struggled to maneuver the fighter into a hard turn,

attempting to escape the danger zone. She risked further damage if she continued her assault in this condition.

She peered out the window and quickly surveyed the situation. Most of the rebels had already taken cover under the forest canopy, which left her with nothing else to target. Leveling her craft, she headed away from the battle.

"Lieutenant Commander Arista Conak of the Meraki Navy reporting from Roget Prison," she said into her radio. "The rebels have destroyed the prison. They've retreated east along the forest line. I suggest the unit dispatched to the prison pursue."

She glanced to her right, taking in the burning prison. Then, lowering her head in frustration, her eyes skimmed over the starburst scar on her hand. She'd been avoiding its pull, afraid of the thoughts and feelings it might trigger if she allowed herself to linger on it. But they were there, regardless.

Stryder had helped her to open up and realize that there were more than missions and combat to her. Because of that, she'd rediscovered another side of who she was, one she thought was lost. She dared to touch on the idea of ever seeing him again. Was he one of the rebels fleeing into the woods, or had she just killed him on the battlefield? And if that was the case, how much would it hurt?

Then Arista's training took over and Duma's voice flooded her mind. *"A good soldier feels nothing: no pain, no pity, no sorrow. No remorse. Those are the things that make you hesitate. Those are the things that get soldiers killed."*

Her feelings were like a live wire right now. If she wanted to survive, it was best to shut them down.

"Returning to Fettis," she said into her comm.

CHAPTER 36

Nathan awoke in bed. The last thing he remembered was crashing through the glass, convinced he'd made a terrible mistake. The entire right side of his body ached like one enormous bruise. That side of his face stung, too. The heat from the laser had cauterized his leg wound, so he didn't have to worry about it bleeding, but it still kept him in constant pain.

"Feeling better?" Vendala said, from a chair next to his bed. Her arm was in a sling, and there were crutches leaning against the wall.

Behind her, a large window looked out at the sea floor. Aquamarine water disrupted by a rising stream of bubbles told him they were back at Riid's base.

Nathan pushed himself up, causing a flare of pain. "I guess. What happened to you?"

"I was shot dragging you out of the prison. Are you hungry? I made you a plate." She handed him a bowl of food from the table next to her.

"Thank you. Looks like I owe you one dragging. You alright?"

"It'll heal. I'm not so sure about your face, though." She grinned.

He put a hand to his face, forgetting how much it still hurt, triggering even more pain.

Vendala chuckled. "Don't worry, you're still a tagat."

"I'll take that as a compliment."

"You do that." She winked. "Now eat."

After eating and getting around, he looked at his face in a

mirror. The right side was deeply bruised from chin to cheekbone. Then he walked the underwater compound, looking for Prymack or Nur. He ran into Cyn, who was much quieter and more evasive than normal.

Nathan was relieved, at least, that all the rebels he knew had made it through the battle alive. It made him think about all they had lost—how this war was all-or-nothing for them. And now that he was part of it, it was the same for him.

Soon, he gave up his search for Prymack or Nur and moved to a firing range, which he found to be the least painful training he could do. The rebels had no medicine or drugs that he knew of that were even close to the technology of the G-booster or ZIPR shells the Meraki had used. He would have to deal with the pain until natural healing ran its course. It had been quite a while since he'd had to tolerate the inconvenience.

It was past sunset when Prymack and Nur found him in the firing range. They led him to a private room and closed the door.

"How did it go?" Nathan said. "The last thing I remember is swinging into that window."

"We found the prisoners held in that nightmare." Prymack pulled a chair out for him to sit. "But we were too late. The Meraki had gassed them. Only one survived."

He heard the words, but they didn't make sense. Slowly, he sat down.

"What? Why?

"They're evil, Stryder. Ruthless. Anything that opposes them is imprisoned and killed. Expect the same for us—or you—if they ever catch us."

Nathan held his tongue. He'd once been one of them, and Arista still was. They couldn't all be like that.

"Did we take any of them alive? They could—"

"No, we have no room for prisoners. We can barely support ourselves. We destroyed the prison camp when we left, so it couldn't be used again for atrocities."

Nathan nodded. "Do you think that this was an isolated incident?"

"No, I'm afraid I don't. Ever since they invaded, they have executed us. Even after the public executions stopped, people have disappeared, taken from their homes—family and friends of the people you fight alongside."

Nathan recalled the pain upon hearing the news of his parents—the shock, depression, and anger. Is that what they faced every day?

"If you're still wondering about the ruthlessness of the Meraki, if you're fighting for the right cause or not, I'll tell you a story." Prymack turned to Nur, who had remained silent. "Could you get us something to drink?"

She nodded and quietly left the room.

"I don't know if I want to hear any more stories," Nathan said, watching the door close behind her.

Prymack took a seat across the table from him. "It was just over six years ago, when the Meraki were planning to invade. A young couple lived in a world of peace with their first child. On his fourth year, there was a small clan celebration. During the feast, a group in battle masks and unmarked uniforms stormed the hall. It was unknown at the time, but they were Meraki agents.

"You see, Dane, the husband, was a high-ranking military intelligence officer, and the Meraki needed codes to disengage the satellites that would warn us if any alien presence had entered our system.

"The group took the hall easily and tortured Dane. Knowing that more than his or his family's lives were at stake, he didn't give them the codes. His only thoughts were to warn someone, to escape. They took a hammer to his knee, but Dane held out. Then they started killing his kin, one by one, until they reached his child."

Prymack paused at this point and stared at him, but all Nathan could see was Susan's body. The implications haunted him. Could he have turned into that had he not broken away from Duma?

"When Dane found the opportunity," Prymack continued, "he killed two of the assailants and grabbed his wife. He knew she could carry a warning, so he made sure she would escape. He sent her to find his commander, to warn them, while he held the agents' attention. The woman escaped, even though her life was shattered. Running from the house, she heard the shots. Her baby was dead, along with her husband."

A cold nausea seeped into Nathan's stomach.

"The Meraki see our lives as expendable, Stryder. They see us as inferior. They will let nothing get in their way of crushing us into submission."

Prymack stopped talking as the door opened and Nur stepped back in with two glasses and a picture of water. When she sat down again, Prymack exchanged glances with her, which seemed to communicate something. She hadn't said a word while they were in the room.

Nathan looked at her again, and for the first time, he saw it. Behind the anger, behind the hate, he saw the sadness. He was convinced Prymack had just told her story. He'd sent her away to spare her from reliving it. Nathan was no longer fighting for himself. Or for Susan. He was fighting for Nur, for the fate of millions like her.

There was a fragile silence for a moment before Prymack spoke again.

"But now, we have to look ahead, to prevent this type of thing from spreading to other planets. To do that, we have to start by freeing Kavka."

Nathan nodded. He understood that now.

"We need to speak with the surviving prisoner to see what she knows," Nur said, her first words since they entered the room. "The only problem is we don't know her language."

"I might—with the translator." Nathan tapped his ear.

They made their way to one of the far-end rooms in the bunker. Inside was a large water tank with glass sides. Walking up to the tank, Nathan spotted something moving underwater.

Through the murky shadows, he could barely make out what it was. When they said "survivor," he'd thought that implied a human, like everyone he'd seen so far on Kavka.

The creature's skin was gray and hairless, camouflaging it in the water and reminding Nathan of a dolphin. It had lower appendages that resembled legs, except a thin patch of skin stretched between them to give the creature momentum in the water. Its upper body had evolved similarly to a stingray's, with large, flexible wings that ended with three thin finger-like digits. Its face and head were smooth and long, with no sign of a nose. From head to feet, it was about a meter and a half in length.

"She is what we call an Esly," Prymack said. "They live in the oceans of Kavka, though we've never had much contact with them. They prefer to avoid us."

"So far, she hasn't said anything," Cyn reported. "Not even a noise."

Prymack motioned to the pool. "Stryder, you're on."

Nathan stepped toward the tank, leaning in as she swam by.

"Does she even come out of the water?"

Cyn shook his head. "Not voluntarily."

The Esly swam around the edge of the pool in a large circle. During her next lap, Nathan put his hand in the water, and she halted at the intrusion. Her legs drifted underneath her. Curiously, she approached his hand, looking it over with expressive eyes. Nathan wiggled his fingers briefly, causing her to dart back, showing no effort or friction in the water.

"She's not going to bite me, is she?"

No one had an answer.

Again, she approached his hand. He held it steady this time. She reached out her webbed fingers and poked it. Gently, she wrapped three fingers around his hand and squeezed. Her head floated to the surface, breaking it without a ripple. Her oversized blue eyes peered around from person to person, curiously. After a few moments, she slipped back underwater again.

"Not much of a talker, is she?" Cyndron said.

Still gripping Nathan's hand, she jerked backward, dragging him off-balance and into the tank. Bubbles fizzed up everywhere, and cold water rushed up his nose as he recoiled at the sudden realization that he was underwater.

Kicking his feet, Nathan tried to regain his equilibrium. He pushed off the bottom of the tank and darted upward. Just before he broke the surface, he heard a quick series of short, high-pitched noises.

"What happened?" was the first thing he heard as he reached the surface, though he wasn't sure who said it.

"I think she's laughing at me!"

"That's good. At least she's not trying to eat you." Cyn snapped his jaw closed, making a chomping noise.

"Eat me?" Nathan looked at Prymack, who looked at Cyn.

"Cyn, stop it," Prymack said in a lighthearted voice. "She won't eat you. Get back under. Try to talk to her that way."

Nathan, eager to understand the creature, was under before he'd finished the sentence.

"Who are you?" she said. Her voice echoed all around him.

As he attempted to answer, his throat filled with water. It pushed its way into his mouth and down his throat. He instinctively swam back to the open air again and coughed out the liquid. Cyn was hushed before he could comment.

Back underwater, Nathan tried again. Keeping his throat closed, he spoke. A distorted, gurgled voice came out in a plume of bubbles.

"I am Nathan. Who are you?"

"Wild Dreams." She paused briefly. "Will you take me home?"

"Yes, I will take you home."

"Please."

He balanced his weight in the water. "How did you get captured?"

She stared at him.

The water around Nathan grew warmer, and images gradually filled his head. He was her, Wild Dreams, and he was climbing out of the water to a rocky shore. A large building stood twenty meters inland, and he could feel her curiosity. As she approached, her skin was already starting to dry out and tingle.

She reached a hill and could see a couple of Meraki working on a small fighter-sized ship with no thrusters. It was triangle shaped, with what looked like a cockpit in the middle and a half dozen stabilizing fins on the back.

A shout to her right sparked fear. Wild Dreams ran back toward the water, but was overcome with fatigue and fell to the ground. Several hands grabbed her.

Nathan blinked and went up for air.

"Stryder, what happened?" Cyn said with a wild arm gesture. "You were down there two minutes!"

"I don't know," he gasped. "I was seeing her memories."

Nur raised her eyebrows. "Like what?"

"I can't explain." He took another deep breath and slipped back underwater.

"When will you take me home?" Wild Dreams floated effortlessly still.

"As soon as we can. Can you take us to that place? Where you were captured?"

"Then you will take me home?"

"Yes, Wild Dreams, then I will take you home."

Nathan surfaced and raised himself to the edge of the tank.

"She's taking us to where she was captured. It could be a hangar. I think I saw one of your fighter planes."

Prymack smirked. "Excellent. First, there is someone we have to meet."

✶ ✶

Major Mir, a rather squirmy man, had finally arrived an hour late, much to Arista's annoyance. She'd had to put her efforts on hold to wait for him. He supposedly had connections inside the rebel forces and could tell her where they were.

Without him, she had no clue where Nath—She mentally scolded herself—where *her target* could be.

"Where are they?" She had no time for introductions.

Mir wore a calm expression. "Fettis."

"Now? Still?"

"Yes, sir." He held out the coordinates on a vid-board.

She snatched the device and quickly skimmed the coordinates. "How do you know that?"

"Sorry, sir. That's classified." His manner was frustratingly calm.

Besides Duma, she wasn't used to knowing less than others. Only the gods knew all the secrets he kept, and it wasn't something she liked.

She marched past Mir, then paused and turned to face him. "You will follow me everywhere from now on."

Mir nodded. "Yes, sir."

Arista gathered her soldiers, and they were ready to move in ten minutes. She rode in the lead vehicle, which was much bumpier than she was used to. As with the fighter, it had been a long time since she'd ridden in anything that didn't use anti-gravity.

It was a twenty-minute ride to the bunkers where the enemy was hiding. They stopped the vehicles a kilometer away. Scanning the layouts, she saw several entrances. Which ones the rebels had sealed off since making it their base was just a guess.

Arista wasn't one to command soldiers. She gave that up to the unit's colonel. He surrounded the area and swept into the bunkers like he had done this a hundred times before.

She was fifth through the hatch. But, by the time she got inside, several rebels were already dead, and the alarm was screaming. It echoed against the hardened walls, which increased the pitch and volume. Quickly, she snaked through seemingly endless halls, with a handful of her soldiers in tow.

They had entered from three points, moving to converge on a large hall, where hopefully the main rebel force would be. The blueprints were old, and the rebels had probably redesigned it for their purposes, so there was really no telling what they might run into.

Movement to Arista's right caught her eye, and she swiftly sprayed the area with lasers. Return fire echoed loudly, ripping into the wall behind her as ingrained reflexes took over, and she rolled to the floor.

Two Meraki soldiers rushed to help. The first tossed in a halo grenade. A series of powerful blasts quickly cleared the room. After the explosions ceased, she jumped to her feet and rushed in. Eyes trained to ignore the consequences of war surveyed the result. With conflicting emotions, she realized that none of the mangled bodies were her target.

The next two rooms were empty, and frustration set in. She had exhausted herself looking for Stryder and was always a step behind. As she reached the door for the next room, it flung open, catching her off guard. Two rebels came bolting out, stopping when they saw her.

The first slashed at her with a blade, which she easily ducked and countered with a hook to his ribs. The second rebel didn't have time to react before she side-kicked him in the throat and he fell backward, grabbing at his neck. Two shots from her sidearm instantly killed them both.

Sweeping through the rest of the bunker, she found nothing. By the time she reached the main hall, the battle there was over.

The Colonel glowed with pride. She didn't need to guess what he was thinking—he would get a promotion for this.

"Our intelligence was excellent, Lieutenant Commander. We have two prisoners." He gestured with open arms.

"Let me see them," she said.

The Colonel signaled for them to be brought in. Two scraggly rebels approached, stripped of armor and weapons. She recognized neither.

"Search the bunker again," she snapped. "We can't afford to miss him."

He waved away her concern. "We just took out a major rebel force. I don't think losing this one unknown rebel is anything to worry over. But to ease your pretty little head, I'll leave a group here to search while we drag the rest back to identify them."

The words made her want to rip out his throat, but she kept her temper in check. He resented her for the authority she had, and that was just his way of getting back at her—belittling her, just like Prinji. They were the same breed. But Arista didn't kill for revenge. She did it in self-defense or because she was ordered to. If not for the war, her hands would have much less blood on them.

Damn the High Command for starting it.

✳ ✳

The rain had come and gone several times in the last hour as Nathan, Prymack, and Nur waited under a partially destroyed awning on the porch of a burned-out bakery.

Before them, sprawled out across four city blocks, was an open-air market. The area was less damaged and more functional than Brevetta. Up and down the street were shops and booths filled with unfamiliar foods. Others sold handmade items as civilians did their best to survive, despite the war around them. To Nathan, the air smelled like a carnival.

Despite the rain, there were probably a thousand people buying and selling goods. There was a sense of normalcy for these people, but the soggy weather was getting rather irritating to Nathan. It reminded him of his parents' funeral. That alone was enough to unsettle him, and now they were waiting for someone who was already late and could be setting them up.

"How long are we going to wait?" Nur asked, apparently just as uneasy as he was. "I feel exposed out here."

"Easy, love." Prymack patted her back. "Sometimes these people are sketchy, but Riid vouched for her."

Nathan scanned the crowd, watching as Meraki soldiers patrolled the market. Being this close to them caused the vise in his chest to tighten. While his skin wasn't tinted orange, and he didn't have a bone head wrap, Prymack assured him he would blend in using the rain cloak he'd given him, which about half the people were wearing, including Nur and Prymack. Even so, he touched the handle of the rifle hidden beneath his cloak, making sure it was still there.

"It'll be okay. Both of you need to breathe." Prymack turned to him. "Stryder, you've been sighing every other minute. You sharp?"

"I'm fine. Riid said she would have something to read the datagem?"

"Not exactly. But this is the Fettis bazaar." Prymack waved his hand out. "On its surface, it's one of the busiest exchanges this side of Lyseum. Its underbelly, though, is the largest black market on the planet—the worst criminals, smugglers, and spies Kavka has to offer."

Nur gestured with her elbow. "That her? A streak of blue?"

A woman covered in a gray rain cloak hurried toward one

of the shops. A blue ribbon peeked out of a stack of boxes she carried, flapping in a cool breeze.

Prymack pushed off the wall and followed. Nur snatched Nathan's arm as he attempted to follow.

"We have to stay back. These people are twitchy. Give him five minutes."

They stood in silence, casually watching the Meraki patrols as they profiled the market pedestrians, occasionally stopping and searching their bags.

"So, what was your job, before this?" Nur asked, awkwardly breaking the silence.

It seemed like a lifetime ago to Nathan. It actually took him a second to remember.

"Nothing, really. I mean, I was a student, but then…" Just thinking of his parents and Susan was like daggers in his chest. He shook his head. "Then, it all got messed up."

"You've been through a lot in a short time, but I can't honestly tell you it will get easier."

Nathan searched her face, wondering if she knew all that he'd been through. After a brief silence, he decided to pry. "Why do you and Prymack fight so much?"

"It's a long story, Stryder. Sometimes things are better left unsaid." She cracked a piece of wood off the railing and threw it to the ground. "Right now, that applies to a lot of things."

Glancing down, he thumbed the starburst scar on his hand and let her avoid the question. There were things he didn't want to talk about either.

To his surprise, she began talking again. "You remind him of his son, you know."

"I don't need him to protect me."

"You have to understand what he's been through. Prymack was an accountant for the government before the invasion. His father was the templar of defense."

She paused. "Never mention this when he's around."

Nathan nodded.

"They blame his father for all this. The invasion, everything. I know it's insane to blame one man for an entire invasion, but that's what the world did."

"Why? What'd he do?"

"He sent our ships to investigate what he thought was a distress signal. No one could have known it was a trap. The Meraki wiped them all out—all the orbital defense we had.

"Prymack is possessed with making it all right again. He's clan, heart and soul, bearing the sins of his father. And he is constantly trying to save everyone and blaming himself when people die. He's great with numbers, but now that all those numbers are lives, he punishes himself for every one he loses."

Nathan pieced it together. "And some of those numbers take a lot of chances."

"Enough talk." She stepped off the porch. "Let's go."

Nathan followed, trying to inconspicuously stop his weapon from swaying under his jacket as he did.

Prymack emerged from one of the shops, talking quietly with a different woman. As Nathan and Nur approached, they picked up their conversation.

"Thank you. This won't be forgotten."

"No, Prymack. You're our last hope. Every day, we thank you. Please take a look at the pictures. There's a lot, but we're desperate."

"I will," Prymack promised, then turned and headed their way.

Nur motioned to a table where Cyn had been sitting and watching them. Nathan noticed Sundiis was also in the crowd behind him. Prymack nodded to Cyn, glancing at the pictures in his hand.

Cyn filled up three glasses from a jug of blue liquid and pushed his noodles into the middle of the table, an attempt to look as much like a family meal as possible.

As the three of them joined him at the table, Cyn was quick to speak.

"Pollo is pulling the track around. It'll be a minute."

Prymack nodded to him. "I've confirmed it. Those were our fighters Wild Dreams saw."

Cyn sipped his glass. "What's the big deal? They don't work."

"Think ahead, Cyn. If we can figure out why, then they would no longer have air superiority." Prymack slid the datagem over to Nathan. "They had nothing to read that. I'm sorry."

Nathan took the datagem and the disappointment that came with it.

"There's got to be some way to read it."

Nur ate some noodles. "Maybe the blockade runner can."

"Blockade runner?" Cyn tilted his head.

Nur and Prymack exchanged glances, then Nur nodded.

"A few months back, Drelmar sent us word he contacted a blockade runner to send us supplies."

"And you think this runner will be able to read this?" Hope rose within Nathan, but by now, he'd learned to moderate it. "That's—"

Heat abruptly rushed through his veins, and a crackling energy pooled in his chest, interrupting his thought. It was a feeling he'd grown familiar with—a sensation he'd once found comfort in. But right now, it was alarming. It was the intense awareness he felt when…

Arista was here.

"Stryder! What is it?" Nur asked, instantly on high alert.

Nathan jumped to his feet. His eyes darted around the crowd, twisting the market into a dizzying whirl as he scanned for her. He spotted four Meraki soldiers flanking their table.

"She's here!"

Prymack stood up, identifying the soldiers. "Shit! Cyn, get the truck!"

Nur, Prymack, and Nathan whipped out an arsenal from

under their cloaks. Handguns, rifles, and knives were now on full display.

The crowd scattered in a panic. Screams and cries of terror filled the market as people scrambled to get clear. Cyn darted away in the confusion.

Prymack opened fire on the soldiers a split second before they could respond, dropping one. Nathan kicked the table over and took up a firing position, killing another with a quick burst of his rifle, then switched targets and focused on the remaining two.

From a garden store, a man in an apron stepped out brandishing a shotgun and blasted a soldier in the back. Prymack waved the shopkeeper back inside as laser and plasma bolts tore up the table next to him.

Nathan dropped the last soldier, and the trio retreated slowly, watching the street for others that were sure to come. Then he spotted a familiar face in the distance. The man looked different, but his smugness was unforgettable.

The last time he'd seen Ajax was in the corridor with Drelmar, right before everything exploded. Now, the man was scarred and giving orders to a squad of soldiers. Two dozen of them fanned out, taking up tactical positions. This was not looking good. And he still didn't know where Arista was.

"Prymack?" Nur's voice was in a panic.

Prymack's face was stone, his eyes probing and calculating.

Ajax's voice boomed over the crowd. "Bury them!"

The soldiers unleashed a barrage of lasers. Nur and Prymack dove to the ground as Nathan dropped to a knee and fired at Ajax. If nothing else, he could blow the smirk off his face.

The shot missed, but it forced him to take cover.

Sundiis shrugged off his cloak, raising two pistols as he did. Alternating shots from each, the element of surprise allowed him to kill two Meraki trying to outflank him.

Nathan rolled right and squeezed off two shots into the

chest of the nearest soldier. In the chaos Nur and Prymack's rapid fire was thumping through the air. Laser bolts spit up dirt near him as he continued firing. He'd have to reload shortly. With a quick glance, he spotted a place that would provide some cover.

More gunfire roared around him as people from the market fired from shop windows and hidden corners at the Meraki soldiers. With some of the attention drawn from him and redirected at their new threats, Nathan saw his opportunity and sprang to his feet.

There was a droning buzz of havoc as the battle roared in all directions. In the middle of it all people were panicked civilians scrambling for safety. Nathan witnessed the shopkeeper Prymack had been talking with earlier slumped over a table, bleeding. The lady with the blue ribbon also lay dead in the street, the ribbon still fluttering in the wind.

He spotted Nur and Prymack and changed direction. Firing as he went, he made his way toward them.

"Fall back to the bakery," Prymack shouted at him.

Sundiis was moving their way as well when several lasers sliced through his chest and he tumbled to the ground. Still alive, he crawled toward his fallen weapon as a fatal shot struck him in the head.

With no time to process this, Nathan took a bead on the soldier. Then—

Arista charged out of the chaos and kicked the rifle from his hands. In the same stream of kinetic flurry, she disarmed Prymack and Nur as well.

Nur drew a knife and lunged at her but was immediately flipped into a booth, sending fruit scattering. Prymack followed up with a mixture of strikes, but was just as easily put down.

"Arista! Don't!" Nathan said. "Leave them out of it."

She turned and squared up on him. There was something

different about her. Her eyes had the gleam of an apex predator.

Orange energy began to crackle and glow in Arista's hands. "You brought this on them. On yourself!"

In disbelief, Nathan readied himself in a defensive stance. He'd never seen her fully wield the glow, the power, whatever it was. He knew what he could do with it, but he still didn't understand it, and on her—in this moment—it was frightening.

He didn't have time to fight her. They were outnumbered. He had to hope Nur and Prymack could escape while he stalled her.

Arista attacked in swift, fluid strikes, her hands surging. Nathan blocked and deflected them, escaping what he could only imagine was enormous power.

He risked a glance at Prymack, who was pulling Nur to cover, but it came at a cost. Arista caught him with a tricky combo that slammed into his chest.

His body seemed to glimmer on impact, but the blow still felt like a sledgehammer, knocking him back a good six feet. Struggling for air, he slipped her next attack and kicked her back leg out from under her, buying him enough time to catch his breath.

"You still don't believe me?" he shouted at her. "I found Susan. She was on the ship! She's dead!" He could feel liquid filling his eyes as the words, the thoughts of her lifeless body flooded his mind. "Duma knew! Did you?"

"Shut up and fight, Stryder!"

From his left came a deafening roar as a massive truck with tank treads rumbled out of an alleyway and lurched to a stop. Pollo manned a heavy-caliber gun mounted on the cargo bed.

There was a brief silence as everyone recalculated the situation. Then Pollo triggered the gun. It spit out metal in swarms, each shot sounding like thunder. He mowed down several of the Meraki soldiers with ease.

Arista dove into a doorway as the weapon swung her way, giving Prymack and Nur time to retreat.

Pollo paused his barrage so the pair could climb onto the truck. The sudden silence was eerily surreal. Nathan's eardrums were ringing, giving him a fuzzy, dreamlike feeling.

"Arista! It doesn't have to be like this," he said.

She stepped into the open and locked eyes with him, but neither spoke.

"Stryder, come on!" Nur called after him.

Nathan gazed at Arista, remembering the feelings he'd developed for her and wanting desperately to embrace them. But he knew it was impossible and reluctantly pulled himself away, climbing onto the truck.

She took a step toward them. Seeing this, Pollo swung the gun around to target her. He racked a round into the chamber, making a hefty metal *clunk* as a warning.

"No! Leave her," Nathan commanded.

Beneath him, the treads growled, and the truck drove off, leaving the confrontation behind.

Arista charged after them, moving quicker and quicker with each stride, until she was in a full sprint, her face emotionless and cold. There was no way she could catch them. Nathan sensed her pursuit was out of sheer frustration. After a few seconds, she slowed to a halt.

The onetime lovers remained locked in an unbroken stare as the truck sped away. Nathan held her gaze, unwilling to turn away until she was out of sight.

CHAPTER 37

THE CRYO CHAMBER that held HaReeka's body was covered in a fine layer of frost as Duma removed it from the entombment vault. It had been kept there until he'd caught up on all the additional duties of an admiral. Among them was to make sure anyone complicit in the destruction and mayhem Drelmar Vinn had caused was found and killed. At least, that was what he had told himself.

In reality, he'd avoided dealing with HaReeka and her funeral because he was afraid to look at her, to see what he had done to her. The warrior caste of Carcosa believed every life you took created a Fury that waited for you, a soul you had to confront before you could find peace in the afterworld. He wasn't a stranger to killing. A horde of Furies awaited him—too many to count—but HaReeka was unlike any before.

The chamber opened as he touched the panel, revealing all that he'd been dreading. As he gazed down on her lifeless body, he knew she had been the closest thing he'd come to feeling love for or being loved by.

And he'd killed her. He'd slid his knife through her ribs and silenced her heart.

But what was he to know about love or compassion? He had a command to fulfill, and she was in his way. It was as simple as that. He wasn't one of the fortunate who got to feel those emotions. They'd trained those out of him at an early age. And if he was honest with himself, they had been gone even before that. Those emotions were for the cattle, for people who didn't carry the burden of power, he told himself.

Sliding his arms under her one last time, he lifted her out of the cryo chamber and placed her into her military issued casket. Duma's movements were gentle as he relived moments of their time together in Sontarey. They had been the best times of his life. But in the end, it was not meant to be.

After setting her in the casket, Duma allowed his fingers to touch her face. The coldness stung, but it allowed him to feel the guilt and shame that he'd wanted to confront. Of all the lives he'd taken, this one touched the last remaining part of his soul.

From there, he leaned over and smoothed out her uniform, then straightened the medals that he'd placed on her chest. The blood stain from his deathblow would be impossible to hide, but he hadn't wanted to. She'd died in battle, like she desired, and he was proud of that.

Water dripped onto the medal of command she'd received from her first flight as a captain. He wiped it dry with his finger and looked up for the source of the liquid. Her body couldn't be thawing already. He felt it under his eye as it dripped again.

Shocked, he used his fingertips to rub any further tears from existence. With the same damp fingers, he pressed the button to seal the casket, leaving a faint impression of his fingerprints. A transparent shield slid over her body and hissed into place.

With deliberate steps, Duma walked the casket to the airlock, and punched in a trajectory to the nearest star. As the casket was exposed to space, the fingerprints froze, accompanying her to her final destination.

"Welcome to the Furies. You will be the hardest to face."

CHAPTER 38

Several days after the confrontation with Arista, Nathan was still reliving it.

He sat on the bow of a small boat, calmed by the sound of the water lapping against the hull. He took in the sky one last time before joining the others. It was close to dusk, and the first time he'd actually had a chance to watch a sunset on another world. The colors were just as stunning—teal, emerald, and yellow, mostly. But among the fading mosaic, he recognized the same rose hue of Arista's eyes, or perhaps he was just imagining it.

He glanced down at the starburst scar on his hand, the only thing he really had to remember her, and wondered if the market would be the last time he would ever see her. Shaking away the thought, Nathan focused on the present—the wind, the gentle rocking, the cold water around him.

They'd left Riid and his forces behind at Fettis and found the approximate location where Wild Dreams had been captured.

Slipping into the ocean, he gathered with the rebel strike force and prepared for the journey. To make the swim, they wore flippers, masks, and re-breathers that could recycle their breaths with no bubbles, the same way a Tanzi could.

They swam for an hour before Wild Dreams stopped and slid her head to the surface. When she came back under, the image she saw rushed into Nathan's mind like a current. It was night now, but they were finally there.

A small group swam with Nathan, Prymack, and Nur, to shallow water. One by one, they emerged, their heads and eyes breaking the surface, followed by the barrels of their automatic rifles. Rolling waves crashed over them as they made their way to the rocky beach. Wild Dreams watched from the sea, then swam back to lead the remaining rebels.

Nathan removed his mask and wiped the salty water from his lips as soon as he lifted the rebreather. He took in a deep breath of the brisk air, filling his nose with the smell of wet sand and seaweed.

To his right, a dock extended away from the gated compound. The main hangar was ahead. A spotlight from a dock tower arced their way, and Prymack signaled for everyone to take cover. Sliding behind an algae-covered rock, Nathan bumped elbows with Nur.

As the light swept by, a cool gust blew in from the water, spraying mist from the crashing waves over them.

"It's clear," Prymack whispered in the dim moonlight.

Nur slid out from behind cover first, followed closely by Nathan. The others emerged from the shadows after Prymack made a slicing gesture with his hand.

"Get the ziplines ready. We're going up there." He pointed to a spot on the wall facing them.

Replacing his wet suit and flippers with a zipline harness and combat boots, Nathan broke for the wall along with the others. There, they shot and secured three ziplines on the roof of the building.

"Pollo, Cyn, Nur, you first." Prymack checked his watch as each of the three rebels fastened lines to their harnesses.

"Stryder, Joesee, we're next. The rest of you, wait here."

Nathan attached his harness to the zipline and flipped it on. The device made almost no noise as the wheels ran up the line, carrying him with it. He held his breath the entire time, fighting the pain in his ribs from when Arista had nailed him in the market.

The roof was clear. The bodies of four sentries lay lifeless in the shadows. He doubted he would ever truly be used to death, but he seemed to handle it better as the days went by.

They searched the roof for a way in. The only option was an exhaust vent. Prymack put his headset on, switching bands.

"Send a breathing tank up here."

As they waited, Nathan strode over to the edge of the roof by Nur. "I'm sorry about Sundiis."

Her eyes scanned the ground, watching over the others and ignoring his words.

"Whoever the woman in the market was, she is your enemy. You must realize that now."

It was a harsh reality, and one he had been avoiding. It was a struggle Nur seemed able to easily pinpoint within him. She'd seemed so different when they talked at the market. There, she displayed emotion and understanding. Now, in the field, she was a different person—cold and battle hungry. He looked her over again. If the story Prymack had told him was about her, then she was justified.

"What did—" The moment he spoke, Prymack called for them. The scout had returned.

"Another time." Nur jogged over to the rest of the unit. Nathan followed.

"As soon as the rest get here, we're going in," Prymack said, offering no explanation.

"What's inside?" Nur pushed for an answer.

"Our missing fighters." Prymack handed his headset to Nathan, along with a long-range scope. "Take these and tell Pollo the minute they arrive."

Nathan nodded and returned to the edge of the roof to scan the shallows.

Thirty meters out from the shore, past the crashing waves, the water was calm and undisturbed. The wind had died down, no longer producing waves. The others would have gone unnoticed, waiting in the tide, unless someone was looking specifically for them, like he was.

They came up one by one at first, each just a slight bump on the gloomy surface of the water. But soon, he could see all ninety of the surfacing rebels as shadowy forms, like demons, rising from the murky depths. Their heads were draped with fine dark netting to conceal their silhouettes, displaying only tiny dots of light that pierced through the veils from their night-vision goggles.

Nathan relayed the news. "They're here."

The group came to the shore with no problem. In less than ten minutes, they were in position. Prymack had set up ten assault ropes on each side of the building. They would swing in through the windows, twenty at a time.

Nathan twisted his body slowly, stretching his bruised torso. His right leg and elbow were still a little stiff, too. This was going to hurt. Looking up, he saw Prymack approaching him and quickly covered up the fact that he was in any pain.

"Stryder, I want you to remain on the roof. You're not—"

"I'm ready," Nathan said. Duma had taught him to push past the pain, the bastard.

"No. I don't want to risk it. You're sitting this one out. We can take this easy." Prymack laid a hand on his shoulder. "Guard our fallback position."

He paused, looking Nathan in the eyes. "You're part of a *team*, Stryder. Tonight, this is your part."

Nathan answered with silence. Insulted, he turned and trudged toward what would be his guard position.

✳ ✳

Valor Krell Duma arrived at Sienna, a planet safely controlled by the Meraki Dominya. Since leaving Kavka, he'd ordered his ships to maintain their current positions, patrolling the High Command borders. Now, here, he could finally release control to the proper command. Someone who wanted to be a lord admiral.

He stepped off the airlock dock to meet a smug woman whose reputation he knew from Lord Admiral Lasal. Some would say her eyes twinkled with life, but Lasal had warned it was only power and greed. She had a long career in the military and then as an instructor prior to this.

"Ambassador Russo." Duma saluted.

The ambassador nodded. "I've heard so much about you, and I am pleased to finally meet you. The man who saw our might and surrendered your world to us so many years ago."

Duma remained silent. That was what they all wanted to talk about. They still believed he'd done it for them, to gain their favor. What would they say if they knew the true reason—to get revenge on the planet, the government, that had betrayed him and his team?

The Meraki invasion had been a perfect distraction. News of it had swept quickly over the planet like a brush fire. He'd heard it quicker than most. Katcha, his mole within the Executive Senate, had arrived at their command meeting bearing the dramatic news.

"They received a reply. They already translated it," he'd said. "They call themselves the Meraki Dominya, and they ask for our unconditional surrender."

Duma looked around the room at his fellow fugitives, observing them one by one. There was Jalin, a man just a few years older than him, who had once been an adversary. Next to him was Holker, one of three still left from his original command, brash and ever questioning. And Katcha, his best covert operative, who was worth more than his weight in platinum. The rest were still on watch, but he considered them as well.

"Just like that? Unconditional surrender?" Holker said.

Katcha handed Duma the official government plan of action. "The Senate voted to fight. They think they can win."

"No," Jalin said flatly. "They think they can inflict enough damage and cause enough casualties that it will be too costly for the Meraki. That it won't be worth the effort or resources."

Duma looked over the plans. "It might work. But it will cost our people millions of lives."

"We're in a tough spot. Both are our enemies." Holker shrugged helplessly.

Duma regarded Holker for a moment. "It's not as tough as it seems. The enemy of our enemy is our ally."

Suddenly, he was surrounded by blank faces.

He sat down, removed a thin piece of cloth from his pocket, and rubbed it between his fingers. It had once belonged to Sain, a man he'd known for a decade. A man who had been the closest thing he had to a family. A man whom their own government mercilessly killed while coming after him.

"The Meraki Dominya has done nothing to warrant becoming our enemy."

Holker asked the question that had changed everything. "So, what do we do, sir?"

This would affect them all, but they all had wanted it as badly as Duma. "We seize the opportunity. We reap our revenge. We overthrow the government."

"Don't you feel the least bit guilty?" Russo's voice brought Duma back to the present. "I mean, that's so many people. You signed their fate without thought or care for their well-being." She grinned in amusement and seemed to enjoy taunting him.

He calmly regarded Russo. "I knew none of them." He kept his icy glare on the ambassador for a long moment, searching her soul.

Russo straightened her robes and moved on. "I've heard rumors you had some problems on the *Kai'den*, yes? Lord

Admiral Lasal's death, of course, and the loss of Susan and Nathan Stryder from Project Asante. Any others?"

Duma said nothing. He knew the problems. Russo was just using them for leverage now, trying to intimidate him, but it wasn't working.

Two high-pitched clicks and a hiss came from the hallway behind Russo. Duma turned slightly to see two of the Vox. They were both of the warrior sect, or Ra'Jran—their robust, spiky contact suits gave that away instantly.

A raspy whisper came from the suit of the lead Vox. Lights gleamed on the suit's built-in translator before a metallic voice spoke.

"The status of the male Stryder. What transpired?" the lead Vox said.

Duma turned to address the Vox. Even among the elite of the Dominya, few knew of them. He knew only two others who did, or had: Ambassador Russo and Lord Admiral Lasal. At one time, he had thought about telling HaReeka. Perhaps if she'd known, they could have worked together and avoided the confrontation that killed her, but that was moot now.

The Vox were ancient, born in a time before most of the known planets had cooled. Their language was much more complicated than others and needed special translators. They secretly worked with the Meraki for their own purposes in exchange for advanced technology. Mostly, they were a mystery, but they gave him power and a purpose.

"The late Lord Admiral thought it best to release Nathan Stryder from the cryo-prison. He later escaped with the help of the saboteur. He knows about Susan and your involvement. I'm afraid there is no longer hope we can convert him with the same success as with the other."

"We didn't scour the galaxy to find him so he could be turned against us," Ambassador Russo injected before the Vox could respond.

Duma directed a stern gaze at Russo. It was doubtful she

had even read the prophecies. She was only out for personal power. There were no delusions about that. The Vox, however, lived by the prophecies, and it was the Vox that controlled the Meraki Dominya, not the Maelidor, like almost everyone believed. Duma could see that clearly. He knew the Vox's concern. He knew what the recent events had birthed. The prophecies had warned of it.

The Asante had been reborn, and they were losing control.

The second Vox whispered, and its translator lit up, processing it. "Eliminate Stryder."

"Understood," Duma said.

"Keetnelir?"

"Regretfully, I'm not sure how, but Keetnelir confronted Stryder and was killed."

"Remains?"

"There are no remains."

The Vox's translator lit up but said nothing.

"There wasn't much left of Keetnelir," Duma reiterated.

The lead Vox stepped forward, its translator whirling. "Arista Conak. Is she unobstructed? Clear of emotions?"

"Definitely clear. Her only thoughts are of killing Nathan Stryder." Duma had made sure of that. "He won't be alive by the time I return to Kavka."

"Make it so."

After Duma finished briefing Russo and the Vox, his orders came in via tightbeam from the Maelidor herself, who was no doubt heavily influenced by the Vox in her presence.

She promoted him to Grand Valor, a rank created for Duma to take command of the battle group. It was not what he wanted or what he had been trained for, but that was the order.

It would upset Ambassador Russo that the *Kai'den* wasn't given to one of the officers loyal to her, which would have put her in a powerful position within the Dominya. Duma really didn't care. He had his orders, and he would carry them out with efficiency. Duma reread the last line of the message once more, absorbing the Maelidor's intentions for the dreadnaught and its support ships.

"The subjugation of Kavka has taken too long. Return with the *Kai'den* and test the Deathwind."

CHAPTER 39

Arista was sleeping when her door buzzed. It was the first time she'd slept in what seemed like days. She didn't have a permanent room anymore. She went wherever Nathan's presence took her, which seemed to be all over the southern hemisphere of the planet.

As she sat up, she eyed the door through the darkness. The room was empty—just a bed, a lamp, and her bags. She'd left all her painting supplies in Brevetta in haste. Peeling off the enhancer from her temple, she climbed out of bed.

By the time she made it to the door, it had buzzed twice more. It could only be Mir. Not only did he have the worst timing, but he was also that annoying.

Sure enough, his slender figure showed up on the door monitor. The door opened when her finger pressed the release.

"Yes?" she said, making sure to relay her annoyance. His eyes looked deep enough to hide just about anything, and she was sure he took advantage of that.

"There was an attack off the shore of the Undercard Peninsula, sir. On the outskirts of Donnay. It's a secret holding base." He paused. "It's where we keep the fighters we captured from them."

"So? Their engines don't work."

"Yes, but as a precaution, we keep the fighters from them. Without reinforcements, we don't have enough air power here to control them if they ever get them to work again."

"So destroy them." She had maps to reference the cities

he'd talked about last time, but now she had no idea where Donnay was. Soon, she hoped, she would be off this planet.

"How far is it?" Arista said, her eyes moving to the clock.

"Too far. Six hours if we take the fighters. Commander Sculic has alerted the nearest base."

"Then why are you telling me this?"

"He wants you to return to Brevetta. He said he has a lead on Stryder."

She closed the door on him.

Life is so painfully ironic, she thought. The only person she could fall for was the man she had to kill. *Are you as eager to kill me, my love?*

She laughed quietly at the vicious irony, but that only brought forth tears. She'd never had pain like this before. It was worse than any knife wound or broken knee. Duma had trained her to suppress her emotions, which she always had until Nathan drew them out of her. At the time, they felt wonderful—tenderness, affection, acceptance…

And love?

Now, her emotions were out of control. Loss and emptiness radiated within her, at times turning to rage. Now she understood why Duma had wanted her to bury them.

Three hours passed before she could sleep again. Much was on her mind, but mostly it was Nathan.

✳ ✳

Nathan could hear the battle beneath him. Every gunshot stabbed at his pride, every explosion was Duma telling him he was too weak. He felt like the coach had sat him on the bench during the playoffs. This would not happen again.

Over the next five minutes, the battle died down. There was no word from Prymack, which no doubt meant that they had easily secured the hangar.

The silence grew, only interrupted now by an occasional

gunshot. Nathan ran a hand down his cheek and over his mouth, trying to pin down his thoughts.

He took a deep breath and exhaled through his fingers. He was convinced he was doing the right thing now, but at what moment had he become so eager to fight? It made him wonder if Arista had gone through the same transformation from civilian to warrior. He'd never really considered her motives, why she'd betrayed him to Duma, only that she had. Was it out of duty? Had she been tricked into thinking what she did was right, as he had?

"You coming down?" Prymack startled his thoughts away.

Nathan turned sharply at the voice.

"Easy, son," Prymack said, questioning his reaction. "What is it?"

The wind blew in from the water and ruffled Nathan's hair. He took in the salty breeze and exhaled slowly. "Nothing."

"If you're mad, it was for your own good. I would rather have you mad at me than dead."

"I know."

"What is it then?" Prymack moved a couple steps closer.

Distant waves crashed against the shore as Nathan organized his thoughts.

"When I was with the Meraki, I had friends…" He paused, not knowing how to say what he wanted.

"I understand. In war, we learn to hate our enemies, even if individually they could be our friends. I have the luxury of not knowing any Meraki personally. What I know is that they came here, they started this fight. They slaughtered us." He stopped to catch Nathan's eye. "You're fighting the cause, not the individual. It's the only way to fight a war."

Nathan took the words to heart and spent the rest of the night considering them. It was similar to what Duma had drilled into him, because he was hesitating. *We are not the judges—we are the executioners.* He could almost hear Duma's voice.

The next morning, they'd packed up the fighters and were leading a caravan of oversized trucks on a quiet back road from the hangar. Prymack and Nathan rode in an armored personnel carrier they'd seized in the raid as well.

Nathan gazed out the window at a cloudless sky that caused the morning to be brighter than usual, forcing him to squint. It seemed to alternate colors between shades of green and blue at different times of the day. He had no clue why, and he never bothered to ask.

Before they left, Nathan had submerged himself into the sea again to say goodbye to Wild Dreams. She'd swum around him excitedly, sending pictures of her home floating into his mind. He wasn't sure of their exact purpose, but he decided that her home was kept secret from outsiders, and revealing even part of it held a sacred meaning for her. He regarded it as a deep thank you for setting her free. He wished he could return the appreciation and send her something as sacred.

Then, he was back in Arista's quarters after the Tithe. A warm sense washed over him. Her smell was exhilarating.

Her voice sang with life. "Nathan, it's okay. I'm just toying with you. It means we have to kiss."

Nathan looked up into Arista's clear rose eyes as she placed a finger to his lips. It slid down his neck, then to his arm. Her touch felt incredible. Finding his hand, she held it.

As abruptly as it had begun, the image ended. Nathan blinked, looking around at the calm water. His lungs burned with stale air.

"You don't have to give me anything, Nathan." Wild Dreams floated in front of him.

"How did you do that?"

"You let your memories out into the water. I just sent them

back to you. I am in your debt. Swift currents, Nathan." Then she swam away.

"Wait!"

But far off, Wild Dreams disappeared into deeper waters.

A flash brought him back to the present, streaking across his vision and smashing into the road next to them. An explosion sent the truck swerving to the right, followed by a fighter roaring by overhead.

The engine revved as Prymack throttled up the speed and turned into the forest. The truck bucked violently, jostling Nathan around. Hopefully, the trees would give them some cover.

They plowed through the thick brush, making a wide path for the other trucks to follow. Prymack and Nathan were thrown around the cab of the truck, bouncing off the ceiling and doors, but somehow Prymack managed to keep control. It felt like one long, never ending car crash.

Prymack clicked on his headset. "Thunderbolt. I repeat. Thunderbolt."

Then he eased the truck to a stop and hopped out. Nathan followed, scanning the trees for Meraki who might be nearby. The rest of the vehicles had stopped as well, and everyone in them was now fleeing into the woods, each with a shovel.

Out of the corner of his eye, Nathan spotted something flying toward him. With no time to think, he snatched a shovel out of the air.

"Follow me," Prymack said and jogged into the forest. About twenty meters out, they stopped.

"What are we doing?"

"Hiding." Prymack stabbed his shovel into the dirt. "Now dig."

Ten sweaty minutes later, they had a two-meter-wide hole dug as Meraki jets crisscrossed above them.

During that time, other rebels had distributed panels of

wood to cover the holes. Piling thin layers of debris on top, they concealed them.

Nathan estimated there were now roughly twenty foxholes in a half circle facing the trucks. Dropping into the hole, he realized it was a lot smaller than it looked. The smell of wet dirt and leaves briefly brought up memories of gardening with his mother, and then the funeral.

Keep moving forward, he thought, before he got dragged into the past.

As Prymack slid the panel over their heads, most of the light disappeared.

"Why are we out here?" Nathan said.

"You tell me, Stryder. Why would we go out of our way to do all this?"

"To ambush the Meraki, but I don't think it's worth giving up the fighters for." Then it clicked. "Unless the fighters aren't in the trucks! We're a decoy. The trucks are empty."

"Not empty." Prymack pulled something out of his jacket.

Nathan recognized the detonator immediately.

"So they'll think the fighters are destroyed."

Prymack nodded. "Exactly. But there is another reason, too."

Nathan eyed him through the shadows.

"A leak. No one knows these trucks don't have the fighters in them, only Nur and me. Everyone else thought, as you did, that I was splitting the fighters up, and taking half while Nur took the other half."

"So whichever convoy got hit would rule out the other half of the team. Then you'd work from there."

Prymack gave him a nod. "You're a quick study, Stryder. It's all about numbers."

"But what makes you think there's a leak?"

Prymack covered Nathan's mouth, pointing up toward the surface. Moments of controlled breathing passed before they heard a twig splinter overhead. Light footsteps passed over them and continued onward.

Slowly, Prymack lifted the cover just enough to peek out. "Damn. What's taking them so long?" he whispered.

"Not them?"

Prymack lowered the cover before Nathan could see. "An animal."

They settled back into the foxhole.

"What makes you think there's a leak?" Nathan repeated, much softer this time.

"I lost contact with Riid. I can only assume they have been eliminated."

"Eliminated? All of them?" It had felt so safe. They'd just left a few days ago.

Prymack removed a bayonet from his pack and secured it to the end of his rifle. "Stay near me if we get into it. I know you can take care of yourself, but I still want you near."

Nathan nodded. "How do you know the spy, or whoever, didn't tell them what we are doing? That we're in these foxholes?"

"Thunderbolt is a standard tactic we train. No one knew we were going to do it until I called it out. Everyone is paired up with someone, so they couldn't reach out without the other person knowing."

Nathan shrugged. "Unless they killed their partner."

The sound of vehicle engines came up from the south, rising in the distance.

"Get ready," Prymack whispered into his headset.

Heavy vehicles rolled by, crushing the underbrush. As they came to a stop, the shuffle of feet replaced the tire noises on the forest floor.

"Search the trucks!" a woman's voice commanded.

Prymack elevated the panel with the end of his bayonet and observed their movement.

Nathan watched the man's thumb as it hovered over the

detonator. Any second it could drop. He felt his way up his rifle and flicked off the safety, hoping Prymack knew what he was doing.

Prymack snapped the trigger, and a roar of destruction followed, thundering through Nathan's body. The shockwave lashed out and jolted him against the dirt. A muted ringing filled his ears.

Prymack tossed off the cover and sprang up, bullets flying from his rifle. All around them, gunfire rattled and thumped, echoing from every direction. The Meraki soldiers, who weren't killed in the explosion, were staggered. They were completely exposed and dying quickly.

Trapped in the middle was the forest. The storm of bullets ripped apart its heavy undergrowth in a hail of leaves and bark. The leafy canopy above, which had been caught in the initial explosion, was now burning in a dome of fire.

Nathan's rifle jerked as he picked off a Meraki from behind them. Adrenaline sped through his body, enhancing his senses.

Along with covering their flanks, there was something else he was looking for. He searched the burning trees and skimmed the battlefield for Arista. If Duma was here, too, they were all dead. Thankfully, he didn't see her. More importantly, he didn't feel her either, like in the market.

Overhead, the burning canopy was breaking up. Flaming leaves drifted down on them in a lazy shower of fire.

Dropping another soldier, Nathan noticed movement from his right. A Meraki trooper jumped Prymack, knocking his gun to the side. Nathan drew his knife and instinctively forced it between the attacker's ribs and into his heart, killing him instantly.

"Ya good?" he called to Prymack.

Prymack nodded, picked up his gun, and called out to the rebels, instructing them to fan out in teams. They had the numbers now.

The remaining Meraki soldiers were scattered and easily overcome by the rebels. Nathan looked over the fallen, scanning the faces for Arista or Duma. It was a pointless act. He wasn't even sure why he did it. If either of them had been here, it would have been obvious.

"Wrap it up," Prymack ordered. "We have to catch up with the others."

✷ ✷

"Nathan Stryder." Ajax repeated the name as he sat at his desk, dissecting the sound of it. He somehow hoped it would help him understand what it was about this man that everyone placed such importance on. He wasn't from a powerful family, educated at an acclaimed school, or in line for royalty. He wasn't even from one of the core worlds of the Meraki Dominya. In fact, he was from a backwoods, self-obsessed planet that thought they were the only life in the universe.

Stryder was a charity case—a poor, unfortunate soul caught up in a war he knew nothing about. Yet Lord Admiral Lasal, and now Valor Duma, treated him with such significance it was vexing. Even Drelmar Vinn, Ajax's onetime mentor, and although he loathed to admit it—friend—had thrown his career away to help this insignificant, unappreciative refugee escape his sentence.

It was something. Something he wasn't privy to that made Stryder meaningful and a splinter in his eye.

As Ajax looked over the intel Major Mir had delivered to him, he attempted to put himself into the mind of the rebel whom they only knew as Prymack. Why had he attacked Fettis Prison? Why steal back the fighters that he had to know wouldn't fly? Was he just a hopeless dreamer, or were his men losing faith? Perhaps he needed a few wins to inspire them again?

Running a hand over his face in contemplation, he was

reminded again how unfamiliar it felt. He wasn't sure exactly how much of it was still him. After the explosion, he'd awoke from the ZIPR shell feeling different. Not only was his vision altered, but his skin was strange and scarred.

He flipped through the files on the vidscreen with his fingertips, hoping there would be more here. The Kavkin society was difficult to penetrate, Mir had told him. They lived by an honor code and didn't trust easy, making it difficult to convince them to spy on their own people. There wasn't much human intel. It mostly came from afar as satellite or drone pictures, data points, and communication intercepts.

His fingers twitched to a stop. Scrolling down the communication intercepts, he spotted three that had not been decoded yet.

Ajax tapped the haloid and brought up Major Mir.

"Is this all you have?"

"Yes, sir."

"There are still communications that you haven't decrypted?"

"Those came from the *Kai'den*, sir. We decrypted them, but they have a cipher that differed completely from the ones the rebels were using and were not like anything I have studied before. But they are from months ago. They were most likely about the attack on the transport when you arrived. Irrelevant information now."

"Nothing is irrelevant, Major. You said they came from the *Kai'den*?"

"Yes, sir."

Ajax clicked off the haloid and stared at the coded messages, contemplating the symbols and shapes that concealed the meaning.

There was only one person they could have come from: his boss, his Gira pal, the traitor—Drelmar Vinn. Playing Gira with him had cued him into his treachery, but ultimately, it had not been soon enough. However, it had given him insight into the man's head. And now, he recalled some of Drelmar's favorite stories.

Rising from his chair, Ajax made his way to his quarters. Inside the closet, on the floor to the right, was a footlocker of Drelmar's belongings. Valor Duma had looked them over already, but for whatever reason, Ajax had felt the need to keep them.

He unlocked the trunk and sorted through the items. Then he found it. For many years, Drelmar had told him legendary myths of the Coda and the Vox. Now, in his hands, was the book they must have all come from. It was full of the same translated stories that Drelmar had told.

But Ajax wasn't interested in the translated stories. Flipping to the back of the book, he found the same stories in their original text—the same symbols and shapes that were in the encoded messages.

Using the book as a cipher key, he decoded the messages. The first two were what Mir thought, all about Stryder and their escape plan. But the third one was not.

After translating the last line, a smirk crept to his lips. He knew exactly where the rebels would be.

CHAPTER 40

Nathan stared out the window of the passenger seat in the remaining APC. He and Prymack were in the cab, while the rest of the rebels from the decoy trucks were in the troop hold. Watching the exotic trees and colors pass by caused his thoughts to wander. With the exception of the Vox, why did humans dominate the Meraki? Arista didn't seem to know about them, and Captain HaReeka said they were made up. But Duma had surely known. It was clear now that their presence was a secret.

"You're a lot like me, Stryder," Prymack said from the driver's seat. "You like to keep things inside."

He paused, as if trying to organize his feelings. "I know how lonely that can be. I also know that eventually you need to trust someone." He smiled. "Nur taught me that."

Nathan knew what Prymack meant—he wanted him to open up about Arista, but why?

"What's her name?"

"Arista," Nathan said, solemnly.

Prymack's gaze stayed fixed on the road ahead.

"I'll never see her again. I don't care," Nathan lied to Prymack as well as himself.

"Make no mistake about it, they killed millions when they invaded. They killed all those prisoners in Fettis for nothing more than making sure we didn't rescue them. If we don't kill them, they come back to kill us. Look at yourself. They were foolish not to kill you. Whoever shot you from the transport just stunned you, and now, how much damage have you caused them? We can't afford that damage." He sighed. "I wish we weren't at war, but we are. You have to accept that and all that comes with it."

Nathan ran his hands over his face, trying to wipe away the turmoil. It didn't work.

The next words spoken between them came two hours later.

"What do you care about Arista anyway?" Nathan said, breaking the silence.

Prymack glanced at him. "I don't. You just need to decide about her before you meet her again. You won't have time to think then. The question is, what do *you* care about her?" He shrugged as they turned off the road into a field. It was growing dark now, the sunset clearly visible on the horizon. "By the time we get there, it will be dark."

Nathan was relieved the topic had changed and eagerly jumped on it.

"So, the mole is in our group. How do we know they won't rat us out now?"

"'Mole?'" Prymack shot him a questioning look. "'Rat?'"

"The spy. The leak."

Prymack chuckled. "I don't. But we can't keep running. There are things we need to do." He shifted gears as they turned into a field.

The APC apparently had no shocks because it lurched wildly the moment they were off the road. Nathan grabbed the handle above him to keep steady. "What are we doing?"

"Drelmar sent us a message before he died. He set up a rendezvous with a blockade runner who's going to drop off supplies for us."

"I thought only the Meraki could fly? How will he get here?"

"I guess we'll see." Prymack shrugged. "If he makes it."

"Will he be human?"

He shrugged again. "Don't know. Though we're human,

you're human, the Meraki are human. I can only assume he will be too."

On the other side of the field, they came to an overgrown dirt path that ran into more forest. The armored personnel carrier trampled through thick grass and bush, making its way to a large clearing. They'd positioned the trucks Nur had taken in a wide circle on the outskirts of the clearing in a defensive position, and Prymack pulled the carrier next to her.

Nathan pressed the intercom button and told their passengers to unload as Nur came up to the driver's window and pulled herself up.

"Well, you didn't miss the party. So far, just us and the termites. Did you have trouble?"

"Nothing we couldn't handle." Prymack opened the hatch and climbed out. "You?"

"No, we dropped off the fighters and came here. How long do we wait?"

"All night. Until he comes. Drelmar made it clear that what the runner was bringing could change everything."

"What is he bringing?" Nathan said.

"I don't know, but I trust Drelmar. So we'll wait."

With that, Nathan sat down on a fallen tree. He pulled the datagem from his pocket and held it up to the brightest moon. He still didn't know what Deathwind was or how to get the information to the High Command.

※ ※

Sitting on her bed back in Brevetta, Arista accepted the fact that there wasn't much to do until the rebels stopped moving and let their guard down. As long as they kept moving, it was almost impossible to catch them. By the time she could scramble people to go after them, they would be gone. That had now happened three times in four weeks. But her only way off this planet, and back to her regular life, was to kill *him*, and she wasn't about to give up.

In the meantime, she'd been training to keep her mind off of her emotions and attempting to work on paintings she'd left unfinished. The paintings were proving difficult to focus on, so she was using her time to learn about the mystifying energy she couldn't seem to control. It had been showing up more often recently, but she wasn't sure why. What she did know was the absolute power she felt when it was there.

Noting the time, Arista knew she had a few minutes before her meeting with Mir and cleared an area in her room. She activated the contact drum with her foot, and a holographic silhouette of a humanoid sprang up from the base.

She took a deep breath and exhaled slowly to clear her mind. Closing her eyes, she focused on how her body felt. Starting from her core, she searched outward. Like an imaginary scan of her body, she attempted to pinpoint where the energy originated, but it was elusive. Several times, she thought she sensed it, only for it to fade.

Opening her eyes, she glanced down at her hands. Nothing—no glow, no tingle. It came so easily in the market. Why couldn't she find it now?

Again, she tried. This time, she imagined herself in a fight and attempted to draw on her anxiety, her excitement, and her fear. The problem was, Duma had trained most of that out of her. He'd taught her to fight without emotion. Drawing that out now proved counterintuitive.

Abandoning this method as well, she opened her eyes once more and threw a combination of attacks at the silhouette. Switching between kicks, punches, elbows, and knees, she tried to trigger the energy within. The silhouette flashed red with every point of contact she made, as it had been designed to do, but her hands did not. There was no glow, no extra power or heated sensation like she'd felt before when it happened.

Arista tapped the base of the drum again, and the silhouette disappeared. In its place was a holographic construct of Nathan Stryder.

She'd loaded it up a few days ago, hoping it would help her visualize what she had to do, but this was the first time she'd dared herself to look at it. It was an image of him as he was when she'd known him. Not of what he looked like when they faced off in the market. There, he was different—chaotic, unshaven, and wearing battered armor.

She circled the hologram, looking it over, pretending it was him. How many times had she punched him before during his training? Yet, now, she could only look at him, wondering what he was doing, what he was thinking.

Behind her, the alarm on her haloid bleeped. Mir was late.

Turning off the contact drum, she waited for him to arrive with his latest report. She didn't know where or how he got his information, but he always seemed to get it late.

Pacing around her room, she examined her unfinished works. Ever since painting the picture of Earth for Nathan, nothing she'd painted felt right. They were all incomplete in some way. She just didn't know why. This planet had a plethora of things to paint, but she just couldn't capture any of it. The colors were off, the shapes were off—*something* was off.

Then she picked up her *Ronya* painting. The canvas was scuffed now, but compared to the others in her room, it felt complete, reminding her of the time, effort, and emotion she'd put into it—it haunted her.

A sudden welling of frustration drove her to the shelf with her paintings. Arista's hands lit up, filling with energy, and with one violent sweep of her arm, she sent everything flying.

Power surged through her, and the paintings exploded into

the opposing wall, splintering around the room. She was in shock. Was it triggered by her anger? Thinking back to all the times it had happened, she tried to catalogue how she felt.

A buzz at her door interrupted her thoughts. She ignored it at first and tried to get back to—

It buzzed again.

Grinding her teeth, she stomped to the door and opened it, expecting to see Mir. She was startled to see Commander Sculic. He stepped deliberately into the room, questioning the ruined paintings strewn over the floor with a grimace.

"Valor Duma will return in the next two weeks. He won't be pleased if Stryder isn't dead," he said as he bent down to pick up part of a busted canvas.

Arista kicked it away from him. "Do you think I need to be reminded of that?" Her patience—with this assignment, with Ajax, with herself—was growing thin. "He'll be dead. If not, I'll deal with Valor Duma."

He handed her the report he'd been holding. "I've taken Mir's data and pinpointed their location. He… missed some things."

"Tell me you know where he is," she said through a clenched jaw.

"We leave in an hour."

CHAPTER 41

It was a bright night with three moons up, bathing the forest in pale light. Six hours had passed with no sign of the blockade runner. It had been a long day, and Nathan wanted nothing more than to sleep. He slowly took in the area, his brain taking longer to compute the images he saw. The others who were on watch with him looked equally tired. Most of them were pacing the perimeter, intent on staying alert. The rest were sleeping.

Nathan's continuous battle against sleep made the minutes tick by even slower. The last time he slept would have been thirty-two Earth hours ago. He kept himself busy with the calculation. To stay awake, he pondered what the runner would look like, and decided it would most likely be human, since it seemed like it would be easier for humans to deal with other humans.

"A pleasant twilight," Vendala said, emerging from the shadowed canopy of the trees wrapped in a blanket and leaning on a crutch. Her arm, still cradled in a blue sling.

Nathan nodded. "How's the arm?"

He'd hoped she would forget their first awkward meeting. She had been drunk and full of lust then. She hadn't been mean to him. She actually seemed nice and thoughtful. He just hadn't felt as he did when he was with Arista.

"Still hurts." Vendala shrugged, causing a flash of pain to cross her face and the sling to fall off her shoulder.

In an attempt to hold it up, she tripped and fell backward onto the ground with a squeal. Her blanket fell partially to the side, revealing the smooth skin of her upper thigh.

"Still haven't gotten used to it yet." She flashed a painful smile as she struggled to stand, then gave up, lying helpless on the ground.

Nathan stepped over to her. She was an attractive woman, he admitted, noticing the way her eyes danced in the moonlight. He lifted the sling back over her shoulder and pulled the blanket up.

She leaned closer to him, her face near his. "I feel like you've been dodging me."

"No, I—" He tried to escape her eyes as she waited for an answer. "It's not you. Please believe that. It's all so jumbled now."

"You think too much. I've been living day to day since the invasion, never knowing if I'll see the next. The only thing we can count on is right now. Do you even know why you're avoiding me?"

Nathan leaned back. Arista's voice was echoing in his head. "*...that you never forget me, or tonight,*" she had asked him to promise at the Tithe. Was that why he was avoiding Vendala? Because Arista haunted him?

"I'm sorry. I'm just not there."

Vendala shook her head with a grin, as if she knew more about him than he did. She rolled her eyes, then placed a kiss on his cheek. "Don't you know? You're stricken."

"Stricken? What do you mean?"

"Bewitched, sloppy, smitten!"

Nathan laughed. "What?"

From the northwest, a light flared against the sky, drawing their attention.

She squinted up at it, then back to him. "I think that's them."

Nathan signaled the others on watch, then stepped over to wake Prymack.

He'd grown accustomed to seeing advanced fighters and

starships that traveled through space in the last several months, from the sleek devil ray ship of Krell Duma, to the large transport that they'd shot down over Brevetta. Now he saw what seemed to be a combination of the two. It was probably four times the size of Duma's ship, with a bulkier V-shape design.

As it approached, the ship's thrusters burned brightly, making it difficult to look at. It set down in the middle of a clearing. Extinguishers whooshed from beneath, expelling a mist to quiet the ground fire caused by the thrusters' heat.

Nathan unconsciously stepped toward the ship, passing Prymack and Nur. The haze floated around his feet and swirled over the ship's scuffed hull, eventually dissipating.

His mind recalled a similar situation back on Earth, in a cornfield, causing his throat to tighten. But it wasn't the Vox in this ship, it was the blockade runner—who might have the technology to read Drelmar's datagem. In a way, bringing Drelmar back from the dead and hopefully helping them rid Kavka of Meraki control.

A wide hatch opened vertically, allowing the exit of two teal skinned humans from the ship. They moseyed side by side toward Nathan. He was shocked to recognize the first—it was Roman, the pilot who'd flown them to Tinook. The second was female and shorter. She was of the same race, wearing a simple flight suit. The co-pilot.

They paused before Nathan.

"Wait. I know you," Roman said. "Weren't you on the other side?"

Nathan cocked his head. "Weren't you?"

"Technically, I'm on my own side."

Prymack stepped forward. "You know each other?"

"Yeah, we met," Nathan said.

"I'm Roman Drake. And by the by, this place is a pain to find." Roman gestured to space. "It just looks like a dead planet from out there."

The woman leaned in and whispered to Roman, who then cleared his throat and nodded.

"And if you don't mind, I'd like the code word."

He narrowed his eyes, looking the three over closely. It was a tough guy act that Nathan totally saw through. The woman was even less skilled in it. A tiny smile formed on her face as she watched Roman put on his show.

"Redemption," Prymack said.

Roman nodded. "Right. Now that we got that out of the way, let's start unloading. Please follow Paola's instruction." He motioned to the co-pilot.

Behind him, the cargo bay doors screeched open, and a ramp extended to the ground.

"You didn't have trouble with your engines?" Nur said.

Roman glanced back to check his ship with a curious look. "No more than usual. Why?"

"Since they invaded, none of our ships have been able to take off," Prymack said, slinging his gun over a shoulder. "You're the first person besides the Meraki to land here."

"Interesting. You're right, though—they have little in the way of air defense. Just what they need to control you."

"And you thought it was your 'persuasive piloting' that didn't draw attention." Paola rolled her eyes at Roman.

"Hey, hey—it still could have been a combination of the two."

"Who are you now, Hawke Mercer?" Paola continued her razzing. "Last I heard, he was racing the Blazer chase on Mignon, not a blockade run on Kavka."

Roman winked at her. "Call me Hawke from now on."

They turned and walked toward the ship, with Prymack, Nur, and Nathan behind them. A scribbling of black paint spelled out something above the cargo door.

"What's the name of your ship?" Nathan asked as they trekked up the ramp.

"The *Freefall*," Roman said with a twinkle of pride.

Once inside the cargo hold, Roman showed them around, opening crates and explaining what Drelmar had ordered. Ten crates held food consisting of dehydrated rations and some longer lasting, age-resistant fruits. Two more crates carried medical supplies, including the G-booster treatments Nathan had used often in his training. The rest of the crates had weapons and what he immediately recognized as plasma detonators—powerful bombs that, if calibrated correctly, could take down a building.

The pain in Nathan's side flared as if telling him it needed a booster. It had been over two weeks since he'd bruised his right side at the prison raid outside of Fettis and then the fight with Arista, but the patches would heal wounds like his and Vendala's in a few hours.

Two crewmen began unloading the crates. Outside, Cyn backed a truck up to the ship, awaiting the cargo.

"I don't know what's up with our cargo sleds, but we'll be doing this by hand, so it's gonna go slower," Roman said.

Prymack examined a sled. "They're antigravity based?"

"Yeah, they were working yesterday."

"They somehow suppressed antigrav engines here." Prymack nodded to Nur, who nodded back. "One more thing."

Roman leaned playfully on Paola, waiting for Prymack to speak.

Nathan jumped into the conversation. "Can you read a datagem?"

Lifting his arm from Paola's shoulder, Roman strolled over to Nathan, sizing him up.

"It ain't free."

Paola waved her hand. "We've already been paid for this."

"Oh. Right." Roman shrugged. "Nothing wrong with a guy trying to make some extra money for his hungry kids."

Paola raised an eyebrow in bewilderment. "Kids?"

"All right, all right," Roman said at last, raising his hands in defeat. "Let me set it up."

By the time they finished unloading, it was nearly daybreak. Nathan slipped the datagem into the primitive haloid, and immediately, Drelmar Vinn's image jumped from the display, dressed in the same uniform he'd worn at the Tithe. A stream of memories flooded Nathan's mind. He sighed briefly and watched as Drelmar spoke.

"I have little time. Duma will be on to me soon enough. I'll try to make this brief. The Vox are real. They took you and your sister from Earth because you are distant descendants of their ancient enemy, called the Coda. Long ago, after their last conflict, remnants of the Coda spread out through the galaxy and integrated with numerous worlds. This is the thread that runs through and binds most of the known races.

"But more than that, the Coda had a caste of divine warriors called Asante. The Asante were trained extensively and given a type of genetic armor that allowed them to do incredible things. The Coda also developed a way for the Asante's memories, skills, and abilities to be etched in their DNA and passed down through generations.

"Stryder—you, your sister, and Arista are all descendants of this warrior caste. The Vox call you the Harbingers. Encrypted in your blood is the complete power of your Asante ancestors. I've unlocked it in you, but only you can fully unleash it.

"You were meant to rise up against the Vox if they ever returned, but they know about you. They've been searching for you. They seek to control you and your power, like they have with Arista. You cannot let that happen. For years, I've tried to free her, but Duma and the Vox had too much time with her. You and your sister were different.

"Stryder, I did everything in my power to save Susan, but I failed, and I am sorry for that. However, your story continues. You have to rise and confront them."

A meter-tall cylinder replaced Drelmar's image, with a line of three red lights above a small keyboard. It rotated and cycled through the schematics and functions, along with all types of other information that Nathan couldn't follow.

"I've downloaded data from a project—a weapon—that the Meraki have developed called Deathwind. It can carry a wave of energy across a planet that targets gene codes to eradicate. In effect, it can wipe a planet clean of a specific race, while leaving plant and animal life intact—a genetic purification.

"I've included a list of possible targets. Kavka is at the top of the list. Earth is there too. I've sent the High Command what I knew about where we were heading, so they should be looking for you and close to the system, but the Meraki somehow cloaked the planet. With luck, all you'll need to do is send a distress signal."

The image faded, replaced with a map of Kavka that showed the locations of the Meraki's forces and facilities. For the first time, Nathan saw where he was. Before, he'd had only a vague idea of the landscape of the planet, but from these pictures, he could see Fettis and the prison camp. The capital, Brevetta, was easily identifiable, outlined in a large red circle.

"Lastly, their main headquarters is in Brevetta. There, you will find the dampening field generator that blocks your outgoing transmissions and grounds your anti-gravity technology."

The map zoomed in on the hexagonal skyscrapers at its center.

"If they use the Deathwind generator, it will need altitude to transmit, so it will likely be in one of these skytowers. By your gods' grace, I wish you luck."

Nathan glanced at the blank faces around him, knowing exactly how they felt. A cold nausea spread through his gut as he realized the sudden danger that was lingering over their heads, like a man strapped to a guillotine who had just looked up to see the blade.

Prymack was the first to speak. "It's worse than we thought."

"We'll find a way to stop it," Nathan said confidently, which surprised even him. He realized, even if it was on an unconscious level, that after everything he'd gone through, there had always been a way forward. Drelmar had saved him in more ways than one, dying in the process, and now he had to make it worth it.

The image began to close in on Brevetta when the sound of explosions rumbled into the ship from outside, followed by the glow of fire.

Prymack drew his pistol. "Damn! They found us again!"

"Paola, burn the engines! Sorry, guys, we have to run." Roman switched off the vid and pulled the datagem out, then shoved it at Nathan. "Looks like I get to do some persuasive piloting after all!"

"Can you distract the air cover?" Prymack hurriedly asked.

Roman nodded. "I'll try."

"Good luck, Roman."

"Thanks, but I've never needed luck." He grinned, then dashed to the cockpit.

Nathan drew his weapon, as did Nur. She nodded at Prymack and charged down the ramp, but as Nathan turned to follow, Prymack stepped in his way.

"You're gonna leave with them."

"What? No." Nathan attempted to push by, but again, Prymack blocked him.

"This isn't your fight, Stryder. We know what to do—we can handle this. I can't let you die here. You heard Drelmar—your destiny is greater than Kavka. You can't stay."

Nathan was blindsided. He couldn't believe what he was hearing. But he knew one thing: this was his fight.

"You're wrong. I can't *leave*—not now. You need me!"

"I'm sorry, but I can't let you die here."

Out of nowhere, Prymack slapped one side of a restraining cuff to Nathan's wrist and the other to a girder, then turned quickly and left without looking back.

Nathan yanked on the cuffs, but they wouldn't budge. He tried again, pulling harder this time, but it still wasn't enough. A rumble vibrated all around him as the engines started. Panic shocked his system. He had to get out.

As the cargo bay doors screeched, he knew time was short. Frantically scanning the area, he spotted a metal rod within reach. Snatching it up, he bashed it against the cuffs, but it didn't even scratch them. Desperation flooded his mind, making it hard to think.

He dropped the rod and closed his eyes. Taking a deep breath, he tried to clear his mind and focus on something specific—ronya. A heated intensity flowed through him as he called forth the ancient power of the Asante within.

Opening his eyes, he found his hands radiating blue energy, only to see them quickly fade.

"Fuck!" He still didn't have control over it.

Scrambling to grab the rod again, Nathan raised it over his head and targeted his thumb. Setting his jaw, he smashed it against his hand.

A roar jumped out of his throat from the sudden and crushing agony as his bones snapped. Jerking against the cuffs again, he twisted his shattered hand free.

CHAPTER 42

In the early morning light, Arista and three fighters soared over the target, circling around for another attack run. Her first pass had taken out two supply trucks. She'd hoped to reach the battle early enough to join the ground combat, but she had just arrived from Fettis. As it was, the ground forces were late, but she couldn't wait any longer to strike.

She spotted an unidentified cargo ship below. It seemed heavily modified, which meant it was most likely a blockade runner—the first she'd heard of on this planet. To stop it from escaping, she would have to move on it quickly. It wouldn't sit still for any length of time.

Keying up a pair of missiles, she set up a new angle of attack. Then, with a twitch of her thumb, Arista launched them at the mysterious starship. She positioned her fighter behind the ordnance, reminding herself that the insurgents would have their anti-ship weapons out by now. Flares and countermeasures were set to deploy automatically.

Her missiles detonated before hitting their target, fire and debris outlining an energy shield that encircled the ship. She followed the missiles with a volley of strafing lasers.

Seconds later, the ship's jets ignited, burning the foliage around it as it rose into the dim morning sky. Its red hull blended with the fires left behind by its liftoff.

Arista couldn't afford to hover like a giant bonfire fly. If she did, the rebels would have a simple time blasting her out to space. Yet flybys gave her little time to do anything but strafe. The alternative was to reduce her speed, giving her time to engage. It would be a gamble, but the shields on the blockade runner's ship couldn't hold forever, and she knew it. To her right, she saw that her wing-mate was following her lead and slowing as well.

She sent two more missiles at the blockade runner's hull, dodging a Spark missile on her right. Again, she pressed in with lasers, trying to slice through the shields before the larger and better armed ship could retaliate.

Deliberately, the rising ship rotated to confront her. From the corner of her eye, she spotted another missile racing in. This was going to be tight. The runner's ship was sure to have guns on it—big guns—and it would come to a front-facing firing position at any moment.

The flare of another Spark being fired caught her caught attention. This was definitely turning into a bad idea. Her wing-mate burst into a ball of fire to her right as a warning light lit up on her control panel, triggering her countermeasures. Hundreds of flares shot out from her wings in a dizzying swirl as Arista jerked the controls to her left, slipping the first missile. Then she pulled back hard on the yoke, lifting the nose of her ship out of the way of the second.

The runner's ship came around and fired two shots. The first was wide to her right, but the concussion still rumbled through her body, rocking her smaller fighter. A second shot struck her wing, blowing it to pieces.

The controls sparked and burst into flames, and the fighter went into a dive. Smoke blackened the canopy, making it impossible to see.

As her last choice, she punched the ejection switch, hoping not to show up too well against the dim sky.

* *

"Oh yeah! I got one!" Roman Drake shouted from the cockpit

of the *Freefall*. His pointed finger tracked the smoking fighter as it spun toward the ground.

Paola was in the seat next to him, too busy controlling the angle of the shields around the ship to share in his excitement.

"Roman, we gotta go. They're sending more fighters, and they might shield the planet!"

Everything she said was in the same cute voice as when he'd first met her, even when she was shouting something important at him. But she didn't need to tell him twice. Other than delivering his cargo to the wrong person, getting trapped under a planet's shield was the biggest mistake he'd made since he started this business, and something he did not want to repeat.

He turned the ship skyward and slid the accelerator forward three notches. The two remaining fighters pursued them, leaving the ground battle behind. Paola angled the shield to the back of the ship protecting them from the trailing fighters.

"Strap in," Roman said into the intercom. "We're going vertical!"

After giving his crew enough time to secure themselves, he rammed the throttle as far as it would go. Instantly, the engines reacted, pinning them all to their seats as gravity shot up to seven times its normal amount. Roman strained to look over at his co-pilot. He wanted to laugh, seeing her adorable face distorted and mushed up by the pressure it was enduring. Paola caught his glance and gazed back at him.

"Wish me luck," he finally said.

She smiled. "Good luck, *Hawke*."

Hawke, Roman pondered. *If only the great Hawke Mercer was here.* But he wasn't, only Roman Drake, blockade runner extraordinaire. Nothing had stopped him on the way in, and nothing would stop him on th—

"Roman!"

He snapped back to reality. "Yeah?"

"You looked like you were daydreaming again."

"Oh. No, I'm good."

"Good, because we have two fighters on our tail and weakening shields."

Her voice was still sweet, even when chastising him. He turned back to piloting, a hidden grin across his face.

Ahead, they could now see the tint of space through the atmosphere. The pursuing fighters were unloading a torrent of lasers to his rear shields.

"Our shields are almost gone!"

Two missiles slammed against the back shield, causing the craft to shudder, as if to emphasize Paola's point.

Roman fought the rising G-forces enough to maintain control as additional turbulence bounced the ship around, causing him to struggle. From behind, the fighters also poured on the speed, reducing the distance between themselves and their prey.

The entire cockpit was rattling out of place. Loose screws were falling from the shelves he'd just put back together this morning. He glanced down to check his altitude, but the altimeter was no longer there, only an empty socket that had once held it stared back at him. He thought perhaps he heard it clanking against the floor behind him.

"Roman! If you're gonna do something, do it now!"

He could make out the desperation in her voice even over the rumble of the engines, but there was no time to reply. Glancing again at his position relative to the fighters, he gritted his teeth and cut the engines.

"Hold on!"

If this didn't kill them, it would work.

The forces pressing against him quickly reversed as the *Freefall* plummeted backward toward the planet. It was a crazy sensation, as if Roman's guts were being stretched in several directions at once.

Paola made a heaving noise next to him.

Through the windows, he saw the fighters shoot by them, their jet wash vibrating the ship. This activated the automatic targeting system, and the fighters lit up red on his display.

Straining against the invisible laws of physics, he fired the ship's air-to-air rockets. Flashes of light streaked forward and smashed into the fighters, creating two deafening fireballs.

Without the altimeter to tell him how close he was to the ground, Roman frantically threw the throttle forward, reigniting the engines. With another jolt in the opposite direction, they were skyward again.

He winked at Paola, whose face was frozen in a mixture of disbelief and nausea.

✷ ✷

Cradling his hand, Nathan made it out of the clearing and to the trees just before the ground assault surged forth. With it came havoc and chaos. The Meraki simply outnumbered them, and there was no hope of winning a battle they hadn't chosen or planned themselves. Survival and escape were the only options now.

Gunfire and lasers blazed all around him, obliterating the calm that had existed only moments before. The battle flickered through the dim forest in convulsive patterns as the thunder of explosions kept an irregular beat. A truck engulfed in flames illuminated the scene in a doom-filled orange glow.

A nearby tree cracked and splintered from a cluster of bullets, and Nathan instinctively dove to his stomach. Lifting his head from the forest floor, he saw four trucks engulfed in flames, and a fifth was speeding out of control into a tree.

Back on his feet, the pain in his ribs resurfaced, joining his throbbing hand. He cursed himself for not using the G-booster patch when he'd had the chance. Leaning against the tree for support, he scanned the forest for his allies.

"There's one!" a voice called from the distance.

Rolling to his right, Nathan evaded a spotlight, but it tracked with him. It was only a matter of time before they started firing.

He crawled around the back of the tree, leaning heavily on it to stand. Out of the glare for the moment, he quickly devised a strategy.

"Flank him!"

Leaning out from behind cover, Nathan took aim and fired two shots, shattering the spotlight. Then he darted north. Everything was tinted in a faded red light from flares that floated overhead. The trees were thick, but he ran as fast as the terrain would let him, dodging everything within view.

Lasers flickered through the forest after him, pounding the tree he'd swept behind as he continued his reckless escape. It was at times like this that he could be thankful for the things that Arista and Duma had taught him. That knowledge was keeping him alive.

Sailing through the underbrush, he hurdled a fallen tree and dashed up a hill. Carrying that momentum forward, he cruised down the other side to a large rock. Pausing, he listened for signs of others in the area, but his breathing and heartbeat drown out everything else. He seemed to have lost everyone, friend and foe.

But he was wrong. His leg folded unexpectedly as a rifle smashed into it, bringing him down hard.

A voice snapped at him. "Get up!"

Surrounded by three vanguard soldiers, Nathan found himself looking into the barrels of their weapons. An adrenaline-fueled mixture of pain, excitement, and fear raced through him.

※ ※

Arista opened her eyes to a soft bed of blankets. The morning sun dared to peek in through curtained windows. As she sat up, she was filled with a familiar cherished sensation; a feeling of heightened existence. It meant Nathan was close.

In fact, he appeared from around the corner with a plate full of breakfast and sat on the bed next to her. With a gentle finger, he pushed back her hair, then kissed her lips. His hand drifted down to her pregnant belly.

No—this wasn't real!

Arista awoke with a jolt and snapped her eyes open from the unconscious delusion. She dangled a good ten meters from the ground, her chute tangled in a tree. The dream was gone, but the sensation remained, rushing through her body. He was here.

Her eyes darted around like lightning, looking for him—her target. Through the sparse branches, she spotted four soldiers below her on the forest floor. In the dim light, she couldn't make out much, but she knew one was Nathan, and the others were probably rebels as well.

She drew the sidearm off her hip and began firing.

* *

A rain of lasers poured down from the tree behind Nathan and tore up the ground. Dirt and leaves sprayed up with each shot like raindrops from a puddle. Caught off guard, the soldiers spun and returned fire at the sniper.

Capitalizing on the moment, Nathan cracked the closest Meraki in the side of the head and snatched his weapon. He released three point-blank shots into the soldier's chest.

Caught between Nathan and the sniper, the remaining soldiers turned to bring their weapons to bear on him. He squeezed off two bursts from the rifle, dropping the soldiers where they stood.

Dashing for cover, he tried to distance himself from the

sniper and the initial ambush, though it seemed every direction echoed with gunfire and shouting.

The brush on his right flared and flickered with a burst of plasma bolts. One struck him in the foot. There was surprisingly little pain, but the force twisted him into the dirt. He rolled over to his stomach to face his ambushers, spraying at the brush blindly.

The returning swarm of shots was uncomfortably close, heating the surrounding air. His blasts crisscrossed with the Meraki's, weaving a lethal pattern of streaking energy. Nathan knew he couldn't hold out for long. Whether by luck or by skill, someone was bound to hit him.

Two bolts landed within an inch of his leg, scorching his pants. Another flew over his back, and one seared his shoulder. Pinned down, Nathan couldn't aim through the blinding barrage, so he was firing just to keep them distracted. Two more shots whizzed by his head.

After everything that had happened in the last year—his parent's and Susan's death, his abduction, his time with Arista—this was it. This was where it ended.

Then, in divine brilliance, the underbrush behind him exploded with light. An armored personnel carrier went airborne as it crashed through, sending bushes and vines flying in every direction. The whine of the APC's engine drowned out everything as the vehicle coasted through the air.

Nathan watched in awe as the vehicle descended on the soldiers who had just threatened him. Cries of pain and surprise erupted from the brush as the soldiers scattered, trying to avoid being crushed underneath the vehicle.

The APC slammed to a stop against a large tree, its hood battered from the impact, spouting flames. The side facing Nathan was marred with blast marks and twisted metal.

Bullets and lasers flashed out from the vehicle's gun slits, keeping the surviving enemies pinned down. Then Nathan was being dragged inside.

Prymack smiled briefly. "Hold tight," he said, ramming the vehicle in reverse and spinning it back around the way they came.

※ ※

Arista had finally worked herself loose from the entangled chute, still monitoring the firefight ahead of her. She'd watched the wrecked and burning vehicle speed under her the first time, and now, it was heading back in her direction. Looking down, she saw a maze of branches and vines between her and the ground, visualizing a way through them.

She detached the chute from her harness and fell. Twisting 180 degrees, she caught a branch and swung forward, dodging the one below it. Releasing it, she swung outside and away from the trunk. At the peak of her arc, she used her momentum to flip into a tight, backward somersault.

The forest spun wildly, but with years of training, Arista could sense the perfect moment to flex. Pushing her legs out and arching her back to slow her spin, she landed feet-first on top of the passing vehicle. Her Tanzi reached out and clamped onto the roof to steady her landing.

She turned to face the front of the truck, crouching down to create a low center of gravity. The APC was speeding through the forest, passing remnants of the ambush. They had surrounded the rebels with tanks and troops, so she had no clue where these people thought they could go. There was no escape.

The truck bounced wildly through the forest. Carefully, Arista took a step forward, keeping an eye out for low branches and hanging vines. The smell of battle and wet vegetation streamed by her. Then the roof jumped as the truck skidded to the side, knocking her to all fours. The terrain was getting worse.

She crept to the front of the roof and drew a thin throwing

dagger from a belt of them on her thigh. Holding it in her left hand, she lay flat on the roof and leaned toward the driver's side window. The blast shield was down, but damaged, leaving a small gap to the cab. She spotted movement through the opening—an arm gripping the wheel.

Knowing she would get only one chance at this, Arista steadied herself. Then, reaching down, she jammed the knife through the gap and into the driver.

The truck swerved, flinging her over the side.

Her right hand lashed out and snatched the railing, whipping her around. She dangled there, bouncing against the door, as she clawed for a grip with her other hand. Once she had it, she hauled herself back onto the roof.

Confused shouting came from within the vehicle and the top hatch swung open. A ragged insurgent climbed out with a pistol in his hand. He shot at her to cover his exit, but it was nowhere close. As she drew her sidearm, the roof bucked wildly, knocking her flat. The pistol tumbled from her hand and disappeared into the forest. She cursed her carelessness. It was mistakes like that which got people killed.

On the roof now, the rebel leveled his gun at her as she slid another dagger from the strap on her leg. Instinctively, she dodged forward the moment she felt he was going to fire, and the shot went high. With practiced grace, she struck quick, flinging the knife. The blade sunk deep in his chest. A whiff of blood hung in the air for an instant before he lost his equilibrium and fell backward off the truck.

Another head popped up from the hatch.

"Mase, you get 'em?" The rebel stopped cold when she realized her comrade was gone. "You bitch!"

Arista's HUD flicked to a higher setting as the truck passed through a long shadow. The rebel fired twice, then ducked back down as two of Arista's throwing knives bounced off the hatch where their target had been only seconds before. A hand shot up and closed the hatch.

Only now that she was out of combat did she realize they had somehow slipped past the perimeter of tanks. The faster vehicles were trailing them in full pursuit. Even given their luck of breaking through the ambush, this mangled APC would never outrun the pursuing army. They were gaining with every second.

Just then, a blinding white light filled her vision, followed a second later by a deafening boom. She knew she wouldn't have time to react before the shockwave hit her, but she recognized the blast. It was a tactical plasma explosion, and it disintegrated the swarm of vehicles chasing them.

When the shockwave hit, she was already encased in the Tanzi. The force flattened trees and ripped up the ground. Even on the edge of the blast radius, it lifted the APC and spun it sideways.

Arista was sent flying, thrown backward from the APC. The effect made it seem as if the world was speeding away from her before the impact turned everything black.

CHAPTER 43

THE REBELS WERE back in Brevetta, and the situation was grim. Of the fifty rebels left to guard the safehouses, only thirty-eight remained. The severity of their position hung heavy in the air, and Nur could see it on Prymack's face. He had called on his supporters—some two thousand in the area—but received little response. They were abandoning him.

The few who had responded met in an abandoned church, each representing their clan. Nur watched on as Prymack tried to convince them that the rebellion was still alive, but they wouldn't hear it. Her eyes drifted to Stryder and Pollo, who stood quietly at the back of the room.

"We've been defeated!" a man called out. "We've lost so many already. By resisting now, we'd only endanger our clans. Risk the death of more innocents."

"No! We are on the verge of winning it all back!" Prymack said. His voice carried an unfortunate hint of desperation.

"You've said that every year since we started these meetings. We must face our fates. We've been short on supplies for months. Every day we get weaker."

"We can't give up. The moment we do, we lose everything. We must stand up or forever live in their shadows. Don't you understand? We are in a do-or-die situation!"

"We've already lost!" a deep voice piled on from a large man in the front.

It was then that they began to filter out. One by one, they got up the courage to leave Prymack and his rebellion behind.

Nur could take no more. She could not stand and watch them throw away the future. She charged up to the dais.

"'From our enemy will come our savior!' That's what Luciian said. Right?" She found Stryder in the room and locked eyes with him. "He's here!" With a swift finger, she pointed him out. "He is with us. And with him, we will be victorious!"

The large man brushed his hand through the air. "Luciian is dead. And so is the resistance."

Nur tried to hide the desperation within her. "Where are you going to go? There is nowhere we can run to anymore!"

"We are going to surrender to them and spare the innocents from this futile war," a woman in priestess robes called out. "Savadon is in three days. We will end this war on our most sacred day."

"You can't justify this shattered world we live in—this nightmare!" Nur's arms flung out in a sweeping gesture of the destroyed church. "The moment we surrender, we are slaves!"

She looked to Prymack for support, but a hollow look of defeat and futility had seeped into his face.

"Won't any of you help us?" Closing her eyes, she willed them to stop stinging. How could these people just walk out and let those murderous bastards get away with this?

"I will," an old woman's voice said.

Nur lifted her eyes. The woman was the only person left. She led a small, local clan. One clan out of thousands who had once been behind them.

"Thank you," Nur said, fighting back tears, knowing it wouldn't make a difference. But she had to stay brave—for the memories of Dane and little Nat.

✷ ✷

The gravity of Kavka pulled the *Kai'den* on an invisible track around the planet. The flagship of the Meraki Dominya had returned from Sienna after two phases. Onboard were the two most dangerous elements facing Kavka—one of the most destructive weapons ever created, and the man whose job it was to use it—yet most of the planet wasn't even aware of their presence.

Grand Valor Krell Duma carefully wheeled the Project Deathwind weapon into the cargo hold of his ship. Since all forms of antigravity would be nullified as soon as he entered the dampening field's range, he strapped down. One by one, he pulled thick belts around the weapon, making sure each one was tight and secure.

Satisfied with the restraints, he moved to the cockpit and started the engines. The bay door opened, revealing the planet below. Kavka looked like a number of other worlds Duma had seen since he became part of the Meraki Dominya, yet somehow it oddly reminded him of his homeworld. For a moment, he stared, remembering Carcosa and its ironic transition into a member of the Meraki Dominya.

It was long ago, the six days he ruled Carcosa before surrendering it to the Meraki. Each day symbolized a member of his team who died as a result of the government's betrayal. Their ghosts would haunt him forever, not because he killed them, but because he failed them. Still, they would join the Furies, waiting for his time to come, so they could tear into his soul.

Duma gripped the ship's controls and engaged the thrusters. He had three stops, starting with setting up the transmitter on the roof of the command center. The stops would be short, but each was necessary for the Deathwind to work. When he was finished, the components would operate in unity to conduct the weapon's power, spreading it over the planet like a technological plague. Kavka would never even know what happened.

Duma piloted his ship out of the hangar and pushed it into a steep dive, plunging through the atmosphere. The turbulence didn't last long, and before he knew it, lights from the pyramid skytowers of Brevetta were in sight. Beacons in the night sky.

Setting the ship down on the roof of one of the superstructures, Duma activated the exterior door. It silently opened and extended a simple ramp. A warm wind brought forth the damp smell of an oncoming storm. He removed the restraints on the Deathwind and wheeled it onto the roof.

Once it was secured in place, he powered it up. Piping on either side filled with muon particles and produced a calming hum. He knew it would kill millions, but there was no redemption for him now—just the endgame. He'd passed the point of no return when he killed the only person he ever cared for. If there had ever been a spot of sentiment in him, it died with HaReeka. Now he could embrace his true nature. He was simply a force of destruction.

Behind him, a subtle ruffle caught his attention. Turning, Duma watched as a winged predatory reptile settled on a support beam. Roughly one and a half meters tall, the creature had a spiked crest that punctuated its elongated head above a fearful maw of hooked, dagger-like teeth.

Duma considered it, beholding the beauty of its deadly design. Was it one of the Furies that awaited him?

"You are early, my foe. Be patient. You will get what's left of me."

CHAPTER 44

ARISTA LOOKED OUT her high-rise window over the city of Brevetta. After being hit with the shockwave of the plasma blast, she was rushed back for medical treatment. Unfortunately, the facilities on Kavka hadn't been furnished with all the equipment of the Meraki Dominya. She guessed it was because they were only helping the local government quell the rebellion, not to fight a full-blown war. Consequently, she had been unconscious for days, and was just now able to walk. The G-booster had done its job, but it was much slower than the ZIPR shells.

Commander Sculic entered the room without ringing.

"You're alive. Congratulations."

Arista turned to face him without a thing to say. Frustration consumed her. She had failed again, and every word Ajax spoke grated on her like wet sand.

"As much as I'd like to bring you soup and talk about your feelings, we are short on time. Valor Du—*Grand* Valor Duma will be here soon."

"'Grand valor?'" The words shocked her out of her mood. She'd never heard of a grand valor before.

"As I've been told, he was promoted by the Maelidor herself. He commands the *Kai'den* battle group now, and he will be here before the day is out. Major Mir will brief you on our current situation."

Mir later informed her that the rebels had hit four installations in the west while she was injured. One of the four, hit today, was a dampening field generator—part of a vast network that linked back to the primary hub here, in the capital. Apparently, this was all just a last desperate effort to get their antigrav fighters working again, or so Mir thought. But she wasn't focused on that—her only mission was to find and kill Nathan Stryder.

Arista headed to the gym to clear her mind. She'd been out of action for too long. Now, she had to get back into fighting form. Two hours of training wasn't a lot for her, but it was all she had before Grand Valor Duma arrived. That was a title she would have to get used to. He'd been her mentor and a valor since she'd started training so many years ago.

After warming up with calisthenics and a two-kilometer run, she spent a half hour in the firing range, then worked between several contact drums with various techniques, alternating speed and direction.

When Duma spoke from behind her, she didn't jump at his voice. Her body had been trained not to make involuntary movements. Instead, she spun and came to a quick salute.

Of course, his first question was about the rebels, though at this point she only knew what Mir had told her.

"They have been active in the west, sir," she said.

"Is Stryder still with them?"

"I believe so, sir."

"Believe so?" Duma stepped closer. "Do you have his body?"

Arista paused before answering. "No, sir. I do not."

"Then your assignment remains incomplete."

"Yes, sir."

Duma's voice switched to a mocking curiosity. "Do you love him?"

Arista, taken totally off-guard, choked on her words. "What? I—"

"Yes, I see," he said accusingly. His eyes drilling into her core.

She blinked. Anger growing from embarrassment. "No!"

"No? Then why isn't he dead? You're making a fool of yourself, Lieutenant Commander! You've let us all down. Do you think he is wrestling with thoughts of you? He used you. His job was to get you away from the Tithe so his partner could kill Lasal without your interference. He kept you occupied."

A fire erupted within her. Blood rushed to her face. "I don't love him! I hate him! I hate him! I hate him!"

"Then you must kill him!"

She pushed past Duma with her jaw clenched and a vengeful, one-track mind.

"I will," she growled.

CHAPTER 45

Prymack moved them back into one of the last safehouses in Brevetta, where they could prepare for their attack. Nathan was in the basement bar where they'd celebrated their first victory together, back when he met Vendala for the first time. It seemed like so long ago.

It was empty now, which was why he came here to eat his breakfast. He was more emotionally exhausted than anything else. There was too much to process and not enough time. The pressure and stress were breaking him down. He could hardly sleep.

Their strikes in the west were a misdirection to spread the Meraki forces out, so they could attack the most heavily defended Meraki position on the planet, the Brevetta skytowers.

They were outnumbered and had no air support. There was a high possibility, he and everyone he knew here could be dead before long. Then there was everything Drelmar had said about the Coda, and Nathan being a "divine Asante warrior," as he'd put it, and all the responsibility that came with it.

Nur's figure appeared as the far door opened.

"This is where you're hiding?" she said, walking over to him and taking a seat at the bar. "What are you thinking, down here all alone?"

Nathan took a deep breath, not even sure where to begin.

She gave him an understanding nod. "I get it. There's a lot going on."

He picked at a gash in the bar, unable to focus.

Nur clasped his hand. "You'll do fine."

"I don't know who you think I am." He forced the words out. "But I'm not your savior."

"No?" she said calmly. "Why not? You streaked from the sky like a comet. You came from our enemy. Those are words straight from the foretelling."

"Nur, I know you want to believe that, but I fell from the transport with a damaged jetpack. I crashed. None of it was divine."

"I do believe it. Why don't you?"

"I don't know. I don't believe in that stuff. I'm just… normal."

"Why are you so desperate not to embrace who you are? You heard Drelmar just like we did." She paused, trying to read his eyes. "Is this because of the woman in the market? Is that why? You don't want to confront her? She has these abilities, just like you. We all saw them. She's not afraid to use them."

"I can't control them," Nathan pulled his hands from Nur. "I don't know what they are."

"Maybe *you* need to believe, Stryder. Maybe you need to accept who you are. Unchain your mind. You may think you're normal, but I've seen you do some incredible things."

Perhaps she was right. He was stuck thinking as if he were still on Earth, where aliens and space travel didn't exist. Maybe there was more to the universe—to him—than he knew. If Arista could tap into the power of being an Asante warrior, then why couldn't he?

"What do I do about Arista?"

Nur tilted her head at him as if he should already know the answer. "You saw her eyes in the market. She would have killed us. Whatever you had before is over. If she stands in our way, she's an enemy. I understand you may have had feelings toward her, but no battle ever ended with a kiss."

With those words ricocheting around in his mind for the rest of the day, his only relief was realizing that whatever happened, this would all be over in thirty-six hours. One way or another.

The night had a different feel than the morning had. It was the eve of the assault on the Meraki stronghold in Brevetta, and Nathan was surrounded by the people he'd grown to care about.

Prymack was on an elevated stage, addressing the crowd.

"Tomorrow is Savadon, and never in our history have we fought a single battle on this day. The Meraki know this. They have known this for the six years they have been here. But tomorrow is different. Tomorrow, we will strike with vengeance." He paused, looking out over the crowd.

"There is no one to fall back on—no one else will help us," he continued, passion surging through his voice. "We are in an impossible situation, but we are Kavka's only hope for freedom. We are the last line of defense against the Meraki Dominya. Their dampening field is in one of the skytowers. By destroying it, we will only need to reach out to the High Command. As soon as they send reinforcements, we will be free.

"We have done so much already. We must look within ourselves for the power to fight this last battle. Everything we have done in the last six years has led to this confrontation. To quit now, as the others have done, would be foolish and disastrous—we have nowhere to go. They have conquered planets before us, but they have not conquered us! I say, we show them what we are made from! I say we stop them here!"

The crowd roared confidently, and Prymack shouted even louder. "When we are finished, the Meraki will know that the moment they landed here, everything they did was all leading to this! It was leading to fire!"

Cyndron jumped on a table and raised his arm into the air

as the rebels cheered. "Leading to fire!" he repeated over and over. "Leading to fire! Leading to fire!"

The crowd joined him, chanting the phrase, crying for Kavka's freedom in one thunderous voice. It was deafening. Determination pulsed through the room, sending chills up Nathan's spine and filling him with hope.

Nur gazed at Prymack with glimmering eyes. He nodded back at her, then turned away. Nathan knew the man had promised her retribution, and now that time had come.

The crowd continued to chant and cheer as Prymack stepped off the stage. Pollo approached him, whispering in his ear. The message seemed to change Prymack's entire demeanor.

The pair slipped through the crowd toward Nathan and pulled him into one of the side rooms. Pollo closed the door.

Prymack paced before speaking.

"I asked Pollo to work with one of our specialists to intercept Meraki communications. While looking for communications, they picked up a signal."

Pollo took a seat. "We discovered a short-range pulse that triggered a tightbeam signal at random intervals. Unless you were scanning the exact moment it was transmitting, you'd never know it was there. It makes it hard to detect, but the information is spotty."

Nathan glanced between the pair. Something was off. "What was it?"

Prymack's hand turned into a fist. "I know who the spy is, Nathan."

"Who?"

Prymack drew a seven-inch blade from his belt with a quick metallic scrape and took a step toward Nathan.

"It's you."

✷ ✷

Arista burst through the door to Ajax's office without caution, ready to erupt. She was done with pleasantries, done with procedure.

Ajax twisted in surprise, drawing his sidearm. With two steps, she disarmed him, and slammed him against the back wall.

Leaning in, she spoke through a tightened jaw. "Where is he?" It was all she could get out.

"They're back. Here in Brevetta."

"Where?"

"Release me, and we can discuss it. There's no reason to be uncivilized."

Her grip relaxed, and she took a step back.

"It's good to see this enthusiasm in you." Ajax said and casually picked up his sidearm. "Now, direct it at our enemies. Currently, we just lost contact. They could be anywhere in the city now."

Her eyes narrowed. "We'll have to flush him out, then."

"Take solace, Lieutenant Commander—preparations are already underway. Tomorrow, we'll remind them who rules this planet."

✳ ✳

Blood poured from the wound in Nathan's leg. The pain cut a path up his thigh as Prymack sliced a ten-centimeter gash. From the wound, he removed a small device.

"Damn it! They've been tracking me since day one! Are we even safe here?"

It seemed the translators and HUD weren't the only thing Dr. Rami had implanted. Now, everyone he'd trusted while with the Meraki had betrayed him.

"We're safe," Pollo said as he wrapped Nathan's leg. "They haven't been able to track us that closely. The safehouses are electronically shielded. The signal can't get out here."

"Pollo, give us a minute," Prymack said, then took a seat as Pollo left the room. "This isn't your fault. No one knew it was there."

"You're wrong. I should have known!" Agitated, Nathan stood up to pace the room, forgetting the wound in his leg. Within two steps, it gave out. He returned to the chair, fighting back a wave of nausea that overcame him. "Fuck!"

"They're devious. Trust me, I know." Prymack sighed. "This war has taken a lot from me, Nathan. It took my family—but it also gave me one. Without that, I don't know where I would be now. You've all kept me human, kept me away from doing things I'd regret, even if you didn't know it. I haven't known you long, but I consider you clan."

Nathan held his gaze. "I think we saved each other."

For a moment, Prymack looked happy, not worried about the upcoming battle or strained by the unbelievable pressure that leading a rebellion must bring. Then, in a measured motion, he opened a drawer and withdrew a wooden box. Placing it on his lap, he looked up at Nathan.

"This has been in the Yiiga clan for generations. I want you to have it."

Prymack opened the box to reveal a spherical medallion on a chain. It had a crystal centerpiece, surrounded by a casting made of intersecting metal circles.

"I can't take this," Nathan said. "Keep it and give it to someone who deserves it."

"No, Stryder. *You* deserve it. It belongs in your hands." He placed it in Nathan's palm and held it there.

"What have I done? No more than anyone else."

"You fight for a world that's not even yours, even after I sent you away. You added hope to us all. There's no discussion here, Nathan. It's yours."

It was the first time Prymack had used his first name. There was no way Nathan could refuse it again. As he gripped the medallion, the gem gave a slight twinkle.

That night, lying on a cot in the safehouse, Nathan went over the plan again and again in his head until he knew every element. Part of it was being prepared, but the other part was trying to keep his mind off all the people who might have died because of the tracking device in his leg.

They were attacking from three sides. The primary team of each force would engage any Meraki forces they encountered. The bomb teams would slip past in the confusion and infiltrate the skytowers which, Drelmar had said, could house the main dampening field transmitter and the Deathwind. Once they were in, they would set a plasma charge on a two-minute delay, allowing themselves time to get clear and retreat. Without knowing which building contained the devices, they would have to blow them all.

Nathan's bomb team was Prymack, Nur, and Vendala. They would storm the tallest building, dubbed "Apex." Sitting up, he gazed through a broken window at his target, which was roughly a mile away, through a wooded area that separated them from the downtown district. He contemplated their defenses. He'd learned some of the Meraki methodology, but mostly about infiltration, not defensive positioning.

Looking down, he realized he was rubbing the starburst scar on his hand again.

Anxiety had him in its grip. There was so much that could go wrong—so many unknowns. He inhaled a deep breath of the universe and exhaled his fears.

✶ ✶

Duma was back aboard the bridge of the *Kai'den*, having accomplished all he wanted planet side. He'd set up the Deathwind weapon and lit a fire under his protégé.

On his monitor was Commander Sculic, who was overseeing the troops on the ground.

"Wave two of the evacuation has started. All non-essential personnel have been withdrawn. The rest are in position."

Duma nodded in satisfaction.

"Sir," Ajax continued, "I feel it's necessary to state that I have serious questions about Lieutenant Commander Conak's emotional conflict with her mission. I have kept sensitive intelligence out of her direct contact for these reasons."

Duma was not concerned. He knew Ajax would have doubts, but the man wasn't aware of everything that had gone into Arista's conditioning.

"If she fails this time, Deathwind will take care of her," he said coldly.

"Sir," the comm master spoke up to his right.

Switching off the haloid, Duma turned to the officer.

"A large group of rebels have gathered in Altec Square on the Tecca peninsula."

"They are just celebrating their holy day." Duma looked at the image of the square on the display screen. What he saw was a disorganized group of unarmed and defeated people celebrating harmony or something equally ridiculous. "No concern to us."

"Sir, they want to surrender—to send a message for peace."

"Surrender? After everything they've cost us?" Duma snarled. "It's too late for that. Continue the systems check. Ready Project Deathwind to go online." He paused. "And realign it to initiate in Altec Square."

CHAPTER 46

As he lifted his head from the windowsill, Nathan realized he must have gotten some sleep. The kink in his neck stung when he moved. Extending it from side to side until the cramp was gone, he followed with more stretching. Then he dropped to the floor for some quick pushups to burn off his nervous energy.

The night had been spent meditating and trying to channel the Asante energy that was locked in his blood. He'd reached a point where he could generate it as a translucent shield, as it had appeared in the market fight with Arista, about half the time he tried. Summoning it into his fits still proved more difficult. Hopefully, it would be enough to face the challenges in the day ahead.

Today was the day that they would either all die or change everything. It was a fulcrum point in Kavka's future—and his.

Down the hallway, he spotted Xantani looking over a blueprint of one of the skytowers. Vendala was with him, but she was staring out the window, lost in her own thoughts.

As the floor creaked under his weight, she turned. Her eyes were distant.

"This could be it, Nathan," she said with a sigh.

He put his arm around her and gave her a quick squeeze. "We got this."

The mood was tense, and the hallways were quiet as he continued his walk. He saw faces he'd come to recognize as friends, rebels who'd overcome so much to make it this far. Some were cleaning their weapons, while others were eating or praying.

He found Prymack and Nur in the room that held their only means of communication with the world outside of Brevetta. It was a low frequency radio, and Prymack was attached to the receiver.

"He's still trying to find more people," Nur said, glancing at the medallion around his neck. Appearing to know its meaning, she flashed him a tender smile.

Nathan nodded in silence. His mind was on the upcoming battle, but that wasn't all.

Haunted by the specter of possibly facing Arista again, he returned to his room to clean his weapons. He'd opted to use a Meraki energy rifle and sidearm he'd picked up along the way. The weapons were familiar, and using them had a certain irony. Like him, they were weapons created by the Meraki, and now would be used against them.

After breaking them down and inspecting the parts, he pieced them back together. Next, he looked over the medallion, rolling it in his fingers. It looked ancient, with scratches on the metal, but otherwise it was unremarkable. Slinging it around his neck, he strapped on the worn and disjointed armor he'd acquired during his time on Kavka and prepared for what could very well be his last day alive.

At sundown, Nathan received the order to meet on the ground floor, where the original bar still stood, boarded up and in ruins.

As he entered, the room buzzed with anticipation. Some rebels seemed excited for the fight, while others stood quietly with their own thoughts and fears. Collectively, they were ready for battle.

"This is it!" Prymack said, silencing the crowd. "All the deaths, all the sacrifice, have led to this. Now is the moment that bares your soul. Now is the time to fight for what you believe in, to fight for the future and refuse to fade into history. I know what many of you are feeling, as I feel it too. Fear.

Anger. Desperation. Grab them now, with me, and forge them into weapons!

"What we do tonight will start a chain reaction that will echo not only around this world, but beyond. Tonight, we usher in a new age!"

✶ ✶

Knowing the rebels were in Brevetta, Ajax was able to create Operation Sundown. It wasn't the most creative name, but it didn't need to be. It was a simple tactic modified from one he'd learned the first week at Ragnakor academy. When it was over, Brevetta would be an inferno and the rebellion would be little more than ash.

The bombers would form a ring around Brevetta and move inward, blanketing the city in Sunfire bombs. Starting on the outside would ensure a perimeter in which none of the rebels could escape the hellfire. Any who managed to stay ahead of the bombing would be driven straight into the meat grinder he'd set up in the center of the circle, the woods around the skytowers.

They had evacuated most of his soldiers, but those who remained he deployed a squad of Cybers for support. Large, heavily armored cybernetic soldiers that should be more than enough to finish the rebels.

After that, he could get off this forsaken planet and take his place in an elevated leadership role within the fleet. He knew Grand Valor Duma was not interested in commanding the fleet long term, which left several openings that he was qualified to fill.

Mir's voice interrupted his thoughts. "Sir, the bombers are in place and awaiting your command."

"Excellent." A smirk creeped across his face. He couldn't have held back his satisfaction if he'd tried. "Start the show."

* *

On the rim of Brevetta, a formation of shadows glided amid the darkening sky. Their wings cut silently through a mist of clouds as they followed their attack vector. Within the cockpits, the comms beeped, followed by Major Mir's voice.

"Razer One, prepare to throw the blanket on my command."

In perfect synchronization, the Meraki bomber squadron dropped from the clouds and opened their bomb-bay doors. Beneath each bomber, a rack of orange spheres lowered into place.

"Razer One, execute."

One after another, the bombers dropped clusters of orange spheres on the city below.

* *

Moments later, a distant boom shook the rebel safehouse. Three more followed, knocking loose debris and dust from the ceiling and onto Nathan's shoulders.

"Xan, see what that is," Prymack said. "Everyone else, you have your assignments. Get ready."

Xantani disappeared up the stairs with a headset. Nathan remained where he was while many others in the room peered through gaps in the boarded-up windows for clues as to what was happening. The crowd held its breath, waiting for Xantani's response. It came over the headset in a crackling tone.

"Bombers, sir. They're blanketing the city from the south, heading this way."

"Damn," Prymack said. "At least they're forcing us the way we're headed. Let's go!"

"Wait, there's something else… something different."

Nathan pushed his way to a window. Coming toward them from the sky was a sight he'd never wanted to witness again.

Their jetpacks gave off a distinctive glow, like red fireflies in the distance. He'd encountered one in a training session. Arista had called them Cybers—hulking machines designed for the simple purpose of killing.

"Listen up," Nathan called into his headset. "They have heavily armored soldiers out there. Use the explosive rounds. Target their backs or go for their joints. They're tough, but we can take 'em."

"You heard him! Let's make some noise!" Prymack swung open the front doors and charged out with Nathan, Nur, and Vendala in tow.

The sky was dark now that the sun had set. It was about two kilometers to their targets—a long two kilometers. Behind them, the bombers were moving slowly, dropping one glowing ball of explosives at a time. They detonated into perfectly spherical shapes like tiny suns, annihilating everything in their radius.

Around Nathan, the rebels were spread out, the main team taking the lead in the formation, and the others following, ready to slip past once the battle started.

Nathan trotted behind Prymack, his senses enhanced with adrenaline and registering the sounds of the forest: snapping branches, shuffling leaves, and animals fleeing from the coming firestorm. They headed through what had once been a park that ringed the city center, now wild with growth.

Flashes from the bombs falling behind them provided enough light to make out the terrain. The subsequent rumbling sent an eerie buzz through the trees. Flaring jetpacks from the Cybers were descending into the forest in front of them. But there was no time to stop or maneuver. The bombers made sure they would run the gauntlet.

They completed the first kilometer in ten minutes, watchful for any sign of an ambush, but none came. The hum of jetpacks ceased, leaving the area relatively quiet. Nathan could hear the whispers of rebels communicating in front of him, between the distant bombs.

Over the headset, Prymack fine-tuned his orders. "Team one, slow down—they're close. Everyone else, be ready to move when the fighting starts. Don't stop until you reach your target."

A sudden explosion shattered the silence and ripped through the forest, followed by a chain of thunderous rattles. Strobing flickers from unseen weapons lit the dark area in rapid succession, making the action in front of Nathan appear like simple snapshots. Before him were disjointed frames of a rebel soldier as he twisted in agony before disappearing in the underbrush.

The first line of rebels dropped to the forest floor and returned fire on the hidden enemy. Nathan dove to his chest, his elbows sinking into the soft dirt. The earsplitting rattle of gunfire echoed in his ears, leaving room for little else. Through the brush and shadows, he could make out the blazing gun barrels of two Cybers methodically flooding the forest with energy pulses.

"Two Cybers! Forward arc!" he called out, then started firing on the closest.

"Explosive rounds!" Prymack said into his headset over the fierce noise. "Keep suppressing fire on them." He turned to check on the proximity of the bombers.

Nathan took a quick glance as well. The bombing had already reached the safehouse, leaving nothing but smoke and flames in its wake. Crawling forward through the underbrush, he flanked a Cyber to get a clean shot at its back. One explosive round to where Arista had shown him, and the machine exploded, creating an opening.

"Move! Move!" Prymack shouted. "Don't engage if you don't have to."

Nathan climbed to his feet, as did Vendala and Nur beside him. Keeping his head down, he crouched to avoid enemy fire. Advancing, he reached a rebel lying on the ground, a seeping wound in her chest. He kneeled beside her but knew the moment he saw the woman's eyes that there was nothing he could do. Several other bodies lay mangled nearby.

Nur looped her arm under his and pulled him to his feet.

"It's too late," she said. Her voice, and everything around him, was muffled and ringing. "We can't stop!"

The bombers were gaining on them. Ahead, Nathan heard more gunfire. Two more Cybers had caught a group of rebels in a crossfire.

"Team one, spread out into groups of ten, ten-meter spread," Prymack said through the headset.

Vendala was now to his left, Nur to his right, and Prymack in front. They passed three more bodies that remained motionless in the dirt. With eyes wide, taking in the carnage, fear tinted Vendala's face. The feeling wasn't solely hers, however. If they didn't win this battle, they would all be in the dirt.

Scattered clashes broke out between the Cybers and the newly formed teams of ten. The bomb teams continued running ahead, relying on the others to protect them. There was only a half kilometer to go now.

Nathan pressed the headset closer to his ear. It was hard to hear over the chaos.

"Sir, this is Xan. We're out of exploding shells."

"They're slow. Try to outrun them."

"Copy."

Fifty meters in front of them, the field lit up as a volley of lasers erupted from the darkness, cutting down several rebels in the front line. Nathan twisted to his right and dropped hard to the ground. Feeling the rough trunk of a tree under his hand, he scrambled to get behind it, banging his knee in the process. A burn shot its way up his leg to his hip.

"Down! Down! Everyone down!" Nathan's voice jumped

from his chest. "They have repeater turrets waiting. Use the grenades if you can get them that far!"

"Xan, flank right!" Prymack said, as a volley of explosions ripped through the night air.

Xantani gave no reply.

"Xan!"

The turrets in front of them continued their fire.

"Manii, flank 'em!"

"Copy."

Nathan fired a burst of four shots, nailing a turret operator in the chest. Another turret exploded to the right, creating a gap.

"Move forward!" Prymack's voice echoed in his ear.

Nathan and the others jumped up and continued their path toward the heart of Brevetta. The forest cover was thinning, allowing the skytowers to become visible through the trees. Behind them was a raging inferno.

Nathan glanced at Nur. Surprisingly, she had kept her cool and not rushed into anything yet. Soon, though, with their dwindling numbers, he knew they would all need to prove their valor. With his heart beating a machine-gun rhythm in his chest, he took another step deeper into the maelstrom ahead.

※ ※

Prymack knew how many rebels were left in his unit, whether by subconsciously keeping track or feeling each one die in his gut. Either way, there were ninety-three left, and it sickened him. The lead team was down to seventy-one, and some bomb teams had lost members already.

This wasn't how it was supposed to go.

He checked to make sure Nur was close. Prymack sensed she was ready to rage and charge off recklessly. He had to trust that Nathan could handle himself now.

The whiz of laser fire to his left caught his eye. Sticking his front foot in the dirt, he pivoted and quickly brought his rifle to bear on the surprise assailant. In his sights was a Meraki vanguard soldier and thankfully not a Cyber.

With his eyes locked on Vendala, the soldier failed to notice him. Without hesitation, Prymack seized the opportunity and squeezed the trigger while the soldier's own rifle blazed with light. His bullets ripped into the Meraki, tearing him apart.

But it was too late.

Vendala's body shook with each hit, her eyes wide and staring at Prymack with a frightened expression, pleading for help. Yet, the life in them faded before she even hit the ground.

Vendala was gone.

It all happened too fast. Another person's blood on his hands, and this time, it was Vendala. She'd been a child when they found her—No, now wasn't the time for guilt. He had to push on. Many had already died, and many more would before this could end.

Another gun cracked twice behind him. Turning, he saw Nur as she downed two soldiers coming from the north. He nodded at her and scanned the chaos for Stryder, whom he found lingering at Vendala's body before moving on.

The bombers' engines were growing louder in the background. The glow of their ordnance now steadily illuminated the area.

Ahead, they reached five rebels pinned down between a repeater turret and several Meraki soldiers. The repeater unleashed a barrage of plasma, sending two of the rebels cartwheeling through the air on impact.

"Stryder, flank left," Prymack said, then turned to order Nur into position, but she'd already taken off toward the turret.

Stryder rolled forward and blasted two soldiers in one

smooth transition. Seeing him move was remarkable, as if he was born for this.

Prymack drove up the middle, drawing the enemy's fire. Four separate streams of lasers stuttered out of sync around him. Diving to the ground, he crawled toward the pinned men. He could see that one was wounded in the leg.

Prymack rolled to the side as the turret gun rattled off another salvo of plasma bolts that ripped up the dirt next to him. Then it abruptly ceased. He stopped rolling and looked up to see Nur standing over the dead turret operator.

The headset crackled to life as he dragged the rebels to safety. "Bombers closing. Mortar shells from the right!"

Just then, two Cybers landed in front of Prymack, targeting his chest. This was definitely not the way it was supposed to go.

But before they could fire, a hail of plasma bolts assailed the cyborgs from the right, destroying one. The other turned to face the threat.

It was Nur.

Standing on her tiptoes behind the repeater, she fired it in a constant stream of energy, howling at the Cyber in her familiar war cry.

Terror ripped through Prymack as the Cyber countered with a relentless barrage of laser pulses. The searing flashes struck her leg and tore through the flesh of her right side. With a gut-wrenching scream, she collapsed to the ground.

Prymack shoved his bomb pack to Stryder. "Take this and stay put."

"Prymack! No!" Stryder clawed at his arm, but he pulled away.

Charging toward Nur and into the hellfire that surrounded her, he caught a glimpse over his shoulder of Stryder laying down covering fire for him.

But the Meraki Cybers were good shots. Within a few strides, he felt something tear through the flesh in his arm.

Adrenaline dulled most of the pain, but the smell was familiar. Another round struck his hip. The booming shots were the only thing he could hear as the rest of the world went silent.

Fighting through the damage, Prymack kept going, dragging his weakening body to where Nur lay, ignoring the lights whizzing by him. Step by unwavering step, he trudged toward her. Everything was slowing down. He couldn't move fast enough.

After an eternity, he scooped her up in his arms, her legs swinging limply under her. He turned and made for a dip in the landscape for cover as another bolt struck him. Immense pain surged up his leg as his knee shattered and buckled.

Reflexively, he jerked his hand down to sustain his balance, staying upright for a few more steps until he collapsed.

As he fell, he cradled Nur with his body so as not to crush her. She lay limp within the safety of his arms. Slowly, she reached out to stroke his face.

The outside world had vanished. Now it was just the two of them. The warmth of her hand on his cheek, and of knowing that she would not die alone, was worth more to him than the rest of his life.

"My love," she cried.

Staring back into her now-glazed eyes, he clasped her hand.

"My life," he whispered.

✷ ✷

Pinned down by a stream of laser fire, Nathan could do nothing more to help. All he could do was watch as Prymack picked up Nur, trying desperately to bring his betrothed to safety, only to be shot again and again as he staggered forward. Prymack's face was a stone carving, his resilience simply heroic, even as he fell. The affection between them was palpable as they held each other's eyes.

"Noo!" Nathan shouted, his stomach filling with dread.

A burst of light followed the high-pitched whistle of an incoming mortar shell, and a ring of explosions sailed through his senses.

Time around him slowed. The blazing flash was all he could see. Slowly, he fell toward the ground, blinded and knowing that Prymack and Nur were forever gone from his life.

Time began again as he hit the dirt.

Nathan roared, a predator's growl rumbling deep inside him.

Before, he had fought with deadly skills that were taught to him by a deadly man. He'd killed in defense, and only when he had to, never because he'd wanted to. Never.

As the deaths of countless rebels replayed in his head, his emotions reached a flash point and burst into the one thing he had lacked, the one thing that kept him from becoming a true warrior: the blazing fire of conviction. Now, he held no doubts and no reservations about unleashing all his skills, all his power, on everything that stood in his way.

Something savage erupted within him and raged through his body. With his sight fully restored, he picked up his rifle, climbed to his feet, and turned to the soldiers still firing on him. Counter to every instinct or training he had, he clenched the trigger and unloaded the clip while running directly at them. The blasts ripped into their flesh, tearing through all three, laying them to waste.

To his left was the Cyber that had killed Prymack and Nur. Nathan tossed the rifle aside, knowing it was useless against its armor. He needed something else.

Drawing his knife, he recalled how Arista had taught him to take a Cyber down. Letting his instincts take over, he charged the monstrosity.

As it turned to face him, he jammed the blade into the joint of the Cyber's knee. It pierced through the flexible armor, sending a cool fluid over Nathan's hand. Retrieving the knife took some effort, but the amount of adrenaline pumping through him made it easier.

The Cyber's arm flung down to fire at him, but Nathan caught it in his off hand, pushing it toward the ground. The arm pivoted as it tried in vain to fire at Nathan. A flurry of laser bolts erupted from the gun port on its arm, slamming into the dirt. The shots had zero accuracy, but the thundering of each round rattled Nathan's brain.

Again, he slashed its knee while fighting off its firing arm with his free hand. This time, the knife hit something more critical, and the Cyber's leg folded.

But just as Nathan thought he'd gained the upper hand, the thing backhanded him in the face. The crushing sting was quickly followed by the taste of blood.

Dazed, Nathan spun the knife around in his hand and thrusted it upward into the mechanical soldier's neck. A splash of liquid ran down his arm as the Cyber began to topple. Nathan followed it down, stabbing it again and again in a berserk rage.

The blade shattered from the force of blows, but that didn't stop him. Nathan's eyes turned to wildfire, revealing the fierce warrior of his lost heritage. His hands began to glow as he continued to thrash the machine. Metal pieces and fragments exploded out with every punch until it was a heap of scrap.

Looking down at the mutilated mechanical beast, he felt a whisper of satisfaction. His fury was running so wildly that he could hardly focus. It was difficult to remember what it was he was supposed to do.

Peering up at the skytowers, his blood-washed teeth dripping red and his hands glowing with energy, his mind was primal. The only thing that registered was his need to destroy.

Forcing himself to pause, Nathan took a deep breath. He

felt the weight of the pack and the plasma explosive inside, pulling him out of his rage. The haze cleared, and he remembered the mission.

The bombs behind him hadn't paused, exploding like drumbeats of some nightmarish soundtrack. Grabbing an extra clip from his pack and the rifle, he ran north toward the skytowers.

Before long, he was within sight of the gate to the Meraki base. It was the only way through the four-meter-high metal walls that surrounded the city center. Scanning the immediate area, there was no movement.

A cool breeze flowed over the grassy field in front of him, making it billow like green waves, rising and falling with the wind and causing a smooth rustling. Throughout the grass were the lifeless bodies of rebels who had made it ahead of him.

Glancing back at the bombers that were still on his trail, Nathan was starting to doubt that anyone had made it inside. But as he approached the gate, he could see blackened and charred pock marks from explosives and the bodies of Meraki soldiers who'd once guarded the entrance lying among the dead.

The once active base that protected the skytower complex was now eerily quiet, like the eye of a hurricane. *This can't be good*, he thought, as the familiar feeling of anxiety settled into his chest. Where was everyone?

Jogging ahead, he slipped through the gate and saw empty guard posts and hastily secured doors flapping in the wind. Even the empty shell of a Meraki tank sat abandoned, still idling. Using the shadows and buildings as cover, he zigzagged through the base until he reached Apex, the tallest skytower. Still, he saw no one.

As Nathan crept through the shallow grass toward the building, each breath he took echoed against the ground, returning louder in his ears. Ahead of him was a meter-high wall, and beyond that he couldn't see.

The bombers were only background noise now, a constant booming that his ears had gotten used to. Intuition told him he was safe from them, as they had probably been ordered not to bomb the base.

Reaching the wall, he pulled himself into a crouched position. Peeking over, he could now see three vanguard soldiers outside the entrance to the Apex building.

There was nothing between him and the guards, which put him in an awkward position. He was too far away for a sneak attack, and he didn't have time to get pinned behind the wall in a shoot-out.

Short on options, Nathan jumped to his feet. He didn't have time for anything else. Each minute the rebel attack was growing weaker, if it wasn't over already.

He rushed the gate in a dead sprint, hoping to get there before they spotted him. The heavy pack on his shoulder bounced with each step, slamming into his back. His breaths grew shorter and quicker as he tried to cover the distance as quickly as possible.

Dipping his shoulder, he shed the pack and flung it to the ground. He was probably ten meters from the guards when the first one turned his way.

Cocking his arm back and then flinging it forward, Nathan released a dagger. It sliced through the air, and on contact the guard twisted violently, dropping his weapon.

By the time the next guard turned, Nathan had closed the gap. The man's eyes swelled when he spotted Nathan charging. Lowering his shoulder into a battering ram, he plowed into the guard. The pain was brief—a sharp pinch down his arm as he connected, his vision turning splotchy as the impact knocked his breath away. The guard's body softened and flew back against the fence.

Using the momentum, Nathan rolled closer to the remaining guard before he could react, stomping on the man's knee. The crunch of the joint would have made him sick a few months ago, but now, it was bliss. He dropped the guard with a quick strike to his throat.

Nathan snapped up a rifle from a fallen guard, shouldered the backpack again, and bolted. The dash to the building drew the attention of more Meraki soldiers. From the guardhouse, four more appeared, raising their rifles.

Without breaking stride, Nathan pulled the zipgun from his pack, lifted it into the air, and fired.

Guards unloaded on him from seemingly everywhere. With lasers crisscrossing around him, Nathan focused on the energy barrier he'd been summoning the night before.

Lifting his arm, a translucent shield appeared. It flickered as it reflected blasts that would have otherwise found his head and chest.

Hoping his aim was close enough, he kept moving and waited for the zipgun harpoon to hit something. A second after sensing the vibration of the projectile striking, he slung his rifle and activated the zipline.

The mechanism whizzed intensely, reeling in the line and lifting him into the air. Clenching his jaw against the force of the ride, he skyrocketed up the side of the building. The world sped by in almost the same way it had when he'd landed on Kavka, except this time he was soaring skyward.

Reaching the end of the cable, the spool locked, jerking him to a stop. High above the guards who were shooting at him, he climbed onto the ledge, detached the zipline, and stowed it in his pack. He'd need it on the way out.

Looking down, he guessed he was around the twentieth floor. The guards below were still firing, but their shots were much less accurate from this distance.

Nathan slipped the rifle from his back and fired two shots into a giant window, causing it to spiderweb with cracks. Then he flipped the weapon around and smashed the stock into the glass, triggering a cascade of shards to burst around him. Shielding his head from the jagged shower with his backpack, he gave it a second to clear before climbing inside.

The hallway was quiet, and emergency lights gave it a desolate glow. He almost couldn't believe he'd made it this far. Pushing away thoughts of running into Arista, he focused on finding a quiet place to set the bomb and get out. That was all he had left to do.

There were a few moments of silence before lasers began whizzing past him from the right. Nathan twisted his body to the floor. His knee and elbow slammed hard as he fell.

Firing off a few wild shots, he scrambled to the corner for cover.

On his stomach, Nathan leaned out from the corner and fired twice to keep the enemy from charging him. Behind him was a long, straight hallway. He wasn't sure if he would have enough time to cover the distance before the guards followed. If he couldn't, he'd have nowhere to hide.

He squeezed off two more shots and decided he had no other choice. Springing to his feet, he turned and sprinted down the hall. He pumped his legs as quickly as he could, trying to cover as much ground as possible before—

Streaks of energy flew past him and slammed into the end wall. An overhead light burst from the stray fire, sending sparks raining down.

Ahead of him, the end of the hall made a sharp right. He dove around the corner as trailing lasers lit up the intersecting wall behind him.

Rolling to his feet, he tried the door to his right—locked.

The next one wasn't.

✵ ✵

Grand Valor Duma watched the progress of the ground forces from the monitors aboard the *Kai'den* with dismay. He regarded their attempts to eliminate the rebels and sighed. How hard was it to kill a few dead-enders? If they took over the skytowers, they could disable the Deathwind.

"They're too close," he said, tension rising in his chest.

The officer at his side nodded. "Yes, sir. Should we—"

"Activate Project Deathwind," Duma interrupted, still staring at his console.

"No, I meant we sh—"

Duma turned to look at the defiant soldier. "Activate Project Deathwind!"

"But—our troops. The last wave will never make it out in time."

Duma stepped up to the officer, grabbed him by the collar, and flung him across the bridge. "We don't *have* time!"

Taking the officer's place at the main console, Duma slammed his fist against the activation button and triggered Project Deathwind. After it swept the planet clean, Kavka would finally be under Meraki control.

CHAPTER 47

Hurrying through the maze of hallways, Nathan was sure he'd lost his pursuers. He continued searching for a quiet room to set the bomb in. After rounding the next corner, he came to a stop.

Ajax stood ahead of him, rifle in hand. His lips forming a smug grin.

"It was a noble effort, but you will not be the hero today," Ajax said, raising his rifle. "Don't try to run. I have control of the building. From the moment you entered, it led you to me."

Ajax strutted toward him, the rifle aimed at his chest. "Put it all down."

Nathan tried to raise the energy shield like he had before, but it wasn't working. Ajax was at the perfect safe distance. Too far to reach, but close enough that his shot would be practically guaranteed to kill Nathan before he could lift his rifle.

With no other options, Nathan dropped his rifle and backpack. "You think you've won, but there's more than just me out there."

"Oh, Stryder." Ajax shook his head. "They're all surrendering. You're the last gasp." He chuckled. "Remember when you thought your little planet was the only one with life on it?"

Nathan inhaled the universe and slowly let it out. Drelmar's words echoed in his mind. *To be resilient, you must keep moving forward. No matter what.*

With lightning finesse, Nathan twisted his body sideways, triggering Ajax's reflex. The move was just enough for the first shot to miss by a fraction. Heat from the laser burned his chest. Then he zigzagged toward Ajax, and the next shots missed him as well.

Trying to be as unpredictable as possible, Nathan leapt at the side wall. With the brief traction his weight and boot treads gave him, he pushed off launching himself higher. Plasma bolts filled the air around him.

Now six feet off the floor, he swung his leg around and connected with Ajax's head. The man's eyes were wild with surprise.

The blow staggered him, sending the rifle to the ground. Nathan landed in a crouch and followed up with two hard body shots.

Quickly recovering, Ajax fired off a series of hand strikes in rapid succession. The counter to each move was etched into Nathan's reflexes, and he blocked them with matching flicks of his arm.

Then, in a fluid transition, he responded with a palm strike, but Ajax slipped to the side.

In a strange way, Nathan was pleased with the challenge. Ajax was good, but he didn't have time to let this get drawn out. It was time to drive full throttle.

Nathan rushed in with simultaneous attacks at Ajax's groin and throat. Both were blocked. Trained senses warned him just in time to sidekick Ajax as he slid in. His foot slammed into the man's lower ribs, forcing out a pain-filled grunt. Pushing his advantage, Nathan landed three more shots to his liver, chin, and temple, causing Ajax to waver.

Without thinking, he grabbed Ajax firmly at the neckline and spun. His body whipped violently and slammed against the wall.

As his foe staggered to his feet, Nathan gave him no time to recover, crashing a flying knee to his face. The blow sent Ajax reeling, blood gushing from his nose and mouth.

Nathan grabbed Ajax by the throat, making his eyes bulge

in panic as he began to squeeze the life from him. In a clouded instant, he forgot about his mission, about Kavka, about everything else. *The enemy deserves everything they get*, someone had once told him.

Then he remembered who'd said it. Krell Duma.

He released his grip and let Ajax fall to the ground, incapacitated.

"Team two here. We've set our bomb," a woman's voice crackled on the headset.

Relief flooded Nathan's body—he wasn't the only one who'd made it. But that relief was short-lived as several footfalls pounded down the hallway. Taking off in the opposite direction, he hunted for a place to set the bomb.

Rushing down the hall, he caught a reflection in the window of Meraki soldiers around the next turn, waiting in ambush. With no time to stop, he lifted his feet from under him and fell onto his back. He slid across the floor, lifting his gun to a firing position, and pulled hard on the trigger.

A storm of lasers crackled through the room as five guards simultaneously unleashed a hail of shots smashing into the wall over Nathan's head. His return barrage fanned out across the narrow corridor, giving them little place to hide.

In a group, three guards fell chaotically to the floor, and Nathan's slide came to a stop. Rolling right, he re-targeted the remaining soldiers and dropped them with two shots each. The smell of burning flesh quickly invaded his nose.

Springing to his feet, he moved to the nearest door. Of course, it was locked. It seemed Ajax hadn't been bluffing. All the doors were metal, and therefore, too sturdy to kick in.

It's now or never, he thought. Closing his eyes, he drew on the power within his blood, the power of generations of warriors before him. Channeling it through the feeling of ronya, his hands charged blue with energy.

Not giving it time to fade like before, he slammed his

fists into the door. It exploded off its rails, sending fragments shooting into the room.

After moving through the carnage, he swept his rifle across the area, looking for any movement. It was empty. A couple dozen support beams broke up the open space. A long computer terminal stretched around the wall, stopping when it came to a full-sized window—just what he needed. Directly across from him was a building perfect for his plan.

Outside, tendrils of smoke entangled the city. In the distance, he could still see some gunfire, but not enough to be encouraging. The remaining rebels were scattered. Beyond that was a strange haze on the horizon. Was it Deathwind? He didn't have time to wonder.

Moving to the terminal, he kneeled on the floor and unzipped the pack, then pulled out the zipline gun and the plasma bomb. The explosive could be set for different effects, but Nathan twisted the dial and set it to blow straight up and down. His fingers ran over the controls and stopped only when it read two minutes. Then he activated it.

After watching the timer for a moment to make sure it was working, he grabbed the zipgun and returned to the window. He fired two shots from his pistol into the glass, cracking it. Lifting a chair, he whipped it against the window. This time, it shattered. He gave it a moment for the glass to fall, then fired the zipline to the adjacent building. It caught on his first try.

As he leaned his rifle against the terminal, a sinking feeling washed over him when he realized he'd forgotten the hook for the zipline in his pack. Rushing back to retrieve it, a voice stopped him in his tracks.

"Your life has come to an end, Nathan Stryder." Arista spoke from behind him. "Savor what's left of it."

He recognized her voice instantly, but not the anger it held. She stood with her legs shoulder width apart, a gun in each fist, ready to kill. Even then, he couldn't help the feelings she triggered in him. It was the first time he'd seen her since the Fettis market. She was no longer the woman he'd fallen for, he told himself. Now, she was the demon's minion, and he would treat her as such.

Slowly, he rose to his feet to fight the battle he knew would ultimately catch up to him.

✷ ✷

In the dim light of a random office stood the man Arista had been chasing around Kavka for the last few months. At one time she thought she loved him, now his name was poison on her lips.

"You're living a lie, Arista," Nathan said.

He was trying to distract her. They both knew he couldn't win. It was obvious, as his eyes searched frantically for a way out.

"Your words mean nothing to me!" she said, trying to block out her feelings like Duma had taught her. It had been easier in the past, but now she struggled.

Darting to the right, he rolled across the floor. She lifted her pistols and squeezed off a rapid burst. But she'd forgotten just how quick he was. Her shots trailed a half-step behind.

In mid-roll, he scooped up his rifle and sent a scattered salvo her way, ripping up the wall behind her. Every instinct she had told her to hit the floor, but she didn't. Instead, she returned his fire, shot for shot.

Then, with the realization that her emotions had overcome her training, she dashed for cover. As Nathan did the same, they sprinted parallel to each other, firing as they went.

It was difficult to get a clear shot between the support columns while running, but she was getting closer with each round. Then he disappeared behind one. Without a target, she ceased firing and took shelter behind another.

"The Vox are in on it, Arista," he called out from somewhere. "They have a weapon called Deathwind that can kill everyone on the planet!"

"Wrong again!" She couldn't believe what she was hearing. Drelmar had twisted his view even more than she thought. "The Vox aren't real, Nathan!"

Keeping her breaths steady, she prowled away from cover, trying to get an eye on her prey. The room was silent, despite everything that was happening outside. Rounding the nearest terminal, she dialed in on how she'd trained him to move. Where to flank, where to—

Quick footsteps to her right interrupted her thought. She spun, but it was too late. A crushing pain flared in her arm and spread to her ribs as Nathan kicked her into the terminal. In the same motion, he swept the weapons from her hands.

Instantly, she flung her elbow out and cracked him in the face. He stumbled backward, creating space between them. Blood dripped from a cut that had opened under his eye.

"Where do you think Lasal got the picture of my family?" Nathan said, wiping the blood away. "He could only have gotten it from Earth, when they took me and my sister."

Arista pulled a throwing knife from the sheath strapped to her leg. Trying to ignore the words, she focused on the one thing she had to do—kill him.

"What about the other picture? Of you and your grandmother in the mountains?" Nathan said. "They tricked you, just like they tricked me!"

"Shut up!" Arista struck out at the lie with her blade, slicing Nathan across the chest.

He winced and stumbled to the right. Pressing in again, she thrust the blade toward his liver, overextending herself in eagerness. Nathan sidestepped the attack and grabbed her knife hand, twisting the blade from it. It seemed she had taught him too well.

Swinging the knife down, he slashed the backside of her hand and sent a biting pain firing up her arm. In one fluid motion, Arista spun and back-fisted him in the jaw, causing him to stumble.

Nathan jabbed the knife at her in a sloppy attack, and he lost it to her quick reflexes. He snapped his arm back a moment before she could break it.

She swung the twice-stolen knife at him in two quick slashes, missing both times. Countering with a straight jab, he again grabbed for the knife. His fingers pressed against her skin, sending a familiar tingling through her body. Clenching her jaw, she tried to ignore the emotions it triggered and forced herself to focus. Damn him, he was distracting her.

Gathering the anger within, Arista pushed against him. The moment he resisted, she used his own momentum and swung him into a terminal. The force made him release his grip, but caused her to lose her handle on the knife, which went scattering across the floor.

She grabbed Nathan's wrist, pulling him off-balance, then sent a kick straight into his gut. The feel of solid contact forced a slight smile to her lips as he floundered backward.

Then, like a bullet, her hand shot to his throat. She squeezed.

"Just tell me why!" The words jumped from her mouth, surprising even her.

Struggling to breathe, he gagged. "You turned me in. I had no choice."

"Lies! Lies! Lies! I never said anything!" She squeezed harder.

Turning blue, Nathan returned the favor and grabbed her by the throat. "I'm not lying. I'm trying to save you."

"Save yourself," she managed to choke out.

A thunderous explosion suddenly rocked the building, flinging the pair apart. The floor trembled, sending equipment dancing across the room.

Focused on Nathan, she pushed the rumbling of the explosion into the background and stumbled unsteadily to her feet before the tremors had subsided.

They circled each other, attempting to gain the line of attack.

"Duma has manipulated us. You're on the wrong side! Come with me."

"Do you think I'm stupid?" Arista said, clenching her fist.

Had her heart been a weapon, she would have plucked it from her chest and used it to kill Nathan Stryder, the only man she had ever loved.

Simultaneously, they charged each other as both of their fists began to glow.

✷ ✷

When Cyndron looked out from the large conference room window at the fire and destruction of Brevetta, it felt as if he were watching a disaster story on a big screen. In the stillness of the room, it seemed like they had all the time in the world. But those were real people out there, friends he loved and a world he cherished—and it was all about to end unless they prevailed.

Around him, busy with purpose, were Pollo, and two other rebels.

"Jaya, Ziil. Guard the door," Pollo said a moment before he smashed the window. Once it shattered, a hot wind whipped into the room, accompanied by sirens and gunfire.

Cyndron pulled the plasma bomb from his pack and secured it to the wall. As he started to activate the device, he noticed an unusual trembling in his hands. Pausing, he shook them out.

"Serenity, Cyndron. Serenity," he said to his inner spirit.

Once again, he started the activation sequence.

"Contact!" Jaya shouted before she fired a burst from her

rifle down the hallway. Laser bolts streamed into the room in return.

Then the building next to them detonated in a violent explosion. Everything went sideways as a concussive blast crashed through the shattered window. An avalanche of energy sent everything into a maelstrom—shrapnel, glass, furniture, and people were all crushed to the wall. The invisible current then whipped them around the confined area like they were dust in the wind.

Cyndron struggled to anchor himself to something as he was dragged and flung around by the vortex. He'd lost track of the bomb and everyone else in the room.

As the surge dissipated, he scrambled to his feet and searched for the plasma device, digging frantically through what was left. Throwing a chunk of the table aside, he found it.

An empty abyss opened in his stomach as he read the timer. The blast had somehow activated it. He struggled to understand how it had happened, but there was no time now—only eighteen seconds.

Seventeen.

"Bloody feck!" Cyndron turned to see who was still alive and spotted Pollo and Jaya. Ziil was nowhere in sight. "We gotta go! Now!"

Pollo dragged Jaya to the zipline and strapped her on. Her legs seemed useless, but she grabbed the handle and began the slide.

"Cyn! You're next!" Pollo said, leaving no room for discussion.

Cyndron rushed to the line, clasped his handle to it, and dove out the window. Glancing backward, he saw Pollo do the same.

CHAPTER 48

Nathan and Arista weaved and dodged through the room in a lethal dance. The swirling glow of orange and blue energy pulsating in their hands flashed and swayed with each attack and counter. Flickers of the armor Nathan had seen before appeared briefly whenever she connected.

He was done talking, and she didn't believe him anyway.

Nathan gauged her actions. She was preparing for an attack. As she shifted forward, he let loose a furious offensive. Arista blocked the first two attacks, but the next got through, slamming into her abdomen and hopefully knocking the wind out of her.

Nearby, the terminal speakers snapped on, broadcasting Duma's voice.

"Lieutenant Commander Conak, return to the *Kai'den* immediately. Project Deathwind has been activated."

Arista didn't acknowledge the message as she charged Nathan with her own flurry of strikes. One slipped by and connected with his liver. A second later, a supernova of agony erupted inside him. He faltered to the side and retreated. Her coaching from the past echoed in his head, "*That's a liver shot. Stay up. Fight through it. Buy yourself time to recover.*"

Pushing her advantage, Arista clutched the back of his neck, limiting his movement, and pulling his head down. She started firing off knees to his ribs and face. Thankfully, the transparent glow of his armor flashed with each blow, taking most of the damage.

He blocked a strike at his head and dove for her legs. He

caught one, wrapping it up in his arms, attempting to twist her to the floor as she'd taught him.

The distinct feeling of an elbow slammed into his mouth as he did. Tasting the blood that came with it let him know that the armor wasn't blocking everything.

Pain was coming at him from all angles. He was losing this fight. There was no illusion about that. In the back of his mind, he realized he only had to hold on for another minute. Then the bomb would go off and… the survivors could contact the High Command.

Another bomb exploded outside, bucking the building's foundation. This time, it worked to his advantage. Equipment hurtled and trembled around the room, knocking Arista off him.

Regaining some strength, he sprang to his feet. Firing off a kick, he caught her on the knee, and she shifted backward.

Nathan risked a glance at the timer. Forty-one seconds left.

He was just trying to keep his distance and buy some time now. Arista seemed to know that and trapped him in a corner. Without warning, she sprang at him, twisting in the air. Her foot caught him in the chest.

The force flipped him over a console, and he landed face-first on the floor. A numb stinging vibrated in his lips, and thick, warm blood rolled down his neck. His tongue had turned into a wad of fur, dry and swollen.

Without delay, Arista hopped the console and kicked him in the ribs.

"Duma was right—you had potential." She spat the words at him as she prepared her deathblow.

Then, for the briefest of moments, the span of time it took for a memory, she hesitated.

Explosions flooded Nathan's ears as another building detonated close by. The room shuddered violently, earsplitting crashes and creaking metal surrounded him. For a moment, he was sure the building was going to collapse even without his bomb. The ceiling showered down, jarred loose by the quake. Pipes, beams, glass, and other debris surged onto Nathan and Arista.

✳ ✳

The Deathwind transmitted its deadly signal to the other three components. Hundreds of kilometers apart, the towers charged up and produced streams of energy that beamed in different directions, then converged together.

In Altec Square, there were thousands of people celebrating peace and surrendering to the Meraki Dominya. They carried signs offering good will and mercy.

Above them, the beams of energy collided and surged together. The crowds, mystified by what they saw, began to panic.

Dark clouds radiated swiftly from the focal point and swirled about, gaining size and mass. Within the storm, lightning sparked with hundreds of bolts a second. The stormfront rolled over the landscape, stretching down to the ground, glittering like a rainfall of silver and green electricity, enveloping the square.

As it reached them, the people shattered on a molecular level, exploding into dust. Within minutes, it had spread like a tidal wave of devastation moving at the speed of sound.

Deathwind raged with power and fury, enshrouding cities and the people within.

✳ ✳

When Nathan awoke face down on the floor, he had no notion of how much time had passed. He struggled to get out from underneath the collapsed ceiling, his wounds burning as he clawed and pulled his way loose. The bomb was buried, so there was no way to be sure how much time was left. It could be mere seconds.

Heaving his left leg free, he limped to the zipline, thanking god it was still intact. He was reaching up to clamp on the hook when he glanced back at the wreckage and the world around him stopped.

There she was—Arista, unconscious and trapped under a blanket of debris. Her motionless face filled his eyes, and his heart wrenched at the sight. Emotions clashed within him, reminding him of what they'd once had, what he'd once felt. It all rose into an uncontrollable intensity, quickly overcoming him.

He loved her. He knew that now. And nothing would change that.

Nathan hurried to her, frantically throwing off debris until he came to a beam that trapped her. Clamping his hands on the jagged metal, he set his feet against the floor. His muscles hardened, and his breathing stopped as he lifted with every part of his being. But it wasn't moving.

Nathan tried again. He wasn't leaving her. If she died in this explosion, he would as well.

Determination flooded his body. Tears slipped from his eyes. His focus was so acute it barely registered that his legs, back, and arms were outlined in his shimmering genetic armor.

A metallic screech and crumbling debris signaled the beam was starting to move. Nathan had all but forgotten about the timer and the bomb. He had one thing on his mind—to save Arista.

The beam rose painfully slow from her body, but it moved enough that he could shove it aside. He grabbed Arista under her arms and dragged her to the window, then scooped her up and threw her over his shoulder.

In one precise motion, he slapped the handle against the zipline, clamping it into place. His fingers still throbbed from lifting the beam as he closed them around the zipline grip. Though unsure whether he could hold on, he knew he had no choice. The bomb could explode at any second, but that didn't matter now. Nothing did—except her.

With his hands firmly in place, Nathan lifted his feet and began the slide down. His hands sent spikes of pain up his arm as he held onto his entire world. The wind rushed by, giving him what little refreshment it could.

They were fifteen meters from the end of the zipline when Nathan saw the reflection of the building he'd just left in the window he was heading for. It ignited, floor after floor, up and down, then burst with a yellowish-orange light as the plasma blast consumed it from within.

A second later, the sound hit him. It was deafening.

The shockwave blew out the windows in quick succession, followed by a blistering heat on his back. The glint of his genetic body armor flared as the concussion blast hit.

The zipline anchor attached to the crumbling building snapped, and the line went slack. The world suddenly lurched downward, ripping the breath from Nathan's lungs.

Arista's body drifted centimeters above his shoulder as they plummeted toward the planet's surface. Nathan clung to the hook, squeezing her between his shoulder and his head, determined not to let go. His insides were in complete chaos. Once stirred by his feelings for Arista and the desperation to save her, they now floated together in one swirling, weightless mess.

In a total freefall, surrounded by an aura of shattered glass, needles of panic stung Nathan from the inside. Arista's hip gently brushed his shoulder, and she began drifting. He tried to turn, but found it almost impossible. There was no leverage. Arista was gradually slipping away from him.

Kicking his leg out in front, Nathan attempted to get into a better position. His body turned slightly, but it wasn't enough. She was completely off his shoulder now, her body floating limply next to him as the ground rushed toward them.

Reaching his arm backward, he flailed out for a grip. The back of his hand brushed hers. His fingers stretched, clawing desperately at her arm as she fell farther beneath him until she was almost directly under him.

Without warning, Arista's eyes snapped open, wild with panic. Their gazes met. She reached out to him.

"Nathan!"

With the world spinning beneath her, he extended his arm, his fingers, and everything else that would stretch. It was still too far!

Then, he felt the gel-like Tanzi that clung to her body as it leaped out at his hand. Wrapping itself around his wrist, it hardened, forming a solid bridge between them.

A heartbeat later, the slack from the zipline still attached to the adjacent building snapped tight, slinging them toward the structure. The sudden jerk ripped at the muscles in his shoulder. He refused to give into the pain, but the combined weight of his and Arista's bodies, multiplied by gravity, and the distance they fell was too much. His fingers slowly pried open, releasing the handle that secured them to the zipline.

Havoc screamed all around them. Shielding Arista the best he could as they lurched and spun through the wreckage, Nathan focused on ronya and projecting the Asante armor. How much of what they were hitting was glass or brick or steel, he had no idea, but he prayed his armor would absorb most of it.

✷ ✷

The bridge of the *Kai'den* was a whirl of movement with officers in the midst of a mass evacuation of their forces. In the center of it all, Krell Duma watched the Deathwind spread its violent rampage on his monitor, not as a grand valor, but as a mere individual. He was in the process of executing a mass genocide on the planet below. There was still time for him to stop it, or at least part of it. Was this something his soul could allow? Briefly, he thought of the army of Furies that would await him.

Then his thoughts wandered to HaReeka. She had been the only thing he'd cared for since as far back as he could remember—the only one he had ever loved. And he'd taken her life without hesitation. Something was wrong with that. He just couldn't capture the feeling that the action must have surely triggered. It slipped away like an eel in the depths. Maybe he was broken. Or maybe that is what made him unique. Either way, he was past the point of no return.

"I'm reading five plasma bomb explosions in the heart of Brevetta! It's gone."

Duma snapped his head to the voice. "Gone? What do you mean, 'gone?'"

"The base, sir, it's destroyed. The dampening field is gone too. They can launch their fighters."

"They don't have enough fighters," Duma said. He was more worried about the other implications—Project Deathwind, and the rebel's widebeam signals getting out.

The cloak was gone. They could call for help now.

* *

From space, the planet of Kavka was marred by a giant storm that glittered and flashed from above, created by Project Deathwind. With the annihilation of the weapon a thousand miles away, the wave of death ceased, and the clouds dissipated, leaving only its destructive wake as evidence.

Plumes of smoke rose from where Brevetta once was, blocking any view of the city that remained. But out of those plumes emerged Kavkin anti-grav fighters streaking through the atmosphere to confront a dreadnaught of the Meraki navy, the *Kai'den*. Several of the fighters were blasted by the colossal ship even before reaching space. Unwavering in resolution, the rest continued their desperate assault.

Along with the fighters, as outside communication was now unfettered, hundreds of signals broadcasted into the night sky, searching for help.

✶ ✶

Nathan was almost afraid to open his eyes, fearing the aftermath that awaited. As he did, he was amazed to see that the shockwave had torn off the top portion of the building they'd collided into. He lay under the open sky with columns of ash and smoke drifting by overhead. Pain flared in every part of his body, but most agonizing was his dislocated shoulder.

Tangled in his legs, Arista was motionless. Her face was smeared with blood, soot, and dirt. After struggling to sit up, Nathan wiped grit from his eyes and eased her to the side. Placing a finger on her neck, he felt for a pulse.

Endless seconds passed before he felt it. It was weak, but it was there. Moving his hand to her face, he stroked her forehead and cheek, expelling a sigh of relief.

When he was little, everything had been so clear. It had been easy to determine black or white, right or wrong. But now, as he looked down at Arista, he saw only gray. She was no more his enemy than he was. Duma had twisted her intentions and beliefs, but how could he make her see that? When she awoke, what would they be? Lovers? Enemies? Whatever the answer might be, he knew he loved her, and that was enough for him now.

Slowly, he stood, his arm hanging limply at his side. His vision swept out over the onetime capital of Kavka, now blanketed in carnage and fire. A giant trail of flames running right up to the edge of the square marked the path that the rebels had taken to get here. The remains of the five skyscrapers and surrounding buildings were spread in every direction. Everywhere, blazes raged, baptizing the city in fire.

Prymack had been right—it all had been leading to fire.

In the sky, Kavkin fighters zoomed off to engage the Meraki overhead. Nathan's battered headset picked up signals from all over Brevetta, calling out to the High Command. He scanned the frequencies, listening to the frantic voices of hope.

"—to anyone listening, we are under Meraki occupation—"

Static, then momentary feedback. "—request any assistance you can give."

"—somebody please!"

"—fourth planet from the sun. I'm not sure how long we can continue broadcasting. I repeat—"

The calls seemed to go on forever, unanswered. The High Command had to respond. Drelmar had guaranteed they were out there, waiting for a distress signal. If they weren't, all the deaths and all the pain would be for nothing. Without the High Command's help, the Kavkin pilots would only be an annoyance.

Then, after minutes of the desperate calls, a reply came that made Nathan's heart skip.

"We receive you, Kavka. This is the Baraska High Command Carrier *Elixir*. Reinforcements have been deployed."

Waves of emotion that he'd struggled to control for months overcame him. Somehow, they had succeeded.

Through the garbled background noise and distress calls that flooded his frequency scanner, another voice forced its way into Nathan's ear, broken by static.

"—out there? Anyone? Team si—All clear. We did it! I can't believe we did it."

Cyndron's voice forced a smile to Nathan's lips. He turned

from the burning city and the battle overhead to limp back to Arista.

✷ ✷

Duma was in awe. He knew the dampening field was down, that the rebels could now reach out for help, but he'd thought it would take the High Command weeks before they could gather any meaningful force in the area. What he saw from the holoscreens projected before him was impossible.

A brilliant mosaic of color swirled out of the blackness of empty space, forming a cosmic vortex. Emerging from the hyperspace tunnel was a Baraska High Command carrier ship. Eight long arms of fighter bays fanned out from it, releasing a horde of star fighters that raced out in organized formations like a hurricane. Behind the carrier, a Battleship and several support ships also appeared from the vortex.

Almost immediately, a large beam jumped from the front of the battleship and drilled into the *Kai'den*. Alerts wailed on the bridge, followed by rumbling along the hull.

Impossible or not, Duma accepted the facts before him and realized he was in a position of disadvantage. While the *Kai'den* was a dreadnaught, and more powerful, it had traveled with a small group of ships intended only to secure Kavka. He was surprised and outnumbered.

"Swivel the guns! Target the carrier! Fire! Fire! Fire!"

The *Kai'den*'s guns rotated to target the carrier and fired. The salvo blew off an arm of the carrier, limiting another wave of fighters, but the barrage's main purpose was distraction.

Duma pointed at a weapons officer. "Ready a static bomb," he said, then turned to navigation. "Open a tunnel."

Their chances in this battle were slim, and the uncertainty of how many more ships would come through the High Command tunnel was troubling.

"Sir, incoming tightbeam transmission," a comm officer said.

"Send it to my channel." Duma strode to the command console and flicked on the waiting signal. It was audio-only.

"This is Admiral Cernurus of the Baraska High Command. You are outgunned and out positioned. Surrender now, and we can end this."

Duma leaned onto the console. "No! This is not the end," he said, ending the transmission with a crushing blow of his fist to the haloid.

The static bomb detonated around the *Kai'den*, dispersing a cloud of ionized dust and preventing anyone from tracking their wake trail. Then, a reddish-purple abyss swirled open, creating a hyperspace tunnel along the ship's path.

Entering the tunnel, the *Kai'den* disappeared in a flash of radiance.

CHAPTER 49

WHAT REMAINED OF the skytowers of Brevetta served as an appropriate and hallowed location for the monument. Black pillars rising from the center of each of the missing buildings, joined together in a swirling iridescent silver spire reaching upward to half the height of the original towers. Symbolically, it represented how the people of Kavka had risen from the ashes to reach for the stars once again.

Niikapollo studied the blueprints of the monument that would stand where so many of his friends had fallen. It would take them months to construct it, but it would be an inspiration to the ones who survived. As acting governor of the territory and now the Deysho of the Yiiga clan, it would be one of several major tests of his leadership. But Brevetta was still in ruins. That was actually the first real—

"Pollo, you coming?" Cyndron's voice shattered his thoughts.

"Yes. Did you find Stryder?"

"Nope."

"Maybe we'll see him there." Sighing, Pollo shifted the decorative chest piece, so it wasn't digging into his armpit.

"Too small?" Cyndron laughed. "It's the only traditional cuirass anyone could find. It's probably the only one left now."

He tilted his head at Cyndron's words. "It should be in a museum, not on me."

"Well, you're the Deysho now. So… enjoy." Cyndron patted him on the shoulder and gestured to the door. "This way, Boss."

The pair strode to the RAV shuttle, that waited to take them to the ceremony.

Even with the doors open and the wind whipping around the inside, the ride was relaxing to Pollo. The hum of the anti-grav engines was a noise he hadn't heard in a long time, a sound he now associated with freedom. It reminded him of a time before the Meraki.

They flew over a sea of what must have been a million Kavkins gathered to celebrate their liberation. It was a rousing sight that filled his chest with a sense of pride and motivation. He only wished Prymack could witness it, and Nur, Sundiis, Vendala, Xantani, Masemada, and the rest. He would rebuild Kavka in their names.

As they landed on the platform, the roar of the crowd was deafening. Cyndron flashed him a smile as he stepped off the shuttle, then thrust his arms in the air. It seemed impossible to imagine, but the crowd cheered even louder.

Around them, banners of each of the ninety different clans flapped in the wind, but the largest ones were of the Yiiga clan. His clan. The boom and spectacle of starburst fireworks began overhead, which sent adrenaline surging through Pollo's body. Reminding himself that the war was over, he realized it would be awhile before he could enjoy any type of pyrotechnics.

As he stepped up to the podium, he looked over the people on stage—the survivors of the final assault on Brevetta. Stryder was not among them.

✶ ✶

Within the temporary detention facilities in Brevetta, every captured Meraki prisoner was housed. Among them all, the most important was the one in cell 46. It was home to prisoner of war Lieutenant Commander Arista Conak of the Meraki Navy.

Every day since the battle of Brevetta, Nathan had visited her around lunchtime. Today, he stopped in the hallway outside her cell to ask the Kavkin psychiatrist—a mindwalker, he assumed—about her condition.

"Physically… " the woman said, then paused with a sigh. "She's recovering. But that's not what I am concerned with. Her mind is strong, yes, but it has been manipulated—programmed even—for years."

Nathan shook his head, knowing it could have been the same for him if not for Drelmar.

"Programmed?"

"I don't use the word lightly, but there is some evidence of chemical involvement. It could take a while, but there may be a future for her outside of here. That's up to her. So far, she's ignored every one of us who's tried to talk to her, as well."

Nathan thanked the doctor and entered Arista's cell. He sat next to the hardened, transparent barrier that separated her from the outside world. Crossing his legs, he started the breathing technique he'd explained to her the first day she was allowed visitors, but like every day, there was no response. He couldn't find a way to get through to her.

Wrapped in a blanket and lying on her bed, turned away from him, she was nearly motionless.

"Life's never easy, is it?" he said, taking a break from the technique. "In the middle of this war, of all these horrible things, I found something rare—someone rare. I haven't sorted out the truth from the lies, but I have faith in who you are. In who *we* are. In ronya."

His next words were ones he'd gone over a thousand times in his head in the last week, ones he dreaded speaking. There was no way to know how Arista would take them. But so far, she hadn't reacted to anything. With an apprehensive breath, he pushed out the words.

"This war is bigger than both of us. And I have to see it

through. I hope you can understand that. Someday, at least." He gazed at the starburst scar on his palm. "I've joined the High Command, Arista. You could too. We could fight side by side again."

Once more, there was no response.

He stood up, and for a few moments, allowed himself to think of what a future with her might look like, a small smile growing on his lips. Then he raised his palm, pressing it firmly to the glass.

"To the future."

He'd found his purpose in the universe, and he'd found her. Though neither was what he'd expected, he knew that soon he would have to fight for them both.

Nathan turned and left, leaving only his fingerprints on the glass.

✴ ✴

Arista unwrapped the blanket from her body and emerged from the sanctuary she had built within it. A tingle climbed up her leg as her feet touched the cold floor. Crossing the cell, she recalled the last time Nathan had spoken those words. A toast, he'd called it, on their first date.

She watched as his fingerprints slowly evaporated. But before they were completely gone, she raised her hand and touched them, matching the impressions to hers on the glass.

For a moment, Arista wondered what life could have been like with Nathan, evoking the dream she'd had while unconscious after ejecting from her fighter. Was that what she wanted? A family? With him?

She withdrew her hand from the glass. It didn't matter anymore. Things had changed, and that was no longer an option. Nathan had thrown that all away. As anger rose in her chest, her hands began to prickle.

Arista slammed her fist—crackling with power and energy—into the barrier.

Hairline fractures raced outward from the point of impact.

EPILOGUE

The datagem in Ambassador Russo's palm filled her with exhilaration. It was not purely excitement though, because if certain people discovered it, they would have her executed. Being an ambassador differed vastly from an instructor at Ragnakor, so much more than she had anticipated. It wasn't just theory anymore. She was able to effect real-world change with her lessons. But her influence was limited in her current position, and she needed to take the next step.

Throughout her life, she'd always felt that she viewed the universe through a different lens than most others. Where they were buried in the uniformity of it, the orderly reality that science and technology had made it, she knew it was ancient and still teeming with mysteries.

But some of those secret wonders were dangerous. The Vox, for example. They were few, but they were like parasites, using the Meraki for their own agenda. And no one seemed to know what that agenda was. Even she could not postulate their true motives, but the dread in her bones told her they weren't noble.

However, there wasn't much she could do about it at the moment. Like a sand viper, she must blend in and wait until the perfect instant to strike. Until then, she would gather her pieces and compose her masterstroke.

In service to that, there was an opportunity two years ago for Russo to slip one of her most trusted agents aboard the *Kai'den*, Cavalon Verdom. Under the guise of the Maelidor's orders and using the alias Shamus Digo, Russo had given Cavalon an additional assignment. That task was to observe and analyze a man who could influence her quest. That part of his position had ended, and Russo held the final report in her hands.

She settled into the chair at her desk, switched on a light, and placed the datagem on her haloid. It decrypted with the pairing key and projected into the air before her.

REPORT SUBJECT: VALOR KRELL DUMA

During the last two standard years, I've observed the subject aboard the *Kai'den* Dreadnaught. At your request, I have made this document as brief as possible, so please forgive any inconsistencies for I deleted unnecessary portions.

:Background:

Krell Duma was born on Carcosa to a peasant family. His father sold him to the Gola crime syndicate of the planet's largest city, Chois. Forced into this world of brutality, the military was his only escape from a life of poverty and abuse. He joined at age 12, the minimum to begin training. Finding security within military structure, he quickly mastered the tactics and skills of warfare and was selected to the toughest branch of the military, a special forces unit known as The Warhawks. Within their service, he learned to embrace violence and to kill without remorse.

Elevating through the ranks, he gained respect through his deadly abilities. But even greater than respect, he earned a reputation that inspired fear. Over time, he was given his own unit, for which he hand-picked the best fighters in the world. Nicknamed The Rippers by others, they were selected for the harshest missions.

Eventually, Carcosa united with a single government and Duma's team was caught in a political dilemma. They took the fall for a botched operation that ended in the death of one of its fortunas (warlords). I was unable to verify how much of the official report was factual, but much of my findings have pointed to fabrications by political enemies. Around the same the time, Duma was diagnosed with a terminal illness called the Echo virus.

To clean up the disgraced "death squad", the government sent a team to eliminate The Rippers. Several members of Duma's team were killed before the conflict ended. Then, Duma disappeared.

Our forces arrived at Carcosa a year after that. The planet inevitably came to resist us, but Duma saw his chance. With little to lose, he led a violent coup against the government. Because of the confusion during our impending invasion, he had the element of surprise. Defeating the military in key points, he captured the capitol and emerged as the Carcosin Invictus.

Duma held the capitol for six days before surrendering it to us. We recruited him and his remaining team. With the help of the Tanzi organism, his disease has been brought under control. In the years since, he is the only member of his team still alive.

:Service to the Dominya:

After his induction into the Dominya, Duma's record has been exemplary, and he has been promoted to valor. His mission success is rated as high as 98. I suggest reviewing his assignments on Sonteray, Drasen Cab, and Winden as prime examples of his work.

Updated - Following Lord Admiral Lasal's assassination, he assumed command of the *Kai'den* by invoking his authority as valor. An armed confrontation with Captain HaReeka ensued, whom he had been assigned to protect only two years earlier, resulting in her death. Reports of this event have not yet been completed, so the reasoning of the skirmish is unclear.

:Conclusion::

He is a man driven by loyalty and duty. Considering the close personal ties to his team on Carcosa and those he brought to join us, their deaths have caused him to become isolated.

In our service, he has an outstanding record of success. There are, however, certain incidents where he has been proven to be short-tempered. No other candidates exhibit anywhere near his level of skill. My conclusion is that he is ruthless, but dependable. He has a strong sense of loyalty and bristles at any form of betrayal. He would be a powerful ally if convinced the Maelidor has deceived her people.

Russo disengaged the datagem and dropped it into her shatterbox. She fastened the lid and activated the device. It vibrated with a soothing rumble as it pulverized all evidence of the report.

Removing her shoes and coiling her legs up to her chest, she contemplated her goals. Her moment was drawing near. Soon it would be time to use her venom.

THANK YOU FOR finishing the book! It's been my pleasure to bring you into this world and share it with you. I hope it was an exciting journey. I'd greatly appreciate your help in bringing it to others. Think of it as being a trailblazer and leading them to their next adventure. Leaving a review is the best way to do that on Amazon, or Goodreads, or YouTube, or wherever else you visit.

There's also a mailing list you can join at bradpaw.com, which will get you a free precursor story to this one called ***War of the Harbingers: Incident at Drasen Cab***. What was Arista like before her world got turned upside down? Find out! You will also get updates and insight into future books.

The story continues in book two…

War of the Harbingers: Starfall

Brad grew up in the countryside of Michigan on the outskirts of the small town of Tecumseh. He graduated from Michigan State University, where he also studied martial arts and started writing his first novel. His home is now Chelsea, MI where he lives with his wife, two daughters, and many rescued animals. Brad is the author of the epic science fiction adventure trilogy ***War of the Harbingers***. If you'd like to know more, visit **bradpaw.com**.

Printed in Great Britain
by Amazon